THE RESOLUTIONS

The

RESOLUTIONS

a novel

BRADY HAMMES

BALLANTINE BOOKS

NEW YORK

Copyright © 2020 by Brady Hammes

All rights reserved.

Published in the United States by Ballantine Books, an imprint of Random House, a division of Penguin Random House LLC, New York.

BALLANTINE and the HOUSE colophon are registered trademarks of Penguin Random House LLC.

ISBN 978-1-9848-1803-4
Ebook ISBN 978-1-9848-1804-1

Printed in Canada on acid-free paper

randomhousebooks.com

246897531

FIRST EDITION

Title page images from istock

Book design by Barbara M. Bachman

For my family

None of us can help the things life has done to us. They're done before you realize it, and once they're done they make you do other things until at last everything comes between you and what you'd like to be, and you've lost your true self forever.

—Eugene O'Neill, *Long Day's Journey into Night*

PART ONE

SAMANTHA

S HE STOOD IN A THICKET of trees at the edge of campus, this place she now called home, a Russian dance company two hundred kilometers northeast of Moscow. The sun hung low in the sky, dropping with the temperature, and her toes were numb from hiking through snow. She'd been gone all afternoon, and now she was late for the dinner party, which posed a significant problem because prolonged absences didn't go unnoticed at a place like this. Nikolai, the director of the company, presided over his dancers with the omniscience of a cult leader, and Sam knew she would need a good excuse to explain her disappearance. Unfortunately, no one was buying her excuses anymore.

Nikolai's father was a steel oligarch who had purchased the estate as a summer retreat for his family, but then the family stopped speaking to one another so Nikolai claimed it for himself. He amassed a roster of choreographers and dancers from across the globe, and hired a team of contractors to refurbish the grounds. He erected a dozen small cottages—little two-bedroom units the dancers shared—and commissioned a famous architect to design the studio space, a three-thousand-square-foot glass cube situated amid dense conifer forest. Nikolai referred to the property as Château Oksana—named for his mother—but everyone else called it campus. Sam imagined it was the closest thing she would ever have to a proper college experience, probably not so different from those fancy private academies in New England. She slept in what was essentially a well-appointed dorm room, attended classes at a rehearsal space rather than a lecture hall, and took her meals in an upscale cafeteria. Even now, in mid-December, everything blanketed in a foot of snow, the grounds were impeccably groomed, the sidewalks brushed and cleared, the trees hung with decorative lights. There was an onsite staff to attend to the dancers' needs, nothing more than a phone call away, yet it was a suf-focating kind of luxury, like being held hostage at Versailles.

At the center of campus was the grand manor, a ten-thousand-square-foot palace that served as the social hub. She watched a proces-sion of black SUVs unload passengers at the entrance, where Nikolai stood greeting a parade of sparkling men and women in formal attire. When he turned to kiss the cheek of an elderly, silver-haired woman, Sam made a break for it, sprinting past the rehearsal space and the gym and finally to her cottage. Once inside, she threw her coat on the bed and removed the small baggie printed with smiley faces. Restraint was not a thing she normally possessed in moments like this, but she was late and she needed to keep her head up through the party, so she stashed the baggie at the bottom of her sock drawer, a reward de-ferred. She moved to the bathroom and did a quick pass of makeup before slipping into a sleeveless black dress. She dabbed concealer on her forearm to mask the bruise, then looked in the mirror one last time, a woman with a question.

Can you do this?

SAM STEPPED OUTSIDE AND HURRIED toward the ballroom, her heels clacking against the sidewalk, her shoulders burning against the wind. She should have brought a coat, but her head was not clear, and when her head was not clear, she forgot things like coats. It had been two days since she'd gotten high, and that was a problem.

Once a month, Nikolai threw a formal dinner party at the estate.

He invited colleagues from the ballet world as well as friends from Moscow, mostly men who enjoyed mingling with the dancers. A few of the guests came for legitimate reasons, but most—the musicians, the minor celebrities, the baggy-suited hedge fund managers—came to gawk and make lewd sexual innuendos about "first position." Sam found the events reprehensible, as if she were part of a parade of dancing prostitutes. At the last party, she poured a glass of Chianti on the head of a sweet-talking investment banker after he put his hand on her ass and whispered *stunning* into her ear. After the incident, Nikolai placed her on an informal probation to ensure a similar embarrassment didn't befall another of his guests. Sam, however, made it clear to him that the best way to prevent future incidents was to instruct his guests to keep their fucking hands to themselves.

She'd been summoned to tonight's party to meet a new choreographer Nikolai had recruited, though most of the names he'd promised had yet to materialize so she wasn't expecting much. The two productions the company had mounted since her arrival had been savagely reviewed, which Sam attributed to their hack choreographers, one of whom was plucked from the Russian equivalent of *Dancing with the Stars*. The company's cachet had taken a blow in recent months, and Sam knew Nikolai needed a win as much as she did.

She entered the hall and scanned the crowd. Her arrival had drawn little notice and for this she felt a speck of relief. An old man was butchering Vivaldi on the piano, and tuxedoed waiters floated around the room with trays of hors d'oeuvres that appeared untouched. A few girls in tall heels and short dresses were huddled at the bar, cocktails in hand, chatting in a language she'd made no attempt to learn. She looked around the room: the crystal chandelier hanging from a forty-foot ceiling, the nineteenth-century watercolors adorning the walls, the Steinway piano. It was all somewhat surreal in its extravagance: the campus, the catered meals and personal trainers, even this dress she was wearing, a dress she hadn't paid for but that probably cost more than most people made in a week, maybe a month. Her talent had shown her so much of the world, taken her so far—Chicago to New York, New York to Moscow—yet she still felt as if she'd been pulled into a terrible black void.

"Sam," came a voice. She turned to see Marie, the only other American in the company, walking toward her. "Nikolai's been looking for you. Where have you been?"

"I went into town," Sam said.

"Is everything okay?" Marie asked.

Everything was not okay, but she wasn't about to open up about it during cocktail hour, so instead she asked Marie to join her for a cigarette.

"It's freezing outside," Marie said.

"We'll be quick," Sam said. "Please? I need to get out of here."

"You just got here."

"Exactly."

They stepped outside and Sam pulled a pack of cigarettes from her purse, handing one to Marie.

"Where's your coat?" Marie asked.

"I forgot it."

"How do you forget your coat?"

Sam shook her head. "I don't know."

"What *I* want to know," Marie asked, cupping her hands around the lighter, "is what you were doing in town?"

"I went to see a friend."

"Who?"

"Just some guy."

"Really?" Marie asked, smiling, wanting more. "You walked all the way to Yaroslavl?"

"It's not that far." Which was true. Thirty minutes round trip if she hurried, which she often did.

"Yeah, but in this weather?"

"I jogged," Sam said with a shrug. "It was a good workout."

"So who is he, this guy? And why am I just now hearing about him?"

His name was Ivan, and he was a twenty-one-year-old high school dropout who cobbled together a living by repairing broken computers and selling heroin from the apartment he shared with his grandmother. Sam had met him shortly after arriving in Russia. It was one of the rare occasions when Nikolai permitted an off-site field trip to a restaurant in town, and Sam had spotted him smoking outside: a skinny, ratty-looking kid with bloodshot eyes. He spoke broken English, but Sam communicated her needs with a little tap on the forearm and a raise of the eyebrows. She ended up getting his phone number and enough drugs to get her through the week. She kept in touch with him after that, sneaking away from campus whenever her supply ran low. "No one," she finally said. "It's kind of over anyway."

"So mysterious," Marie said, extinguishing her cigarette. "You almost done? I'm freezing."

Inside, the conversation had quieted and Nikolai was instructing everyone to move to the dining hall for dinner. As the crowd filtered out, he approached Sam and put a hand on her shoulder. "You're late to the party," he said.

Nikolai was close to six and a half feet tall, with a mane of blond hair working its way toward white. He wore a tuxedo and an ostentatious watch and glossy crocodile shoes. Everything about him seemed to be cut from the finest, most expensive cloth, and he made sure to flaunt this air of elegance to everyone he met.

"I went into town," Sam said. "For personal items."

"We have drivers for that."

"I felt like walking."

"You've been here long enough to know that's not how it works."

"Sorry."

"You know there's a reason they call it a company, Samantha. I try to run it like a business. I take care of my employees, provide help when they need it."

Sam plucked a glass of champagne from a passing waiter. Nikolai stared at her, waiting for a response. "Samantha?"

She took a sip. "Yes?"

"Do you need help?"

She shook her head.

Nikolai looked at the purple mark stamped across the inside of her forearm. She'd missed her vein a week ago and the bruise lingered, despite her rushed attempt to conceal it. "What happened to your arm?"

"I fell," she said, turning slightly away from him.

Nikolai scoffed.

"I slipped on some ice walking down the stairs and hit it on the handrail." It was a quick, convincingly crafted piece of fiction, for which she felt a small burst of pride. "You should talk to the maintenance guys about that. It could have been much worse."

"You know what it looks like to me?" Nikolai asked.

"Like it hurts? Not too bad actually. It did right after it happened, but not so much now."

He shook his head, unamused. "We have a zero tolerance policy here."

"Got it," Sam said, hoping to end the conversation. Nikolai wasn't worried about her well-being so much as the troublesome press that would result from one of his dancers dying of a heroin overdose. Sam had become a liability, a neighborhood kid sneaking onto his trampoline, and his interest was only in preventing an incident that might reflect poorly on the company. Nikolai treated his dancers like collectible glass figurines, and it was laughable to imagine he was concerned about anything other than protecting the value of his assets.

"There are people you can talk to if you don't think you can do it on your own," Nikolai said. "I can bring someone in to meet with you. No one has to know."

"I fell, Nikolai," she said, growing exasperated. "I don't know what you want me to say. It's winter. It's icy. I'm a klutz."

"You're not a klutz, Samantha," he said evenly. "You're a dancer. And I suggest you start acting like one." He turned and walked toward the dining hall.

Sam downed her champagne and looked around the room, wondering how she ended up here. Not just at this dinner—it was an unavoidable obligation—but rather Russia of all places. It had seemed like a reasonable idea a year ago, when she was treading water in New York, bouncing between different companies, not really advancing in any measurable way. Moscow: the epicenter of dance, the place that represented a certain kind of glamour in the mind of a twenty-five-year-old girl from the Midwest. A darkening had come upon New York, the city that once sparkled in her mind, and she hoped a change of geography might summon the sun. Yet here she was, on the other side of the world, experiencing no discernible change aside from the color of the clouds.

At eighteen, Sam was offered an apprenticeship with the New York City Ballet. She said goodbye to Chicago, to her family, and settled in Manhattan. She lived in the residence hall, rarely veering from the path between her dorm room and the rehearsal space at Lincoln Center. After a year, she was invited to join the corps de ballet. She advanced quickly within the company, and it was while rehearsing for her first solo role that the unraveling began. She'd been practicing one morning when she felt something tear inside her knee, a jolt of pain that sent her to the ground. A torn meniscus was the diagnosis. The doctor recommended surgery, which left her bedridden for three weeks. It was the longest she'd ever gone without dancing and she couldn't help but feel as if she'd prematurely arrived at the end of her career. *You'll be back soon enough,* people told her, but every day away from the studio diminished her relevance within the company. Her role was given to her understudy, a girl named Abby, who sent a bouquet of flowers and a helium balloon with the words *Get Well Soon* written in some obnoxiously cheery font. The subtext was clear: Get well soon, but not *too* soon.

If they offer pills, take them. If they offer more, take those too. Her brother had told her this when he called to check on her after the surgery. She'd taken his advice, both parts, but found she needed more still, despite the doctor's warning, delivered in a condescending tone, that she use them sparingly, only when necessary. *Define necessary.* The pain in her knee was minor compared to the disappointment of losing something she'd been working toward for years. So yes, the pills were necessary, because the pills made her feel better. They were a necessary consolation to counteract the injustice of her injury.

She spent the rest of the summer hobbling around the city on crutches, riding urine-smelling elevators to subway platforms. She met a guy named Atticus at a barbecue hosted by a friend. He arrived on a skateboard, with a backpack full of sweet corn and a cast on his arm, which he'd acquired after attempting to clear the stairs outside a PetSmart. They bonded over their respective disabilities and the pills that kept them afloat. They spent their days together, touring bars, day drinking in parks. Her knee slowly healed, and in time she returned to the studio, carefully testing the limits of her fitness. Her form was slow to return and the progress was frustrating. Her discipline and commitment began to wane. She didn't lose interest in dance, but she did draw a line between the dance world and her personal life, which began to include all the things she'd sacrificed in her youth. Lincoln Center became her office, and she treated it as such, arriving on time every morning but also leaving promptly at the end of each day. She spent less time with the other dancers, who came to feel more like co-workers, the kind of people with whom the only possible conversation was the one she wasn't interested in having.

She and Atticus moved in together that fall. She returned home from the studio one afternoon to find him lying on the living room floor with a needle in his arm. She'd thought he was dead at first, but when she began shaking him, he opened his eyes and smiled and said, *What a nice surprise.*

Maybe this was a mistake, she'd said later that night, as they lay in bed together. She didn't want to be in a relationship with a drug addict. He'd assured her it was just an occasional thing, something to tide him over until they could find more pills, but there was nothing recreational about what she'd seen. It was a macabre scene, her boyfriend lying unconscious on the floor of their home. But then, slowly, almost imperceptibly, because that's how these things happen, she too began to slip. The first time was on a Friday night, after returning home from a bar, when she smoked a little with Atticus just to see what it was all about. The verdict: unalloyed ecstasy.

In time, the pills became harder to find, the heroin easier. But never needles. That was what she'd told herself. That was a bridge too far. But then one day she crossed that bridge and that was that. As she and Atticus lay in bed, decoding the grain patterns of the hardwood beams of their bedroom ceiling, she knew that something terrible had been set in motion. The architecture of her life began to crumble. She was soon spending whole afternoons melting on their apartment floor. Calls from her fellow dancers went unreturned. Rumors circulated. Offers of counseling from the company were rebuffed. She was suspended for six weeks, in the hope that she might pull herself together, but when that didn't happen, she was fired. Two days later, she woke to find Atticus dead on their living room sofa, and the untenability of her savage lifestyle fully revealed itself. Atticus's father arrived with a U-Haul trailer a week later, and together they packed up his belongings, which were trucked back to Virginia, effectively erasing him from her life. She spent the next three months privately mourning in her apartment. Friends stopped by with flowers and food, but she lacked the stomach for small talk, so she thanked them and accepted the offerings and closed the door to the outside world. She had hoped Atticus's death might be a turning point, what people referred to as rock bottom, but her sadness only plunged her deeper still.

A few months later, she received a call from Marie, a fellow dancer she'd met when they were both fourteen-year-olds attending a summer dance intensive in Los Angeles. It had been Sam's first extended time away from home, and the two had shared a dorm room, where they would stay up late discussing boys and their dreams of becoming professional dancers. It was a brief friendship, something akin to a summer romance, but she'd bonded with Marie in a way she hadn't with other dancers. Marie had recently landed a spot with the Pacific Northwest Ballet in Seattle, dancing supporting roles in the old standards. She told Sam about the rich Russian she'd met after a performance of *Giselle*. The man, Nikolai, was on a tour of North America, poaching apprentice dancers from other companies. She insisted that Sam meet Nikolai when he came through New York, because, she explained, *how fucking cool* would it be if they were both dancing at the same company, in Russia of all places. There was also the money, she added, almost as an afterthought, a guaranteed salary three times what she was currently making. Sam was intrigued but also suspicious. She told Marie to give the guy her number, that she'd listen to his pitch over dinner.

Nikolai arrived in New York on a Friday and sent a car for her later that evening. They went to a sushi restaurant in the West Village, where she ate a few hundred dollars' worth of fish while Nikolai explained his plans for the company, crowing about his relationships with some of the most innovative names in contemporary dance. By this time, Sam had become a pariah in the New York ballet world, and while she'd heard murmurs that Nikolai was nothing more than a mildly handsome charlatan, he possessed a desperation she recognized in herself. Their reputations were both in need of repair, and by the time the check arrived, she knew she would follow him wherever he led her, because *he* at least had a plan, while she did not.

AND THIS IS WHERE it led her, to this bizarre dance company in rural Russia, where she now joined the slow migration to dinner. The dining hall was a cavernous rectangle bisected by a thirty-foot walnut dining table, and the walls were cast in the kind of ornate gilded carvings she associated with European royalty. Marie had disappeared, so Sam took a seat next to an elderly woman draped in pearls.

"You are dancer?" the woman asked in a heavy Russian accent. She had the grave, insistent eyes of someone with many questions and little time.

"Yes," Sam said.

"I met Nikolai when he was very young. At Vaganova."

Sam flashed her a curious smile. "Nikolai danced at Vaganova?"

She'd known he was a dancer in his youth, but she never imagined his talent being so great as to allow him entrance to such a prestigious academy.

"He was small talent," the woman said, making a little pinching motion with her fingers. "A favor for the wealthy."

Sam laughed. "Right."

The woman smiled back. "He is better off-stage."

Sam made a face. "Jury's still out on that."

A waiter arrived with their food: a breast of duck flanked by butternut squash and grilled asparagus, a dish Sam knew she wouldn't touch, her stomach churning and unsettled, her mind racing and unmoored. The woman draped her napkin across her lap and began surveying her plate, rendering silent judgment on the meal. Sam downed her second glass of champagne and motioned to the waiter for another.

It was his voice that first caught her attention: North American English with a subtle Canadian accent. He looked a little older than her, maybe mid-thirties, with sharp cheekbones and a rush of black hair. He sat across the table, chatting with a few of the dancers, his gaze alternating among them in the charitable manner of someone trying to pay his listeners equal attention. Through some not so subtle eavesdropping, Sam learned that his name was Max and that he was working on a new piece for the company. Then he laughed, saying he was unsure if that was information he was allowed to divulge. Sam listened closely, maybe a little too closely. After a moment, he interrupted himself to acknowledge her gaze. "Hello," he said. "I'm Max."

"I know," Sam said.

"You've been listening."

"Is that okay? I'm bored." The other girls eyed her suspiciously, seemingly annoyed by her entrance into the conversation.

"Bored with my story or bored with the dinner?"

"The dinner mostly." She raised her hand in greeting. "I'm Sam by the way."

"Yes," Max said. "I believe we'll be working together."

"Something new I hope?"

"Yes, though I'm not sure I should be discussing it." He looked around the table. "Here at least."

"Because it's top secret?"

He smiled. "Something like that."

"Max's Top Secret Ballet."

"It's a working title."

"I should hope so," Sam said, punctuating the conversation with a sip of champagne.

Dinner proceeded slowly. There were five courses, followed by coffee and a toast from Nikolai, who thanked everyone in that disingenuous tone of his, which was really meant as veiled praise for himself, the man responsible for everything around them. When dinner adjourned and the crowd filtered back into the ballroom for another round of cocktails, Sam ordered a vodka tonic and settled into a quiet corner of the room, wondering how much longer she had to suffer through this before making her escape. A moment later, Max wandered over, holding a tumbler of whiskey. "I didn't mean to be cagey," he said, "but it didn't seem wise to get into the specifics with the other dancers around. I know how competitive these places can be."

"We aren't a very competitive group," Sam said. "Mostly because there hasn't been much to compete for."

Max finished what was left of his drink. "I'm sorry to hear that."

"Me too."

They stood next to each other in awkward silence, watching the party swirl around them. Max jostled the ice cubes around his empty glass, then tried to take a drink.

Sam laughed. "It's all gone."

"What?"

"Your drink," she said, nodding toward his glass. "It's empty."

He looked down at his tumbler. "It is."

"Then why did you drink from it?"

"I don't know," he said. "A nervous tic, I guess."

"Why are you nervous?"

He shrugged.

"Maybe you need a refill," she said, pouring a splash of her cocktail into his glass.

"*Za zdorovie*," he said, touching his glass to hers. "It's the only Russian I speak."

"It's all you really need."

"Has Nikolai told you anything about my piece?" He leaned back against the wall, which seemed to put him at ease.

"Nope." She looked down at his shoes: black leather cap toe oxfords with white rubber soles. A girlfriend had once told her to judge a man by his shoes, so she was doing it now. She ruled in his favor.

"I'll explain it to you when we meet tomorrow," he said. "But I'm excited to get started. I've been wanting to work with you for some time."

"Really?" she asked.

"Of course. Why do you think I came here?"

"I assumed for the cheery weather."

"There was that, of course, but I've actually been watching you dance for years. I remember seeing you in *Scotch Symphony* a couple years ago and was impressed. But then it seemed like you disappeared for a while. You got injured, right?"

"That's right." *Injured, addicted, fired, shunned.* All appropriate descriptors, none properly capable of articulating her downfall. Word traveled fast in the insular world of dance, even internationally, so she was grateful he'd chosen injury as the explanation for her absence.

"Earlier this year, Nikolai reached out to see if I had any interest in working with the company. We met through a mutual friend—a fellow choreographer in London. I was ambivalent, but then I saw your name and it made me reconsider. You immediately came to mind when I started imagining this particular role. There's something about you I find irresistible."

Sam's face warmed.

"I meant about the way you move—your body," Max stammered. "Not your body—just the way you dance." He downed the remainder of his drink. "Sorry, I'm making this super awkward. You know what I mean."

It had been a long time since anyone had paid her a compliment, and she wasn't sure what to do with it. But before she had a chance to savor the kind words, Nikolai arrived and broke the spell. "I take it you two had a chance to meet," he said.

"We were just getting acquainted," Max said, smiling, quickly recovering his composure.

"Wonderful!" Nikolai placed a hand on Max's shoulder. "I know Sam is ready to get to work. All of the dancers are. The company is fortunate to have you here."

"I hope I don't disappoint," Max said.

"I'm not worried about that," Nikolai replied.

"I should get going," Max said, "but I'll be in the studio at ten." He looked to Sam. "I'll see you then?"

"You will." She watched Max disappear into the crowd.

"What do you think of our new guest?" Nikolai asked. The faux cheeriness he'd displayed around Max was replaced with the disapproving tone Sam had come to expect.

"He seems great," she said. "Not sure why he agreed to come here, though."

"You came."

"Mistakenly." For the briefest of moments, Sam had been warmed by Max's presence, but Nikolai's arrival brought back the familiar dread that had infected her life in Russia.

"Whose fault is that?" Nikolai asked, staring down at her. In addition to his imposing height, Nikolai had the annoying habit of standing uncomfortably close when he spoke.

"Mine alone."

"Have you thought about our conversation?"

"Was that a conversation?" Sam asked, avoiding his stare. "It seemed like a threat."

"Let's call it an ultimatum." Nikolai waved to a guest across the room, then turned his attention back to Sam.

"Call it whatever you want," she said, "but he already told me I'm a big part of why he came here. So I'd say that gives me the upper hand."

"Don't flatter yourself. There are a lot of great dancers here. You're replaceable."

"Maybe," she said. "But *he's* not."

"You're right about that. Which is why you should clean up your act before you ruin what little bit of goodwill you have left."

Sam finished her drink, then stalked across the room and out into the night. Her relationship with Nikolai had always been contentious, but the animosity between them had intensified. The unfortunate reality was that they needed each other—Sam being one of the most talented dancers at the company, and Nikolai being the only person willing to give her another shot. She'd worked with difficult men before—that wasn't a problem—but it was the constant harassment that she found so infuriating. She didn't need to be lectured about her drug use, especially from someone like Nikolai, whose penchant for scotch and cocaine was equally noxious. Besides, she was already planning to stop using. She'd gotten herself into this situation and she would get herself out, and no amount of badgering was going to expedite that process. She would do it on her own terms, when *she* was ready. Just not today. Or tomorrow. Maybe after the New Year. Maybe that would be her New Year's Resolution. *A resolution for the irresolute.*

She hurried back to her cottage, past the frozen duck pond and the maintenance building, where, in warmer months, the gardeners played dominos. It was cold and getting colder. Having grown up in Chicago, she was used to winter weather, but this Russian winter was a whole new thing: the snow deeper, the days shorter, the mood darker. When she arrived at her place, she shook the cold from her body, went to her room, and closed the door. Tomorrow she would arrive at the studio on time and commit herself to the work in a way she hadn't in a long time, because hope had arrived in the form of a handsome choreographer who believed in her talent. Good things would happen tomorrow, but tonight she needed to regain her equilibrium. She needed to clear her head. She dropped her dress on the floor and changed into sweatpants and a T-shirt, then grabbed her makeup bag from the dresser and arranged her tools on the bed: the spoon, the needle, the rubber tourniquet, and, most important, the drugs she'd spent her afternoon in search of. She set a flame to the spoon and brought a dose to boil, then let the needle drink it up. She tied the tourniquet above her elbow, tapped a good vein, and shot a stream into her arm, feeling suddenly, impossibly pleased.

JONAH

S O FAR TO GO AND so little light to guide him. The sun was almost down, the trail fading quickly. He was returning from town, slightly drunk, enjoying the high of human contact, his first in almost a week. He'd left camp early that morning to recharge the equipments' batteries at a restaurant owned by his colleague, Laurent, but the drinking had interfered with the mission and he'd forgotten to grab the batteries before returning to camp. This just meant he'd have to go back tomorrow, which would be Thursday. Or would it be Friday? No idea. *What are days anymore?* he wondered. *Long stretches of loneliness,* he answered. He then counted the letters in loneliness: 10. One zero. *One is the loneliest number,* he sang to himself, then laughed because its loneliness was nothing compared to his. "What's lonelier than a man living alone in the forest?" he asked aloud, but there was no one around to answer. *Precisely,* he thought.

Jonah had come to Gabon four months earlier to assist Marcus, his thesis advisor at Vanderbilt—a quiet man with tenure and no family, his lifestyle the kind that afforded six-week sojourns into the forests of West Africa. Marcus had spent the past decade studying the vocalization of forest elephants, planting ARUs—Autonomous Recording Units—in the trees to capture the elephants' communication. As his research took shape, he convinced some of his behavioral ecology students—Jonah being one of the more eager—to help analyze the hours of recordings. Jonah spent countless days staring at spectrograms in the lab, extrapolating some very interesting things and relaying those things back to Marcus in the field. They linked the sounds they recorded with the behavior they witnessed, shedding light on the relatively unknown complexities of elephant communication. Jonah and his colleagues drafted what they referred to as *The Elephant Dictionary,* a compendium of their findings, a sonic key to the elephant dialogue. Their work began garnering attention—articles in scholarly journals, followed by an increase in funding—and Marcus offered Jonah a position as a field assistant, a welcome relief from the grinding tedium of lab work. But shortly after Jonah arrived in Gabon, Marcus contracted malaria and returned to the States, leaving Jonah to spearhead the research. There was talk of sending someone to assist him, but it was difficult to find anyone willing to abandon university life for one spent in the forests of Gabon.

He looked to the sky. Maybe rain? Rain might be nice once he was back at camp, settled in for the evening, drinking what was left of the duty-free scotch he'd picked up at the airport in Paris. He watched a wire-tailed swallow swoop past his head and land on a tree branch. He nodded at the bird, bid it good day. The bird chirped something that sounded like his name. "How can I help you?" Jonah asked, but the bird didn't respond. He wondered if he misheard the bird. Or perhaps the bird misspoke. *Better to pin it on the bird,* he thought. Or maybe there was a third option. Maybe the bird just said *Jaja,* which would make more sense because *Jaja* wasn't a word, just a bird sound. "Am I losing my mind?" he wondered aloud. "No," he answered. "You're just lonely."

It was nearly dark when he finally returned to camp, which was nothing more than a two-person tent pitched in a small clearing. He had no electricity, no running water. What he had was a whole arsenal of electronics—laptop, DSLR camera, ARUs—all of which, without batteries, were essentially useless. He powered up the camera to find that he had three bars left, enough for an hour's worth of shooting at most. He decided he'd get up early tomorrow, make the trip back to town, retrieve the batteries, email his sister. He'd arranged his flight home so that his layover in Paris might coincide with Sam's, who had planned to fly from Moscow on the same day. They had discussed trying to arrive at Charles de Gaulle around the same time so they could wander around the city together, try to see as much as possible before the final leg back to Chicago.

He wasn't particularly close with his sister, but he had hoped this impromptu rendezvous might change that. He attributed their distance to the five-year age difference, but the truth was that they didn't have that much in common. When he was in high school, Sam was his annoying kid sister. And when she did get to the age when they could enjoy a beer together, she was caught in the winds of the dance world while he was mired in academia. It was different with his older brother, Gavin. There were only four years separating them; they'd been best friends as kids. But even now it was hard to find anything to talk about with his brother. The older they got, the more their personalities seated themselves at opposite ends of the room. Gavin and Sam had grown closer over the years, and Jonah was a little jealous of their bond. They could talk for hours about art and obscure movies and bands Jonah had never heard of, only looping him into the conversation out of courtesy. His mother used to say they were the artists and he was the scientist, which Jonah always took as a slight, though he wasn't sure why. He had more advanced degrees than either of them, Gavin having graduated from a small liberal arts college in Illinois and Sam having forsaken higher education for dance, but he still felt as if his life were only half as interesting as theirs. Gavin was acting in TV shows out in L.A. and Sam was dancing in Moscow and he was living by himself in the forest, drinking too much and accomplishing very little.

But still, he thought, the idea of home stirring his heart. *It'll be nice to see them, my family.*

———

JONAH FIRED UP THE butane camp stove and set water to boil. He emptied a package of noodles into the pot and watched the last bit of color drain from the sky. He had expected this extended bout of solitary living to result in some kind of enlightenment, but most of his thoughts were occupied by images of nude women doing dirty things. He'd kept a journal for the first month, but abandoned the idea when he finally got around to reading what he'd written. It was mostly a lot of uninspired musings about how *distant* everything seemed, how *disconnected* he felt. He was certainly no writer and looking back at those old entries made him cringe at the teenage drama and hyperbole. *No shit,* he thought, *of course you feel disconnected, of course everything seems distant. You live alone in the forest.*

His camp was six kilometers from Franceville, the closest thing to a proper town. The train ride from Franceville to Libreville, the capital and location of the only international airport, was somewhere between ten and sixteen hours, depending on the condition of the track and the mood of the conductor. To say that he lived in a remote part of Gabon was inaccurate. It was more like camping on the moon.

He removed the noodles from the heat and strained them into a small plastic bowl, then added soy sauce and settled in for the only dinner he knew. His diet had been reduced to that which didn't perish: lots of pasta and oatmeal and dried fruit. On trips to town he'd sometimes treat himself to meat—smoked fish or Laurent's famous poulet nyembwe—but the longer he lived without it, the harder it became to stomach. He'd grown up backpacking with his father and was used to living for days in the wild, subsisting on trail mix and protein bars, but life here was a prolonged version of that, without the daily change in scenery and the calming assurance that a warm shower was only a few days away. Now he bathed in the stream if he bathed at all. He worked alone, ate alone, slept alone. He'd always assumed he was built for a life of solitary scientific inquiry, but now he wasn't so sure.

At thirty-one years old, Jonah had spent the past twelve years in academia, rarely venturing outside the confines of campus. His time in Gabon was the longest he'd spent away from libraries and lecture halls, and though he was loathe to admit it, he was beginning to suspect this expedition was an effort to shirk the responsibilities of graduation. His dissertation—"The Grieving Patterns of West African Forest Elephants"—was due in two months and he had very little besides a title and fourteen hundred hours of raw data. For the past few months, he'd been observing an elephant calf named Kibo, whose mother, Jonah worried, had been killed by poachers, and he planned to compare the sounds Kibo made when alone to those he'd produced when accompanied by his mother. He suspected the elephant was mourning.

During his time in the forest, Jonah had become interested in the phenomenon known as *emotional contagion,* where a calf mimics the emotional state of a fellow distressed elephant. He'd witnessed instances of an elephant placing a trunk in another's mouth, a soothing gesture that suggested they were capable of radical empathy. Demonstrations such as these were rare among animals—the behavior, until now, witnessed only in apes—and Jonah hoped to prove that elephants possessed similarly complex cognitive abilities. It was good, important work he was doing, but it was also lonely work, the kind that drove a man to drink more than he should and talk to birds and forget the batteries for his electronic devices. He'd arrived in Gabon with a clarity of purpose and, although he'd lost some of that focus in the past few weeks, his commitment to the elephants was steadfast. He resolved to do better in the new year.

AFTER DINNER, HE GRABBED his water purifier and walked to the stream to pump drinking water. The trail was well worn and even with only a splinter of moon, he made his way easily, as if walking half-asleep to the bathroom of his childhood home. With the sun down, the jungle orchestra began firing up: the hooting owls and

burping frogs and the guttural, orgasmic moan of the tree hyraxes. It
was a place where life was heard more than seen, a chorus of disembod-
ied sounds raining down from the forest canopy. For all the discomfort
of his lifestyle, he'd become rather attached to this small part of the
forest and would miss it once he was gone. His plan was to return to
Chicago for Christmas, treat himself to a couple weeks of easy American living, then return refreshed and ready for work. But with Marcus
no longer in the field, the grant money was in question and there was
the very real possibility that his departure would be permanent.

When he reached the stream, he pumped two bottles full of clean
water and began hiking back to camp. As he approached his tent, he
heard what sounded like footsteps. He stopped, set the water down,
turned off his headlamp, and crouched in the leafy growth of a maid-
enhair fern. It was quiet for a moment, then he heard it again, unmis-
takably footsteps. He grabbed a stick and approached camp, unsure
what kind of damage he could inflict but certain he would find a way
if that's what it came to. As he got closer, he heard the sound again,
but the footsteps were quicker now, fading into the forest. He scanned
the tent with his light and noticed that his camera was gone. "Moth-
erfucker," he muttered.

He circled the perimeter of the camp, but the thief had vanished.
Poachers, he guessed. After discovering a battlefield's worth of massacred elephants last year, the president of Gabon dispatched a military unit to make periodic sweeps through the parks, hoping their
presence might slow what had recently become an epidemic. Jonah
was skeptical. While the poaching in the forests around his camp did
subside, he suspected they'd just been chased to other corners of the
country. The ivory trade had been raging for years, and Jonah held no
illusions about the government's ability to eradicate it, so his goal was
to protect, by whatever means necessary, his own small jurisdiction.
Marcus had given him a Beretta 9mm before he'd left, but Jonah,
thinking the danger had subsided, traded it for beer and groceries
with a man in town, an exceptionally shortsighted decision he now
regretted.

He crawled inside his tent, slid into his sleeping bag, and tried not to think about the possibility of the poachers returning to cut his throat. He tried not to think about what that would feel like, all that blood pouring forth, the days and weeks his corpse would lie undiscovered while jackals snacked on his decomposing body. He tried to think of more pleasant things, like single malt scotch and breakfast burritos, but his mind kept circling back to the image of his lifeless corpse seen from above, by a helicopter or a bird of prey or the eye of God. Realizing this was an unhealthy kind of thinking, he grabbed his notebook and headlamp and began drafting a letter that he hoped would shepherd his thoughts into sunnier pastures. He tried to think of someone to write, but there were few options besides his colleagues (who were busy with their own research) and his mother (who was better left in the dark, particularly involving matters such as the one this evening). He decided to compose a letter to Sam that he would then translate to email when he returned to town.

Dear Sam,

This place is everything and nothing like I expected. In terms of my research on elephant communication, I've accomplished very little. In terms of drinking too much and feeling sorry for myself, I've been wildly successful. Today, I hiked six kilometers into town to recharge my camera batteries, then returned to camp without the batteries. An hour later my camera was stolen, which made my earlier failure irrelevant. Needless to say, this new development will make future research difficult. And by difficult, I mean impossible.

    I work with a nice man named Laurent, who also happens to be my only friend. He's originally from the Bantu tribe, which is a group of indigenous people who have been friendly, if not a little skeptical as to the reason for my visit. They often ask me why I traveled so far to listen to elephants, and sometimes, particularly as of late, I have wondered the same.

How are things in Russia? Do you still want to meet up in Paris? I have a twelve-hour layover, which seems like enough time to drink a bottle of wine at a café and snap a few pics of the Eiffel Tower. Let me know if you think it might work out. If not, I'll probably just sleep on the floor at the airport because I'll be exhausted and Paris intimidates me.

Love,
Jonah

GAVIN

HIS DAY BEGAN WITH AN earthquake, a sharp jolt that catapulted him out of bed like a spooked drunk, swatting at floor
lamps and stubbing his toe on the coffee table. He threw open the
front door and stepped into his yard, looking for signs of life but finding only the fuzzy shapes of his neighbors' houses. The shaking had
now settled and everything seemed strangely tranquil. The birds were
yelling at the dogs and the dogs were yelling at the sprinklers and the
world appeared as it should, which made Gavin wonder if he'd imagined the whole thing, if what he felt was just a physical extension of a
bad dream, his body kicking itself awake. He went back inside to get
his glasses, then did a quick pass through the house. Everything was in
its proper place until he reached the kitchen, where he discovered a
cabinet's worth of dinnerware lying in small pieces on the floor. He'd
anticipated a shit week, and in the four minutes he'd been awake, it
had exceeded expectations. *When life rains shit, go umbrella shopping.*
That was something his grandfather once told him and it seemed like
solid, actionable advice. Last night, he slept alone for the first time in
a year, which coincided with the first significant earthquake in the
same amount of time, and he was certain those two things were related, but the elusive *how* remained a goddamned mystery.

Renee, his girlfriend, had left the day before after an argument over his unwillingness to support her activism. She'd recently been spending a good portion of her time wading through the social media sewer, subsisting on the intoxicating cocktail of hyperbole and self-righteousness. She'd begun hosting Twitter Meetups at their house, where she and her fellow activists strategized ways to manifest their outrage, which was alternately vague and bottomless. Two of her friends—unwashed men who traveled around the country in a minivan—had spent the previous three nights sleeping on the floor of their living room. Renee had assured Gavin it was a temporary situation—just some fellow comrades in need of a place to lay their heads—but in addition to their insufferable body odor, they'd also eaten most of the food in the house. For people with such a strong distaste for the capitalist machinery, they had a real soft spot for single-origin coffee and eleven-dollar juices. So when Gavin returned home to find three more strangers drinking his beer and Photoshopping memes on their laptops, he pulled Renee aside and suggested it was time her friends found a new home. The argument escalated from there. Renee accused him of being a politically apathetic yuppie, and Gavin accused her of promoting a toothless brand of activism, at which point Renee rounded up the group and left the house. When Gavin asked what time she'd be home, she slammed the front door and yelled something that sounded like *maybe never*.

He cleaned up the mess of broken dishes, then went for a jog around the lake, passing the street fruit vendors, the homeless sleeping off hangovers, the ducks fighting over French rolls. It was a sharp, smog-free day, a rarity in the city, and he could see the San Gabriel Mountains very clearly, the snowcapped peak of Mount Baldy glowing in the distance. As a thirty-five-year-old actor on a fledgling television series, Gavin found himself with an extraordinary amount of free time and nothing constructive with which to fill it. His show was in its last week of production before hiatus, which meant that his only responsibility was to be in Burbank for a 3:00 P.M. wardrobe fitting. The show—a half-hour abomination on a second-tier cable network—filmed five days a week, but he was usually only required for two or three of those days, typically for no more than six hours at a time. There were certainly people who deserved a hiatus, people who did actual *work*—the grips and electricians and baby-faced PAs running around like caffeinated squirrels—but Gavin was not one of those people. He'd always felt guilty about how the industry delineated between those above and below the line, the way the term *work* shifted between verb and noun depending on one's role in the production ecosystem.

He was no stranger to hard work. At fourteen he got his first job detasseling corn, waking before dawn to board a school bus that hauled him to the fields of rural Illinois, where he spent mindless, soul-crushing summer days ripping tassels from the stalks of sweet corn for five bucks an hour. After three weeks, his hands were stripped raw and his face so badly sunburned that his mother demanded he find a less punishing line of work. But he made six hundred dollars in those three weeks, and he used the money to buy the Trek mountain bike he'd been eyeing for months. He remembered it as a transformative experience; the supreme gratification of knowing that his suffering had been rewarded with something he wanted very badly. The next summer, he graduated to air-conditioned work, scrubbing dishes at a local diner alongside men twice his age, making only slightly more than he did as a field hand, but still feeling that same exhaustion after a long day of work, the thrum in his heels, the sweet relief of being granted permission to sit. But that was a long time ago; he was a kid then.

When he returned home from his jog, he checked his email and found a note from Renee.

> To: gavinb870@gmail.com
> From: reneeketchem@gmail.com
> Subject: Xmas
> I don't think I'm going to Chicago with you after all. I
> don't like where things stand with us right now, and I
> don't think spending time with your family is a very

good idea until we decide if we have a future together.
I'm going camping for a few days in Joshua Tree with
some friends. They're picking me up tonight. I'm sorry
to disappoint your parents, but you sort of did this to
yourself, so you can explain what happened. I'll be
home later this afternoon to pack. Maybe I'll see you
then.

       —R

Gavin's parents had recently moved to downtown Chicago from
the quiet northwest suburb in which he'd been raised. They'd spent
the past thirty years in the same house before deciding, somewhat
spontaneously, to see how they felt about urban living. They bought
a small condo at State and Jackson, under the watchful eye of the gar-
goyles perched atop the Harold Washington Library, and for the first
time ever he and his family had planned to spend the holidays in the
city by the lake. Gavin had purchased round-trip tickets for Renee
and himself, but now she'd decided she might prefer the company of
revolutionaries to her boyfriend's family. It seemed that whatever had
transpired between them last night was significantly more serious
than he'd imagined. For her to abandon a trip they'd been planning for
months meant that he'd really screwed up.

He began composing a response, but it came out angry and com-
bative, so he deleted it and searched for a better approach. When
nothing came, he scrapped the idea, thinking he'd try to smooth
things over when he got home that evening. Instead, he took a quick
shower and left for his fitting. He took the 101 North, which the
Audi's GPS assured him was moving. It was mid-December, sunny
and seventy-two, twelve days before Christmas. He stepped on the
gas and blew past a small pickup stuffed full of lawnmowers. Five
minutes later, he was at the studio gate, showing his ID to a man who
didn't recognize him. People rarely recognized him.

"Always late," Daphne said. "And not even a little late. Always fifteen, twenty minutes late. Why?" Daphne was a costume designer from Prague, a dinosaur in the industry, but not the kind that garnered any respect.

"Traffic," Gavin said.

"No matter, anyway," she replied, steering a wardrobe rack. "Shooting got pushed."

"Till when?"

"January."

This was news to Gavin. The show, *Makin' It,* documented the romantic and social transactions of a group of entry-level grunts working at a music label. It was set at a hip bar in Silver Lake, where they met for Trivia Night once a week and usually ended up getting drunk and sleeping with one another. The show was highly improvisational, full of halting, inarticulate speech intended to mirror the characters' confused inner lives. There were lots of circuitous conversations about the difficulty of navigating the real world, how *relationships are hard, you know*. It was like *Cheers* meets *Friends,* updated for the twenty-first century, but without the canned charm of the former and the easy, familiar humor of the latter. It was pretty terrible, but Gavin wasn't allowed to say that, which was okay because the critics said it for him.

"Where's Jake?" Gavin asked.

"He's with the writers."

Jake was the creator, the showrunner, the man in charge. The show was blatantly autobiographical in the most insufferable way, and Jake liked to impress aspects of his personal life onto the characters. There had been instances of Jake rewriting scripts as they were shooting, claiming that a particular event hadn't actually happened the way it was being filmed. His entourage was usually on set, acting as a kind of group quality control, making sure the actors were remaining faithful to the real-life individuals they portrayed. When one of the staff writers confronted Jake about his insistence on factual accuracy at the expense of narrative consistency, he was promptly fired. For Jake, the show was his diary broadcast to the world, a photo album of all the crazy shit he and his buddies got into. For everyone else, it was unwatchable.

"So is there any reason for me to be here?" Gavin asked.

"Not unless you want to help me fold clothes."

"Would have been nice if someone could have told me that before I drove all the way over here."

Daphne shrugged.

Gavin stepped outside to call his agent, a worthless MBA dropout named Michael Badger.

"Hello?" Michael answered after a few rings.

"What's up with the show?"

"Who's this?"

"It's Gavin. I was supposed to have a fitting today, but when I get here, the wardrobe broad tells me shooting got pushed. Is that true?"

"Someone should have called you," Badger said.

Gavin watched two men guide a leashed cow across the backlot. "So when are we back?"

"Could be a while."

"What's that mean?" The men led the cow toward a red barn, outside of which sat a vintage John Deere tractor. The men tied the cow to a C-stand weighted with sand bags. The idea that someone, somewhere in America, might watch whatever transpired in this scene and accept it as an authentic portrayal of rural farm life was astonishing.

"It's a tricky thing, you know," Badger continued.

"No, I don't know."

"Tricky how these things work. There are so many moving parts, so many people with opinions. Some people like the show, others not so much. The ratings tell us the audience is part of the not-so-much crowd."

"So they're pulling the plug?"

"You could say that."

"Which means I don't have a job."

"You've got a decent face, Gavin. You'll bounce back."

"What about the rest of the episodes? Don't they have to finish out the season?" Now there was a farmer in denim overalls standing next to the cow, while the camera assistant held a light meter up to his face.

"Yes, but they don't require you."

"What do you mean?"

"You died in a boating accident," Badger explained. "Lake Travis. While you were at South by Southwest. I'm sorry, but you were drunk and reckless and it ultimately served as a teachable moment about the dangers of drinking and boating, so—"

Gavin tapped off his phone. He should have known better. He should have known better than to sign with a man whose last name was a member of the weasel family. He should have known better than to believe that such a poorly written show could ever maintain a steady viewership. He should have known better than to expect class from an industry that had somehow squeezed six seasons out of a reality program called *Celebrity Dog Wash*. He shoved his phone into his pocket and walked back to his car. As he passed the barnyard scene, he noticed the farmer sitting on a bale of hay, drinking a green smoothie and scrolling through his phone. "Last looks!" a voice called out, and suddenly, like vultures upon carrion, four heavily armed hair and makeup artists descended upon the farmer.

The drive home was torturous. He'd been on the freeway for thirty minutes and had moved exactly four miles. The motorcycles continued zipping past, squeezing through unmoving lanes of traffic, mocking his progress. He felt his phone vibrate and fished it from his pocket to find Renee's smiling face staring back at him. "Hey," he said.

"Where's my sleeping bag?" she asked, her voice contrasting sharply with the smiling woman on his home screen.

"It's in the garage. I'll be home shortly—I can get it for you."

"I'll find it."

"Can you at least wait until I get home before you leave? I'd like to see you."

"Depends on when you get here," she said.

"I'll be there shortly, traffic's really moving."

"Right," she said, and hung up.

HE ARRIVED HOME THIRTY MINUTES LATER. Renee was hustling about the house, throwing the last of her things into the backpack she'd excavated from the tub of camping gear in the garage, seemingly annoyed that her boyfriend had the nerve to return home at this particular moment. She wore frayed jean shorts and an unbuttoned flannel shirt over a vintage Michael Jackson T-shirt Gavin had bought her at a thrift store in Houston. Her wavy auburn hair was tied carelessly on top of her head.

"Need any help?" he asked, trying to suppress the venom he'd accrued after swimming through heavy traffic.

"No."

"Why are you being so rash about this?" Gavin asked.

"I'm not being rash," she said, finally turning to him with a look of exasperation. "I've been unhappy for a while now. I've told you this repeatedly, but you either didn't care or assumed I wouldn't do anything about it. But now I am."

"Is this because I asked you not to use our place as a flophouse?"

Renee scoffed. "Give me a break. I was helping some friends who needed a place to stay. It's called hospitality. It's about committing to something larger than yourself."

"So *that's* what this is about?"

"That's part of it, yes." She moved to the kitchen and began rummaging through the cabinets. "It bothers me that we don't share the same values."

"That's absolutely not true." He and Renee *did* share the same values—he'd never voted anything but Democrat—but she was more of an activist, the type who spent her Saturday mornings canvassing outside Whole Foods. As much as he admired her passion, Gavin sometimes felt she was fueled more by her own rage than a real understanding of all the things she railed against. She got her news from the dark corners of the Twittersphere, and her grasp of the issues was primarily formed by the talking points she picked up from other people. Last year, a group of Evangelicals protested outside Planned Parenthood, and Renee commented that it was probably a good thing she didn't own a gun because she might be tempted to mow down every last one of the Jesus Freaks. The following week, she attended a summit by a group trying to reinstate the assault weapons ban, and it took some serious restraint for Gavin not to comment on the irony of her activism.

"Look," Gavin said, his voice projecting into the kitchen. "I respect what you're trying to do, but I don't understand the tactics. If you want to make a difference, then run for city council. That's something I can get behind. But posting memes and screaming into the void seems a little misguided. I think you'd be better served focusing on policy rather than sloganeering."

She reappeared from the kitchen holding a canteen. "This is what I'm talking about, Gavin. You shit on everything I do."

"I'm not shitting on it, Renee. I'm just questioning your method."

"You don't take anything seriously," she said, stuffing the canteen into her backpack.

"I take this relationship seriously."

"I'm not sure you do."

"Really?"

She turned to him, her face softening into something like pity. "Maybe this hasn't occurred to you, but my unhappiness is primarily a result of your all-consuming selfishness—your inability to consider anyone or anything other than yourself. You claim to take this relationship seriously, but I think you take it seriously only insofar as you believe it's the appropriate trajectory for the life you have mapped out in your mind. You're more in love with the idea of marriage and a family than you are with me as a partner. Our relationship feels hollow, Gavin. It feels like it exists purely out of convenience for *you*."

"That's a shitty thing to say," he said, though part of him worried it was true.

"I'm not trying to be cruel," she said. "But we aren't young any-more, and I think it's time to face the reality that maybe we just aren't right for each other. Maybe we want different things out of life. And maybe that's okay. I don't think I can give you what you're looking for, and I don't want to keep you from finding someone who can."

A honk sounded from somewhere outside. "I'm sorry," she said, grabbing her backpack and making for the door. "We can discuss this more over the phone. Tell your family I said hello. I hope you have a nice Christmas."

And like that she was gone. Their relationship had been wonderful in the beginning, when they'd see live music a few nights a week, or spend half their Sunday at brunch. They traveled extensively: a long weekend in Banff, a wedding in Portugal, an extended visit to Mexico City for a friend's gallery opening, followed by two weeks driving up the coast of Baja, eating ceviche and camping on the beach. And even the more quotidian activities, like making dinner together or walking around the lake on a Saturday morning, were charged with the simple satisfaction of having done them together. But then something hap-pened, a distance opened up, and their lives took parallel tracks. It happened slowly, incrementally, a slow drift that made it difficult to place blame on either party. Gavin retreated into his acting, Renee into her activism, and before long they became more like roommates. They hadn't had sex in weeks, maybe months, it was hard to remem-ber. He supposed he still loved her in some abstract way, though maybe it wasn't the right way, or maybe he didn't love her enough. He knew there was always a cooling period with long-term relationships, a settling of emotions, but he also believed there should be something beating beneath the stratum of domestic tedium. And that thing, he now knew, had gone dormant.

Maybe we don't want the same things out of life. That part was certainly true. Gavin had always imagined he would be a pretty good father, but Renee wasn't the maternal type. He'd held out hope that she might come around to the idea if she met the right kid. Last month, he'd offered to babysit for a mutual friend of theirs. He and the boy—a

three-year-old named Simon—spent the evening building an elaborate Lego castle while Renee sat on the couch reading *Mother Jones*. It
was apparent this wasn't a lifestyle that interested her, and he should
have known there were certain things a person couldn't change. But
here he was, thirty-five years old, not getting any younger as his
mother liked to remind him, and he worried that if he waited much
longer his sperm would be reduced to a flush of tiny, swimming cof-
fins.

He cracked a beer and stepped outside. It was a cool evening and
the air was filled with woodsmoke from his neighbor's chiminea. He
had to admire Renee's follow-through. She'd threatened to leave and
she'd done just that, which would have been remarkable in anyone
other than Renee. Part of him thought he should go out rather than
sitting around feeling sorry for himself, but most of his friends were
either raising small children or preparing to raise small children. He
called Tim, his last unmarried friend, to see if he wanted to meet for a
drink, but he was out with his new girlfriend, Jess, a twenty-five-
year-old he'd recently met at a show at the Hollywood Bowl. Gavin
told him about Renee's decision to leave and the loss of his job.

"Sorry, pal," Tim said. "Sounds like you had a rough day. Jess and
I have dinner reservations tonight, but you should meet up with us
afterward. We're going to a holiday party in Silver Lake. It's one of my
buddies from the dodgeball team. I'm sure there'll be lots of nice girls
for you to meet."

"I'm not feeling very sociable," Gavin said.

"You can't just sit home alone all night. That's not healthy."

"I don't know."

"Don't be a snooze," Tim said. "I'm texting you the address."

IT WAS A NICE HOUSE: a mid-century rectangle with a wall of windows overlooking the reservoir. The place was carefully appointed
with an assortment of modern furniture and handmade textiles acquired on someone's tour of Central America. Christmas ornaments

hung from an artificial tree and the kitchen table offered a selection of baked goods.

Gavin did a lap through the house, but Tim was nowhere to be found. He went to the kitchen to try to find a home for the beer he brought, but the fridge was gorged with other people's booze, so he made his way out to the deck, where he drank two beers in quick succession while surveying the traffic of a distant freeway. *So this is what it's like,* he thought, *the single life.* He'd spent most of his adult years in relationships, "a serial monogamist" he liked to say, and he now realized he was ill-equipped to be alone. For someone who made his living as a performer, he was painfully shy around strangers and had little patience for small talk. He wanted to believe the situation with Renee might somehow repair itself, though the more rational part of him suspected otherwise.

"There's my pretty boy," a voice called. He turned to see Tim approaching, wearing a ridiculous Christmas sweater with blinking lights.

"Nice sweater," Gavin said.

"Festive, right?"

"Where have you been?" Gavin asked.

"Over there," Tim said, pointing to a patio table where a small group presided over a field of spent cocktails. "Come on. I'll introduce you to some of Jess's friends. I think one of them could be your next ex-girlfriend."

As they approached the group of strangers, Gavin recognized one of the women as Mariana, his sole experiment with online dating. Five years ago—during one of his blessedly brief periods of bachelorhood—he'd impulsively joined an online dating club, which he referred to as a club because it was free and therefore slightly less repugnant than the pay sites. Gavin signed up, contacted three women, and went out with the first one to respond, an Argentinean girl from old cattle money. Her parents owned a ranch on the Patagonian Steppe, a little family-run *estancia* along the Malleo River that, in addition to hosting trout-starved fly fishermen during the winter months up north, provided select cuts of meat to the toniest restaurants in Buenos Aires. Mariana, the eldest of three girls, had attended boarding school before earning a scholarship to study theater at UCLA. After graduating, she moved to Santa Monica, and through the circuitous ways of the Internet, met Gavin for a glass of wine at a bar in Westwood. He'd pretty much forgotten about her until now, when he extended his hand in greeting, the slightest look of recognition blooming on her face.

"Hey there," she said.

"Hi."

"Gavin, right?"

"Yeah."

"You guys know each other?" Tim asked.

"Yeah," Gavin said. "But it's been a while." She looked just as he'd remembered: flawless complexion, with long black hair that fell past her shoulders, and a posture that defied the norms of their generation. She projected a radiant optimism, and Gavin felt better just standing in her presence.

"How do you know all these people?" Mariana asked, glancing around the crowded deck.

"I don't." He pointed to Tim, who had now inserted himself into an adjacent conversation. "I know him."

"How's your show?" she asked. "I've seen a few episodes. It's funny."

"It's not, but that's kind of you to say."

She laughed. "You're right, it's not. But *you're* good in it."

"*Was*," he said. "The network canceled it, which seems like a reasonable business decision."

She frowned. "I'm sorry to hear that."

"It's okay," Gavin said, and he sort of believed it.

"So now what?"

"I think I'll teach myself to cook," he said, because it sounded like the kind of thing people did when they found themselves with a surplus of time.

"Do you ever do any theater work?" she asked.

The last piece of theater he'd been involved with was shortly after he'd moved to Los Angeles, when he naïvely auditioned for what the ad in *Backstage West* described as "a daring new piece of underground theater by one of the city's most subversive directors." The subversive director had been curiously absent from the audition, so he ended up reading a monologue from *The Cherry Orchard* at a rehearsal space in West Hollywood. A few days later, he received a call from a producer offering him the part, but when he pressed for details he was told to arrive at the theater at seven that evening, at which point he would meet the director and be given the script. The script turned out to be a three-act bondage piece about a naïve young gay man who goes to work for a butcher and ends up becoming enslaved by the man before exacting revenge by removing his head with a bone saw and hanging his corpse from a drag hook in the meat locker. The director described it as a morality play for the LGBT community, some pretentious bullshit about sexual repression, but it seemed to Gavin more like a stage version of the torture porn being pedaled by the studios. After a night of serious deliberation, he committed to it only because he had nothing else booked and they offered him a thousand bucks for the three-week run. When the production ended, he found an agent specializing in commercial work, booked a couple ads for Verizon Wireless, and said farewell to the stage. "Yeah, you know," he finally said. "A little bit—here and there."

Mariana smiled. "I actually have something you might be interested in."

"Oh yeah?"

"Two problems though," she said, holding up as many fingers.

"Okay."

"The first is that you'd have to shave the beard."

"Not a problem. I think it's time for a new look anyway." Perhaps it was the beard or his penchant for designer flannel, but for whatever reason he was often cast as the grieving lumberjack, the heartbroken longshoreman, or, in the case of *Makin' It,* the hapless folk singer. He had a face casting agents described as Americana, whatever that meant. Renee had once told him he was *accessibly good-looking,* which she described as handsome but not so handsome that a woman might be too intimidated to approach him in a bar. "What's the second problem?" he asked.

"You'd have to relocate to Taos, New Mexico—at least temporarily."

"That's not a problem."

"I live there now," she explained. "I'm just back here for the weekend. I met a local guy—now my fiancé—and we're getting married in a couple weeks."

"Congrats."

"Thanks. Anyway, I've been doing some directing at a small theater there. It's certainly not Broadway, but it's fun and I'm proud of the work we've produced. We're in the process of putting together a production of *Long Day's Journey into Night.* The guy who was supposed to play Jamie just bailed and I need to find a replacement. I came back here to hold auditions since my pool of actors is pretty small, but the session today was a bust. I'm wondering if it's something you might be interested in?"

"I'm interested," Gavin said, perhaps a bit too enthusiastically.

"Yeah?"

"Absolutely."

"Great," Mariana said. "We have a house we can put you up in. There isn't a lot of money, so we can't offer much in terms of payment. But we could cover most of your expenses. And besides, Taos is beautiful. It's not the worst place to spend a few weeks."

"I know. I've been." When Gavin was in high school, his family went to Taos for a ski vacation during spring break. Back then Gavin didn't understand why they had to go to New Mexico when all his other friends were headed to places like Winter Park, Colorado, which seemed like the obvious choice for a ski trip. He associated New Mexico with deserts, and Taos with a brand of taco seasoning his mother used. But when they pulled into the valley at dawn, Gavin woke to the snowcapped peaks of the Sangre de Cristos glowing orange, and the scene struck him as quintessentially alpine, more Colorado than Colorado. "I love Taos," he said. "And *Long Day's Journey*. I actually played Jamie in a production back in college. It's a role I know well."

"Fantastic," she said, removing her phone from her purse. "The play doesn't start until mid-January, but we've been rehearsing for the past few weeks. I'd love to get you in the mix as soon as possible."

The last month had been one long string of unproductive days. He needed a change. Actually, what he needed was a new girlfriend, but that wasn't about to happen so he'd have to settle for a change of scenery instead. The idea of a few weeks in the mountains sounded nice. And besides, if today's earthquake was any precursor, L.A. would soon be reduced to rubble and he'd like to be as far away from that mess as possible. A house in the mountains of New Mexico seemed like a good place to ride out the apocalypse. "Let me know when to show up," he said.

"Perfect." Mariana consulted her phone. "Are you still at the 323 number?"

"Yeah."

"I'll call you in the next day or so, and we can hash out the details." She finished what was left of her wine and placed the empty glass on the table. "I have to split, but I'm so glad I ran into you. I think this could be great for both of us." She gave him a friendly hug and disappeared into the house.

"What happened?" Tim asked, reappearing from across the deck.

"She left."

"Why didn't you go with her?"

"I'm going to," Gavin said. "I'm leaving for New Mexico."

"New Mexico?" Tim said, baffled. "Why?"

Gavin shrugged. "Because I have nothing else to do."

SAMANTHA

ORNING CAME AND IT WASN'T so bad. Gone was the anxiety from yesterday, the incessant gnawing at her nerves. She was hopeful about the day in a way she hadn't been in months. Marie was in the shower, her laptop broadcasting *Morning Edition*. They were discussing a North Korean missile test and rising interest rates and trouble at the IMF, but Sam was interested in none of it. Since arriving in Russia, she had failed to keep up with the news from home. The only contact she had was the weekly phone call with her parents and the emails her brother sent with links to new music. She tried reading the online version of *The New York Times,* but even that seemed irrelevant, like studying a language no one else spoke. Besides Marie, no one here was concerned with America, and Sam had begun to share this feeling.

Like most children with talent, Sam had been encouraged. Encouraged to spend the hours after school at dance class rather than drooling over teen magazines with her girlfriends. Encouraged to spend her summers at dance camp instead of running around the neighborhood, sneaking beers and making out with boys. When she entered high school and the extent of her talent had begun to manifest—successful auditions, praise from her instructors, offers from prestigious dance academies—she was encouraged to try homeschooling in order to preserve her afternoons for dance. Unlike many girls with dreams of becoming a ballerina, she had the innate talent to make a legitimate go of it. When she was sixteen, she was invited to the Joffrey's trainee program. She'd meet with a tutor from eight to noon every weekday, then hop on the Metra and travel into the city for a three-hour block of dance instruction. Still in high school, she was already fluent in the language of urban living. She was riding trains and hailing taxis and drinking enough coffee to power small appliances.

In December of that year she was selected to perform the Sugar Plum Fairy role in *The Nutcracker.* She was praised in the *Tribune*'s review of the production, the critic calling her a dancer of exceptional promise. The following spring, she danced the butterfly in *A Midsummer Night's Dream,* and followed that with a turn as Odette in *Swan Lake,* a role that further cemented her standing as one of the principal young dancers in the city. It went like this for almost two years—rehearsing endlessly, performing beautifully—and she regretted none of it. Unlike many child prodigies, she was free to step away whenever she pleased. There were no unrealistic demands, no "stage mother" directing her career. Her parents encouraged her without compelling her. They often made a point, particularly as the dance world began absorbing all other aspects of her life, to make sure she was still having fun, that it hadn't become the kind of mechanized routine that causes most kids to burn out before they reach their full potential. And it never did. Sam loved to dance. She loved the difficulty, the hours of strenuous training, and it was this unstoppable work ethic, inherited from her father, that separated her from most every other girl with pointe shoes and inherent grace.

SHE ARRIVED TO FIND Max alone in the studio, marking through steps that seemed almost improvised, his body moving elegantly around the floor, as if blown by the winds of some beautiful brainstorm. She watched his body wind down, then applauded when the music stopped.

"Hello," Max said, wiping his forehead with a towel, a small patch of sweat darkening the neckline of his Henley. He reached for his water bottle and took a drink. "How long have you been standing there?"

"Long enough to be impressed," Sam said.

"That's the clunky version. I'm hoping you can inject some grace."

"What's the music?"

"It's by a Danish composer. What do you think?"

"I like it."

"Me too. He'll be here after the first of the year to adjust the timing, so I'm hoping to have the piece in a solid place by then. Not sure if Nikolai told you, but we open the first weekend in February, so I don't have a lot of time."

"I'm here to work," Sam said, dropping her bag on the floor.

Max's cellphone rang. He walked to the other side of the room to take the call. Meanwhile, Sam removed her boots and put on her pointe shoes. She tried to eavesdrop on his conversation, which she imagined was about her, based on the hushed manner in which he spoke. After a moment, he hung up and walked back to her.

"Everything okay?" she asked.

"All fine," he said, setting his phone on the bench. "Should we get started?"

Max performed a sequence of steps completely foreign to her, part of a physical vocabulary she wasn't familiar with. She watched closely, trying to follow along, but her mind struggled to keep up. He repeated the steps again, this time with Sam clumsily mirroring the moves back to him. After a moment, she stepped away, overwhelmed by the complexity of his choreography. "That's a lot to remember," she said.

"I just want you to get a sense of the blocking. We'll refine the movement over time."

"Yeah, but . . ."

"Is there a problem?"

"No," she said through a pained smile. "No problem." But that wasn't true. *Focus* was the problem.

Soon the other dancers arrived and began stretching at the barre. Max gathered everyone together and began explaining the conceptual aspects of the ballet before narrowing in on how they related to the specific choreography. He spoke with an authority that suggested the piece would come together nicely so long as the dancers executed his vision. After a year of false starts, this was Sam's chance to be a part of something meaningful, yet as much as she wanted to right her crooked path, she didn't entirely trust herself. She wasn't sure she could resist the beastly urges that had come to dominate her life.

As Max continued his instruction, Sam noticed Nikolai enter the studio with a young woman Sam had not seen before. She was a dancer no doubt: tall, svelte, a body designed for movement. She had the eager, wondrous look of a new recruit, and Sam recognized something of her former self in the girl. Nikolai escorted her over to the other dancers.

"Sorry to interrupt," Nikolai said, "but I wanted to introduce everyone to our newest dancer, Marguerite. She was a soloist at the Paris Opera Ballet, but she's decided to join us here. She's a great talent, and I'd like everyone to make her feel welcome."

Sam knew exactly what Nikolai was doing. This was an intimidation tactic, a thuggish way of letting her know the precariousness of her position. If Marguerite really was a soloist from the Paris Opera, she obviously had chops, which begged the question as to why she had defected here. Sam guessed it had something to do with Max's name, coupled with a substantial amount of money.

"Very nice to meet you," Max said. "Feel free to join us. I'm giving everyone a quick overview of the piece." He turned his attention back to the group and signaled for Sam and Mikhael, one of the male dancers, to join him on the floor. They stepped through the first few moves, while Nikolai observed from across the studio. A moment later, Max cut the music. He put his arm on Sam's back and guided her through the steps.

"You're going horizontal when it should be diagonal," he explained. "You have to match him. It's good in the beginning, but you're overextending at this point. It's too much. Let's go back to one."

Sam repeated the steps, but Max soon cut her off once more. "No, no. That's not it."

"I'm sorry," Sam said. "It's just not in my body yet."

"Perhaps you'd like Marguerite to give it a try," Nikolai suggested.

Sam ignored the comment. She wasn't typically a spiteful person, but she resolved to make sure Nikolai regretted ever having doubted her ability. "I've got it," she said. "Let's go again."

LATER THAT AFTERNOON, she returned to her room to find a manila envelope sitting on the kitchen counter. It was covered in a collage of postage, and in the upper left corner was a Christmas-themed return address sticker that read JEFF AND CYNTHIA BRENNAN. She opened the envelope and pulled out a DVD and a handwritten note.

> Sweetie —
>
> Not sure if you even have a DVD player over there, but I thought I'd send this to you anyway. It's the latest episode of your brother's show. He says it's terrible (no comment) but I can't help but be proud of everything you kids have accomplished. I can't tell you how excited I am to have you all home for Christmas. I've been trying to come up with fun things to do, but let me know if you think of anything in particular you'd like to do while you're here. Your dad and I have been looking at flights for February. Please let us know when you have dates for the ballet. We wouldn't miss it for the world! Love you!
>
> —Mom
>
> P.S.—Email me your flight info so I know when to pick you up!

———

HER MOTHER'S LETTER ALLUDED to two things that weren't wholly true. The first being that Sam had already bought a ticket home for Christmas (she had not) and the second being that she was going to dance the leading role in a new ballet (she was not). The second one was a lie that had recently acquired some truth. There *had* been a ballet scheduled—a horrid, uninspired piece of garbage—but it now seemed likely that Max's piece would take priority, which meant that perhaps it wasn't a lie after all.

Sam's mother had been a dancer herself, a serious talent according to her father's stories. Cynthia had been raised in a small factory town outside Pittsburgh. As a kid, she'd taken private dance classes with a Ukrainian woman, cleaning the studio in exchange for instruction. She eventually landed a spot with the Washington Ballet in D.C., but her career quickly ended when she became pregnant with Gavin at twenty-three. What amazed Sam was that her mother harbored no bitterness, especially considering how hard she had worked just to gain access to all the opportunities Sam had already squandered.

The front door opened and Marie entered, followed by her boy-friend, Owen, a twenty-four-year-old dancer from Ottawa. He was basically a third roommate at this point, which Sam didn't necessarily mind. She enjoyed the presence of a nonthreatening male in the house.

"How was rehearsal?" Marie asked. "Did you work with the new choreographer?"

"I did. He's nice enough. Little demanding, but that's probably a good thing."

"We're heading to the bowling thing tonight," Owen said. "You interested?"

The bowling thing was Nikolai's way of building camaraderie among the dancers. He hosted social activities once a week, though Sam found most of them to be superfluous and a bit corny. She didn't normally attend, but she'd spent most of the past week alone in her bedroom, so she figured it might be nice to log some face time with other humans.

THE EXISTENCE OF A bowling alley in Nikolai's home was just another example of the absurdity of his wealth, more reason Sam would never be able to relate to him on anything close to a human level. The place was hopping when they arrived. A deejay was spinning bad EDM beneath a disco ball, while the female dancers sipped martinis on angular leather sofas, the irony of the scene seemingly lost on everyone but Sam. She'd only been bowling at birthday parties as a kid, but even she knew that martinis were as anathema to bowling culture as beef jerky was to ballet. She selected a pair of designer bowling shoes from a shelf, then followed Owen over to a rack of bowling balls, all of them lovingly polished and free of prints. They were a far cry from the gold-speckled ones at the alleys back home, most of those chipped and faded, their insides sticky with God knows what.

"You'll probably want something in the twelve-pound range," Owen said, surveying the selection.

Sam found one she liked and carried it to the lane. Owen programmed their names into the electronic scoring system, while Sam and Marie laced up their shoes.

"I didn't think you'd come," Sam heard a voice say. She looked up to see Max standing above her, holding a matte black ball against his hip.

"There isn't much else to do on a Friday night," she said.

"Do you bowl a lot?"

"Nope. You?"

"I was actually in a league when I was a kid," he said with a giddiness that suggested he, unlike Sam, was tremendously happy to be here.

She glanced up at the electronic scoreboard. "How many strikes have you made?"

Max held up four fingers. "Two hundred and five is my personal best."

"That's good, right?"

He shrugged. "I like to think so."

"You're up, Sam," Owen said.

Sam stood and lifted a ball from the cradle. She stepped up to the line, then looked back to Max. "Any advice?"

Max tapped his index finger against the side of his head. "Focus."

"Right." Sam took a few awkward steps and heaved the ball down the lane, where it quickly found its way into the gutter. She looked back to Max. "What else you got?"

When the ball reappeared, Max picked it up and cradled it in his hands. "Let's start with the basics," he said. "First thing is learning how to handle it properly. It's not a melon, okay? Ring and middle fingers in the holes, left hand to steady." He situated the ball in Sam's hands, then positioned her a few steps behind the line.

She took two large steps and launched the ball down the alley. It started right then leaned back to center, downing all but one pin. Marie and Owen clapped. Sam looked to Max.

"See . . . ," he said.

"It wasn't focus," she said.

"Then what was it?"

"Chance."

SAM WENT TO GET a glass of wine and returned to find Owen doing a little celebratory dance. Sam told him to stop gloating, then handed her wineglass to Marie and rolled two more gutter balls, putting her total at nine points through the first two frames, a score that prompted Marie to suggest she get another drink. Owen rolled another strike and then one more after that, putting his total at a number yet to be determined, which he explained was due to the machine not being accustomed to such heavy math. Sam rolled her eyes and another gutter ball, then flashed a middle finger at the pins and went outside for a smoke. She was standing under a heat lamp when Max appeared holding a half-empty wineglass. "How's it going in there?"

"No strikes," she said.

"How do we fix that?" Max asked, setting his drink on the ground and pulling on a stocking cap.

"Not sure." Sam took a drag from her cigarette.

"Can I have one of those?"

She pulled the pack from her clutch and handed him one.

Max fumbled with the lighter before Sam stepped in to help. She lit the cigarette, then stepped back and watched as he took a long, awkward drag, which immediately resulted in a protracted coughing fit.

Sam laughed. "You don't actually smoke, do you?"

"I do not," Max said, covering his mouth.

"Then why are you out here?"

"Because you are," he said, tossing the cigarette on the ground. "Sometimes I wonder if I shouldn't have come."

"You could have waited inside. I wasn't trying to escape, though I have been known to do that."

"No, I mean *here*," Max said, motioning to their surroundings, the large, fortress-like buildings, the trees weighted with snow. "To Russia. To this company."

"Why's that?" Sam asked. She had her own opinion on the toxic nature of this place, but she was curious to hear a new perspective.

"You don't find the atmosphere slightly odd?"

"Oh, of course," she said, motioning with her cigarette to the thirty-foot-tall aluminum dragon standing sentinel in the courtyard, Nikolai's idea of fine art. "It's fucking bizarre."

"I don't mean to sound unappreciative. Yesterday I got a sixty-minute massage and a two-hundred-dollar bottle of wine delivered to my apartment."

"Ply 'em with booze and back rubs. That's Nikolai's style."

"It feels more like a resort than a dance company."

"Like Club Med for the Jonestown crew."

Max snorted into his drink. "I wouldn't go that far."

"You just got here, Max. Wait and see." Part of her wanted to tell him to run, to escape while he still could, but the other part, the selfish part, wanted him to stay, because she was so lonely and he was so handsome.

"I already feel strangely disconnected from the world." He blew into his cupped hands and looked to the wall of trees surrounding the campus. The door opened and Sam watched two female dancers rush out into the cold, dragging with them the remnants of a thumping bassline.

"So why did you come?" Sam asked, turning back to Max.

"My options were limited," he said with resignation.

"Last night you said you met Nikolai through a mutual friend—another choreographer."

Max hesitated. "That wasn't entirely true."

Sam smiled, equal parts confusion and intrigue. "What's the entire truth?"

"I had a wife and son in Toronto. I still do I guess, though only technically."

"Right," Sam said, because she suspected she already knew the rest of the story. A silence ensued.

"Aren't you going to ask what happened?"

She shook her head. She didn't need to, because she could guess. Infidelity most likely, probably with a dancer, probably a girl a lot like herself. In another life, she may have winced at the indiscretions of a man like Max, but not in this one. She too had done some things she wasn't proud of. "Did you grow up in Toronto?" she asked, attempting to recalibrate the conversation.

Max explained that he'd been raised in a suburb of Montreal, the only son of a welder with no interest in the performing arts. His was a youth of trout fishing and first-person shooter videogames. His father was an amateur hockey player, and most of Max's boyhood had been directed toward capturing the glory that had eluded his old man. In high school, he began dating a girl who attended the local performing arts high school. She showed him a television production of Pina Bausch's *Café Müller,* and he was floored by the recklessness of the choreography, the bodies collapsing onstage. Realizing that dance could be more than tutus and *The Nutcracker,* his interest grew and before long he traded his hockey skates for canvas slippers.

"And what about you?" Max asked. "What brought *you* here?"

"Poor decisions."

He paused, waiting for her to continue. "Care to elaborate?"

"I'd rather not."

She'd felt a droning unease since arriving here, though she knew the drugs were to blame for most of that. But there was also a lot that couldn't be blamed on the drugs, the parts of this place that were just weird and insular and way outside any normal person's notion of a dance company. But what could she do, where could she go? New York was unhealthy, but this place had become unhealthy as well.

"It seemed like you were fast-tracked to become a principal in New York," Max said. "What happened?"

"I got injured. Then I went through a bit of a funk where I wasn't sure I wanted to do this anymore. And by the time I snapped out of it, I'd been replaced. I spent some time wandering before Nikolai wooed me here."

"Are you happier now?"

"Not really," she said evenly. "Though I wasn't happy in New York either. I'm not sure I'd be happy anywhere."

"Are you depressed?"

She eyed him suspiciously. "Are you asking as a therapist or a friend?"

"Friend."

"I don't know. Let's just say that at this particular moment I'm happier than I've been in some time." Which was true. Max had a soothing effect on her, the ability to lozenge the scratchy despondency of her life in Russia. She'd felt unmoored since arriving here, but Max's arrival had brightened her mood. What she needed, she realized, was a partner, someone in whom she could confide. There

was Marie, of course, but Marie was now Owen's girlfriend, a desig-
nation that trumped her relationship with Sam. Almost everyone at
the company had paired off in one way or another—as lovers or
friends, dance partners or understudies—while she stumbled alone
through this foreign land. It was only now that she realized how ill-
equipped she was to find her way back, and she wanted to believe that
Max could help. "Are you enjoying this?" she finally asked.

"I'm sorry," Max said, taken aback. "I didn't mean to pry."

"No, I mean this bowling shit." Through the clouded, frozen windows, she could see the outlines of people dancing. "You wanna get
outta here?"

"Is that allowed?"

"No, but that doesn't mean we shouldn't."

"What did you have in mind?"

Sam flashed him a mischievous smile. "You have a car, right?"

WHAT SAM HAD IN MIND was a dive bar in Yaroslavl, where a handful of local men were watching a drag queen sing a groggy karaoke
version of Whitney Houston's "I Wanna Dance with Somebody." A
neon sign above the stage read: IMPERIAL DREAMS.

Sam sidled up to the bar. She ordered two vodka tonics and ferried
them to a folding table surrounded by plastic lawn chairs. They sat
and watched the singer transition to a Linda Ronstadt song while
drunks threw popcorn on the stage.

"It must be hard for you to be so far from home," Max said.

"It was my choice to come here."

"But still. You don't get homesick?"

"I miss my family, but that's about it. You?"

"I miss mine very much," he said, casting his eyes down toward his
drink. "But I don't think they miss me."

Sam exhaled something like a laugh, then realized he wasn't trying
to be funny. "Sorry," she said, composing herself. "So what happened—
your wife left?"

Max smiled awkwardly. "She went to Vancouver with our son. And her co-worker. I was not invited."

Sam felt a pang of guilt for assuming *he* was to blame for the dissolution of his marriage, followed by another, stronger pang of disappointment that, unlike herself, he was actually the victim of his circumstances.

"I thought I'd bury myself in the work," Max continued, "but I'm not even sure the work is very good."

"I liked what I saw."

Max looked to the stage, where an elderly, balding man was dancing with the drag queen. A chorus of hollers erupted from the crowd. "You haven't seen much."

"Isn't insecurity part of the deal? As my dad would say, this is the life you chose." Max's face, in profile, contained a sadness she'd only now noticed.

"I suppose," Max said, turning back to her. "I've been trying to get this ballet off the ground for so long now that I was starting to think it wasn't meant to be. But then I imagine someone like you performing the moves and it becomes the exact thing I had in mind all along. It's even more perfect, in fact."

"You're probably reconsidering after my performance today."

"It's the first day. You'll get there. It's Nikolai that worries me. I understand he doesn't have a great track record."

Sam laughed. "Let's just say there have been some false starts."

"Like?"

"Like the fact that he's only managed to mount one production, which wasn't exactly *critically acclaimed*."

"Then why do you stay?"

"Because I don't have anywhere else to go. Look, I don't have any illusions about the work that's being produced, though of course you give me hope. This isn't New York City. Christ, this isn't even Los Angeles. But I was promised a second chance, which wasn't something anyone back in New York was willing to give me." She finished her drink. "So here I am."

Sam heard the first notes of Sonny and Cher's "I Got You Babe" and looked to the stage where she saw someone grab the microphone from the emcee. Her chest tightened. It was Ivan, her drug dealer. In the dim light she could see the crude spiderweb tattoo scratched across his neck. He motioned for Sam to join him onstage.

"You know that guy?" Max asked, confused.

Ivan stepped off the stage and walked toward Sam, extending his hand.

"What are you doing here?" she hissed.

"Sing with me," Ivan said, eyes glazed, clearly high.

"Please," Sam said. "Not now."

"What's going on?" Max asked. He seemed unsure if he should intervene.

"Who is he?" Ivan asked, nodding at Max.

The microphone feedback cut through the song, prompting boos from the crowd.

"You need to go home," Sam said, standing and putting a hand on Ivan's back, directing him toward the door.

Ivan reached into his pocket and pulled out a small baggie. "I have a gift for you."

"I don't want it," she said, slapping his hand away. She turned back toward Max. "Let's go," she said, taking hold of his arm and leading him toward the exit. When they reached the door, she looked back one last time and saw Ivan holding the microphone in one hand, a gram of heroin in the other.

JONAH

H E AWOKE THE NEXT MORNING grateful to be alive. He stepped outside and breathed in the new day, which, even at this early hour, was already choked with a suffocating heat. He ate a breakfast of oatmeal and bananas, then washed it down with a cup of instant coffee. Life here was lived in the singular. He had one bowl, one cup, one spoon. He had a three-foot length of rope that doubled as a clothesline and a belt. He had a dishrag that he sometimes used on his face. He owned twenty-three items, twenty-two now that his camera had been stolen.

He shouldered his backpack and set off for the bai, the forest clearing where the elephants gathered each day. It was a quick layover on his way to the village. A nest of clouds shielded him from the sun and the hiking was easy, almost enjoyable. When he arrived at the bai, he saw a few dozen elephants slurping water from puddles that had sprouted from last night's rain. There were several familiar faces: Goldie and her youngest calf, an ornery, bowlegged runt Jonah had nicknamed Scooch; Rango and her two babies, neither more than a few weeks old; and Silver Ears, whose semi-translucent ears gave her an extraterrestrial appearance. Jonah climbed the stairs to the observation deck, a wooden treehouse perched thirty feet above the forest floor. Without his electronics, his work would be limited to what he could record with his eyes. He did a quick head count, twenty-three, and noted the attendance in his journal. The numbers had been slowly declining over the past few weeks—fifty-eight on November 27, forty-four on December 4—and he hoped this was a statistical anomaly rather than a fundamental change in visitation rates. Either way, it was an alarming trend and he would have to come up with a way to explain it to Marcus when he got back to the States.

He noticed two new adult female elephants, who, unlike the rest of the herd, did not have tusks. He'd heard about tuskless savannah elephants in Kenya and Mozambique, but he'd never seen such a trait in forest elephants. The thinking was that the lack of tusks was an evolutionary adaptation due to the pressures of poaching. As the larger tusked elephants were killed for their ivory, only the smaller ones were left, which meant that through years of breeding, the size of the tusks continued to decrease until there were significant populations born without them. He couldn't be certain this was what was happening here, but he wished he had his camera so he could document the animals to show to Marcus, who might know what to make of it.

Once he'd finished his daily count, he treated himself to a mid-morning snack and set off for the village. He followed a trail carved by the elephant foot traffic, part of a grid of pathways weaving through the forest. During his first month here, he'd marked the route with cairns, but it wasn't long until he was able to navigate by memory. It was three quarters of a mile to the giant *okoume* tree, where he turned right and followed a wide swath of trail leading to the footbridge over the Ogooué River, then the final quick, unbending mile along the logging road that emptied into the town of Franceville.

As he approached Laurent's restaurant, he heard the metronomic ping of someone beating thin metal. He spotted Laurent and his sole employee, Mateo, pounding away at the bar's sheet metal roof, the sun reflecting off their hammers. It seemed like every time Jonah visited town, Laurent was at work on some new renovation to the restaurant, and most of the jobs were either half-finished or completed with such haste so as to make the place seem in greater disrepair than before he began.

Laurent had grown up on a coffee plantation in the hills east of town. As a boy, he tracked animals in the forest, keeping detailed records of the size and color of each one, the location and time of day. He was the eldest of four boys, and it was assumed that he would take over the family business after high school, but he'd received a scholarship to the university in Libreville and wasn't about to forgo his own dreams for those of his father. It was while studying for his MS in ecology that he met Marcus, who invited him to assist with fieldwork during one of his initial trips to the area. Laurent's knowledge of the forest—and the elephants that inhabited it—was unmatched, and he soon became a permanent fixture on Marcus's team.

During one of their layovers in town, Laurent reunited with Helen, a childhood classmate who now worked at the restaurant her father owned. The relationship progressed, and a year later they were married. When Helen's parents passed away quite suddenly, she—and by extension Laurent—inherited the restaurant and all the attendant responsibilities. Laurent now lived with Helen and their four-year-old son, Clement, in a two-bedroom house behind the restaurant. For a while, he assisted Marcus with fieldwork, but with a small child and a business to run, his role had been reduced to that of consultant. He still assisted Jonah with data management and analysis, but his life had acquired a new shape that could no longer accommodate weeklong journeys into the forest.

"*Bonjour, ami!*" Jonah yelled. He'd taken four years of French in high school, and though the version spoken in Gabon was a far cry from his textbooks, he'd acquired a base-level competence that served him well.

"Hello," Laurent called back, looking down at Jonah from his perch on the roof, his wiry frame backlit by the sun. "Got a bit of a leak in this roof. Mateo's got some ideas on how to fix it."

"I thought you did that last week," Jonah said.

"Apparently, it didn't work so well," Laurent said, descending the ladder.

Mateo was responsible for everything from washing dishes to basic handyman work. He was in his mid-twenties, a good decade younger than Laurent and considerably less friendly. He was almost clinically averse to eye contact, and for a long time Jonah assumed he was a mute, an assumption that was quickly disproved when he caught him singing a Lady Gaga tune while scrubbing dishes.

"Why are you back already?" Laurent asked, stepping onto the ground and making his way toward the front door of the restaurant. "Miss me?"

"Somebody stole my camera last night," Jonah said, following him.

"Really?"

"Yep."

"Have you told Marcus?"

"Not yet. It just happened."

"This is a problem," Laurent said, stepping through the door.

"Yeah, to say the least," Gavin said, following him inside. "Can I borrow your computer? Need to send some emails."

"Sure," Laurent said, carrying a couple empty glasses to the kitchen. "You know where it is."

Little Clement sat at a table, hunched over a coloring book. "Hey, bud," Jonah said, but the boy was too engaged with his art to acknowledge Jonah's presence.

The restaurant wasn't much to look at. There were a dozen small plastic tables draped with floral tablecloths and a makeshift bar constructed from cinder blocks and scrap plywood. Mounted on the wall were family pictures and an old Zenith television that showed whatever football match the antennae could find. But what the restaurant lacked in design and aesthetic continuity, it made up for with the cheery, welcoming disposition of its proprietors.

Jonah walked to the kitchen, where Helen was chopping vegetables while listening to the BBC on a small radio. "Good morning," he

said, grabbing a Fanta from a small commercial refrigerator embla-
zoned with an eighties-era Pepsi logo.

"You back already?" Helen asked. She was a few years younger
than Laurent, with the poise and austerity of someone who doesn't
suffer fools. Jonah sometimes wondered if she considered him one of
those fools.

"I forgot my batteries," he said.

Helen shook her head and made a little *tsk* sound before returning
to her work.

Jonah stepped into a large closet that doubled as the restaurant's
office and grabbed the batteries from the charger plugged into the
wall. He then sat down at the desk, which contained an ancient IBM
laptop Marcus had brought from Vanderbilt when he first arrived.
Despite being almost a decade old, the computer was surprisingly
useful so long as you didn't need anything more than a word pro-
cessing application, a few simple games, and a spotty Internet connection.

Jonah logged into his email account and found a message from his
mother: *How are you feeling? Are you getting enough to eat? Are you wearing
bug spray?* He skipped the questions he didn't plan to answer and got to
the paragraph where she filled him in on the news from home. Apparently, Gavin's TV show had been canceled, which didn't surprise her
because she never did understand what it was about, which wasn't a
knock on Gavin, whose performance was actually quite good, much
better than his co-stars in her opinion, and though he's a little bummed
about the whole thing, she's certain he'll bounce back. She wrote that
Sam wasn't returning emails and she had no idea if she'd even booked
a flight back yet, which was beginning to worry her, because the idea
of not having all her kids home for Christmas was enough to break
her heart. Jonah rarely spoke with his siblings, usually relying on his
mom to keep him updated on their lives, and since moving halfway
across the world, his connection with them was essentially nonexis-
tent, which was why he was looking forward to rendezvousing with
his sister in Paris. He wrote back to his mother letting her know that

everything was going well, that he was excited to come home. He hit send, then began transcribing his letter to Sam.

When he was done, he took a seat at the bar. The television was broadcasting a football match between the Ivory Coast and Cameroon, the sounds of the game distorted by static, the picture nothing more than a swamp of muddy colors. It was a slow, scoreless game, so he decided to go for a walk. The town was relatively quiet. There was a woman hanging clothes out to dry and a skinny dog chasing a rooster down the street and some kids acting out a scene in which one of the boys held a toy gun to the other's head, while a third one filmed it with what appeared to be Jonah's video camera. The gunman had the smaller boy in a headlock, the gun pressed to his temple, and Jonah quickly realized that some kind of fictional hostage situation was taking place. He ran toward the kids, yelling, "Cut, cut, cut!"

"*Que diable?*" the cinematographer said, looking up from his viewfinder. "*Nous faisons un film.*"

"Where'd you get the camera?" Jonah asked the kid, who looked to be about fifteen years old.

"Not your business," the kid shot back in surprisingly good English. "Who are you?"

"Who are *you*?" Jonah said.

"I'm Oliver."

"Well, Oliver, *I'm* the owner of that camera."

"This is *my* camera. My dad gave it to me for my birthday."

"No, it's not." Jonah grabbed the camera from his hand and pointed to the small sticker on the bottom. "See that sticker? It says PROPERTY OF VANDERBILT UNIVERSITY, which is a college in the United States. This camera is for documenting elephants, not making amateur action movies. I'm very sorry, but I have to take it back."

"I'm telling my dad."

"Oh yeah?" Jonah asked, turning and walking back to Laurent's. "Who's your dad?"

"Your worst nightmare," Oliver yelled after him.

Jonah did a little pretend shaking motion, then laughed to himself. "Whatever, pal."

WHEN JONAH ARRIVED BACK at the restaurant, Laurent and Mateo were eating smoked fish at the bar. "Where'd you run off to?" Laurent asked.

"Went for a walk," Jonah said, holding up his camera, "and found this."

"Where?"

"Some kids were using it to make an action movie."

Mateo had been enthusiastically tearing at his fish, but he looked up when he heard Jonah's explanation.

"And you just took it?" Laurent asked.

"Of course," Jonah said indignantly. "It's *my* camera."

"I understand," Laurent said, sounding concerned. "But maybe that wasn't the most diplomatic approach."

"What was I supposed to do?" It seemed to Jonah like the obvious course of action, and he didn't understand why Laurent thought otherwise.

"I don't know. But probably not that."

Mateo nodded his assent, then returned to his fish, spitting a sliver of bone onto the ground.

After Laurent's comment, Jonah replayed the scene in his mind, wondering if he'd been too cavalier in his handling of the situation. He convinced himself it was fine, just some smart-ass kids, nothing to worry about.

Laurent and Mateo finished their meals and carried the dishes to the kitchen. The day's heat had settled on the town, cooking the metal roof to a temperature better suited to making waffles. Laurent said they'd have to wait till tomorrow to finish that particular job, but in the meantime, they could try to figure out what was going on with

the toilet that had stopped flushing after Mateo's extended visit with
it earlier in the day.

Jonah grabbed the camera and began scrubbing through the video.
There was a quick, frenetic montage of the young gunman arming
himself, followed by a prolonged chase scene in which he stalked his
target through the surrounding forest, into a hair salon, and finally to
the open stretch of dirt road where Jonah had found him and his buddies. He rewound another ten minutes and hit play. He watched a
shaky hand run with the camera through the dark forest, followed by
a few minutes of black during which two voices were heard speaking
in French and then, a minute later, a sight that made his heart sink. It
was hard to make out at first, but as the camera moved closer he recognized his own sleeping body in soft focus. The camera lingered for
a moment, then moved closer, revealing his face in the weak light, his
mouth open wide, his snoring light but steady. It was alternately familiar and terrifying. He immediately recognized the mistake he'd
made by repossessing the camera, a mistake that snapped into chilling
clarity when he saw a man on a motorcycle approaching from down
the road.

The bike coughed to a stop, and the man dismounted and dropped
it on the ground like an old bicycle. Jonah guessed he was close to
fifty; muscular, with cheeks pocked with acne scars and a fleshy, bulbous nose acquired from heavy drinking. He wore camouflage army
fatigue pants, a Tupac Shakur T-shirt, and the displeased countenance
of someone forced to attend to business for which he doesn't have the
time. "You took my camera," he said in toneless English.

"Excuse me?" Jonah said.

"That's my camera," the man said, pointing to the camera in Jonah's hand.

"I actually think this is mine," Jonah said. "Well, not mine, exactly, but the college's. It's for research. For the elephant research. For
the college." He was stammering, clumsily casting about for an explanation that might appease this indignant fellow.

"I know about your research," the man said. "I've seen your camp in the jungle. My brother, he is the police chief, and he tells me about you and the elephants. I try not to cause any problems with your elephants, but then you steal my camera so now I don't know." He summoned something phlegmy from the depths of his throat and discharged it into the dirt. "What happened to the other elephant man?"

"Marcus?" Jonah said. "He went home."

"So now it's just you?"

Jonah nodded.

He exhaled loudly as if dissatisfied with Jonah's answer. "I liked the other elephant man better," he finally said. "He didn't cause me trouble."

Jonah took a step back, imagining how he might weaponize his camera should the man lunge at him. "Honestly, the last thing I want is to cause you trouble."

The guy looked off in the distance, as if considering where he wanted to steer the conversation. "Tell me again why you are here."

"I'm doing research on forest elephants," Jonah explained.

"Yes, but why. What do you wish to know?"

Jonah wasn't sure how detailed an explanation the guy was looking for, so he said, "I'm studying how they communicate. Vocal patterns, things like that."

The man smiled condescendingly. "So you go into the forest to talk to the elephants? Is that right?"

Jonah knew he was being made fun of, and he hoped that some gentle teasing might be the extent of the man's wrath. He adopted a more conciliatory tone. "If you feel like I've stolen your camera, we can speak to the police." He then remembered the man's claim that his brother was the chief of police.

"Yes," he said. "I think I may do that. I'll speak to my brother and see if we can find a happy ending to this camera." He clapped Jonah on the back, causing him to flinch. The man laughed, then picked his motorcycle up off the ground, kicked it to life, and rode away.

Jonah went back inside the restaurant, where Laurent was standing by the door, holding a broom in his hand, apparently eavesdropping on the exchange.

"Who was that guy?" Jonah asked.

"He's a bad man," Laurent said, shaking his head. "A very bad man."

"Yeah," Jonah said. "That's sort of the impression he gives. Do you know him?"

"I know *of* him." Laurent explained that the man's name was Lionel, but everyone called him Slinky. As a boy, Slinky had acquired his nickname by trapping large snakes with his hands. He soon realized that in addition to the thrill of the hunt there was a substantial amount of money to be made. A few years ago, he joined forces with two Rwandan men with connections to exotic animal collectors across the globe, and together they formed one of the largest black market animal smuggling rings in West Africa. Slinky and his team of hunters were responsible for acquisitions, while the Rwandans handled sales and delivery.

"So this is an organized thing?" Jonah asked.

Laurent nodded.

"And he more or less gets away with it?"

Laurent explained that as the chief of police Slinky's brother had connections with the Gabonese minister of the interior, which ensured that the appropriate heads would be turned at the appropriate moments, allowing Slinky and his team complete freedom to transport an almost limitless number of wild animals. A year ago, Slinky trusted a relative newcomer to the business, a Nigerian man named Gibby, with moving six Nile monitor lizards from his home in Benin to a Finnish dealer in Cameroon. When Slinky arrived at Gibby's apartment with the delivery instructions, he found his product snacking on the corpse of his newest employee, Gibby's midsection picked clean by the eight-foot lizards. Slinky packed what was left of the man into two large suitcases, which he dumped in the Gulf of Guinea. Slinky considered the whole ordeal a minor hassle, but his Rwandan partners—rattled by the graphic realization that one could actually be *eaten alive* by lizards—abandoned the exotic animal trade for the relative safety of the diamond business. With his connections gone and no support structure to help with a line of work as logistically complex as his, Slinky made a career move of his own, this time into the ivory trade, realizing that animals were easier to deal with dead than alive. Now he spent half his time interfacing with brokers in Libreville and the other half hunting elephants in the forests outside Franceville. As its unofficial mayor, he presided over the town with the unbending discipline of a warlord. When a man from a neighboring town reported Slinky to the authorities, the man was taken into the forest and given a backwoods colonic with a three-foot elephant tusk.

"Of course," Laurent said, "this is all just gossip. Who knows how much of it is true."

This last part was little comfort to Jonah, because he knew that if *any* of it were true, if even part of Laurent's story was indicative of the kind of man who would not only steal his camera but then have the audacity to return in the middle of the night to film, with chilling objectivity, his sleeping body, then surely this was a man *not to be fucked with*. For the first time in his life, Jonah became acutely aware that someone might have a reason to kill him.

"Why is this the first I've heard about the guy?" he asked.

"He hasn't been around much," Laurent said. "I thought maybe he'd been arrested."

"And the kid?"

"That's his son apparently, though I believe he lives in Libreville with his mother most of the time. He goes to some fancy international school. I think his mom sends him out here during his breaks."

Clement approached with a page torn from his coloring book, a purple rocket ship arcing over a yellow sun.

"*C'est bon!*" Laurent said, inspecting the drawing.

It was getting late in the day, so Jonah collected his batteries from the office and placed them in his backpack. "So what do you think I should do?" he asked Laurent.

"Well," Laurent said, pausing either for effect or because he genuinely wasn't sure what to say. "If it were me, I would probably do whatever he asks."

GAVIN

HE LEFT BEFORE DAWN, before the freeways filled, heading west through the L.A. sprawl, past the factory outlets and the big-box retailers, over the Cajon Pass and through Barstow, where he once spent three terrible weeks shooting a low-budget horror film about desert zombies. He shook the city from him and entered the emptiness of the Mojave Desert, the interstate unrolling before him like so many miles of clean track.

This whole thing had come together quickly, maybe too quickly. He'd committed without really thinking it through, which, in the past, had often landed him in trouble, though he wanted to believe this time would be different. But he also had very little to lose, so there was that. As far as he could tell, the worst-case scenario was that he'd put an extra two thousand miles on his car. Mariana had followed up with him the next day, sketching out her thoughts on the play. From a directorial standpoint, she seemed far more intelligent than most of the hacks he'd worked with in L.A. She lived in Taos with her fiancé, a general contractor who also helped run the theater, though his involvement, she assured Gavin, was purely administrative. She didn't want him to think this was some kind of crazy husband-wife directing duo. She financed the productions—typically one per season—through grant money and ticket sales. The casts consisted of locals, sometimes kids from the schools, *hobbyists* she called them, though occasionally she was able to lure a professional like himself from one of the coasts, a face the audience might recognize, someone whose legitimacy could be confirmed with an IMDb search. He wanted to tell her that an IMDb credit was about as legitimate as a child's pilot wings, but he figured there was no point in negotiating against himself.

The winter production of *Long Day's Journey* was a first for the theater, considerably darker than most of their previous work, feel-good puff like *Annie* or *The Sunshine Boys*. Mariana was worried it might be a struggle to draw the kind of crowds needed to square the bank account, which was why his involvement was so crucial. At least she'd have a name to hang on the marquee, though Gavin doubted many of the town's residents would recognize a part-time player from a recently canceled show on a second-tier cable network. He'd done some research online, and for a community theater it seemed reputable enough; lots of poorly photographed headshots of the principal actors, a calendar of events with links to future productions. There was even a write-up in the *Albuquerque Tribune,* the theater critic calling a recent production of *Our Town* delightfully unexpected, praising Mariana's empathetic direction. And if it was terrible, he'd find some excuse for why he couldn't return after the holidays, though his conversation with Mariana gave him hope that it might be pretty good, certainly more satisfying than his previous role as an executive assistant with dreams of becoming a folk singer.

HE PASSED INTO CENTRAL ARIZONA, the sun setting behind him, a collection of clouds building up ahead. He was a hundred miles from Flagstaff, where he planned to treat himself to a beer and a nice dinner. Before the trip, he imagined stopping at roadside diners, chatting with locals and documenting his journey through photographs, but thus far his only meal was at the Jack in the Box in Needles, California, where he ate a hamburger while watching a Styrofoam cup blow across an empty parking lot. He'd tried to chat up the gas station attendant in Kingman, Arizona, but the man had little interest in another Californian passing through. All he could see from the interstate were hundred-foot-tall McDonald's arches and Chevron logos, and he realized he'd foolishly mistaken Interstate 40 for Route 66.

As he crossed into Arizona, his mind circled back to Renee. He'd tried calling her a couple times, but it went straight to voicemail, which made him think that maybe she *was* camping. Renee was the most nature-averse person he'd ever met, so it was a little curious that she'd decided to spend the holidays in the high desert. Their shared experience in the outdoors was limited to a hike she and Gavin had done while vacationing in Big Sur. She'd spent the entire afternoon scanning the forest for bears, despite Gavin's insistence that there were no bears in the Ventana Wilderness. Gavin imagined her slogging through desert scrub brush, regretting her decision to spend Christmas in rattlesnake country.

Apathetic. That's how Renee had described him before she'd left, and he knew there was some truth to the accusation. There was a time, maybe five years ago, when his career had been clicking along quite nicely. He'd spent his first four years in L.A. working for pizza on student films and campy horror movies. But then he starred in a low-budget coming-of-age film that won the Audience Award at Sundance. That led to a supporting role in a Danish film that premiered at Cannes. It was while doing press on a hundred-foot yacht in the south of France that it seemed as if he'd finally made it. There was no turning back now, he'd graduated to the next level, the hard work had paid off. But then he spent the first half of the following year auditioning for leading roles he didn't get. He finally took a job on a CBS procedural to pay the bills, but it was canceled after the first season. His agent at CAA jettisoned him in a cruel display of infidelity. He cashed in on a few commercials before succumbing to the empty promises of Michael Badger, who secured him the role on the flaming piece of garbage he was now fleeing. So *yes,* maybe he was a little apathetic. Maybe he *was* a little frustrated with the trajectory of his career. At his age, he was forced to confront the reality that maybe this wasn't going to happen after all, that maybe he'd already peaked and what awaited him was a slow descent into irrelevance.

GAVIN'S PLAN WAS TO drive through the night, hopefully arriving in Taos by dawn. But as he climbed toward Flagstaff, the snow began falling in earnest and he realized he wasn't going to make the kind of time he'd expected. The road soon turned white and he worked hard to keep the car in the single track of asphalt carved by the SUV ahead of him. He was doing twenty on the interstate, being passed by semis that sprayed his windshield with a thick wintery paste. His wiper blades had frozen over, and before long it was like trying to navigate through an empty jar of mayonnaise.

When he arrived in Flagstaff, he stopped at an Olive Garden and ordered fettuccini Alfredo and a glass of cabernet. From his booth by the window, he watched a rising tide of snow build on the hood of his car. He ate slowly, then ordered dessert and coffee. It was now close to nine, and the snow wasn't letting up. Pressing on meant possibly spending the night in a ditch, so he picked up a six-pack and booked a room at a Super 8. He changed into his pajamas and flipped through the meager selection of channels, finally settling on *60 Minutes,* where Anderson Cooper was reporting on the opioid epidemic. Checking to see what time it was in Moscow—11 A.M.—he attempted to Skype his sister, but she didn't pick up. He hadn't spoken with Sam in over a month, and he was looking forward to spending some time together back in Chicago, maybe catching a show at the Hideout.

Back in college, when Gavin would return home to Chicago for the summer, he used to drive Sam into the city to see shows at the Fireside Bowl, a grimy, all-ages punk venue that smelled of beer and vomit and adolescent perspiration. It wasn't the kind of place he imagined his sister would enjoy, but Sam was taken by the scene, the band thrashing onstage, the heaving, pulsing crowd. It was the antithesis of ballet, but Sam had the most catholic taste of anyone he knew so her reaction wasn't completely surprising. They spent the rest of that summer listening to records in the cool dark of their basement before venturing into the city a few nights a week to experience live versions of the music that soundtracked their summer. They'd wander the streets of Logan Square beforehand, nipping at the flask of whiskey Gavin smuggled in his backpack, and then, at the end of the night, catching the last train back to the burbs, sweaty, ears ringing, bodies thrumming with the residue of live music.

GAVIN AWOKE THE NEXT MORNING, filled his thermos with coffee from the motel's continental breakfast, and was on the road by eight. He followed the signs for I-40 east. The interstate had been cleared overnight and the driving was effortless. He polished off the balance of Arizona and made his way into New Mexico, gassing up in Gallup, then pressing on to Santa Fe, where he stopped for lunch. He was about seventy miles from Taos, which he figured he could do in ninety minutes. After two full days of driving, he was looking forward to his arrival in this quiet mountain town that would be his home for the next week. As he sat in the warm sun of a Chipotle dining room, he checked his phone and found a message from Mariana:

> Call me when you get this. Something came up.
> Hope you haven't left L.A. yet.

THE HOUSE WAS A two-story adobe structure at the end of a long gravel road. Ponderosa pines bent with the weight of new snow, and a man, Mariana's fiancé, Gavin guessed, was clearing the driveway with a snow blower.

Gavin parked on the street and walked along a path of cleared concrete, lifting a palm in greeting. "Hey there."

"Welcome!" the man said. He cut the blower and walked to Gavin, removing his leather work gloves. He extended a meaty, calloused hand and shook with the force of a trash compactor. He was shot through with a blue-collar ethos, the sturdy frame of a guy who spent his days working outdoors. "You must be the actor."

Gavin laughed uneasily. "I guess so."

"Mariana's inside," he said. "Go on in."

Mariana greeted him at the door. "Come in, come in," she said. "I'm so sorry about all this."

Gavin removed his shoes at the door and hung his coat on a pair of antlers mounted to the wall. The house had a southwestern modern aesthetic: sharp lines and desert hues, a slightly incongruous mix of local and contemporary art. A few logs smoldered in the fireplace, and a wall of windows looked out at a herd of cattle milling on the valley floor, the uneven peaks of the Sangre de Cristo sparkling above them. "Quite a view," Gavin said.

"It never gets old," Mariana said from the kitchen. "Can I get you something? Water? Coffee?"

"I'm okay. Thanks." Gavin wandered into the living room. The coffee table was littered with wedding invitations and playbills. Yellow tulips sprouted from empty wine bottles wrapped in decorative twine, centerpieces he guessed.

"For some reason, I had it in my head that you weren't leaving L.A. until this morning. Sorry for the confusion."

"It's cool. So what happened?"

"It's kind of a mess," she said, shaking her head at the insanity of it all. "There was a fire at the theater the night before last. No one was hurt and the damage isn't terribly extensive, but it certainly throws a wrench in my schedule. The guy who owns the building is a friend of ours, and he's hired Jesse to do the renovations, but it's hard to say how long it'll be until we can get back in there. So basically, we're kind of in a holding pattern. We obviously won't be opening in mid-January like I'd planned. Maybe not at all, though I'm trying to remain optimistic."

Gavin smiled and looked out the window. It seemed he'd driven a thousand miles to stare at cows.

"The house is yours for as long as you want. I'd still like to rehearse just in case we do get up and running. The high school has offered to let us use their theater for rehearsals. I know you're heading to Chicago in a few days, but I'd love to at least introduce you to the rest of the cast, maybe do some table reads." She grabbed an envelope sitting on the kitchen counter. "I also have some free lift tickets if that entices you to stay. You a skier?"

"I am," he said. "Skis are in my car."

"Great," she said, feeding another log to the fire. "I'm really embarrassed. I don't want you to think this is some disorganized hillbilly theater thing we're running here. This is just about the worst possible thing that could happen. It's also a little crazy trying to plan a wedding *and* mount a production."

"I get it. I've worked on far more disorganized productions, believe me."

"Why don't I show you up to the house, let you get settled?"

"Sure."

The door opened and Jesse entered, stomping his boots on the rug. "Clean drive," he announced.

"I'm taking Gavin up to the house," Mariana said. "You want to come along?"

Jesse planted himself in a leather club chair by the fireplace and rubbed his hands together in the exaggerated motion of a homeless man over a trashcan fire. "I think I need to sit by this fire and drink two glasses of bourbon before I get up to much."

"There's leftover lasagna in the fridge," Mariana said, grabbing her keys from a clay bowl on the counter. "I'll be back in a bit."

GAVIN FOLLOWED HER JEEP out to the highway and through the historic old town of Taos, a quaint little community that seemed to be constructed entirely of adobe and the positive vibes of Kokopelli. They turned up Highway 64 and wound their way to the base of the mountain. The lifts had powered down for the day, and a mass of ex-

hausted skiers waited for the shuttle to carry them back to their cars. A
funk band had set up on the deck of the lodge, jamming out après-ski
tunes for a group of laconic skiers with their boots cracked open, beers
in hand. They continued up a service road, past a shed housing heavy
snow machinery, and finally to a newly constructed house at the end
of the road. Aside from some new construction going up a couple hundred yards down the way, it was the only home for a quarter mile.

"So this is it," Mariana said, pushing open the front door. "Not
bad, huh?"

It wasn't large or extravagant, though it did have a hot tub off the
deck and a view of the catwalk that funneled skiers to the base. It had
the feel of a staged home, fully furnished but not lived in, a rarely
visited second or third residence. Mariana explained that it had been
built less than a year ago for her friend Nikki, an interior designer
who spent most of her time out of the country. She was in Japan for
the next six weeks, decorating the home of a Sony VP, and had given
Mariana permission to use the house as guest quarters.

"It's perfect," Gavin said, taking in the place. "It's more than perfect, actually."

The sun had disappeared behind the mountains, staining the sky a
creamy purple. Gavin looked out the window and saw the headlights
from a snowcat printing lanes of corduroy on the mountain. Mariana
turned the thermostat to seventy and showed Gavin where to find
fresh towels. She warned him he might have trouble getting the Internet up here and that there wasn't much in the way of television,
though he was welcome to dig into Nikki's record collection, which
consisted mostly of old country albums. She'd stocked the fridge with
beer and food—a pan of lasagna and a six-pack of local IPAs—enough
to tide him over until he had a chance to visit the grocery store. On
her way out, she showed him where Jesse had stacked a few cords of
firewood, then bid him good night and said she'd check in tomorrow.
She disappeared down the road and Gavin was left standing in the
driveway, still for the first time in two days, unsure what to do with
himself now that he'd arrived.

He went inside and grabbed a beer, thinking that was a good place to start, then carried his bag to his bedroom and changed into his swimming trunks. He got the lasagna going in the oven, then stepped out onto the patio and removed the lid to the hot tub. A wall of steam splashed his face, like opening a dishwasher, and he grazed his toe along the water's surface, which was very hot. He scooped a handful of snow from the deck railing and dropped it in the water, a purely symbolic gesture. When the water had reached a tolerable temperature, he lowered himself in and admired the stars, a whole map popping against black.

Thirty minutes later, the oven's timer sounded. Gavin dried himself off and went inside. He changed into his pajamas, slid a square of lasagna onto a plate, and planted himself on the couch. Two beers, nine thousand feet, and thirty minutes in hundred-degree water had reduced his bones to saltwater taffy, ground his brain into an alpine sludge. He annihilated his dinner while listening to "Blue Kentucky Girl" by Loretta Lynn, then, on a drunken whim, called Renee. It went to voicemail again. "It's me," he said into the phone, to no one. "I'm in New Mexico, in the mountains of New Mexico actually, and it's very cold here. I came to do a play, but now I don't know if that's going to happen. Maybe if you get this, you'll want to give me a call?" He tapped off his phone. Why was he even calling Renee, who had no interest in him? Loneliness, obviously. Everything had happened so quickly: Renee leaving, meeting Mariana at the party, then packing up his car and driving to a small mountain town.

Perhaps it was impetuous, certainly a little impetuous, but that's what happens to a man with no anchors. At thirty-five he should have anchors. He should have a wife, a couple children, a mortgage. At thirty-five his own father had three kids and a job traveling around the Midwest selling insurance, and while Gavin didn't know what his dad used to do in his free time, he was fairly certain it didn't involve crossing state lines in the name of community theater. He imagined whatever spare time his dad found outside of trying to provide for a family of five on thirty thousand dollars a year was spent in a far more admirable way, like playing catch with his boys or barbecuing with the neighbors. And if Gavin wanted to go back a generation further, he could examine the life of his grandfather, an Irish immigrant who settled in rural Illinois, working a couple hundred acres of farmland until he keeled over at the age of sixty, a man as familiar with the concept of a vacation as he was with the Internet. But Gavin? His whole life was a vacation, though not a particularly interesting one. Back in L.A., his days were spent sleeping till ten, followed by coffee, a half-assed workout of some kind, lunch, a nap, more coffee, a beer, dinner, more beer, an hour of television, and bed. And now he was here and, with the exception of television, there was nothing to suggest a variation to that routine. There was nothing to suggest his life would be any different.

SAMANTHA

SHE HAD A TWO-HOUR WINDOW and while that seemed like enough time to terminate the relationship and still make it back for rehearsal, there was no accounting for the emotional terrorism Ivan was likely to inflict. Last night's episode had shown that despite his utility as a supplier of narcotics, the collateral damage engendered by their partnership rendered it wholly unsustainable, both to her professional ambitions as well as her health. She knocked twice and resolved to make this quick.

"Yes?" Irina said, opening the door.

"Where's Ivan?" Sam asked, stepping inside. Ivan and Irina, his grandmother, lived a life of controlled squalor in a two-bedroom unit on the top floor of an old Soviet-Bloc apartment complex at the edge of Yaroslavl. The kitchen was stained with five decades of careless cooking and the bathroom's shower glass was lacquered with soap scum that Sam once spent an entire weekend trying, unsuccessfully, to remove. But it was the smell that she couldn't get over. Everything else was just aesthetics, the hallmarks of an unkempt home, but the odor was alive and it burrowed into her nose and stayed there. The place was a sharp contrast to her own apartment, which, though small, was tastefully decorated and regularly cleaned by someone other than herself. With the old woman's worsening dementia and the boy's crippling heroin addiction, there didn't seem to be much hope for the two of them, yet Sam still found herself returning at least once a week. She cleaned, though she knew it wouldn't last, and she cooked, though she knew it wasn't appreciated. She did these things partly in exchange for drugs, but also because it provided her with a concrete task for the day, manual labor masking as atonement for the mess she'd made of her own life.

"Irina," Sam said again. "Where's Ivan?"

"Not here," Irina said. She wore woolen slippers and a threadbare housecoat, her pockets overflowing with used tissues.

"When will he be back?"

"Soon."

Sam pulled her phone from her pocket and set the timer. If he wasn't back in twenty minutes, she was leaving.

"Pasta?" Irina asked, taking a seat on the living room sofa.

Last time she was here, Sam had made a spaghetti bolognese, one of the few recipes she'd picked up from her mother. While it wasn't traditional Russian cuisine, it was at least made from scratch, which was more than could be said of the canned soup that typically constituted Ivan and Irina's dinner.

"Irina?" Sam asked.

Irina was silent, her eyes fixed on the television. She was prone to moments of sudden abstraction, which appeared to be happening now.

"Irina!" Sam said, clapping her hands together. "Where's your grandson?"

Irina snapped to attention. "Huh?"

Sam lowered herself to Irina's level, looked her directly in the eyes. "Where did he go? Ivan?"

"At store. He come home soon."

Sam took a seat on the other end of the couch and looked down at her phone. Seventeen minutes. She grabbed the remote and began flipping through the channels. She landed on a montage of a dread-locked man twirling a flaming baton in front of a campfire. Another man stood knee-deep in the ocean, stabbing at fish with a wooden spear.

"This is good one," Irina said. "*Last Hero.*"

Last Hero, Sam realized after watching a few seconds of the show's title sequence, was the Russian version of *Survivor,* with cruder camerawork and a less sophisticated graphics package.

"When is Chicago?" Irina asked.

"Soon," Sam said, watching a group of half-naked islanders deliberate around a campfire. She glanced down at her phone. Fifteen minutes.

"Take care of Ivan. He never leave Russia."

For some reason, Irina was under the impression that Ivan would be accompanying Sam back to Chicago, though Sam had made no mention of such a plan, so she wondered how Irina had gotten that idea. For the last few weeks, Irina had, on more than one occasion, said things that suggested there was some kind of romantic involvement between Sam and her grandson. Sam wasn't oblivious to the affection Ivan had shown her, but she attributed it to an innocent crush, a local boy's infatuation with the exotic American. Ivan had tried to kiss her a couple weeks ago but she'd escaped by fielding a text on her cellphone. He tried again last week and she allowed it this time, only because he was so sincere with his words, and she couldn't stand to break his heart. She also couldn't imagine where she might find more drugs, though she didn't want to believe that had factored into her decision. But she was leading him on; she knew that. She was leading them both on—the grandmother wanting nothing more than for her grandson to marry this pretty girl who treated them both so kindly—by not being forceful enough in her protestations. Her entire life up to this point had been an effort not to disappoint anyone, a kind of gentle acquiescence that only exacerbated small fires that could have been extinguished with the firm placement of her foot, an emphatic *I don't think that's the best thing for me right now.*

———

THE DOOR OPENED AND Ivan entered with a sack of groceries. His cheeks were red, his eyes bloodshot, as if he hadn't slept since she last saw him.

"We need to talk," Sam said firmly. She looked down at her phone. Eight minutes. "I don't have much time."

"I have lunch," Ivan said, moving toward the kitchen.

"It can wait," Sam said, following behind him.

"What?" he asked, setting the groceries on the counter.

"In private." Sam walked down the hall, then into his bedroom, which resembled the scrambled innards of a hard drive. The ceiling was webbed with extension cords and Ethernet cables and blinking Christmas lights. There were modems stacked upon routers and the remains of a disemboweled computer scattered on the floor. In one corner was a twin bed with no frame, above which hung an eighties-era Apple poster. "What happened last night?"

"What do you mean?"

"At the bar," she said. "You ambushed me."

"I wanted to sing with you," he said plainly.

"You can't do that shit, Ivan. You can't stalk me like that."

"I was not stalking," he said.

"Whatever this is between you and me—it's over."

"What about drugs?"

"No more drugs. I'm done. *We're* done. Do you understand?" Sam checked her phone: six minutes. She walked to the bedroom window. In the distance, two men stood around a pile of burning garbage.

"But I have more," Ivan said.

"I don't want it."

"Just take," he said, extending his hand. "You already pay for it."

This was true. She'd given him money the last time they met. Despite her assertion that she was done with drugs, she figured it might not be a bad idea to have a pinch in reserve. And if she didn't want it after a couple days, down the toilet it would go.

"Fine," she said, "but this is it. I appreciate what you've done for me, but it was a mistake to become friends with you. I accept the blame for that. I shouldn't have confused the boundaries." She put on her coat and checked her phone. Four minutes. She looked back to Ivan. "I wish you nothing but the best, but please don't ever contact me again."

She closed the door behind her and walked through the living room. Irina had fallen asleep in her chair. Sam turned off the television, placed a blanket over the woman, and stepped into the bathroom to pee before the long walk back to campus. There was dried piss on the toilet seat and empty toilet paper cores scattered across the floor. The mirror, which she looked into as she washed her hands, was smeared with toothpaste. *So long to all this,* she thought. She knew she was being cold, but there was only so much one person could do for another, and she had reached that limit. She needed to take care of herself now. She dried her hands on her pant leg, then walked to the door and turned the knob, but it didn't move. She tried again, but the resistance was real. "Ivan," she called. She worked the knob a few more times, but nothing. "Ivan!" she yelled. She pounded on the door, but there was no response. "Goddamn you, Ivan!" she yelled again. "You little fuck!" Her phone vibrated in her pocket. Time to go.

She walked to the window and looked outside. It was a good thirty feet to the ground, with no fire escape to assist her. She pulled her phone from her pocket and dialed Max's number but it went straight to voicemail. She left an unconvincing message about how she wasn't feeling well and wouldn't be able to make it to rehearsal, though she knew there was almost no chance he would believe her. She tried the door again, but it was still locked. She yelled for Ivan, then for Irina. No response. She rummaged through the bathroom drawers looking for a key or some tool to help her break the lock, but instead she found a canvas toiletry bag filled with Ivan's paraphernalia. Not what she was looking for, but it would at least help offset the frustration of being locked in her drug dealer's bathroom. She sat on the floor and removed the drugs from her pocket. There were a dozen reasons not to get high, but none were strong enough at that moment. She fixed herself a dose and shot it into her arm. *That's better,* she thought, feeling that familiar rush of warmth, as if whatever had tethered her to this world had been cut.

SHE HEARD THE DOOR click open and looked up to see Irina standing above her. She wasn't sure how much time had passed.

"What are you doing?" Irina asked, looking down at Sam sitting on the floor.

Sam stood. She felt nauseous, her legs unsteady. "Why the fuck is there a lock on the outside of the door?"

Irina shook her head, not understanding.

"Never mind," Sam said, pushing past her. She walked down the hall, then stepped outside, where the snow was blowing sideways, making it difficult to see. She quickened her pace, hurrying past the train tracks and into the forest, following the trail back to campus. She wanted to believe that all was not lost. She wanted to believe she could still make this right.

Her phone rang when she arrived back at her apartment; it was Max. "Hello?" she said.

"Where are you?" he asked.

"Did you get my message?"

"I did."

"I'm sorry, but I wasn't feeling well. I'm starting to turn the corner, though. I think I'll be fine tomorrow."

"We should talk. I'm at the studio. Can you come by?"

"Now?"

"Yes."

"This really isn't a good time." She'd been looking forward to spending the balance of her high listening to music in bed.

"I'll rephrase that," Max said. "I need you to come here. Now."

———

THE STUDIO WAS A glowing yellow cube in the forest. Max, alone with his laptop, looked up when Sam entered.

"Sorry," she said. It was an empty offering, but it was all she had.

Max closed his computer and slipped it into his bag. He looked tired and frustrated, and Sam knew that she was likely the reason for his distress. "Nikolai stopped by. He asked where you were."

"What did you say?" she asked, moving slowly toward him. She wanted to put a hand on him, tell him how sorry she was, but she wasn't sure how he might respond to the gesture.

"I said I didn't know, which reflects poorly on me. It makes it look like I don't have any control over this production." He rubbed his forehead. "Which is sort of how I feel."

"I'm sorry."

"I need more than that, Sam. You not only wasted *my* time, but the time of all the other dancers."

"I've been working through some personal shit, but I know that's no excuse. Tell me what I can do to fix this."

"I want you to focus," Max said. "I want you to attend rehearsal. I want you to convince me that you're committed to this production. I've got four weeks to get this ballet into shape, which is about half as much time as I need." Max walked to the window and looked out at the darkening forest. "Every day counts. I can't move forward wondering if my lead dancer is going to show up to rehearsal." He turned back to her. "I've seen you dance, Sam. You're very good. Extraordinary really. No one's arguing that. But you're worthless if I can't count on you."

"You can count on me," she said, unsure if she believed it. "I swear this won't happen again. I want to do this. I want to be a part of whatever you're doing."

"Nikolai has serious concerns about you dancing this role."

"What did he say?"

"That he's not sure he can trust you."

"Is that all?" She searched his face, trying to determine what else he knew, whether Nikolai had said anything about the drugs. She wouldn't put it past him, even though he'd assured her that no one else had to know. Max was the only constructive figure in her life right now, and she couldn't afford to lose him.

"He said you have self-destructive tendencies. He thinks I should replace you. I'm trying to make a case for why you're essential to this thing, but you're making it difficult."

"I'll do better. I promise."

"Look," Max said. "I know you don't like Nikolai and I can see why. He *is* kind of a dick, like you said. But he's also our boss, which means we have to produce for him. We have to make him happy."

"I get it," she said, nodding vigorously, making clear that she understood the gravity of the situation. "I really do."

Max smiled, which Sam took to mean that he was satisfied. "You technically still owe me some rehearsal time."

"Now?"

"What do you think? Do you want to dance with me?"

She very much wanted to dance with him, but she wasn't sure her body would cooperate. While the initial rush had worn thin, she still felt the drug coursing through her body, entombing her in that gummy warmth she'd come to crave.

"Okay," she said, slipping off her shoes. "Sure."

Max hit play on the stereo and took her hand. He led her through a few quick steps, the same ones he'd shown her yesterday. It felt different, since she wasn't dancing on pointe, but still, she was surprised by how much she remembered. Despite her high, or maybe because of it, her body transitioned seamlessly as she treaded water, then rotated once, twice, her leg going vertical, back arched against his hand, the weight of her body falling into his arms. Everything moved slowly, and she attained a focus that had eluded her for the longest time. Outside, the cold Russian winter blew snow against the glass, but inside the studio she was wrapped in the arms of a good and kind man. She remembered now what she had always loved about dance, and it crystallized her resolve to get clean, because this, this right here, was all she wanted. Max then lifted her by the waist and spun her in a circle and slowly lowered her to the ground until she was supine on the floor, their faces nearly touching. She smiled and he smiled back, but when he leaned in for a kiss, a large rock crashed through the glass and skidded across the floor.

J O N A H

RETURNING TO CAMP SEEMED UNWISE, so he spent the night on the observation deck. With its location three kilometers from camp, disguised by camouflage netting, Jonah figured it would make a good safe house until the situation with Slinky could be smoothed over. He hiked through the grinding heat of late afternoon, swatting at insects, a large A/V backpack strapped to his back. The trail was faint, the undergrowth thick and grabbing, and Jonah moved in slow, belabored strides, hacking a path with a folded tripod.

By the time he arrived, a light rain had begun to fall. He scaled the ladder and began assembling his jungle studio, mounting the camera on the tripod and affixing a 400mm telephoto lens. He was pleased to find that the camera still worked after its brief stint filming Gabonese action films. He snapped some pictures of what he guessed was an African finfoot alighting from a branch above his head, then stole a couple shots of a red-billed firefinch darting between trees. He'd never been much of a birder, though Marcus, during their many hours together on the deck, had tried to educate him on the various winged creatures that made a home in the forest: African pied wagtails, black-casqued hornbills, African grey parrots. Marcus had left behind his tattered copy of the *Collins Field Guide to the Bird of West Africa,* which Jonah devoured during the mindless hours spent waiting for elephants to do stuff. He wasn't expecting accolades from the Audubon society, but he'd begun to take a certain pride in the ornithological knowledge he'd acquired, the ability to differentiate between a cerulean kingfisher and a common kingfisher, based on the color of its plumage.

When Jonah was eight, he attended Zoo Camp at the Lincoln Park Zoo in Chicago. He and three other second graders were assigned to a "creature-teacher" named Eric. Most of the creatures Eric taught them about were the kind Jonah had seen on his grandparents' farm—goats, box turtles, barn owls. They were fine—all animals were special in their own way, Eric told them—but it wasn't until they visited the elephant enclosure that Jonah felt he'd encountered something truly magnificent. It wasn't just their size, which he'd learned about in books, but the grace with which they moved, the elegance of something so large.

After high school, he studied conservation biology at Boston University. The summer after his junior year, he took his first trip to Africa, volunteering at an elephant sanctuary in Kenya. The organization's mission was to rehabilitate orphaned elephant calves to the point where they could be reintegrated back into the wild. Jonah was initially tasked with menial jobs like shoveling manure, but in time he learned the basics of animal husbandry and was eventually assigned to the nursery, where the youngest, most fragile calves were nursed back to health. Most of the elephants that arrived had been orphaned after their mothers were killed by poachers. They were usually found half starved and wandering alone through the savannah, and it was the job of people like Jonah to help them through this intense period of mourning. Toward the end of his time in Kenya, he was assigned to a three-month-old female calf named Laki. She'd been found standing next to the decomposing body of her mother, dehydrated and on the verge of death. Jonah spent that first night lying alongside Laki, rubbing his hand along her back, waking every few hours to feed her from a bottle, trying to impress upon her the understanding that she was safe now, that she was loved. It was the closest he'd ever felt to any kind of paternal instinct, and during the long dark hours that he watched the animal sleep, he imagined finding the man responsible for Laki's grief and smashing a rock against his head.

Jonah fixed himself a meager dinner of rice and beans and dined in the fading light of a discouraging day. He wasn't sure what to do about the whole Slinky situation, though he suspected a shakedown was headed in his direction, the extent and severity of which he could only guess at. He'd courted danger before—a run-in with a disagreeable bush pig being one of the more terrifying instances—but this was the first time he'd felt truly threatened. He held on to the slight hope that his new nemesis might forgive the whole thing, dismiss it as a minor affront unworthy of his time, though Laurent's description did not suggest a man brimming with mercy.

The sun was nearly gone when Jonah heard the trumpet call and saw a family of elephants emerging from the forest. He spotted the matriarch first, but something about her slow, halting movements seemed strange. She stopped every few feet as if she'd smelled something offensive, then continued carefully, like a soldier navigating a minefield. It seemed like she was trying to camouflage herself in the forest growth, but when Jonah grabbed his binoculars and looked closer, he noticed that it wasn't her massive body she was trying to conceal but her tusks. It was both shocking and heartbreaking. Not only did she associate the human scent with poaching, but she seemed to be cognizant of the reason someone would want to kill her. He'd never witnessed such behavior, and it was a stark reminder of the intelligence of his subjects, as well as how dispiriting their situation had become.

The matriarch led the others to a shallow pool, where they slurped mineral water percolating from the ground. As the night wore on, Jonah set up a thermal imaging camera that he and Marcus often used to track nocturnal visitation patterns. The video had shown that a lot more was happening than anyone had previously suspected, and Jonah looked forward to reviewing the footage from this evening, discovering what he'd missed after falling asleep. He grabbed his notebook and jotted down some observations, the names and faces that were familiar to him, as well as those that were not. He was relieved to discover Kibo standing beneath his mother, whom Jonah had assumed was dead. A dozen more soon filtered in, and now there were close to forty, an encouraging increase from the morning's count. A few of the younger ones locked tusks, roughhousing, while the adults congregated in little subsets, drinking and socializing in the manner of good-natured suburbanites. It was a festive scene, full of bonhomie and goodwill, one that reminded Jonah of a spirited forest block party. As he unfurled his sleeping bag and settled into bed, he paused to savor the moment, how fortunate he was to spend an evening with such noble and sentient creatures.

JONAH AWOKE WITH A BUTTERFLY on his face, which he interpreted as a good start to the day, though a moment later he saw it swallowed by a toad and was forced to reexamine the omen. He put together a quick breakfast, then collected the ARUs from the trees, which required some elementary ropework he'd learned during an introduction to rock climbing class back at Vanderbilt. He had two hundred hours of new media to decipher during his time in Chicago, and he hoped there might be something in there that would jump-start his thesis.

He packed up his equipment and started back to camp. His flight left in a little over a week, and his plan was to spend the intervening days collecting data before heading back to town, where he would catch the train to Libreville. It was a lot of traveling, but he knew it would be worth it once he was back in Chicago, surrounded by deep-dish pizza, cold beer, and the familiar faces of his family.

HE FOUND HER IN a dry riverbed, bathing in a pool of her own blood, surrounded by Kibo and four other grief-stricken elephants. They paced circles around her, laying their trunks on her collapsed body in the style of a funeral procession. Though he was a good twenty yards away, there was no question it was Kibo's mother. There was also no question that the slaughter had been carried out by Slinky, who had likely butchered the animal as a warning. Once the elephants had disappeared into the forest, Jonah approached the corpse. Her face had been removed by crude machete work and the rest of her body lay rotting in the sun, sizzling with flies, emitting an odor that made Jonah's stomach buck. He considered trying to conceal the corpse with palm fronds, but the vultures were hovering overhead, and he knew it was only a matter of time before there would be nothing left but clean, white bones. He snapped a few photos for evidence and then, fighting back tears, continued back to camp.

He hiked for another hour, experiencing a sadness he could not have anticipated. He'd grown close to these animals in his time here, had come to know them not only through their vocalizations, but also their physical attributes, the subtle markings on an ear, the curvature of a tusk. Most of his time was spent observing these animals, and he appreciated their company more than most humans. *But what was it all for?* he wondered. What was the point of his research if he couldn't provide basic security for his subjects? He'd always believed his presence had shielded the animals in some way, provided cover, but that was obviously just a comforting myth. Since Marcus left, his time here had been nothing but a series of escalating failures culminating in this, the death of something like a pet. He could notify the government rangers, but he knew Slinky was tracking his movement, and any act of vigilance might be dealt with in a similarly gruesome manner. He could send an email to Marcus, but there was only so much he could do from back home, a dead elephant from an obscure African country not exactly the kind of thing that made the evening news. Marcus would probably just send another email to his friend at the World Wildlife Fund, who would respond in the same exasperated tone, saying *I know, I know, we're doing everything we can.*

So his options were limited.

Approaching his camp, Jonah saw what looked like two large teeth hanging from a tree. Immediately, he realized they were tusks, washed and drying in the sun. A motorcycle was parked next to the tusks, and a moment later he saw Slinky emerge from his tent, raising a hand in greeting. "Hello, friend," he called. "You have a good night in the forest? I wait here all night for you, but then I get so tired and sleep on your air mattress. Very soft."

"Look," Jonah said. "If you really want the camera that bad, you can have it. This is insane."

"No," Slinky said, as if he'd recently soured on the idea. "I don't want your camera anymore."

"Then what *do* you want?"

"Mateo tells me things," Slinky said, drawing near.

"Mateo?" Jonah had always had a bad feeling about the guy, so it made sense that he was friendly with Slinky.

"He tells me you set up your cameras to film us," Slinky said, clapping Jonah on the shoulder. "He says you show these videos to the government."

"That's not true," Jonah said. "I only film the elephants."

"Mateo tells me not to trust you. He says I should have killed you a long time ago."

"And why didn't you?" It was a question that had occupied Jonah since they first met, and he was genuinely curious to hear Slinky's answer.

"Because I got to thinking that maybe there's a way we can work together. There's something you can help me with. A small favor." Slinky motioned for Jonah to walk with him, then began laying out what he had in mind. He told him that with Mateo's help, he'd been selling his ivory to a Chinese national who worked for a mining company in the northeastern part of the country. The Chinese guy, Slinky explained, had been flying back and forth between Libreville and Guangzhou—"*very easy*," Slinky said, clapping his hands together and smiling—until two weeks ago when his partner was apprehended with eighty pounds of raw ivory at the Singapore airport.

Jonah wasn't sure where Slinky was going with his story—or even what physical direction they were headed—but it seemed unwise to interrupt, so he continued listening, hoping he wasn't being led to a shallow grave in the forest. Slinky explained that with his Chinese connection temporarily severed, he was forced to find a new place to unload his product. He said he had a cousin in the United States, a former student at DePaul who now owned a jewelry store in Hyde Park. The cousin, Andre, was living in the States on an expired student visa, which meant flying back to Gabon to retrieve the product wasn't an option. Slinky said he'd considered doing it himself, but after a few run-ins with INTERPOL, it wasn't a risk he was willing to take. Which was where Jonah came in. The plan, according to Slinky, was for Jonah to ride with Mateo back to Libreville, where he would take possession of a hundred pounds of ivory before catching his flight back to the States. In Chicago, he would transfer the ivory to Andre in exchange for $50,000, with which he would then return to Gabon after the New Year. And if all that happened without any trouble, without any *dérangement,* then Slinky would leave Jonah to study his elephants in peace. He said that despite Jonah's impression of him, he was a very honest businessman. "So what do you think?" he asked.

The question was obviously rhetorical. It wasn't a proposition so much as a directive. "I don't think that's possible."

"Why not?" Slinky asked, seemingly perplexed that Jonah hadn't jumped at the offer.

"Because I'd get caught."

"Ahhh," Slinky said, swatting away his concern. "But how do you know until you try?"

"I don't know how it works in China, but I can assure you the U.S. government is extremely intolerant of ivory smuggling."

"Not to worry. I have a long list of tricks. Besides," he said, pointing to the tusks hanging from the tree, "too late to put this one back together." Slinky spit out a hearty laugh and reached for his cigarettes. He lit one and exhaled a cloud of smoke in Jonah's face.

"Take whatever of mine you want," Jonah said, shaking his backpack from his shoulders and tossing it in his tent. "Hell, go ahead and shoot me if you have to, but I'm not helping you smuggle ivory." He grabbed his canteen and water purifier and began walking to the river to pump drinking water.

"I don't want to shoot you, my friend," Slinky yelled after him. "I want to convince you. And I will. You'll see."

GAVIN

H E WOKE TO THE CONCUSSIVE blow of the ski patrol mortaring the guts out of West Basin. He rolled out of bed and went to the living room. A foot of snow had fallen overnight, and the lanes of corduroy were now blanketed with pillows of white. He found a nearly empty box of Cheerios and some milk and washed it down with two cups of strong coffee. Afterward, he changed into his ski clothes, poled out to the slopes, and glided to the base of the mountain. The lifts weren't open yet, though a few dozen anxious skiers were queued up, chatting with one another. "Hey," a woman's voice called to him. "Where'd you come from? Mountain's not open yet."

Gavin saw Mariana lift her goggles and wave her ski pole at him. She wore slim black snow pants and a purple Patagonia parka, her black hair spilling out the back of her helmet. Gavin ducked beneath the lift rope and slid in line next to her. "Morning!"

"I thought about calling you," Mariana said, "but I wasn't sure you'd be awake."

"The bombs woke me up."

"Want to make some turns with me?"

"Sure."

The lifts soon jolted to life, and a few minutes later they reached the front of the line, where a chair arrived and seated them with a swift kick to the back of the knees. A moment later their skis lifted off from the snow and they were ferried up the mountain.

"Do you ski every day?" Gavin asked.

"Almost," she said, tucking her poles beneath her thigh. "It's like my gym. I usually go for an hour or two in the morning."

"Must be nice."

"It is. Jesse doesn't ski though, which is kind of a bummer. I usually end up going by myself."

"How are the wedding preparations coming along?"

"Fine, I guess. I'm just assuming everything will fall into place."

"New Year's Day, right?" Gavin asked. Below him, a father coached his young son down the mountain.

"Yeah, it's kinda terrifying."

Gavin paused, unsure what to make of her comment. "Not exciting?"

"No, it is," she said, as if realizing how it sounded. "I guess it's both, if that's possible."

"I think so." A gust of wind kicked up, and Gavin turned his back to shield her from the blowing snow. "And afterward? I assume there's no honeymoon planned."

"Not right now at least," she said. "Not with the play happening. Assuming the play actually happens."

"You guys think you'll stay in the area?"

"I don't see why not. We both love it here. It's a good place to raise kids."

"So kids are part of the equation?"

"I think so. I've always imagined I'd be a pretty good mother."

"Yeah," Gavin said with a smile. "I don't doubt it."

Mariana waved away the thought. "But that's getting ahead of myself. Right now, I'm just focused on pulling this wedding together. We're doing most of the planning ourselves. And by *we,* I mean me."

"That's ambitious, considering the play and all."

"I have a hard time relinquishing control. I've always considered it an admirable quality, though lately it's become a problem."

Gavin smiled at her. "Maybe you're just a woman who knows what she wants."

"Maybe." Mariana tapped her skis together and watched the snow float to the ground. "What about you? Got a girlfriend?"

"I did," Gavin said, hoping that might be enough to appease her.

"What happened?"

He hesitated, unsure how to explain the dissolution of his relationship. "She went camping."

Mariana laughed. "And what, never returned?"

"She was trying to prove a point or something."

"That being?"

Gavin shrugged. "That I was expendable? I don't know what she was thinking, to be honest. It apparently wasn't working though, so it's probably for the best."

"How long were you guys together?" she asked.

"Four years."

"So it was serious."

"I thought so."

"Was there talk of marriage?"

"By me. Not so much by her, which should have been a sign."

"I'm sorry," Mariana said. "That must be hard."

Below, a man in blue jeans and a Dallas Cowboys parka barreled down the hill with no poles, his skis pointed inward in a kamikaze pizza pie. He hit a mogul and shot into the air, face-planting directly beneath the lift.

"Beautiful," Mariana said. "Really solid form."

GAVIN FOLLOWED HER DOWN a gentle cruiser called Porcupine, carving figure eights in the untouched snow. They made their way back to the top of the mountain, then dropped over to the east side,

bombing down Ash Pond and Walkyries Glade, Gavin working hard
to keep up. She floated through the trees as if on tracks, working a line
she seemed to know by heart, whereas Gavin had to stop every hundred yards to catch his breath and rest his quivering thighs. She led
him to some untouched runs off lift four, and they skied those until
they were tracked out. On the ride back up, she leaned close, her
breath on his cheek, and directed his gaze toward a flock of bighorn
sheep congregating on a saddle ridge in the distance. The sky was a
luminous shade of blue, and everything was covered in new snow,
and there was this woman sitting next to him, this woman who smiled
a lot and didn't complain much, an unflappable beauty who would
soon marry someone other than himself. He tried to broker peace
with this fact, but its inconvenience annoyed him, so instead he swept
it aside in order to enjoy the unsustainable reality of the present moment.

They stopped in the lodge for Irish coffee, clomping their way in
ski boots to the nearly empty bar. The holiday crowds would soon
descend upon the mountain, but now it was quiet, aside from a woman
vacuuming the floor.

"I have a question for you," Mariana said, staring into her coffee,
as if afraid to ask. "But you don't have to answer."

Gavin smiled uncomfortably. "What's that?"

"Why didn't you call me again?"

"What do you mean?"

She took a drink and looked him in the eye. "All those years ago.
After our date. Why didn't you call me?"

"I believe I did call you," Gavin said, wondering where she was
going with this. "And you didn't call back."

She shook her head. "Not true. Because I would have called back."

"Are we sure about this?"

"Absolutely."

"I don't know," he said softly, acknowledging the missed opportunity. "I honestly don't remember. I think I was in a weird place then.
I still am, I suppose."

"I guess I'm just curious. Most people want to know why they were rejected."

"Whoa," Gavin said. "I did not *reject* you."

"Then what was it?" Her questioning had been slightly teasing, almost playful, but now it acquired a sharper edge, as if she wanted an explanation.

Gavin tried to summon some recollection of the date. He was so much younger then, so inflexible in his standards. He approached potential partners with a list of requirements, and anyone who didn't satisfy his obnoxiously rigid criteria was immediately tossed aside. "I don't know," he finally said. "But it certainly wasn't rejection. I think it was looking for someone who only existed in my mind."

Renee snorted into her coffee. "Did you find her?"

"I did not," he said resignedly.

She rolled her eyes. "Shocking."

"There was also the matter of geography," Gavin said, trying to lighten the mood. "I had a rule back then about not dating girls on the west side."

"That's dumb."

"In hindsight, yes, very dumb. My loss appears to be Jesse's gain."

Mariana smiled.

"Does he know about our history?" Gavin asked.

Mariana laughed and shook her head. "We met for a glass of wine one night five years ago. I'd hardly call it a history."

SHE INVITED HIM TO dinner that night. The rest of the cast came as well, a meet-and-greet, though Gavin was the only one doing the meeting. He picked up a bottle of wine on his way over, along with a lemon meringue pie from a bakery located next to the liquor store. Mariana greeted him at the door, taking his offerings and shepherding him inside. She introduced him to Don Stuckler, a sixty-something retiree in a Pendleton jacket and large silver-rimmed glasses, who would be playing James Tyrone; as well as Pat, a gray-haired woman with a faint Texas accent who joked that it might not be a bad idea to start calling her "Mama." Colin, the actor playing their son Edmund, a redheaded high school kid, was cuddling on the couch with his girlfriend, Madison, who, Mariana explained, would be playing Cathleen, the maid.

Jesse, who had been working out in the garage, came through the door as they were sitting down to eat. He took his place at the head of the table, appearing slightly uncomfortable among the room full of thespians.

"I can't say I'm too familiar with your show," Jesse said to Gavin, shoveling salad onto his plate, "though Mariana tells me you're quite good in it."

"I've seen it," Colin said. "It's kinda lame, no offense. What's with all the stammering? Does everyone in L.A. have a speech impediment?"

"What's the show called?" Pat asked.

"It *was* called *Makin' It*," Gavin said. "But it's no more. Canceled."

"Oh no," Pat said, looking unnecessarily distraught.

"Trust me. It's for the best."

"I thought about moving out to Hollywood," Colin said, "but I'm not sure I'd like it."

"You know what they say," Don said. "There are two kinds of people in Hollywood. Those who think they want in, and those who know they want out."

Mariana turned to Gavin. "Which one are you?"

"I'd argue there's a third camp," Gavin said. "Those who'd like to get out but can't because they have no other marketable skills."

"You could always move here," Pat suggested. "That's what Don did."

"I slummed it in Tinseltown back in the seventies," Don said, "but nothing came of it, so I set up shop out here and haven't looked back."

"Seems to have worked out pretty well," Gavin said.

Don smiled. "I wouldn't trade it for anything."

"How long have you been working with Mariana?"

"Oh, gosh," Don said, looking to the ceiling for an answer. "I guess since the beginning, right? Two years now."

Mariana nodded.

"I was involved with some church productions before she showed up," he said. "All in all I guess I've been subjecting the nice people of Taos to my hammy performances for close to thirty years."

"Don is as bashful as he is talented," Mariana said, refilling her wineglass.

"So what's going on with the theater?" Colin asked, sawing at his meat. "A kid at school said the place nearly burned to the ground."

"That's a bit of an exaggeration," Mariana said. "But it may be a little while before we're back in there. We're waiting for the fire marshal to clear the place, at which point Jesse and his guys can get started on the restoration."

Pat looked to Jesse. "How long will it take to fix something like that?"

"It's hard to say until we get in there and have a look," Jesse said. "But it could be a while."

"Such a shame," Pat said. "It was such a beautiful old theater. But I'm sure you can whip it back into shape."

"We'll see," Jesse said. Something about Pat's comment seemed to rub him the wrong way, as if he were tired of playing the role of maintenance man, the blue-collar laborer whose job was to construct stages on which the actors could perform.

"I'm looking for alternative venues," Mariana said, "but there aren't a lot of options. Since we can use the high school theater for rehearsals, I'd like to meet there tomorrow around two. Don, Pat, and Gavin can read through the first half of act one, and then we can run through the whole thing once Colin gets out of class."

"Works for me," Gavin said.

HE WAS NEARLY PASSED out in the hot tub when he heard what he thought was the doorbell. He wrapped himself in a towel and hurried inside, trailing water on the hardwood floor. He opened the door to find Mariana holding his cellphone. "You left this at my house."

"Oh," he said. He'd acquired a slight paunch over the years, which he tried to hide by shimmying the towel up his waist. "I was in the hot tub."

"Obviously," she said, smiling. "I've been ringing the doorbell for the past five minutes."

"Sorry," he said. "You want to come in?"

Mariana stepped inside, removing her boots. "I tried calling the landline, but I must not have the right number, because I kept getting some confused kid." She helped herself to a seat on the couch. "I figured I'd better just bring it to you since it's your only link to the outside world."

The truth was that no one had called him in the last twenty-four hours. His services—as an actor, as a boyfriend—weren't in high demand. But still, it was nice of her to return it, though the timing was certainly curious.

"You want something to drink?" he asked from the kitchen. "I picked up a bottle of wine on my way home."

"If you're having some."

He wasn't planning to. He was planning to go to bed and wake up without a hangover, but he couldn't retract the offer. He poured two glasses, then slipped on a T-shirt and joined her on the couch.

"Thanks for putting up with the blue hairs," she said.

"Blue hairs?"

"Don and Pat."

"Oh yeah. They seem nice enough."

"Don's a legit actor. Pat will take some work, but I think I can get her there."

"And the kid?" Gavin asked.

"Colin's putty. I can make him do whatever I want, and for the most part he sells it pretty well. Plus, with that red hair and those sunken cheeks, he's got the kind of sickly countenance that's required of Edmund. That boy is consumption personified."

"Is his girlfriend any good?"

"Not really, but that's kind of a throwaway part. Those two are inseparable, so I knew that if I cast Madison, Colin would have a reason to show up for rehearsals."

"You're a very cunning director."

"That's half the job, isn't it?"

Mariana inched closer to him on the couch, her leg brushing against his. There was no denying something was working its way to the surface, an adulterous kind of magma that threatened to do irreparable damage. Not only the way she kept looking at him at dinner, but also more innocuous things like the way she referred to it as *her* house, as if Jesse were just a tenant living month to month. It seemed like a conscious distancing tactic, and while he wasn't certain what her intentions were at this late hour, he suspected they'd been decided upon well in advance. He leaned in to kiss her and she didn't refuse.

MARIANA WAS GONE WHEN he awoke the next morning. Gavin found a note on the kitchen counter, telling him to meet at the high school at 2:00 for rehearsal, and so here he was. He couldn't remember the last time he'd been inside a school, but the halls of Taos High resembled his own memories from so many years ago: long rows of beige metal lockers, a trophy case, aspirational posters taped to cinder block walls. He passed the gym, where the basketball team was running wind sprints, then made his way through some kind of common area, where a handful of kids were sitting on the floor, communing with their phones.

"Do you guys know where the theater is?" Gavin asked, and the kids, without looking up, pointed down the hall.

The theater was small, about the size of a classroom, more like a black box than a proper auditorium. Don, Pat, and Mariana sat at a table in the center of the room, surrounded by rows of metal folding chairs.

"There he is," Don said. "There's my good-for-nothing son. How are you, boy?"

"I'm well," Gavin said, unsure if he was expected to arrive in character.

"You found us," Mariana said. She was wearing black leggings and a chunky wool sweater, and she looked just as lovely as she had the night before. Maybe it was a result of being in a high school, but Gavin was reminded of walking into English class on the Monday after he'd lost his virginity to Jill Lehman during the senior camping trip, and knowing that there was something between them now, that their relationship had changed in a fundamental way.

"We were just going through the first few pages," Mariana said, "but let's push on now that you're here." She smiled at him and he smiled back. Just seeing her again, in this new environment, strained his focus, which he hoped went unnoticed by his castmates.

"Sounds good." Gavin pulled up a chair and paged to the beginning of act one.

"Let's pick it up with Mary calling for the boys," Mariana said. "I'll read Edmund's lines until Colin gets here."

They made their way through the first part of act one, haltingly at first, but then, once Colin and Madison arrived, much quicker than Gavin had expected. Mariana made adjustments as they went, but for the most part the actors executed their lines with surprising precision, and if anyone seemed rusty it was Gavin. Colin was what Gavin had expected: slightly naïve, but also completely believable and pleasantly sympathetic. Don was appropriately animated, while Pat possessed the detached desperation required of her character. Mariana had a clear idea of what she wanted, but she conveyed her direction with a deft, almost maternal touch. After four hours, Gavin felt thoroughly reinvigorated, shaken to life by an enthusiasm for his craft he hadn't felt in a very long time. As they were packing up, Don suggested a trip to the pub.

"I don't know," Gavin said. "I feel like I should go home and work on my lines. You guys are making me look bad."

"Come on," Mariana said, pulling on her coat. "It's not every day the people of Taos get to rub shoulders with a big Hollywood star."

THEY SET UP AT a table in a quiet corner of the pub, far away from the bluegrass band installed on a small stage by the entrance. Mariana returned from the bar with a pitcher and four glasses. "I want to thank everybody for all their hard work," she said, distributing the beer. "Nobody's getting rich from this, but I hope we can create something we're all proud of."

"Cheers," Don said, raising his glass.

"And cheers to Mariana," Pat said, "for directing a play while also planning a wedding. It's a Herculean effort. You must be exhausted, sweetheart."

"I'm a little fried," Mariana said, "but the end is near."

"The *wedding* is near," Don said, "but the real work begins the next day. As my father used to say, a wedding is a day but a marriage is a lifetime."

Mariana looked to Gavin and offered a nervous smile. Gavin took a sip of his beer.

"What about you, Gavin?" Pat asked. "I take it you aren't married."

"Not yet."

"People in L.A. don't get married till they're forty," Don said.

"Then you've got some time," Pat said.

"Not if you ask my mother," Gavin replied.

"Look who it is," Don announced.

Gavin looked up and saw Jesse clomping toward the table. "Howdy," he said with a solemn nod.

Gavin, who had been seated next to Mariana, stood up from the table. "Here. Take my seat."

"That's okay," Jesse said.

"No, no. Sit next to your fiancée." Gavin felt the sudden need to remove himself from the situation.

"You're fine," Jesse said. "I'll pull up a chair."

"What do you want to drink?" Gavin asked. "I'll get this next round."

"You're our guest," Jesse said. "Let me buy *you* a beer."

Fuck this guy, Gavin thought. The only thing that might ease his guilt was the assurance that the man whose fiancée he had slept with was a monstrous asshole. But he wasn't, and it only compounded the terrible shame overtaking Gavin like a heavy fog. Jesse had been nothing but kind and Gavin had been nothing but covetous, and the disparity of their moral codes was alarming.

Jesse walked to the bar to fetch another pitcher, while Pat excused herself to visit the ladies' room. Don turned his attention to the band.

"Did you know he was coming?" Gavin whispered to Mariana.

She shook her head.

"I should probably go."

"Don't be silly," she whispered, her eyes trained on the band.

Jesse returned with a pitcher and took the seat next to Mariana.

"How'd it go today?" she asked, turning to him.

"Got the all clear from the fire marshal," Jesse said. "We'll get started on the cleanup tomorrow."

"How bad is it?" Don asked.

"Could have been a lot worse," Jesse said. "They were able to contain it before it spread too far."

"How long do you think until it's back to normal?"

"Hard to say. Maybe three or four weeks if we hustle. Not sure how much I'll get done with the wedding coming up." Jesse put his arm around Mariana and pulled her close, kissed her on the cheek. "That's the most important thing right now."

"Cheers to that," Don said, raising his glass.

Gavin watched the glasses go up, then raised his own in a half-hearted salute.

THE DAYS PASSED IN cloudy disgrace. Mariana would stop by his place in the morning, under the pretense of work, and they'd ski, then have sex in the hot tub before heading to the high school for rehearsals. It was a nice little rhythm and despite the illicitness of the affair, Gavin was happier than he'd been in some time. He knew he should pull back, but he wanted to believe there was a way for this to work out without any collateral damage. It had been years since he'd felt this close to Renee, if in fact he ever had, and it only highlighted the hollowness of their relationship. Everything she'd accused him of was true. Theirs *was* a relationship born out of convenience, particularly when viewed in the context of his feelings for Mariana, which were visceral and all-consuming. He'd squandered his opportunity with her once before, and now, five years later, in a small mountain town in New Mexico, he'd been presented with a second chance.

SAMANTHA

SHE ARRIVED AT THE STUDIO, but Max wasn't there. She ditched her bag and joined the other dancers stretching at the barre. As she went through her routine, she noticed a couple maintenance men patching the broken window with a sheet of plywood. Nikolai, who had been chatting with one of the private security guards who typically patrolled the grounds, approached Sam. "Can I have a word with you?"

He led her to a quiet corner of the rehearsal space. "What's this?" he asked, handing her a piece of notebook paper. Written in black marker were the words: *Stay away from her!* "I found this taped to the door when I showed up this morning. What's going on?"

He'd done it. That little fucker Ivan had thrown the rock through the window yesterday. The kid had lost his mind. She thought she'd made it very clear to him that he wasn't supposed to show up at the company, yet there he was, not only vandalizing property but also destroying a rare chance at intimacy. She would kill him. Strangle the fucker. Dead.

"Sam." Nikolai grabbed the piece of paper from her. "What's this about?"

"I don't know."

"You don't know who threw a rock through my window?"

"Just some kid," she said, her voice betraying her. "He's harmless."

"Do you owe him money?" Nikolai's tone was eerily calm. She would have preferred that he just scream at her and get it over with.

She shook her head.

"Then why is he breaking the windows of my studio?"

"I don't know." It was the first honest thing she'd said. "He's obviously nuts."

"Yet he's a friend of yours."

"Not anymore." She caught the reflection of her fellow dancers in the wall mirror, and while they pretended to be immersed in their stretching, it was obvious that the collective gaze was fixed upon her.

"Do you remember my ultimatum?" Nikolai said.

"I don't need a lecture," Sam said. "I've got work to do."

"There's no work for you here."

She looked up at him for the first time. "What do you mean?"

"Go home, Sam." There was a finality to his directive.

"Please, Nikolai. I'm sorry. It won't happen again."

"You're no longer welcome here."

"Please. I'll make it up to you. I want to make this happen. I'm ready to work." She was groveling. She could see that. She didn't care.

"Pack your bags and leave. I'm done with you." Nikolai turned and walked out of the studio.

Sam turned her back to the other dancers and placed her head in her hands.

Marie, who had been stretching at the barre, approached and touched her shoulder. "What happened?"

Sam glanced up at the wall mirror. Her mouth hung open and tears ran down her face. "It's over," she said. "I'm done."

SHE RAN THROUGH THE FOREST, chest throttling, fingers burning, her anger like a current. She arrived at the highway and followed it until she reached the gravel road that led to the farm. It was an old Soviet-era peasant plot with a small house and barn ringed by a few acres of scorched farmland. Dead cornstalks poked through the snow and some loose cows were huddled next to a chicken coop, hiding from the wind. A truck, two motorcycles, and Ivan's bicycle were parked out front. Back behind the house, Gregor, the owner of the place, was splitting firewood. He'd inherited the land from his parents, and enlisted local junkies to help him work it in exchange for a place to get high, a kind of shooting gallery for farmhands. The house was littered with spent needles and burnt spoons, and the roof was pocked with holes offering views of the daytime skies. It depressed her to come to this place, with all these broken, dead-eyed addicts. She'd always surrounded herself with the ambitious and the talented, what she referred to as the bright, shiny people of New York, yet these people were its inverse. These people were sad and directionless, and she'd always felt that her career, the fact that she was actually doing something with her life, was what prevented her from sliding into their debased orbit, but the truth was that she'd become one of them.

Sam walked over to Gregor, who held an ax in one hand, a cigarette in the other. "Where's Ivan?"

Gregor pointed to the barn, where she saw the lower half of Ivan poking out from beneath a pickup truck.

Sam walked over to him. She grabbed a shovel and struck him hard on the shin.

"Aye!" he yelled, sliding out from beneath the truck. "What?"

She attempted another blow, but Ivan caught the shovel and wrested it from her grip.

"You fucker!" she yelled. "Do you have any idea what kind of damage you've done? You ruined my life with your crazy shit. I told you I didn't want to see you anymore. Why don't you understand that?" She waited for a response but nothing came. "Answer me!"

"I wanted to see you," Ivan said pathetically.

"And you thought throwing a rock through a window was a good way to get my attention?"

"Who is he?"

"It's none of your business who he is."

"Do you love him?" he asked.

"What's it matter, Ivan?" she yelled. "Why do you care?"

"Because *I* love you," he said.

"Well, I'm afraid the feeling isn't mutual," she said, and started down the road. "Don't ever look for me again," she yelled back. "I'm done with you. I'm done with all this shit."

SHE RETURNED HOME TO FIND Marie and Owen snuggling on the couch, watching a Russian dubbed version of *Die Hard*.

"Hey," Marie said, standing from the couch. "Where did you go? I've been looking for you."

"Don't," Sam said, stepping into her bedroom and pulling the door closed behind her.

"Sam!" Marie yelled. "Can we talk?"

Sam opened the door. "What?"

"Can I come in?"

Marie closed the door behind her and sat on the edge of the bed. "Nikolai pulled me aside after rehearsal and told me what's going on."

"Then what else do you want to know?"

"I want to know why you never told me. I want to know why you didn't feel like you could ask me for help."

"Because I'm not looking for help, Marie. I'm looking for people to mind their own fucking business. Which should be easier now that I'm leaving."

"Where are you going?" Marie asked, unfazed.

"Chicago, I guess. I don't know. I don't really have a master plan."

"Do you think you should talk to someone about it?"

"No, I don't," Sam snapped. "You're beginning to sound a lot like Nikolai, and I don't like it."

"I'm sorry, but I'm worried about you."

"Yes, that seems to be a theme around here." She had tried so hard to conceal it, and she wasn't sure if she was more devastated by the loss of her job or the fact that she'd been found out.

Sam's phone rang. It was Max. "I need to take this."

Marie left the room, and Sam answered the phone. "Hi."

"I tried," Max said. "I did."

"I didn't mean for this to happen," she said, trying to hold it together. "I'm sorry."

"Me too."

Sam walked to the window, where she watched a deer high-step through the snow. "I haven't been honest with you."

"I know," Max said. "Nikolai told me everything."

"I'm such a fuckup," she mumbled. The tears were flowing now. She had trouble getting the words out. "I let you down. I'm so sorry."

"Don't worry about me," Max said. "I'll be fine. I want you to do what's best for *you* right now. You're a beautiful dancer, Sam. There will be other ballets, and when you're ready there will be a role for you. All I want is for you to get better. We'll work together again. Maybe not here, but somewhere else. I know that much."

"I'm sorry," she said. "I know I keep saying that, and I know it probably doesn't mean much, but that's really what I am. I'm just sorry."

"I know you are."

There was a moment of silence as she considered what else she might say.

"Goodbye, Sam," he said gently. "I wish you nothing but the best." The line went quiet. "Fuck!" she yelled, throwing her phone across the room. Despite his assurance that they would work together again, there was an obvious finality to the call. The false little world she'd constructed was crumbling around her.

She grabbed the bag of drugs from her dresser. She considered the white powder that had caused her so much grief. She knew she needed to quit. She also knew it wouldn't be easy. But she must. She must come to terms with the fact that once the drugs were gone she would step through an imaginary door into a life of sobriety. But even thinking about a drug-free life brought forth a torrent of future cravings. How could anyone expect her to not partake in something that her body now required, something as essential as oxygen? Resisting heroin felt like being handed a glass of cold water at the finish line of a marathon and being asked not to drink it. It was like dropping a mouse in a snake's cage and asking the snake to babysit while you run some errands and then returning to find the mouse gone and the snake gorged and loafing in a nest of wood chips, with a pleased look that said, *Really? Did you really think that wasn't going to happen?* That's how insane it was, the idea of her life without drugs.

She guessed it was about a quarter gram. She considered saving a little, but that would dilute the high and since this was her last time doing this shit, she figured she might as well treat herself to the kind of oblivion-grasping, checkout high she deserved; a ceremonious, firework-filled close to a pretty shitty chapter of her life. And afterward, the drugs would be gone and she would be finished, forever. But just the thought of going a whole day without drugs was terrifying. And this fear of a day without drugs compounded her distress, because it meant this whole thing ran a lot deeper than she wanted to admit.

She opened her computer and found an email from her mom.

> To: sambrennan362@gmail.com
> From: cynthiabrennan0762@gmail.com
>
> Subject: Flights
>
> I don't mean to nag, but that's what mothers do! You still haven't sent me your flight info. I hope it isn't because you haven't booked it yet. Jonah gets here the 23rd and Gavin said he should be here soon after that. He's going to New Mexico for some strange reason. He's very elusive about the whole thing. Did I tell you his show got canceled? He's a little sore about it, so please don't say anything unless he brings it up.
>
> Let me know what time your flight gets in and Dad will pick you up at the airport. Also, I just read an

article in the Tribune that the baggage handlers at the
airport are stealing Christmas presents. So if you did
any shopping, make sure you carry them on the plane
with you ;)

—Mom

She clicked over to a travel website to see how much this visit
would cost her. Moscow to Chicago three days before Christmas was
not a cheap flight. She knew she shouldn't have waited this long—
only fugitives and the bereaved bought last-minute plane tickets. She
considered going to New York, where she could hide out at her friend
Nikki's loft until she was ready to confront the disappointed faces of
her family. But as much as she dreaded the fallout from this visit, the
idea of spending Christmas alone was even more depressing. She
found a one-way ticket that left Sheremetyevo at 9:00 A.M., $1470
USD. She plugged in her credit card info and hit submit, knowing
that she would be paying off this visit, both financially and emotion-
ally, for a very long time.

JONAH

"MERRY CHRISTMAS!" LAURENT BELLOWED. He was wearing a Santa hat and decorating an anemic, three-foot-tall silver Christmas tree. Two patrons sat in the corner shooting dice, while Clement doused the tree with packaging peanuts meant to represent snow. A limp string of flashing lights hung above the bar and "Little Drummer Boy" blasted from the stereo in the office. The place reminded Jonah of a failed office Christmas party. It was the first visual indication that the holidays were near, and he was reminded of his reason for returning home. He'd packed up his camp earlier that morning and schlepped his belongings back to town. His plan was to spend the night at Laurent's, who would then drive him to the train station the next morning. He'd been looking forward to going home for weeks, but his encounter with Slinky cast a pall over the trip and he worried about the fate of his elephants while he was gone.

He ditched his bags in the office, then joined Laurent and Clement, who were now hanging the tree with ornaments. "Nice-looking tree," he said.

"Thanks," Laurent said. "It's not real, though."

"Get out," Jonah said. "I figured you made a trip to the North Pole over your lunch break."

Clement crowned the tree with a lopsided star he'd cut from blue construction paper.

"Perfect tree for us," Laurent said, beaming. He took a step back to admire their work. A moment later, the door to the restaurant swung open and Slinky and Mateo stumbled in, their voices amplified by booze.

"Hello, Elephant Man," Mateo shouted. "You ready for our big trip tomorrow?" Mateo's surliness had been softened by a night of heavy drinking, and as far as Jonah could remember, this was the most he'd ever said to him. Slinky, meanwhile, had found the remote control and was flipping through the channels, finally settling on a soccer match between Kenya and Ethiopia, which he watched with the intensity of a man with money on the line.

"I thought I was taking you to the train?" Laurent said to Jonah.

"You are," Jonah said. "I don't know what he's talking about."

"No no no," Mateo said, grabbing a beer from the refrigerator. "No need for the train. I have to go to Libreville to see my mother, so you can come with me."

"No thanks," Jonah said.

"No . . . !" Slinky yelled at the TV, which showed the Ethiopian goalie lying on the ground with his hands over his head while the Kenyans pawed one another in celebration.

"Fucking Ethopians," Slinky said, abandoning the match for a French-dubbed version of *How the Grinch Stole Christmas*. The smile on his face indicated he was familiar with the movie and derived a great deal of pleasure from it.

"Elephant Man," Slinky said, motioning for Jonah to come over. "I have something of yours."

Jonah walked over to Slinky, who removed Jonah's passport from his own back pocket. "I found this in your tent."

Jonah felt something collapse inside of him. He'd assumed his passport was still tucked in his backpack. He hadn't considered the possibility that it had been taken along with his camera. He sensed the situation closing in around him, his options dwindling.

Slinky leaned toward Jonah. "I told you I would convince you to help me," he said. "Here's how this will work. Mateo will pick you up at ten tomorrow morning and drive you to Libreville."

"I told you I'm not doing this," Jonah whispered. He was trying, unsuccessfully, to shield Laurent from their conversation.

"You don't have a choice."

"I'll get another passport at the embassy," Jonah bluffed. He knew the embassy wasn't open on weekends and that his flight left in less than forty-eight hours. He just wasn't sure how much of this Slinky knew.

"Suit yourself," Slinky said, tucking the passport back into his pocket.

There was no way Jonah could smuggle ivory, but he also knew he wasn't getting home without a passport. Getting caught with ivory would result in a prison sentence, though refusing the request could result in a death sentence, either for his elephants or himself. He did the mental arithmetic but couldn't come up with a satisfying solution. "What happens if I get caught?"

"I told you not to worry about such things," Slinky said. "Just make sure you're ready to leave tomorrow morning. Once you're back in Chicago, my cousin Andre will be in touch. He'll arrange for a meeting. You give him the ivory, he gives you the money. Then you return it to me after Christmas. If there are no problems, you go back to talking to your elephants in the forest." Slinky stood up from the bar and clapped Jonah on the shoulder. "Very easy for you. No problem." On his way out the door, Slinky stopped to admire the Christmas tree. "Nice tree," he said to Laurent.

"What was that about?" Laurent asked as soon as they were gone.

Jonah shrugged. "I guess he's giving me a ride to the airport."

"Jonah?" Laurent said, his face demanding an explanation.

Jonah had considered telling Laurent everything, but there was nothing he could do to help. "I'd rather not get into it."

"I don't like the look of this," Laurent said, sweeping the empty beer cans off the bar.

———

JONAH WOKE EARLY THE next morning and logged onto Laurent's computer to fire off a few emails. He sent a note to his mother informing her that he would arrive at O'Hare on the afternoon of the twenty-third and that he'd take a taxi into the city. He still hadn't heard back from Sam, which was fine, since a whirlwind tour of Paris was about the last thing he felt up for. At three minutes after ten, he heard a honk and looked out the window to see Mateo approaching in a battered Toyota pickup truck with a camper shell over the bed. He grabbed his bags and told Laurent goodbye, promising to email pictures of snow.

Outside, Jonah loaded his bags in the truck, then walked to the passenger door and noticed another man sitting shotgun. Mateo, from inside the truck, nodded toward the back. *Perfect,* Jonah thought, *ten hours in the bed of a pickup.* Slinky hadn't mentioned that he'd be riding with the cargo, which consisted not only of a crate of tusks, Jonah discovered, but also four burlap sacks of coffee beans and three caged chickens. The road was rough and punishing, and the chickens were squawking and cawing at such a crushing pitch and decibel that Jonah briefly considered suffocating them with his T-shirt. Soon, the small cab window slid open to reveal a bearded man with rotten teeth and a goofy smile. "*Chaud?*" the man asked.

"Yeah, it's a little hot. Maybe you could keep the window open."

"*Poulets,*" the man said, pointing to the birds. He spoke with the wonder and awe of a toddler.

"*Oui,*" Jonah said. "*Ils sont à vous?*" He nodded and the man did the same. "Did you fellas do some Christmas shopping?"

The man continued nodding, though he obviously didn't understand a word of English. "Bought your girlfriends coffee beans and live chickens?" Jonah continued. "That's very sweet of you. *Très romantique.*"

Mateo's hand reached across and slammed the window shut. Jonah banged on it a couple times before sitting back down. The chickens were still carrying on, so he threw a handful of coffee beans at the cage, which he immediately regretted. Caffeine, he realized, probably wasn't the best sedative.

They drove through the afternoon, stopping every couple of hours to bribe officials at checkpoints. Twice they let Jonah out to stretch and both times he considered running into the surrounding forest. Mateo would usually disappear momentarily before returning with additional cargo—marijuana, automatic weapons, an aquarium containing a six-foot python—until Jonah wondered whether they planned to shoot him, feed him to the snake, or some combination of the two. Jonah was battered, filthy, sore, despondent, and ultimately alone. If he weren't alone, he might have tried to overtake Mateo and his goon, but he possessed neither the energy nor bravery to stage such a coup.

At dusk, they arrived at a concrete structure that advertised itself as a Nightclub Pizzeria. Jonah's heart jumped at the possibility of pizza and cold beer, but the club was empty save for an elderly woman who emerged from the kitchen with a tray of charred songbirds. In a precooked state, he might have been able to educate the men about their dinner, but now, as he lifted one of the birds from the tray and cracked its wings and tried to extract what little meat was available, he felt as though he might vomit. When the tray made its way around a second time, Jonah politely declined and went outside to eat his last granola bar.

After dinner, they piled back into the truck. Jonah moved the cargo around to create a rectangle of empty space in which to sleep. He stacked the crate of marijuana on the aquarium to ensure the snake didn't wander around in the night, then unrolled his sleeping bag, balled a couple T-shirts into a pillow, and crawled into bed. He was no stranger to crude sleeping arrangements, but between the bouncing and pounding of the dirt road, the noise of the chickens, and the threat of the giant python staring at him through a half inch of glass, he knew whatever sleep he found would be intermittent. He almost wished he'd been taken at gunpoint and shoved into the back of the truck and *forced* to do this thing that violated every tenet of his moral code, because at least then he'd be a legitimate hostage rather than a feckless grad student without the balls to demand a proper seat.

MORNING ANNOUNCED ITSELF WITH a rectangle of sunlight to the face. Jonah crawled out of the truck and into the concussive din of a fast-moving city. They'd arrived in Libreville sometime in the night. Jonah spotted Mateo sitting on a curb some distance away, shouting into a cellphone. Taxis and motorcycles sped past, and two men were arguing in front of a wheelbarrow filled with oranges. It was a blunt transition from the quietude of forest life, like being shoved half-asleep into a coliseum.

Jonah walked over to Mateo, who was now scribbling something down on a piece of notebook paper. "What's the plan?"

"Come with me," Mateo instructed.

"Where are we going?"

"Don't worry," Mateo said, walking a few steps ahead of Jonah.

"I have a flight to catch," Jonah said. "I don't have time for sight-seeing."

"We'll get you to the airport. But there's something I must take care of first."

Mateo led Jonah to an abandoned garment factory down the street. Inside, the skeletons of wardrobe racks were stalled between rows of postwar sewing machines and cast-iron blocks that reminded Jonah of car engines. At the other end of the factory floor, a group of men sat on rolls of uncut fabric, smoking cigarettes and listening to American hip-hop on a small boom box. An elderly man emerged from a room somewhere behind them. He appeared to be in his sixties, with the stoop-shouldered posture of someone stuck in a permanent flinch. Despite his meager comportment, he possessed an aura that suggested he was in charge of whatever the hell was going on here. When he saw Mateo he summoned him to his office, closing the door behind him.

Jonah sat on the floor and picked at the rubber peeling on the sole of his shoe.

It was tempting to wonder how he ended up here, though he knew that line of questioning would only send him into an existential spiral. He was a long way from the elephants, a long way from the path he'd prescribed for himself. He'd made a choice, and that choice had informed another choice, and somehow, without much consideration as to how it would end, he'd gone from being a Ph.D. student monitoring elephants to a foot soldier in an ivory trafficking ring.

A few minutes later, Mateo reappeared from the office.

"Who was that?" Jonah asked, standing.

Mateo ignored him, walking toward the truck, his face indicating he was pleased by whatever he'd learned inside the office.

"I thought you were taking me to the airport?" Jonah asked, hurrying to catch up.

"Wait here," Mateo said, charging forward.

Jonah was sick of waiting, sick of not knowing what the hell was going on. He looked back at the men smoking and laughing at the other end of the factory floor. He counted eight in total, most were in their twenties, all were wearing brightly colored soccer jerseys plastered with logos for cellphone companies. Jonah wasn't sure if he'd stepped into the meeting of a West African crime syndicate or the postgame celebration of a victorious soccer club.

Mateo returned with the python around his neck, flaunting it like an expensive scarf. He dropped the snake in the middle of the room and the men gathered round, poking at it with lengths of metal conduit. Mateo finally parted the crowd and unsheathed his machete, lifting it high above his head and dropping it on the snake, removing the head in one clean slice. He peeled back a six-inch slab of skin and motioned for one of the guys to give him a hand. An eager boy with bad acne grabbed hold of the skin while Mateo held the snake's body with both hands, and together they pulled in opposite directions, as if peeling a very large banana. Once the snake had been disrobed, it was hauled off to another room, then returned twenty minutes later in the form of breaded strips that looked like chicken tenders but smelled far worse. The group made quick work of the snake, and Jonah wondered why the obvious meal, the chickens, had been spared.

After their feast, the men divided up the guns and began departing in small groups. Jonah looked at his phone. It was ten till eleven and his flight was scheduled to leave at 12:20, which meant he needed to be at the airport very soon. When Mateo returned, Jonah politely reminded him of his time crunch and said that although he hated to interrupt whatever the hell they were celebrating, he really needed to get going. Mateo nodded, and together they walked back outside to the truck, where Jonah began transferring the tusks to his rolling case. "Don't bother," Mateo said. "It stays here."

"What do you mean?" Jonah said.

"With me."

"No," Jonah said, shaking his head. "That wasn't the plan."

"It is now." Mateo grabbed the tusks from Jonah's case and began putting them in an empty duffel bag.

"Fine," Jonah said, suddenly relieved that he might not have to follow through with this after all, "but I need to confirm that with Slinky first."

"Slinky isn't in charge anymore." There was an uncertainty in Mateo's voice, as if he wasn't sure he believed what he'd just said.

"Says you?"

Mateo stared into the distance, and Jonah could sense he was struggling with his betrayal. "Yes."

"I don't think you want to do this," Jonah said firmly but without judgment, as if talking a stranger off a bridge.

"That's not your concern," Mateo said, removing the last piece of ivory from Jonah's case and placing it in the duffel.

"What am I supposed to tell Slinky when he asks why I didn't deliver the ivory?"

"Tell him it got lost." Mateo zipped the bag shut.

Jonah shook his head. "I don't think he'll buy that."

The factory doors swung open and Jonah turned to see the old hunched guy motioning for Mateo to come near. Two heavily armed men stood at his side.

Mateo handed Jonah his passport. "Wait here. I'll be right back."

Mateo left the duffel in the back of the truck and walked over to shake the crippled man's hand. Jonah's instinct was to run, but he knew he wouldn't make it far on foot, so he hesitated, waiting to see what happened. Though he couldn't hear the details of their conversation, Jonah could see that Mateo was speaking quickly, gesticulating in the manner of a desperate salesman, pointing back to the duffel. The old guy allowed him to finish his speech, then nodded to the taller of the two bodyguards—a heavyset young man with light, freckled skin—who grabbed Mateo from behind and ran a knife across his neck. Jonah involuntarily released some hybrid of a whimper and a dog bark.

It was a shocking turn of events and his immediate reaction was to flee, which he did, his legs carrying him into the cab of the truck. The men began chasing him, but Jonah locked the doors, turned the ignition, and stepped on the gas, charging the truck down a narrow alley lined with dumpsters. He checked the side mirror and saw a quick succession of muzzle flashes before the mirror exploded and his pursuers disappeared in the shattered glass. Another shot ripped through the tailgate and a couple more wheezed past the driver's-side window. He drove erratically, weaving back and forth in a clumsy attempt at evasion, a useless tactic he'd picked up from watching too many action movies. When he reached the end of the alley, he made a hard left onto a busy street and slipped into the camouflage of midday traffic. A heavy rain had begun to fall and people darted through the streets, seeking shelter. He couldn't find the lever for the wiper blades, so he rolled down the window and wiped the windshield with his hand. He'd been in this city only once before, when he first arrived four months earlier. He hadn't paid much attention during the taxi ride from the airport to his hotel, and he now found himself wishing he'd been a little more cognizant of the city's layout. He eventually found the L101, the main coastal boulevard, and saw a sign with a picture of an airplane pointing north out of town. *Finally,* he thought, *pictures, the language of idiots.*

He looked in the rearview mirror to see if anyone was tailing him, but there was only the water-blurred shape of a city bus. He eventually arrived at what appeared to be either a long-term parking lot or a car dealership. It made no difference really. He ditched the truck next to a decommissioned taxi and began loading the tusks into his rolling case. He then shouldered his backpack and pulled the case of ivory through an archipelago of parking lot puddles. He finally saw the DÉPARTS sign and made his way to the Air France desk, where a surly Gabonese man checked his luggage through to Chicago before presenting him with two boarding passes. He cleared security and hurried to the gate, where the last of the passengers were filing onto the plane. Jonah handed over his boarding pass and settled into his seat. His hands were shaking, and he kept expecting the police to storm the plane and apprehend him, but minutes later the doors closed, the engines charged to life, and they were quickly rising through moisture-thick clouds. Jonah finally took a deep, satisfying breath, knowing that somehow, despite everything, he had made it out alive.

IT WAS SNOWING IN Paris. He spent the first thirty minutes sitting at the gate watching flakes gather on the tarmac. It was close to 9:00 P.M. and his next flight didn't leave until 8:30 the following morning, which meant that unless he ventured into the city, he would have to spend the night at the airport. If Sam were here, he could be talked into walking the Champs-Élysées or catching some obscure film she'd read about, but she'd never responded to his emails and he wasn't about to venture into an unfamiliar city by himself. Instead, he went to a bar at the end of the terminal and drank two glasses of cabernet. Afterward, feeling pleasantly buzzed, he went searching for dinner, and ended up at a Pizza Hut in Terminal 2B. He ate with a speed and ferocity that astonished him. It felt good to be in this place that was not Gabon and not Chicago, this middle ground, where he could exist in a kind of suspended reality, far from the problems awaiting him in the States and those that had chased him out of Africa. Of course, tomorrow he would be forced to confront his actions, but tonight he was a man with no responsibilities, nowhere to go, and so he staked out a piece of real estate at Gate 21 and spread his sleeping bag on the floor. Before long the wine got the best of him, and he drifted off to sleep.

HE AWOKE TO A group of French schoolchildren dressed in matching blazers staring down at him. They spoke among themselves, like a congregation of tiny sophisticated assemblymen. Jonah slid out of his sleeping bag and retrieved a new T-shirt from his backpack. He'd brought seven shirts with him to Gabon, one for each day of the week, but he hadn't the time nor the mental acuity to wash them before he left Laurent's. As he changed, the kids began giggling and shooting disparaging looks in his direction. The chorus of giggles grew louder, the kids making exaggerated fanning motions with their hands, hiking their shirts up over their noses, alternately amused and disgusted with the foul-smelling American sleeping on the ground. One of the kids, a soft-spoken, curly-haired boy, approached Jonah. "*Monsieur*," he said. "*Tu sens mauvais.*" The boy turned and ran into the giggling mass of schoolchildren, where his bravery was rewarded with high fives. Jonah felt an intense shame, not only about his moral failings, which were many, but also that he'd let himself become the kind of foul-smelling American ridiculed by French schoolchildren.

He gathered his belongings and went to the men's room to freshen up. He washed his face in the sink and dabbed his armpits with damp paper towels. He brushed his teeth with hand soap smeared across his index finger. He went searching for deodorant, but was unsuccessful. He considered purchasing a small bottle of cologne from the duty-free store, but he didn't have enough money, so instead he settled for a pack of chewing gum, which masked his odor very little. He spent his last two euros on a coffee, then hurried back to the gate and boarded the plane that would take him home.

He got stuck in the middle seat, between two of the kids that had teased him earlier. They were now flipping through the pages of the in-flight magazine, disinterested in the man they had once found so amusing. A flight attendant at the front of the plane was going over the emergency procedures when one of the boys finally set his magazine down and looked to Jonah. He had small metal-rimmed glasses and an intense side part. There was just something about the kid's smug precociousness that reminded Jonah of Harry Potter. "You are American?" the kid asked in charmingly accented English.

"Yeah."

"You live in Shee-cago?"

"Sort of."

A flight attendant approached Jonah as they taxied from the gate. "Mr. Brennan?" she asked.

"Yes?"

"The airline would like to have a word with you when you arrive in Chicago. Apparently, there's an issue with your luggage."

"Uh-oh," Harry Potter said with a wry smile. "You in *beeeg* trouble."

GAVIN

THE MORNING BEFORE HE WAS to head back to Chicago, Gavin and Mariana drove to Albuquerque to look for costumes. They rummaged through thrift stores searching for clothes that could pass for twentieth-century fashions, then visited a used bookstore and picked up a few dozen ancient hardbacks to use for props. It all felt very domestic, just a normal couple out running errands, the only problem being that they weren't a couple. He wasn't sure what they were, because they'd never discussed their relationship. Gavin knew it would be an awkward and unpleasant conversation and so, like all the other awkward and unpleasant conversations in his life, he chose to bury it in the hope that it might magically resolve itself.

Back in town, they stopped by the theater, where Jesse and his team of contractors were hanging drywall, the floor littered with power tools and fast-food wrappers, a small boom box blasting top forty hits. The damage wasn't as extensive as Gavin had imagined. The building, a large adobe structure, appeared unharmed from the outside, and most of the interior damage was confined to the lobby. It seemed to Gavin as if they'd already made significant progress since they began working a few days ago.

Gavin walked over to Jesse, who was taping a section of drywall. "You've been busy."

"As have you," Jesse replied without looking at him.

"What do you mean?"

"With the play. Seems like you and Mariana have been burning the midnight oil. I hardly see her anymore." The friendliness from a few days earlier was replaced by a more hostile tone.

"Yeah," Gavin said. "There's a lot to get done."

"Apparently."

Mariana approached from the stage area. "Are you planning to paint the walls in there?" she asked Jesse.

"We'll do as much as we can with the time and money we have."

"Okay," Mariana said. "But I feel like it needs a fresh coat of paint."

"Noted."

"Come on," Mariana said to Gavin. "I'd like to get your thoughts on the set design."

"The salmon was delicious," Jesse said as they walked away.

"What?" Mariana asked, turning around.

"The salmon," Jesse said. "She did it with a nice honey-lemon glaze like we discussed."

"Shit," Mariana said. "I totally forgot."

"We had an appointment with the caterer this afternoon," Jesse explained to Gavin. "Final tasting before the wedding. I brought home a little platter for Mariana to sample, but feel free to help your-self. It's in the fridge back at our place. There's a cab franc in the wine cellar if you guys need something to pair it with."

Gavin sensed a controlled rage in his voice, a violence awaiting release, and he figured it was best if he removed himself from the situation. Outside, he sat down on the steps of the theater and awaited the fallout of what he'd set in motion. If it involved physical violence to his person, then so be it; he accepted that as the just punishment for sleeping with another man's fiancée. But part of him hoped Mariana would just do the difficult work of coming clean with Jesse, telling him everything so that they might settle into their own future to-gether.

A moment later, she appeared. "I think you should probably go," she said. "I need to do some damage control here. I'll call you later tonight."

GAVIN RETURNED TO THE house to pack up his things. His plan was to leave in the morning. He consulted the map on his phone: a touch over twelve hundred miles, nearly nineteen hours. It was three days before Christmas, so he'd have to hustle to make it in time. His mother had texted him twice in the last day, asking if he'd left yet, and he'd conveniently neglected to respond. Nineteen hours was too much to do in one shot, so he'd have to spend the night somewhere in Nebraska. As he was deciding on a good layover spot, his phone rang.

"Hey," Mariana said.

"What did he say?" Gavin asked.

Mariana sighed. "He said he doesn't feel good about what's going on between us."

"So he knows?"

"He suspects something."

"Maybe it's time to tell him."

Mariana scoffed. "I can't tell him."

"Why not?"

"Because we're getting married in less than two weeks."

He hesitated. "What if you called it off?" He knew it was a long shot, but it was all he had.

"I can't call off the wedding," she said tonelessly.

"Why not?"

"I'm in too deep."

Gavin felt something turn inside of him. This was the conversation he'd feared, because despite their time together—the mornings they spent skiing, the afternoons at rehearsal—Mariana had said nothing to suggest she wasn't going to marry Jesse. And he'd resisted broaching the subject for fear of breaking the wonderful little spell they'd cast. "I'm sorry, but I think that's a bit cowardly."

"Gavin, I've got a hundred and twenty people flying here to watch me get married. I can't just back out now. That shit only happens in the movies."

"This isn't about them," Gavin said. "It's about *you.*"

"I know that. But still . . ."

Gavin walked to the window and looked out at the skiers on the mountain. He felt something rising within him. "So this was just something you needed to get out of your system?" he said sharply. "You just needed to fuck another guy before settling into married life?"

A wounded silence. "That's a horrible thing to say."

"Yet true."

"You know very well that isn't true."

"I *don't* know. Apparently, I don't know anything about you, because I thought you had feelings for me."

"I do! But I'm also engaged to another man. And I don't know how to reconcile those two things."

"I just told you how!" Gavin tried to compose himself.

"I can't call off my wedding to run away with a guy I barely know," Mariana said.

Gavin looked at his bags sitting by the front door of this home that wasn't his. "Do you love me?"

"I think so," she said carefully.

"Then you should call it off," he said, as if that settled it.

"But I love Jesse too," she replied.

"It doesn't work like that."

"Yes it does, Gavin. Love isn't an absolute."

"Well, I believe it is."

"Then you don't know much about love."

"And you don't know much about fidelity."

The line went silent. Gavin thought he heard a whimper on the other end. "Don't cry," he said, "you brought this on yourself."

"I know that! Fuck, Gavin! What do you want me to say? I'm a shitty person. I'm a cheating whore. Is that what you want to hear?"

"I should go," Gavin said. "I need to finish packing."

"So this is it?" she asked, her voice catching.

"Apparently."

"Will you be back?"

"I don't know yet. I'll be in touch. Enjoy the wedding." He tapped off his phone and stared at the sun sliding behind the mountains. There it was. The thing he'd feared had come to pass. And how could it not? He was a fool to believe otherwise.

HE COULDN'T SLEEP, so shortly after midnight he got in his car and left. He dropped the key to the house in Mariana's mailbox and began the drive to Chicago. Fuck it, he thought. He'd do the whole thing in one straight shot. Like a long-haul trucker. Like a brokenhearted long-haul trucker. Fifteen miles outside of Taos, his phone rang. It was strange that anyone would be calling him this late at night, stranger yet that it was an international number.

"Is this Gavin?" the voice asked. It was a female voice.

"Yeah," he said.

"Hey, Gavin. You don't know me. My name's Marie. I'm Sam's roommate at the dance company in Russia. I need to talk to you about your sister."

PART TWO

SAMANTHA

SHE ARRIVED AT O'HARE AT 1:20 A.M. on December 23rd. The newsstands were boarded up for the night, the restaurants all closed: TGI Friday's, Cinnabon, Dunkin' Donuts, that windy city staple. She collected her bags and followed the signs for trains to the city. She fed a twenty to the ticket machine, grabbed her Ventra card, and boarded a nearly empty carriage toward the loop. There was a man sleeping at the front, his head resting on a backpack wedged between his shoulder and the window, and across the aisle sat a Korean businessman with a small rolling suitcase, his face reflecting a strain of exhaustion Sam recognized in herself.

When she'd finally emailed her itinerary, her mom had written back offering to pick her up at the airport, but Sam knew it would be an ungodly hour, particularly for her mother, who rarely stayed up past ten. Sam had told her not to worry, she could take the train, simpler for everyone really, to which her mom had acquiesced more easily than she'd expected. But as Sam made her way down empty corridors hung with portraits of stoic Native Americans, she'd secretly hoped to find her mom waiting at baggage claim, ready to whisk her home and tuck her into bed, make her soup and stroke her hair while she spent however many days it would take to claw her way out of this awful pit of despair. But she also knew how unrealistic that was. It would never happen, because she was too ashamed of what she'd become, of how she'd failed, so she would continue hiding, deflecting, obscuring, in the hope that the unspeakable truth would never be revealed.

When the train finally bolted to life, Sam watched the soft edges of the city reveal themselves. It was a seamless continuation of her life in Russia, white and cold and carelessly lit. As the train gained speed she held tight to her suitcase, which pulled away from her in the turns. Through the window, she saw warehouse distribution centers outlined in colorful lights and a thirty-foot-tall wooden reindeer standing sentinel outside a Best Buy. She watched a snowplow carve a swath of black down the Kennedy Expressway, a line of cars following close behind like obedient schoolchildren. It was a forty-minute ride into the city, so Sam put on a pair of headphones and listened to orchestral post-rock, reliving childhood memories in the poorly attended theater of her mind.

When she was fourteen, she attended a four-week summer dance intensive in Los Angeles. Her instructor had encouraged the program as a way to maintain focus during the summer months, when most students abandoned the studio for indolent afternoons back in their hometowns. The program was based out of Pepperdine, in Malibu, a private university with glamorous views of the Pacific. Sam brought the glossy ten-page brochure home to her parents, who looked it over one night after dinner and, to Sam's surprise, agreed to let her go despite the two-thousand-dollar price tag. As far as her parents could tell, their daughter had no hobbies outside ballet, and they worried that if she didn't fill her summer with dance, she might be lured into some kind of unsupervised teenage underworld. So on the last Monday in June, Sam's mom dropped her off at O'Hare with a hundred dollars' spending cash and instructions to remember why she was going to California. Sam smiled and kissed her mom goodbye and disappeared through the sliding glass doors, feeling gloriously free. It was her first time traveling alone, and she arrived at her gate far too early. She bought a latte and the newest issue of *Vogue,* and sat at the airport terminal like the sophisticate she aspired to be.

Her roommate at the camp was a girl named Marie, whose father had sent her to L.A. under the misguided belief that a month in Malibu might cure the wild streak she'd acquired after her parents' divorce. But Marie wasn't into the idea of wasting her summer indoors when the gentle wash of the Pacific beckoned from across the highway. She spent her days marking through movements in the studio, but after dinner she'd disappear down to the beach to hang out with whatever cute boys offered her beer. One day she met a surfer named Rusty, the son of a music producer, an exceptionally handsome boy whom Marie described in exquisite detail later that night. Sam had been militant about her dance, remembering very clearly her mother's instructions. She was aware of what this trip was costing her parents, and she didn't intend to squander the opportunity. But she was also a curious fourteen-year-old away from home for the first time in her life, and it seemed crazy not to allow herself even a taste of the California lifestyle.

For the first few days, she towed a fine line between sticking to her dance commitments and providing cover for her roommate's adventures. Marie returned to their room one day with a page she'd torn from a surf catalog. It featured a shirtless teenage boy with an Al Merrick board tucked under his arm staring longingly out to sea. This, Marie explained, was Rusty's best friend, Teddy, amateur surfer and professional catalog model. Sam was excited by the idea of a double date, especially if he looked anything like he did in the picture. Marie told Sam that Teddy was totally her type and arranged for them to meet the following night at a party at Rusty's house. After curfew, they snuck out of the dorms and walked a half mile south along the PCH. The house was empty when they arrived, and Sam suggested they go home, watch a movie, and call it a night, but Marie wasn't interested in that. She let herself into the house, Sam following close behind, and walked out to the deck, where they found Rusty and Teddy firing bottle rockets into the sea. Rusty explained that the party was kind of a bust due to his forgetting to invite people. He apologized by whipping up a pitcher of margaritas, which Sam enjoyed more than she would have expected. She'd never tasted alcohol aside from a couple sips of her grandpa's beer, but the yellow Slurpee-like things Rusty was serving went down surprisingly easy. After a couple rounds, Rusty suggested they go for a moonlight swim.

Feeling the pleasant effects of good tequila, Sam followed Marie and the boys down to the sand, where they shed their clothes and skipped into the water. Under more sober circumstances she would have balked at the idea of undressing in front of strangers, but she figured this was just how they did it in California, and she didn't want to be the prude who sat on the beach while everyone else frolicked in the sea. She peeled off her tank top, dropped her jean shorts, and, wearing only her underwear, jogged sheepishly toward the water. Teddy, who had swum a good distance out, was now trudging back to shore, his member, Sam could clearly see, standing at full attention, like a fleshy periscope breaching the water's surface. It was the first time she'd ever seen the male organ in such a pronounced state, and there was something unsettling about the way it protruded upward, defying gravity. Instead of acknowledging this thing that seemed to her like a new, uninvited member of the party, Teddy simply grabbed her by the hand and escorted her back into the water. She dove beneath a breaking wave and surfaced on the other side, but Teddy was gone. She could see the soft outline of Marie and Rusty a hundred yards down the beach, locked in a serious make-out session. Teddy finally surfaced and grabbed her by the waist, pulling her close, both of them treading water. "I'm really glad I met you," he said, a big goofy grin breaking across his face.

Was he though? she wondered. Because in their two hours together, he hadn't asked her a single question aside from her name, which she wasn't even sure he remembered. He didn't ask her about dance camp or where she was from or what she thought of California. The entirety of their so-called "date" had consisted of the two girls sitting awkwardly on the couch, while Teddy and Rusty recounted the summer's most epic waves.

"I'm glad you're so chill," Teddy said, wrapping his legs around her waist. "Most girls I meet aren't nearly as chill as you."

Sam wasn't sure what to do with that compliment. In fact, she wasn't even sure it was a compliment. It had a hollow ring to it, the kind of canned charm she'd seen in movies, and she fought the urge to roll her eyes. It was also hard to take him seriously with his penis bobbing against her thigh.

"I think I'm gonna head back in," she finally said, and swam back to shore. She dried off with Teddy's towel, slipped back into her clothes, and scanned the beach for Marie and Rusty, who had disappeared, leaving her alone with this dim boy. Teddy arrived a moment later and spread his towel on the sand. "Have a seat," he said. "The stars are pretty sick tonight."

That was when she should have bid Teddy farewell and hightailed it back to campus. That was when she should have written her phone number on the palm of his hand and said to call if he ever matured into a gentleman looking for a proper date. But instead, she joined him on the towel and watched him remove a glass pipe from his backpack. "You smoke?" he asked.

"Like cigarettes?"

Teddy laughed. "No. Weed."

"Oh yeah," Sam said, though the truth was that she did not.

Teddy handed her the pipe. She put it to her mouth, inhaled, and coughed a few times. "Good stuff," she said, handing it back.

"Sativa," Teddy said. "Very heady."

Sam waited for something to happen, but all she felt was a burning sensation in her throat.

"Lie down," Teddy said, patting the towel. She leaned back and stared up at the sky, listening to Teddy spout some questionable facts about the Big Dipper. *Why?* she wondered. Why did she just do that? Why did she just smoke something she knew nothing about? It had all happened so quickly, and now this drug was swirling around inside of her, doing unknown things to her body, staining her organs in ways that would probably register on some future drug test she hadn't even considered. *Shit, shit, shit!* She felt the regret crash over her as Teddy's hand worked its way up her leg.

And now, as Chicago's skyline presented itself, she recognized that night on the beach in Malibu as a sort of pivotal life event. It wasn't so much that she'd smoked pot, which she knew was an inevitable teenage rite of passage, but rather the circumstances in which it had occurred, the way she had let it happen with so little consideration. She had been careless then and she was careless now, and almost all the anguish in her life could be attributed to this crucial flaw.

The train stopped at Clark and Lake. She hurried down the metal stairs and began the short walk to her parents' apartment. Technically, she was returning home, though she'd never visited her folks' new place, and she had to reference her phone for directions, an irony that hinted at some greater meaning she couldn't articulate. She headed south on State Street, past the Joffrey, where she'd spent so much time as a kid, the origin of her doomed journey. She felt as if she'd come full circle, though not in any sort of conclusive, satisfactory way. Looking up at her old practice space made her realize how far off course she'd drifted, framed with chilling clarity the magnitude of her miscalculations.

She passed beneath the gilded trumpets perched above Macy's. The mechanical Christmas vignettes in the large picture windows had powered down for the day, but Sam stopped to have a look. A young girl sat atop a reindeer, while Santa watched benevolently from a wooden rocking chair. She'd always enjoyed Chicago during the holidays, though she wouldn't admit that to anyone. She liked wandering downtown, seeing the skeletal trees veined with yellow lights. She liked watching the ice skaters at Millennium Park and the tourists posing for pictures next to the lions outside the Art Institute. For a girl her age, with her interests and her left-leaning politics, it was terribly unhip to find comfort in the *yuletide-industrial complex,* but she did. Or more specifically, she *had*. Maybe she'd outgrown those feel-ings or maybe she'd just been away for too long, but Christmas held no allure for her now. Right now, nothing seemed very appealing, which was the simplest way of explaining her condition. She'd been lying to herself for months, convinced that whatever happened next would be the catalyst for some grand transformation, but nothing ever came, and now she wasn't sure if she deserved anything other than the dark cast her life had acquired.

WHEN SHE ARRIVED AT the condo, the door to the building was locked so she pounded on the glass, rousing the doorman from sleep. He walked to the door and cracked it enough to stick his head out. He wore a suit and a wool fedora.

"Hi," Sam said. "My parents live here. Six oh eight. I think my mom mentioned that I was coming."

"Right," the doorman said. "You must be Sam. Come in, it's cold out there. Sorry, I fell asleep for a minute."

Sam entered the lobby. The walls were hung with framed faux-vintage posters for the 1893 World's Fair. There was a tiny koi pond surrounded by white leather armchairs. "Your mom's pretty excited to have all of her kids home," the doorman said, leading her toward the elevator. "She's been talking about it for weeks. You have some brothers coming too, right?"

"Yeah," she said, a little taken aback by how much he knew about her family. She imagined her mother chewing the poor guy's ear off, exaggerating her children's accomplishments, bombarding him with motherly anecdotes about each one. She felt a rush of mortification followed by another rush of guilt for being embarrassed by her moth-er's love. The truth was that her mom missed her, and she missed her mom too, and if she could ever get over the stupid guilt she felt about being born into a family that loved one another without condition, then maybe she could enjoy her time here.

She got off at the sixth floor and dragged her suitcase down the hall. The door was unlocked, so she entered quietly, careful not to wake her parents. Inside, it was dark, the only light coming from the glow of a Christmas tree planted in the corner of the living room. It was now close to 3:00, her parents no doubt asleep, her brothers yet to arrive. She walked to the wall of windows looking out toward the lake. It was an incredible view, unobstructed despite being only six stories aboveground. A sliding glass door gave way to a sliver of balcony, which was blanketed with an inch of untouched snow.

"Hi, sweetie," came her mother's voice, softly.

She turned and saw her mom standing in the door to her bedroom, squinting in the dull light, smiling through her sleepiness. Sam stood and walked to her, put her arms around her. "Hi, Mom."

"Did you just get here?"

"Yeah."

"What do you think of the place?"

"It's great," Sam said, looking around.

"It's perfect for your dad and me," her mom said. "A little small with all you kids home, but I guess we'll survive."

"We will," Sam said, wondering if it was true.

A silence settled between them. "Well," her mom finally mumbled over a yawn. "I'm going back to bed. Let's catch up in the morning. You're in the little room, first door down the hall."

"Good night," Sam said.

"I'm glad you're home," her mom said, closing the door behind her.

Sam pulled her suitcase to her room, unpacked enough to find her pajamas, then went to the bathroom to wash her face. The exhaustion she'd felt after landing had given way to a second wind, so she went to the kitchen, where she found a corked bottle of wine, which she helped herself to. She moved to the living room and sat on the couch and looked out toward the lake. The giant Ferris wheel on Navy Pier had gone into hibernation for the winter and most of the city looked strangely dark. Unlike New York, Chicago shut down at the end of each day, the businessmen and women fleeing to bedroom communities west of the city. She watched a man in a puffy down jacket and pajama bottoms lead a small dog outside to pee, but otherwise there were few signs of life at this late hour. Even the heartiest of the homeless had retreated to church beds once the sun dropped. The thermometer on the end table displayed an outside temperature of nine degrees, while on her side of the glass it was a comfortable seventy-two.

She was drinking her wine and staring at the shining city by the lake when she saw two men standing in the street below. They looked like they were involved in some business that might interest her, so she stepped onto the balcony and called down to them. The men scanned the street for a few seconds before they located the voice above them. "Hey," Sam yelled softly, careful not to wake her parents.

"What?" the tall one asked, squinting to get a look at the woman standing above him.

"What are you doing down there?"

"None of your business," the tall one said.

"Don't talk to her," the shorter one said.

"I have a question for you," Sam said. "Wait there, I'll be right down."

GAVIN

H E MADE IT TO DENVER then continued east, wondering
what exactly to do with everything he'd learned about his
sister. Heroin? Who the hell gets hooked on heroin? He hadn't exactly
been a shining example of a drug-free lifestyle, but he always understood there to be an invisible yet implied line separating recreational
drug use from the dark underworld of intravenous abuse. How could
she be so careless? He felt a flush of anger that was quickly replaced by
the kind of deep fear that forced him to imagine, with great clarity,
the death of someone he loved. Because there was no way to think
about his sister doing heroin without imagining his sister overdosing
on it. He knew very little about the drug, aside from what he'd seen in
movies, but it was enough to know that it killed people, very easily,
often due to some careless measuring.

He considered his options. He couldn't tell his parents, at least not
until he spoke with Sam first. He couldn't tell anyone really, and
that's what troubled him most. This wasn't something that could be
sorted out with a phone call. Marie had been fairly vague regarding
the extent of Sam's use, though it was obviously troubling enough to
warrant a phone call. If she was truly addicted—and by now he'd
convinced himself she was—she would find more drugs regardless of
whatever obstacle he threw in her path. He didn't want to do any-

thing that might alienate her, destroy his opportunity to talk some sense into her, and so he decided he wouldn't call, at least not right now. He needed to think this through, formulate a plan, though he had no idea what that might be. His relationship with his siblings operated best when it avoided confrontation, which had been the default arrangement for most of their adult lives, though now it seemed they were headed for some kind of reckoning. What that might look like Gavin couldn't say, though he suspected it would involve acknowledging his own complicity in Sam's drug use.

As a teenager, Gavin had been unpopular by most social metrics, and a good portion of his high school years had been spent trying to remake his image into that of someone desirable and hip. He quickly realized that the most effective way to accomplish this was through the consumption of drugs and alcohol, which he enjoyed mostly for the social currency they provided. And while his stories about smoking pot at the movie theater or barfing in the McDonald's drive-thru helped him ascend the ranks of Palatine High, they fell flat when recounted to his little sister, whose commitment to dance was absolute. But now, thinking back on it, he wondered if he'd planted some toxic seed that had lain dormant for a time, finally blooming all these years later. Because *he'd* been the one to extol the magic of pharmaceuticals after her dance injury, and *he'd* been the one to offer nips from his flask when they went to shows at the Fireside Bowl. The memories came flooding back, and he felt something cold lodge itself in his chest, blotting out his romantic concerns, which now seemed annoyingly inconsequential in light of his sister. But as much as the news was awful and terrifying and guilt-inducing, it was also liberating in a strange way, because he now felt a sense of purpose, something that needed his attention. He bumped the cruise control to eighty, switched lanes, and overtook a Walmart tractor trailer.

He guessed he was about twelve hours from Chicago, eleven if he pushed it. This stretch of Nebraska was a flat, dry charge through fields of corn, and after hours of uneven mountain, driving it seemed easy, almost automatic. He usually enjoyed mindless interstate driving, but what had begun as a meditative silence had devolved into a harrowing anxiety over all the things he couldn't control. Overhead, the sun was a dull splotch obscured by clouds. The flat, colorless horizon seemed like an apt approximation of his inner life, and he felt justified in his sulking, as opposed to in L.A., where he was expected to purge his sadness by gallivanting in the sun.

His phone rang. It was Mariana. "Hey."

"You left," she said. This was an accusation, not a question.

"I told you I was leaving."

"I assumed you would say goodbye first."

"I thought I did."

She sighed. "So what's your plan?"

"I'm driving to Chicago," he said, watching cows congregate around a half-frozen pond.

"Obviously. I meant after that."

"I don't know yet."

"But not back here?"

"It seems unlikely," Gavin said. "I think we're both better off if we don't see each other for a while."

It was quiet for a moment. He hoped maybe she was changing her mind about the wedding. "I guess I can't blame you if you decide not to come back," she finally said. "I would love for you to be a part of this play, but I know that's not fair of me to ask."

"You're right. It's not."

"I'm sorry. I didn't mean for it turn out like this."

Gavin knew he shared responsibility for the situation, but he was enjoying his righteous indignation and didn't want to ruin the moment by acknowledging his own complicity. What was it that made him so toxic to women? He remembered Renee's critique that he was more in love with the concept of marriage than he was in fostering a relationship that might result in marriage. It was a pretty damning indictment because the truth was that he did in fact have a very specific future mapped out in his mind—marriage by thirty-six (that deadline quickly approaching), first child by thirty-seven (preferably a boy) followed by a second (girl) a year or two later. And the fact that these milestones were all measured by *his* age rather than that of his partner was further evidence of his unmitigated selfishness. When presented this clearly, it was easy to see how he'd ruined two relationships in less than two weeks. "I should go," he said, because there was nothing left to say. "I'm about to lose reception."

HE MADE GOOD TIME through Nebraska, then passed, without notice, into Iowa. He stopped for a late lunch at what the billboards described as the World's Largest Truck Stop, where he was greeted by a chubby hostess in a miniskirt. "Hi there," she chirped. "Table for one?"

Gavin was led to a booth by a large window looking out at rows of gas pumps.

"You need a minute to look over the menu?" the waitress asked.

"I'll have the tenderloin sandwich," Gavin said.

The waitress nodded. "Something to drink?"

"IPA?"

"How about a Coors?"

"Sure."

"You look familiar," the waitress said. "Like someone I've seen on TV." She studied him for a moment before delivering her verdict. "Jim."

"What?" he asked.

"That's who you look like. Jim. From *The Office*. You look like Jim with a beard."

"John Krasinski," Gavin said.

"Huh?"

"The actor's name is John Krasinski."

"Anyway, Jim," she said, turning to leave. "I'll be back with that beer."

Gavin's phone rang. He pulled it from his pocket: Home. "Hey, Mom."

"It's your sister."

"Sam?"

"You only have one sister."

"You're back?" He heard voices and a television in the background, the familiar sounds of home.

"Yeah. Where are you?"

"I'm at the World's Largest Truck Stop," he said, looking around the restaurant. "In Iowa."

"The world's largest, huh? How do they measure such a thing?"

Gavin was pleased to find his sister capable of engaging in conversation. Just knowing that she was alive was a relief. "I don't know," he said, "but if you could see the place, you'd understand."

"Why are you driving anyway?"

"I've been in New Mexico. It's a long story. I'll explain when I get there."

"And when will that be?"

He looked at his watch. "Sometime this evening."

Gavin heard a voice calling to Sam, followed by his sister's muffled voice saying, "What?"

"Sam?" he said.

"Mom wants to know if you'll be here in time for dinner."

"It's unlikely."

"She says to hurry up and get here." There was a pause. "But don't speed."

"I'll call you guys when I'm close."

He hung up. It was nice to hear Sam's voice after so long. He realized just how much he missed her, how long it had been since they'd spent any prolonged time together outside of the holidays. It must have been two years ago, when he'd spent six weeks shooting a film in New York. It was the directorial debut of a guy he'd met through an improv group, and the two of them had worked on the script together for nearly a year before they began filming. It was a melancholic comedy about a twenty-eight-year-old magician finding his way after his young wife dies from ovarian cancer. The script was a strange assemblage of scenes, alternately hilarious and heartbreaking, and Gavin felt genuinely proud and excited for what might result. He was staying at a friend's apartment in Chelsea, working during the week and spending his weekends touring the city with his sister.

As a kid, Sam's social circle consisted of polite, carefully groomed young women from the dance world, but in New York she was living in some kind of hipster B&B run by a merry band of musicians and artists. She introduced Gavin to her boyfriend, Atticus, an anorexic-looking guy who spoke with the flat, measured drawl of a ranch hand. He reminded Gavin of a young Tom Waits.

They spent a Sunday afternoon day drinking with Sam's friends at a dark bar in Williamsburg. Gavin was surprised and a little taken aback by the community she'd created, how her interests—which had always been singularly dance-focused—now encompassed so many things outside of ballet. These friends of hers, these shaggy-haired philosophers with dyslexic outfits—one of whom wore Winnie the Pooh pajamas under an orange windbreaker—seemed a little suspicious of Gavin's art and the disagreeable fact of him being from Los Angeles, a city none of them had visited but which they viewed as a cultural abomination that deserved to be cast into the sea.

"So you're shooting a movie here?" Atticus asked Gavin.

"Yeah," Gavin said, "a little indie film." He hoped the "indie" qualifier might engender some artistic currency, but the group seemed unimpressed.

"They were shooting something in my neighborhood the other day," a pixie-haired girl announced. "They closed down my entire street for three hours. I fucking hate that shit. I mean, why do you have to shoot your shitty Sandra Bullock movie in Greenpoint?"

The rest of the group nodded in vigorous agreement, as if they too had suffered the injustices of the entertainment industry. Gavin felt them turning on him. They seemed to view him as a foot soldier in Hollywood's evil empire, despite the film's microscopic budget of five hundred thousand dollars, a pittance by Hollywood standards. He considered relaying this fact, but he suspected it was futile to defend himself. "It's just a paycheck," Gavin finally said a little dismissively, hoping to insulate himself from the group's collective wrath.

"That's not true," Sam put in.

"What?" Gavin asked.

"It's not *just* a paycheck," she said to him with a level of defiance that surprised him. "You know it's not." Then, to the others, she said, "I visited Gavin on set the other day and met the director, who's a super talented dude. He told me a little about the story and it sounds amazing. And my brother is a phenomenal actor, so I know it'll be great."

Sam stood from the table to go retrieve another round of beers. "Also," she said, "I fucking *adore* Sandra Bullock."

GAVIN FINISHED HIS MEAL, then explored the grounds of the world's largest truck stop. Knowing that his sister was alive and safe at home eased the sense of urgency he'd felt earlier, and he took some time to stretch his legs before the final push to Chicago. There was a movie theater and a dental practice and a barbershop. The place looked like a frat house for long-haul truckers. He walked past the arcade, where two men were locked in an intense game of *Cruisin' USA,* talking a good amount of shit between them. He heard the voice of a man shout, "Holcomb, shower's up," over the intercom, and the idea of a hot shower after twelve hours in the car seemed like a wonderful idea. He asked the man at the counter how it worked and was handed a clipboard on which he wrote his last name. He went back to his car and retrieved his Dopp kit and a clean pair of underwear. He bought a hotel-size bar of soap and a bottle of shampoo from a vending machine and used the two remaining quarters to play a clumsy game of pinball. When his name was finally called, he went to the bathroom and washed himself in lukewarm water, listening to the grunts of sleepy truckers struggling at the urinal.

When he was done, he helped himself to some gas station coffee and explored the gift shop, which wasn't a gift shop so much as a Walmart in miniature. He made a lap through the store. There was a mannequin dressed in head-to-toe leather—boots, chaps, vest, even a leather cowboy hat—as if he'd murdered a cow and crawled inside. He hadn't done any Christmas shopping yet, so he went searching for a few last-minute gifts. He bought a silver bangle for his mom and a wool blanket for his dad. He grabbed the leather cowboy hat for Jonah, a nice addition to the Indiana Jones image he believed his brother was cultivating. He picked up a pair of moccasins for Sam, ones very similar to the kind he'd seen people sporting back in Echo Park. Gavin hauled his wares to the woman at the register. "You need anything else, sweetheart?" she asked.

"This'll do it," Gavin said, placing his credit card on the counter.

The woman ran the card and then stuffed his items into a white plastic bag. "You have yourself a merry Christmas," she said.

Gavin smiled. "Let's hope."

JONAH

His case was gone. The carousel coughed up a planeload of luggage, but his bag never arrived. He watched his fellow passengers gather their suitcases and make their way toward customs. After thirty minutes, the belt finally sighed to a stop and he was left staring at an unclaimed stroller. There was always the possibility that it had been misrouted to another airport, where it sat in a holding cell with other lost luggage. Or there was the more likely possibility that it had been singled out for inspection by a snoopy German shepherd with a nose for raw ivory and was now being examined by a team of customs agents, who were connecting the dots from the case to its owner. He imagined trying to explain to Slinky that his cargo was now in the possession of the U.S. government. He could sketch out a semi-plausible story involving X-ray machines and airport security and possibly jail time, but even if Slinky spared his life, there was almost no possibility he could return to Gabon. There was almost no possibility this would end well, and he had no one to blame but himself. The fact remained that there was only one way out of this airport, so he grabbed his backpack and joined the line for U.S. Citizens. It was shortly after noon when he reached the kiosk. The customs officer—a doughy fellow with a buzz cut—took his passport and declaration form and inspected them for what seemed like an inordinate amount of time. "Where are you coming from?"

"Gabon. But I had a layover in Paris."

"What was the reason for your visit?"

"Research. I'm a student. Graduate student."

The man studied his passport, then looked back up at Jonah. "Apparently, there's an issue with your luggage."

"Okay."

The officer motioned to another uniformed man for assistance. The second man was a decade older and gave the impression of being in charge of deciding who was allowed back in the country. He looked over the printout, then down at Jonah's passport and finally back to Jonah. "You're missing a suitcase, Mr. Brennan." It was not a question.

Jonah nodded.

"Come with me."

So this was how it would end: at the airport, two days before Christmas, culminating in a sad phone call to his mother explaining why he wouldn't make it home for Christmas, how he'd be spending the next ten Christmases in prison. It was ridiculous to think he could get away with such a foolhardy plan. The customs official led him through baggage claim, but instead of a holding room, they arrived at the Air France baggage office, where he was greeted by an austere female airline employee. "Mr. Brennan," she said, typing something into her computer. She didn't bother looking up.

"Yes?"

"It's about your suitcase," she said evenly.

"What's the problem?"

She continued punching violently at the keyboard, apparently engaged in a few different tasks. "It's too heavy."

Jonah wasn't sure he heard her correctly. "What?"

She finally looked up from the computer. "Your case weighs over eighty pounds. The limit is fifty. We usually give a little leeway if it's a few pounds over, but yours is much too heavy."

The misunderstanding racked into focus, and Jonah felt a weight empty through his shoes. He was not being arrested after all.

"I'm afraid we're going to have to charge you for a second bag," the woman continued. "It's thirty-five dollars. I'm very sorry. Someone should have informed you about this in . . ." She looked down at her computer screen. "Libreville. I'm not sure why that didn't happen."

His assumption of prison time had been replaced by a fairly reasonable demand for thirty-five dollars, and he wanted to throw his arms around the woman and cheer. "Of course," he said. "I'm sorry about that. I've got all my camera equipment in there, which is why it's so heavy."

The woman smiled disinterestedly. Jonah handed over his credit card, and she disappeared into another room. She returned a moment later pulling his rolling case. "Thank you for understanding," she said, handing back his card.

"Not a problem." Jonah grabbed his case and smiled at the woman. "Merry Christmas," he said, then turned and walked away, feeling alternately proud and ashamed at having successfully smuggled eighty pounds of raw ivory into the United States of America.

He powered on his phone as he made his way toward the exit. In the four months since he left, he'd received only three voicemails. The first was from the librarian at Vanderbilt asking him about an overdue book whose whereabouts he could not recall. He guessed it was probably packed away with the rest of his junk in a public storage unit in Nashville. The second was from Marcus, asking him to check in once he was settled. The last one was from his mother, left sometime in the last few minutes, saying that she was almost at the airport.

His phone rang: *unknown caller.*

"Hello?" Jonah said, weaving his way through a rush of travelers.

"This is Andre. Slinky's cousin."

"I'm still at the airport. Can I call you later?" He'd been on American soil for less than an hour and Slinky was already keeping tabs on him.

"You have my address?" Andre asked.

"No," Jonah said.

"You know the South Side?"

"No."

"I'm gonna text you my address," Andre said. "Make sure you're here by four. I got the Bulls game tonight."

"I can't be there by four," Jonah said. "I just landed. Can we arrange something for tomorrow please?"

"I don't know about that, Johnny."

Jonah's phone beeped with an incoming call. "Can you hold on a second?" He clicked over. "Hello?"

"There you are," his mom said. "I've been trying to call you."

"Hi, Mom. I just landed."

"I'm pulling up now. Air France, right?"

"I told you I'd take a cab."

"Too late," his mother said. "I'm already here."

Jonah heard honking through the phone, followed by a few seconds of muffled dialogue. "Mom?"

"Cop," she said. "I have to go. I'm pulling up now . . . in the Mazda."

Jonah passed through the sliding glass doors and stepped into a kind of weather he'd almost forgotten about. The temperature was somewhere far below freezing and he had no coat, an oversight that now became painfully clear. He'd been wearing the same torn corduroys and T-shirt for the past three days, which for the most part had been sufficient. But he hadn't considered this thing called winter. He hadn't considered that he might need more than seven T-shirts and a rain slicker fashioned from a plastic trash bag. Bracing himself against the cold, he hustled out into a river of slow-moving traffic, fielding curious looks from other travelers.

His phone rang again. Same number. "Hello?"

"You hung up on me," Andre said, annoyed.

"Sorry, but I can't really talk right now. Can I call you later?"

"Are you through customs?"

"Yeah."

"And you have the product?"

"Yeah."

Jonah saw his mother's car approaching and he waved her down. She pulled to a stop and hopped out. She wore fur-lined snow boots and a chunky red scarf over the black pea coat he'd bought her for Christmas last year. For years she'd dyed her hair brown, but now it was a natural shade of gray that he thought looked quite nice on her. "Where's your coat, bozo?" she said.

"My cousin says I should keep you on a very short leash," Andre said. "He's worried you may try something funny."

"I don't have one," Jonah whispered to his mom.

"You don't have what?" Andre asked.

"Look, I really have to go," Jonah said into the phone. "I'll call you tomorrow." He clicked the phone off and slipped it into his pocket.

His mother approached and threw her arms around him. "I missed you, kiddo."

"I missed you too," he said, feeling suddenly warmed by his mom's embrace. Thirty hours of air travel were immediately forgotten in that moment.

She walked to the rear of the car and popped the trunk. "Who were you talking to?"

"Work," Jonah said, tossing his backpack in the trunk.

"Don't they know you're on vacation?"

"Apparently not."

"Lordy, sweetheart," Cynthia said, trying to lift his rolling case. "Did you bring one of your elephants home with you?"

Not funny, Mom. He grabbed the case from her and hoisted it into the trunk.

"Do you want to drive?" she asked, handing him the keys. "I don't do well on these icy roads."

They escaped the airport and merged onto the freeway. Everything was cast in a flat light and the sky felt low, the clouds cupping the city in a gray dome. It was his first time behind the wheel of a car in months, and he drove carefully, the feeling slowly returning to him.

"Sam back yet?" he asked, glancing over his shoulder before changing lanes.

"She got in late last night."

"And Gavin?"

"He's driving from New Mexico. He should be here this evening."

"What was he doing in New Mexico?"

"He was there for a play."

A taxi cut in front of their car. Jonah hit the brakes, causing the car to slide momentarily before he regained control. "Jesus, asshole!"

"Jonah . . . ," his mother said.

"What? That guy's driving like a moron." Jonah took a deep breath and tried to compose himself. "What happened to the show?"

"What show?" His mom was now texting someone on her phone.

"Gavin's."

"Oh, it was canceled," she said, punching at the phone. "I thought I told you."

"Maybe you did."

"I don't think anyone's too surprised," she said. Her phone dinged with an incoming message. "Did you ever see it?"

"I don't have a television in the forest."

"Oh, right," she said, typing again. "Anyway, he's still pretty sore about it, so please don't bring it up."

"I wasn't planning to."

Her phone dinged again, then once more after that. "Who are you texting?" Jonah asked.

"Your brother," she said. "Trying to figure out what time he'll be here." She tossed her phone into her purse and turned her attention back to Jonah. "So what's the latest with your elephants? You figure out what they're jabbering about?"

"To be perfectly honest, Mom, I haven't really gotten much work done lately."

"Why's that?"

"The situation on the ground hasn't been conducive to research."
He hoped that would be enough to appease her.

She frowned. "That's a shame. I thought everything was going so
well out there."

"It was until about a week ago."

"Then maybe it's a good thing you came home."

"Maybe." The car smelled strongly of flowers. Jonah looked in the
rearview mirror and discovered a back seat filled with bouquets of
poinsettias and holly. A couple wreaths sat on the floor between the
seats. "What's with all the flowers?"

"They're from the shop. A bunch of the girls and I had lunch
today, and we divided up everything that hadn't sold. Quite a haul,
huh?" She giggled to herself, though Jonah wasn't sure what was so
funny.

Before his parents moved downtown, his mother had worked part-
time at a flower shop in Palatine. The store was owned by one of her
girlfriends, who staffed it with other friends from the neighborhood,
and in this way the store became a sort of meeting place, a social club
for the empty nester subset. They each worked a few short shifts every
week, but most of their time was spent enjoying wine-heavy lunches
like the one his mother had apparently just attended.

"Boozy lunch?" Jonah said. "Is that why you wanted me to drive?"

"No," she said a little defensively.

"You haven't had anything to drink today?"

She shrugged. "I had a glass of wine. Big deal."

It really wasn't a big deal, but he liked to give her grief about it,
probably because he was jealous of her social life, the fact that she was
undeniably more popular than he'd ever been. Jonah's image of his
mother had always been of the woman who ran the vacuum while
they watched cartoons, the woman who carted them around to
sleepovers and sporting events and dance class, the woman who
awaited him at the kitchen table every morning. This other woman,
the one who spent her afternoons drinking with friends and traveling
the world, this was a very different person. Her kids were gone and so

was the big house in the suburbs, along with all the requisite house-keeping that had occupied so much of her time. She now had whole days and weeks to do whatever she pleased. One of the girls from the flower shop came from a wealthy Italian family that owned a villa at Lake Como, where his mother and her posse of girlfriends spent a couple weeks every summer. It seemed like every time he spoke to her she was either returning from an overseas adventure or preparing to depart for one. In the past year, his mom had taken a riverboat tour down the Danube, followed by a week spent touring the coast of Croatia. It was as if she'd found herself, at fifty-eight years old, on perpetual spring break.

They arrived downtown a half hour later. She directed him toward the apartment, which turned out to be a fairly new building stacked atop a Walgreens. It seemed as though almost everything in Chicago was stacked atop a Walgreens. He parked in the underground garage and followed his mother into the elevator. They got off at the sixth floor and walked down the hall and into their apartment, where Christmas music was playing for a seemingly empty home.

"You and Gavin are sharing the big bedroom," Cynthia said. "I put Sam in the small one."

"Where's Dad?" Jonah asked.

"Probably out doing some last-minute shopping."

Sam appeared from the bedroom looking as if she'd just awoken from a nap. She was skinnier than he'd remembered, though she'd always been thin. She wore black stretch pants and a hooded sweatshirt, and her hair was uncombed. He noticed her eyes were bloodshot, though his were as well, an unavoidable result of international travel.

"Look who I found," his mother said. "Returned from the jungle."

"You smell like it too," Sam said, embracing her brother.

His mother sniffed audibly. "I didn't want to mention it in the car, but it's really quite bad, Jonah."

"I know, Mom. They don't have showers where I've been."

"You could have showered at the airport," Sam said, twisting a fallen strand of hair around her index finger.

"If you'd ever been to the Libreville airport, you would know that's not an option."

"What did you do in Paris?" Sam asked.

"Exactly what I said I would. I drank two glasses of wine and fell asleep on the floor."

"Whatever happened to your plan to meet up?" their mother asked.

"She never got back to me," Jonah said.

"Sorry," Sam said. "It was kinda hectic at the end there."

"I'm gonna go take a shower for you ladies, okay?" Jonah said, walking to the bedroom. He closed the door and sat on the twin bed he'd slept on as a kid. It was strange seeing elements of their old suburban home restaged in this unfamiliar space. In the corner of the room was the bureau he and Gavin had plastered with skateboarding stickers when they were kids, though someone, their father he guessed, had refinished it in a dark walnut stain. As he sat on the bed, he listened to the metronomic tick of the small table clock on the nightstand. The last few days had been so loud, but now it was so quiet and he found the silence unsettling.

There was a knock at the bedroom door. "Jonah," his mom called.

"Yes?" he said.

"What's in this giant suitcase? I thought you were only staying a week."

"Don't open that!" he said, swinging open the bedroom door.

"What is it?"

"Your Christmas present." There were few things his mother held more sacred than the surprise of a Christmas gift, so he figured this would be an adequate deterrent.

"Okay, okay," she said, turning and walking back to the living room.

Jonah shut the door again and went to the bathroom that connected the two bedrooms. He got the shower going, then undressed and tossed his dirty clothes in a pile by the door. There wasn't much hope for those old things, so he added *new wardrobe* to the mental list of supplies needed for his time in America. He looked at his naked body in the mirror for the first time in four months and was pleased with what he saw. Beneath the dirt and grime was a surprisingly toned thirty-one-year-old male, defined chest and ropy arms, contoured thighs and bulging calves. A plant-based diet and some daily hiking had vanquished the gut he'd acquired back in Nashville, and for the first time in his life he felt like a man in control of his body.

When the water reached a comfortable temperature, he stepped in and basked in the glory of a warm shower. A buffet of shampoos and conditioners and body gels was lined on the shower rack, and he smelled each one carefully before making his selection. He'd almost forgotten how simple life could be, how he could turn a knob and stand for however long he wanted beneath a stream of clean hot water, and then step out of the shower and dry himself with an absurdly luxurious towel. *My God,* he thought, what a life he'd been missing, what a perfectly comfortable way to exist.

Afterward, he dressed and went to the living room, where Sam was sitting on the couch with her laptop.

"What's really in the suitcase?" she asked, clapping the laptop shut and placing it on the end table.

"Poor choices," he said, plopping down next to her. He picked up the remote and began flipping through the channels.

"So you haven't actually done any Christmas shopping?"

"There was a Best Buy in the village. You're all getting thumb drives."

"I'm going shopping tomorrow if you want to come along."

"You know how I feel about crowds."

"I'll bring a flask."

Jonah smiled. "We'll see."

He stood and walked to the kitchen and opened the refrigerator. He nearly wept at the bounty it contained: four varieties of cheese, pasta salad, gourmet sausages, a crisper stuffed with assorted vegetables, three bottles of sauvignon blanc, and six different kinds of beer. He studied the beers carefully before grabbing a pilsner and rejoining his sister on the couch.

"How long are you back?" Sam asked.

"Supposed to be a couple weeks," he said, cracking the beer. "But it's still up in the air. You?"

"I told Mom the twenty-ninth, though I actually just bought a one-way ticket home."

"You aren't going back?"

"To be determined."

Jonah took a drink of his beer. "So what's Moscow like?"

"I'm not actually in Moscow. I'm in a little nothing town about a hundred miles northeast of Moscow. It's a lot like suburban Illinois to be perfectly honest. Maybe a little colder but equally boring."

"I take it you don't like it?"

She shrugged. "It's fine, I guess. Not sure how much longer I'll stay."

"It's nice to see you," he said, putting his arm around her.

"Yeah," she said, smiling. "Nice to be seen by you."

THEIR DAD RETURNED HOME later that evening with a collection of shopping bags. "Welcome home, pal," he said, giving Jonah a quick hug, then went to the bedroom to hide his gifts. He returned a moment later. "How was the flight? Or flights, I guess."

"Long," Jonah said. *Fraught* was more accurate, but that would invite a line of questioning he wasn't interested in addressing.

Later, they gathered around the kitchen table for chicken piccata and a couple bottles of Malbec. For the first time in almost a year, the entire family, minus one, was together, and Jonah found it slightly annoying that the two living overseas had managed to make it home, while the third, the unemployed actor, was nowhere to be found.

His mother finally joined them at the table and began circulating the dishes.

"So what are you doing out there?" Jonah's dad asked him.

"What do you mean?" Jonah said.

"In Gabon. What do you do there all day?"

Jonah didn't see the need to lie. He'd already lied to his mother about the ivory, so he figured he might as well be honest about the indolent nature of the last few weeks. "I'm supposed to be studying elephants, but lately I've just been drinking with my buddy in town."

"That doesn't sound very productive," his mom said, trying, unsuccessfully, to modulate her displeasure.

"It's not," Jonah admitted.

"How much longer do you expect to be there?" his dad asked.

"Hard to say. At some point I have to return to the States to work on my dissertation. My advisor thinks I should graduate."

"And that's the guy who lives out there with you?" his mother asked.

"*Lived,*" Jonah said. "Remember I told you, he got sick and went home a couple months ago."

His mom shook her head. "You didn't tell me that."

"Pretty sure I did."

"So now it's just you?"

Jonah could hear the worry in her voice. "Yeah."

"What happens if there's an emergency? If you fall and break your leg?"

"He'll make a splint out of tree branches," his father said matter-of-factly. "Which he's very capable of doing."

"Exactly," Jonah said. When the boys were young, their dad had started them in Cub Scouts, which Jonah excelled at, unlike Gavin, who dropped out after attaining the unimpressive rank of Bear Scout. Jonah enjoyed the weekend camping trips and nature walks. He enjoyed the science that went into constructing the Pine Wood Derby cars, calculating force and axle resistance in order to shave a few tenths of a second off his time. He enjoyed long weekends in the woods, where he learned wilderness survival techniques, many of which had served him well in Gabon.

"I don't like this at all," his mom said. "Now I have one more thing to worry about."

"What are the other things?" Jonah asked.

"Well, I just read an article in the *Tribune* about all the poaching going on over there. Is that happening where you are?"

Jonah shrugged.

"It sounds like a war zone. Apparently, some rangers were killed in Cameroon last week."

Jonah turned to Sam. "Tell us about this ballet you're working on."

"No," Sam said, refusing to take the bait. "Don't change the subject."

"I think you should have a gun out there," his mom said.

"I have a knife," Jonah countered.

She shook her head. "I don't think that's enough."

"Then get me a bazooka for Christmas."

The front door opened and they all turned to discover the final missing family member entering with a duffel bag slung over his shoulder.

"You made it!" his mom said, standing and moving toward the door. "I didn't think you'd get here so early."

"I made good time," Gavin said, dropping his bag and embracing his mother.

Jonah approached and clapped his brother on the back. "What's new, Hollywood?" Gavin looked more or less how Jonah remembered him. Ripped denim jeans most likely purchased that way, colorful, presumably Japanese, sneakers, and an expensive-looking haircut.

"Not much," Gavin said. "You?"

Jonah headed back to the table and took a long pull of his wine. "Enjoying some first-world luxuries," he said, saluting him with his glass.

"Are you hungry?" their mom asked Gavin. "Make yourself a plate and come sit down."

Gavin emerged from the kitchen and joined them at the table, where most everyone had finished eating.

"How was the drive?" his dad asked. "Hit any weather?"

"It was fine once I got to Nebraska."

"So tell us about this play," his mom said.

"Not sure if it's actually gonna happen," Gavin said.

"Why's that?"

"I had a falling out with the director."

"That's too bad. Is he a jerk?"

"*She's* very nice, but it doesn't seem to be working out between us." Gavin took a drink of his wine. "Mmm, that's good."

"It's a Malbec," his dad said. "From the northern Maipo region in Chile. Sort of a Bordeaux-style."

Their father had become a bit of an oenophile in his later years, and Jonah, deep into his second glass, was enjoying the fruits of his dad's new hobby.

"What's the play called?" his mom asked. "Anything I've heard of?"

"*Long Day's Journey into Night,*" Gavin said.

"Isn't that an old play?"

"Yes."

"I think I saw it on TV once," his mom said. "Kind of depressing, right?"

Gavin shrugged. "It's not *The Producers* if that's what you mean."

"We saw the most depressing play the other night," his mom continued. "At the Steppenwolf. August something."

"*August: Osage County,*" Gavin said.

"That's right," his mom said. "Have you seen it?"

"I have."

"My god, it was depressing. It's hard to believe anyone's family is that dysfunctional."

"You'd be surprised," Jonah said. He'd been silent throughout the exchange, but now the collective gaze turned toward him.

"What's that supposed to mean?" his mom asked pointedly.

"Just that it's all relative," he said. "They only seem dysfunctional because they aren't *your* family. They seem like crazy people because you don't know them. When it's your mother or brother or sister, you have a way of justifying their craziness, which of course never registers as craziness. It's just someone going through a rough patch. *Challenging times.* Isn't that what people say?" He felt a warmth rising within him, so he stopped to take a drink of wine and compose himself.

His mom made a face. "No need to get so defensive about it. I was just talking about a dumb play."

GAVIN

SHOPPING ON CHRISTMAS EVE WAS only tolerable under the influence, which was how they ended up at Joey's, drinking cheap beer with the regulars. They'd made a pact that for every retail store they were forced to fight their way through, they would reward themselves with a stiff drink. It was midafternoon and the bartender was fixing rounds of a gin-based cocktail called Santa Juice. Joey's was tucked into a quiet stretch of real estate just north of the river, surrounded by steak houses and parking garages. It was the kind of bar a man found himself in after being thrown out of other, more sophisticated establishments.

Gavin had been trying to think of a good way to talk to Sam about the drugs, but he still hadn't decided on the appropriate angle. He'd been debating whether to tell Jonah, who, as far as he could tell, didn't suspect anything. Jonah was so disengaged when it came to family matters that Gavin worried his involvement would only complicate the situation. Yet there was strength in numbers and Jonah—being the more even-tempered of the two of them—might come across as less confrontational. It would certainly be easier to include Jonah, although the involvement of more than one person might make it seem like a formal intervention, which he hoped to avoid. He wanted it to come about casually, though he had no idea how to design such a discussion.

He looked over to Sam, who was rocking back and forth on her barstool. She'd barely touched her drink, and she had a faraway look in her eyes. She still wore her coat and stocking cap, despite the warmth of the bar. "Are you cold?" he asked.

"Little bit," she said.

"Do you feel okay?"

"I'm fine," she said. Her phone, which was sitting next to her on the bar, vibrated with an incoming message. Gavin tried to steal a look, but Sam picked it up and began typing a response.

"Who are you texting?" he asked.

She shot him a look that suggested it was none of his business. "I'll be right back," she said, sliding off the barstool and walking outside.

Jonah motioned to the bartender for another drink. "You want another one?" he asked Gavin.

Gavin declined, not wanting to cloud his mission with too much alcohol. He was struggling with how to broach the subject, so he decided to tell Jonah everything he'd learned about their sister. "You know how I asked earlier if you thought Sam seemed different?"

"Yeah," Jonah said, his eyes fixed on a basketball game on the television above the bar.

"I got a really strange phone call from her roommate at the dance company. This was a couple days ago, when I was leaving New Mexico."

"Okay," Jonah said, immersed in the television.

"Can you look at me, please?" Gavin asked.

Jonah turned to him. "What?"

"She said Sam's been doing heroin."

"Really?" Jonah said with more surprise than concern.

"Yeah," Gavin said.

Jonah had always been unflappable in the face of bad news, but Gavin sometimes found his nonchalance infuriating. He wasn't sure if

this was because Jonah figured there was usually a simple way to resolve the situation or because he just wasn't that interested.

"Do Mom and Dad know?" Jonah asked.

"I think we would have heard about it if so."

Jonah took a sip of his drink and exhaled a long sigh. "Well . . .
have you said anything to her?"

"I've been trying to figure out a way to broach the subject, but I
haven't come up with much. I thought maybe you could help."

"You want *me* to talk to her?"

"I thought we both could."

Jonah shook his head. "Nothing we say is going to convince her to
stop doing drugs. She's going to have to arrive at that decision on her
own."

"I get that. But I also think it's *our* responsibility to push her in that
direction."

"I'm not sure it is."

"You understand what's at stake, right?" Gavin asked, annoyed.

"Of course I do. But I don't see how anything I say is going to
change her mind."

"Maybe not. But we have to try."

"Then *you* do it," Jonah said, turning his attention back to the television, as if to absolve himself of responsibility.

"You're unreal."

"Don't blame this on me. If Sam's legitimately addicted to drugs,
then why the hell are we at a bar? This seems like the worst possible
place to be."

It was a valid point, and one he'd been grappling with all day. As
much as Gavin wanted his sister clean, he loathed the idea that they
might never again be able to drink together. Most of the best times
he'd had with Sam involved alcohol, and he couldn't picture their relationship without it. He understood the selfishness inherent in his
line of reasoning, but he still held out hope that he could work something out.

"Look," Gavin said. "I could really use your help with this. I'll do all the talking. I just need you to be there with me."

"I can't think of any possible scenario in which that conversation ends well."

"Neither can I, but we have to try."

"Fine," Jonah said. "But I'm blaming everything on you when she freaks out. And she *will* freak out."

The door swung open and Sam reappeared, dragging with her a blast of arctic air. She climbed back onto her barstool.

"What's the plan?" she asked, her spirits seemingly lifted. "I still need to find a gift for Mom."

Jonah looked to Gavin, waiting for him to say something.

"Sure," Gavin said. "Where do you want to go?"

Jonah shook his head. "I thought you had something you wanted to talk about."

"What?" Sam asked.

"We can discuss it later," Gavin said. Whatever resolve he'd felt was slipping away. Besides, a dive bar probably wasn't the appropriate place to have the conversation.

"In that case, I need to run an errand before it gets too late," Jonah said.

"Okay," Gavin said. "Then I'll go with Sam."

"But I need your car," Jonah said.

"Take the train."

"The train doesn't go where I'm headed."

"Take a cab," Gavin said.

"That'll cost a fortune. Why can't I use your car?"

"Because you've been drinking all day," Gavin said, his voice rising.

"Then *you* drive me."

"I don't want to drive you."

"You told me earlier I could use your car."

"That was based on the assumption that you'd be sober enough to drive it."

It was frustrating to see that Jonah hadn't matured much over the years. Gavin was reminded of his junior year, when his date with Megan Moore—the exalted beauty of Palatine High—was canceled because their mother insisted that he retrieve Jonah from the Junior Geology Expo at the convention center. Apparently, Jonah had been separated from his group of fellow rock hounds and found himself calling home from a pay phone in some foreign neighborhood. At sixteen Gavin had been blessed with the keys to his parents' Pontiac, but it was a conditional arrangement that stipulated that he was also responsible for ferrying his siblings to their extracurricular activities. It took him an hour to get downtown, where he found his brother standing in an empty parking lot, surrounded by four shoeboxes filled with small rocks. That was a long, uncomfortable ride back to the burbs, Gavin driving in a steely silence while Jonah babbled on about the crystallization patterns of igneous rocks.

"It's fine," Sam finally said to Gavin. "You go with Jonah and I'll meet you back at the house before church."

"What time is church?" Jonah asked.

"Six," Sam said, "but we're supposed to be there early."

"Because it might sell out?"

"Something like that," Sam said, making for the door.

"You handled that well," Jonah said to his brother once she was gone.

Gavin's phone buzzed. He fished it from his pocket and saw Mariana's name. He hadn't expected to hear from her, so he walked to a relatively quiet corner of the bar to take the call. "Hey there," he said.

"Gavin, it's Jesse."

"Oh, hi."

"I found your number in Mariana's phone, and just wanted to call and thank you."

"For what?"

"You exposed some strains in our relationship," Jesse said. "I wasn't a very attentive fiancé, and I can see why Mariana was attracted to you. I wasn't giving her what she needed, and I accept the blame for that."

"She told you?" Gavin couldn't believe it. She'd assured him there was no reason for Jesse to know what had transpired between them.

"She did. And the interesting thing is that despite whatever passed between you two, Mariana still wants to marry me. I'm sure that must be difficult for you to accept. It was obviously just a passing thing, and I'm glad it's done with. I guess what I'm trying to say is that you don't need to call here any more, okay?"

The line went dead and Gavin stood staring at a framed Bud Light poster.

"You ready?" Jonah asked. He had borrowed a sweatshirt from Gavin and a fleece jacket from their father, both of which he'd shed during their time in the bar. He was now awkwardly reassembling the layers.

"Yeah," Gavin said, still spinning from the news. He put on his hat and followed his brother toward the door. "I don't understand why you didn't bring a coat."

"Because I've been living at the equator for the past four months," Jonah said, pushing open the door.

"So where exactly are we going?"

"South Side," Jonah said. "A quick trip to the South Side."

JONAH

THE ONLY TIME JONAH HAD ever ventured this far south was when his fourth-grade teacher took his class on a field trip to the Museum of Science and Industry in Hyde Park. It was a two-hour bus ride from Palatine, and he was amazed at the city's reach, how it stretched forever along the lake, the buildings becoming shorter, like stairs descending southward. But now, sitting in the passenger seat of his brother's fancy European car, transporting a trunk full of massacred elephant parts, he was thinking only about how to offload his cargo and still make it back in time for church.

"Thanks for doing this," Jonah said.

"I don't actually know what we're doing," Gavin replied.

"I'm dropping off some equipment with a colleague."

"I would ask what a colleague from Vanderbilt is doing in Chicago, but I already know you're lying so I won't bother."

"What makes you think I'm lying?"

"Because you're nervous."

"I'm not nervous."

"Sure you are." Gavin nodded toward Jonah's leg, which was hammering away.

"I do that when I drink," Jonah said.

"Maybe. But you also do it when you're nervous."

They stopped at a red light, and Jonah watched a man push a wheelbarrow filled with stuffed animals across the street.

"So," Gavin said, "who are you meeting down here?"

"I told you. A colleague."

"From Nashville?"

"He's from Chicago originally. Just like us. Just like lots of people who happen to be home visiting their families during the holidays. It's not unprecedented."

"What's his name?" Gavin asked.

"Andre."

"What does he do?"

"He's a research assistant. He works in the lab. What's with all the questions?"

"Just curious."

Jonah glanced down at his phone. "Take the next right."

Gavin turned into a strip mall on the corner of Fifty-Third and Harper. Andre's store—Elegant Impressions—was wedged between a tanning salon and a Baskin-Robbins.

"So your colleague has a part-time job at Baskin-Robbins?" Gavin asked.

"It's actually the jewelry store."

"Better yet," Gavin said, pulling the car to a stop.

"Pop the trunk," Jonah said. "This won't take long." He stepped out of the car and hauled the case of ivory out of the trunk. As he wheeled it to the entrance, he waved back to his brother in a half-hearted attempt at reassurance. The alcohol had dulled his nerves, and he felt brave enough to pull this off without incident. A CLOSED sign hung in the window, though the lights were on. He knocked loudly and a moment later, a very attractive woman opened the door. She appeared to be roughly Jonah's age, wearing a leopard-print top and a denim skirt. "Yes?"

"I'm here for Andre," Jonah said, suddenly intimidated by the woman's beauty.

"What's your name?" she asked.

"Jonah. He's expecting me."

Satisfied with his explanation, she stepped aside and allowed him to enter. Jonah glanced at the display cases glowing with expensive rocks. He'd anticipated a much seedier place, something like a pawnshop, but despite its location next to an ice-cream parlor, the store actually lived up to its name. "Do you work here?" he asked.

Without acknowledging his question, the woman pointed to a door at the back. "Go in," she said.

Jonah entered what appeared to be some fusion of an office and a speakeasy. There was a baby grand piano in one corner and a bar cart stocked with an assortment of liquor decanters. An African American man of about thirty, dressed in a gray suit, was sprawled on a velour sofa, watching SportsCenter on a plasma television mounted to the wall. His eyes were large and penetrating and a shrub of hair sprouted beneath his bottom lip. "Johnny," he said, standing. "Please, come in. Very nice to meet you."

"It's Jonah."

"Of course." Andre cleared a mess of papers from a large mahogany desk and took a seat behind it. "Please sit," he said, motioning to a well-worn club chair.

Jonah sat and looked at Andre across the desk. He looked more like a mortgage lender than an ivory trafficker, and the intimidation Jonah had initially felt was replaced by a mild annoyance at having to drive all the way down here on Christmas Eve.

Andre smiled and leaned forward with his elbows on the desk, a man with a terrific offer to share. "One day you're with my cousin in Gabon and the next day you're here with me in Chicago. Very small world."

"Yeah," Jonah said, "I guess."

Andre stood and walked to the bar cart to refill his tumbler of gin. "Can I get you a drink? How was your flight? Any trouble?"

Jonah wasn't sure how much Andre knew. He wasn't even sure how much Slinky knew. Surely Slinky would have gotten suspicious when Mateo failed to return to the village, though there was no way for him to know that his number one man had been cut open after trying to screw him out of fifty thousand dollars' worth of ivory. Andre's tone made it seem as if the ordeal had gone off without a hitch, and he didn't see any reason to clue him in on the bloody details. "Flight was fine," Jonah said. "Everything's in the case. Where's the money?"

"We'll get to that soon enough."

"I'd prefer to get to it sooner rather than later, Andre. It's Christmas Eve and my brother is waiting for me outside."

"Of course. I understand." Andre walked over to the case and opened it slowly, carefully, as if there were something in there that might bite him. "Perfect," he said, glancing at the tusks. He carried the case to a digital metal scale and frowned at the results. "And the rest of it?"

"This is everything," Jonah said.

"This is eighty pounds."

"Yes."

"I was told to expect one hundred."

"This is what I was given."

"Now, Jerry," Andre said, his mood turning.

"Jonah."

"Forgive me, Johnny, but the problem is that I was told to expect one hundred pounds, and you only brought me eighty. You must understand my situation."

"Look," Jonah said. "I smuggled this into the country, against my will, without getting caught, which is no small task." Because of Jonah, Slinky had been able to eliminate his Chinese middleman and sell his product for a substantial markup. The real money in the ivory trade was made by those capable of getting it out of the source country, which Slinky had never been able to do himself. Jonah knew that his Chinese partner paid him only a fraction of what he was later fetching at the shops and bazaars in Asia. He'd made Slinky a tremendous amount of money in a relatively short amount of time, and it seemed to him like Andre could be a little more appreciative.

"I understand the risk you took in bringing this here, and I want you to know that my cousin and I both appreciate it. But that doesn't entitle you to keep some for yourself."

"I don't know what your cousin told you, but I have no interest in keeping this. I find it reprehensible." There was a moment, albeit a brief one, when he'd considered turning himself over to the customs agent in Paris, confessing to everything that had happened and hoping it might result in some kind of mercy. But the more rational part of him knew how unlikely that was, and so he'd scrapped the idea.

Andre stood and made a lap around his desk, running his fingers along the veneer surface. "I think we must make a phone call to my cousin. Hopefully he can sort this out."

"Let's do that," Jonah said, eager to conclude the visit.

It was almost midnight in Gabon, but Slinky picked up after a few rings. They exchanged pleasantries in French before Andre passed the phone to Jonah.

"Hey," Jonah said.

"Elephant Man," Slinky's voice boomed. "My cousin tells me there's a problem."

Jonah paced around the room. "I delivered the ivory like you asked."

"He says you only bring eighty pounds."

"That's what I was given," Jonah said evenly.

"Not true, Elephant Man. I gave Mateo one hundred."

"You'd have to talk to Mateo about that." Jonah looked to Andre, who was watching him from across the room.

"He's not answering his phone," Slinky said.

Jonah plucked a mint from a bowl on the coffee table, plopped it in his mouth. "There's a reason for that."

Slinky went quiet, which Jonah took as permission to continue. "I don't think Mateo was quite as trustworthy as you thought. When we got to Libreville, he tried to sell the ivory to some guys who didn't feel like paying for it. So they killed him. They had planned to take the ivory themselves, but I was able to get away with it. You should actually be thanking me right now."

"This doesn't sound right," Slinky said, a shade of uncertainty entering his voice.

"It's the truth."

Slinky exhaled audibly through the phone. "And how do I know this?"

"I would tell you to ask Mateo, but that isn't possible."

"Who are these people Mateo visited?"

"I don't know," Jonah said. "It was a bunch of dudes in a garment factory. Some old hunchbacked guy."

The silence on the other end of the line suggested that Jonah had struck upon the very detail he needed to validate his story. "Osman," Slinky finally said in the dejected manner of someone whose fear has been confirmed.

"Who is he?" Jonah asked.

Slinky explained that Osman was a Nigerian ivory broker and member of the terrorist group Boko Haram. Slinky had never met the man, since most of Osman's dealings had been with poachers along the border with Cameroon. But he'd heard that Osman had intentions of expanding his network into Gabon, though he'd been told, incorrectly, that those plans were merely hypothetical. Slinky guessed that Mateo had tried to pledge his loyalty to a man who wasn't interested in such things and learned a difficult lesson in the process. "But I'm not like them," Slinky said. "I don't kill innocent people."

"Just elephants," Jonah said.

"Look, Elephant Man. Just bring me my money, so we can finish this. You've already done the hard work. Now you just have to return my money."

"Sure," Jonah said, though he wasn't sure it was that easy. He'd heard stories about mountaineers who died on their way down Everest, the ones whose sense of accomplishment became their fatal flaw. He was determined not to become one of those people. "I'll call you when I get to Libreville," he said, handing the phone back to Andre, who walked to the other end of the room, where he spoke in hushed tones.

Andre occasionally looked over at Jonah, who was now relaxing in the club chair with the poise of a man in firm control of his situation. A moment later, Andre hung up and began filling a backpack with stacks of banded bills from a safe under his desk. "Sounds like you had a big adventure," he said.

"I wouldn't call it that."

"This is fifty thousand dollars," Andre said. "I expect you will take all of it—not one dollar less—back to my cousin."

"I'll do what I can," Jonah said.

Andre handed him the backpack. "Do better than that."

Back outside, Jonah walked to his brother's car and got inside. Gavin was listening to some kind of audiobook in which the narrator was describing, rather ornately, the musculature of a racehorse. "What are you listening to?" Jonah asked, pulling the seatbelt across his chest.

Gavin lowered the volume. "What's in the bag?"

"Books," Jonah said.

"What kind of books?"

"Textbooks."

"Can I see?" Gavin reached for the backpack, but Jonah pulled it away.

"Let's go," Jonah said.

"Not until you show me what's in the backpack."

"Drive."

"No."

"Really?" Jonah had hoped to keep his dealings with Andre private, because he worried his brother might use this dark knowledge as leverage for something.

"I'm not going anywhere until you show me what's in the backpack," Gavin said. "I drove you down here. I'd like to know why."

"Okay, sure, have a look." Jonah unzipped the bag and peeled back the top flap, revealing the banded stacks of cash.

"Jesus," Gavin said. "How much money is that?"

"Fifty thousand dollars."

"Are you selling drugs?"

"I'd feel a lot better if I were."

"What the fuck, Jonah? Why do you have all that money?"

"You know, Gavin, the thing I really appreciate about our family is that we don't discuss our problems. I'd prefer to keep it that way." Jonah zipped the bag shut and tossed it in the back seat. "Let's go. We're late for church."

BECAUSE THEY WERE LATE and because it was Christmas Eve, the church parking lot was full, so Gavin parked in the lot of a liquor store three blocks south. Jonah stashed the backpack in the trunk, then locked the car and followed his brother down the street, a fierce wind cutting at his face. Despite his assemblage of outerwear, he lacked the mental fortitude for this kind of meteorological assault. "How much farther?" he called to Gavin, who charged unaffected through the cold.

"We've only gone one block," Gavin said.

"It's shockingly cold right now. I'm not used to this."

"Neither am I, but I'm not complaining."

Jonah knew that the only reason Gavin wasn't complaining was to avoid the accusation—rightfully earned during their fourteen years under a shared roof—that he was a perpetual complainer. As a kid, Gavin had complained about everything, to everyone, everywhere they went. On a summer vacation to Los Angeles, he complained that the air was too dirty, the beach too sandy, the freeways too crowded. He complained when he didn't catch a home run ball at the Dodgers game and when their visit to Universal Studios resulted in zero celebrity sightings. He complained about the thirty-two hours in the car, then complained that he was being unfairly maligned when their mother suggested he stop being such a whiner. So the fact that Gavin wasn't complaining about the cold didn't mean that it wasn't affecting him, just that he'd learned to shut up about it.

The church was at capacity, the overflow of parishioners sitting in rows of folding chairs at the back. The priest stood at the altar, leading the congregation in the Penitential Rite. "As we prepare to celebrate the mystery of Christ's love," he pronounced, "let us acknowledge our failures and ask the Lord for pardon and strength."

Jonah located their parents and squeezed into the pew. The voices in the church rose, and together said, "I confess to almighty God. And to you, my brothers and sisters . . ."

"You're late," their mom whispered to Gavin.

"His fault," Gavin said, nodding at Jonah.

"That I have greatly sinned, in my thoughts and in my words, in what I have done, and in what I have failed to do . . ."

"Where's your sister?" his mom asked.

Jonah shrugged.

"Through my fault, through my fault, through my most grievous fault," the priest recited.

"Gavin," his mom hissed across the pew. "Where's Sam?"

"She said she'd be here," Gavin whispered back.

"Therefore, I ask blessed Mary, ever virgin, and all the angels and saints, and you, my brothers and sisters, to pray for me to the Lord, our God."

"Amen," the congregation chorused.

"Amen," Jonah said.

"Unbelievable," their mom said.

SAMANTHA

S HE BATTLED HER WAY THROUGH cosmetics, dodging women
spraying clouds of perfume at her face. She passed the shoe department, which had been ransacked by derelict shoppers, then
through lingerie, and finally to a quiet corner of the store, where she
found a stray wardrobe rack hung with loungewear. She rifled through
the robes, running her hand across the downy cotton, appraising the
threads of each one. She and her mother used to be the same size, but
Sam had lost so much weight over the last year, though how much
that was she couldn't say because she refused to step on a scale for fear
of what she might learn. She chose a simple, white terry robe by
Ralph Lauren, size two, and carried it to the dressing room.

"Excuse me," she said, intercepting a female employee about her
age. "Can I try this on?"

"The bathrobe?"

"Yeah."

"You can slip it on out here if you'd like."

"I'd prefer a room."

Annoyed, the employee led her to the dressing rooms. "Let me
know if you need another size," she said, pushing open the door.

The floor was littered with discarded sewing pins, which Sam
swept away with her shoe. She slipped into the bathrobe and cinched

the sash tight around her waist. She looked in the mirror and mouthed *don't* three times over, but the decision had already been made. She removed the drugs from her purse, spread her utensils on the small bench in the corner of the room, and fixed herself a dose. Leaning against the thin dressing room walls, she shot herself full of the one thing she could no longer live without, a flush of warmth going through her body, a faint smile stretching across her face. In the room next to her, she heard giggling female voices that slowly faded as her eyes flickered twice and closed.

"MA'AM?" THE VOICE CALLED. It was followed by a pounding at the door. "Please open the door or I'll have to open it myself."

Sam nodded awake, as if surfacing from somewhere deep underwater. Her face was flushed and she had sweated through the bathrobe. She looked in the mirror and tried to place herself.

"What's going on in there?" the voice said again. It was a male voice, authoritative and annoyed.

"Just finishing up," Sam said. She stuffed the drugs back in her purse and returned the bathrobe to its hanger. She stepped out of the room and came face-to-face with a man she guessed was the manager.

"What are you doing?" he asked.

"I was trying this on," Sam said, holding up the bathrobe.

"She said you've been in there for thirty minutes." Standing behind him was the female employee, looking alternately smug and annoyed.

"We're closing in fifteen minutes," he said.

"I'm done anyway," Sam said, slipping out of the room and hurrying toward the register.

After paying for the robe, she pushed through the revolving doors and stepped outside, where a light snow had begun to fall. She made her way south on State Street, then across the bridge, past a homeless man lecturing the river. She pulled her phone from her purse to check the time, but her battery had died and she wasn't wearing a watch.

The streetlights were snapping on and she guessed it was well past six, which meant she had missed Mass.

How would she explain that? she wondered. It was the lying that was so exhausting, yet she wasn't ready to admit the truth, at least not to anyone other than herself. Because if she was being honest, then she must acknowledge that it was her choices that had led to this moment, and that's what troubled her. It was the element of personal responsibility, the conscious decision she'd made to dive into a pool of unknown depth. It might have been excusable, or at least expected, had she come from a broken home or been abused as a child or any of the other false reasons for believing drugs can fix the sad feelings. But she'd experienced nothing but the plain love of parents who had sacrificed greatly, and yet somehow, despite her easy fortune, she had devolved into the kind of girl who nodded out in department store dressing rooms. Her life was a lie that begot other lies, a bad decision that spawned other bad decisions, which, if one connected the dots, would sketch an accurate portrait of the young woman now walking the streets of Chicago, alone and despondent in the winter twilight.

She eventually arrived back at Joey's, the only place that was still open, and ducked inside to warm up. She took a seat at the bar and looked around, but most of the faces from earlier were gone.

The bartender approached and tossed a cocktail napkin on the bar. "What are you drinking?"

"Vodka tonic," she said.

The bartender studied her for a moment. "Weren't you in here earlier?"

"Yeah."

"What happened to the other two guys?"

Where were *the other guys? Where was everyone, really?* She'd somehow isolated herself from the world, from everyone she loved, so that now, when she was finally ready to explain herself, to come clean in every imaginable way, there was no one to talk to but an elderly bartender.

"My brothers," she said. "They're at church."

"But not you?" he asked, running a rag across the bar.

She shook her head.

The bartender laughed softly. "You an atheist or something?"

"No."

"Agnostic?"

"I don't know what I am," Sam said. "Just guilty, I guess."

The bartender smiled. "You've come to the right place."

GAVIN

AVIN AWOKE AT DAWN, unable to sleep. He walked to the kitchen and poured himself a cup of coffee, then spiked it with a shot of Bailey's, a little Christmas morning tradition. Sometime in the night, his mother had placed three stockings beneath the Christmas tree, each filled with candy and a random collection of personal items: lip balm, socks, and a pack of razors even though he hadn't shaved in two years. He took his coffee and walked to the large window overlooking the city. All was quiet except for a couple taxis parked along the curb and two young men pulling suitcases along the sidewalk, heads bowed to the wind. He tried to read the first chapter of the John Huston biography he'd picked up at a bookstore in Taos, but his mind kept bouncing between the women in his life. He wanted to call Mariana, but there was nothing left to discuss. She'd made her decision and he would have to live with it, whatever that involved. Acceptance, he guessed, though he wasn't ready to accept anything aside from how profoundly unfair it all was. It was strange that he hadn't heard from her again, though maybe considering Jesse's phone call yesterday it wasn't strange at all.

"Merry Christmas," his mother said, emerging from her bedroom, cinching her robe tight around her waist. "You're up early."

"I couldn't sleep," Gavin said, setting down his book.

She yawned. "Too excited to open presents?"

"Something like that."

His mom walked to the kitchen and poured herself a cup of coffee, adding a shot of Bailey's. She lifted the bottle as an offering.

"Beat you to it," he said, raising his cup.

She pulled a skillet from the cabinet. "Since you're the only one up, you can help me with breakfast."

"Sure." Gavin walked to the kitchen and washed his hands. "What should I do?"

She placed a sack of potatoes on the kitchen island. "You can start by peeling these."

Gavin pulled the vegetable peeler from a drawer and went to work.

"So what happened with Renee?" his mom asked. "We were looking forward to seeing her."

"I think that relationship might be over."

"I'm sorry, sweetheart."

"It was sort of inevitable."

"I'm sure you'll meet someone else."

"Yeah, maybe." Gavin considered telling his mom that he already had, and that he'd somehow managed to botch that relationship as well, but there was no point in compounding his humiliation.

"I don't mean to be insensitive, but I never felt like Renee was right for you."

"She apparently felt the same way." Gavin peeled the last potato and looked to his mother. "Now what?"

"Quarter them and then parboil for six minutes," she said, handing him a large knife. She grabbed two eggs from the fridge and cracked them against the lip of a glass bowl. "There's a young woman who works part time at the flower shop who's quite pretty. And single. You'd have to move back here, though."

"I'm not sure I'd find much work in Chicago."

"There's always theater work."

"I tried that. It didn't go very well."

His mom shrugged, as if she didn't have a ready opinion on that. "What do you plan to do now that your show is canceled?"

"I don't know."

"Maybe it's time to start thinking about something else."

"What do you mean?" Gavin asked. The question struck him as an affront.

"Just a more traditional career," she said, attempting nonchalance, though Gavin knew she was easing toward some larger point. "Something a little more stable—with a fixed income."

"You think I should quit acting?"

"Of course not," she said defensively. "I'm just saying you might want to think about finding a full-time job and doing the acting thing on the side."

"That's a polite way of telling me to give up, Mom."

"It's absolutely not. I just worry about you making a living doing this given your age. And if you really do want to start a family, acting doesn't seem like the most financially stable profession."

Gavin finished cutting the potatoes and tipped them into a pot of boiling water. "Would you say the same thing to Sam about dance?"

"No, but that's because Sam is much younger than you."

"And more talented." Gavin had always known that his sister's talent was far greater than his own. It had been evident since she was young: the comments from other people, particularly strangers, who felt no obligation to dispense with flattery. There was genuine astonishment in her audience, an admiration he'd never experienced in his own line of work. Which was fine. He was nothing if not realistic when it came to appraising his abilities, which were more akin to a skilled tradesman, someone valued for his ability to perform a specific task with a certain baseline competence. *Greatness* was not a word often associated with his career.

"That's not true at all," his mom said. "I think you're both exceptionally talented, but a career in the arts isn't the most financially secure path. I learned this when I was younger. You know I stopped dancing when I got pregnant with you. And while I don't regret the decision, it certainly wasn't an easy one to make. But that's life. That's growing up."

These were all realities Gavin had already wrestled with and, to some extent, accepted. He knew there was a timer on the acting thing, and he suspected that the cancellation of his show was the death knell to a spectacularly mediocre career. Which would have been fine if it meant settling down with Mariana somewhere high in the mountains, but the circumstances of his personal life made it harder to accept.

"Maybe you've heard," she said, "but your friend from high school—Tony Stanton—he just started his own real estate company. He's apparently doing quite well."

"Are you suggesting I go into real estate?"

"Just an idea. Real estate is all about relationships and charisma. You're certainly charming enough. People generally like you."

"Not as of late." Gavin strained the potatoes and dumped them into a large baking pan, then added olive oil and salt before sliding the pan into the oven. Roasted potatoes were one of the few things he knew how to make, though Renee used to tease him that it was pretty difficult to botch such a rudimentary dish. But he was no longer sure that was true. Lately, he'd destroyed everything he'd touched, and he had no reason to believe the potatoes would be spared.

His mom shook her head. "Now you're just feeling sorry for your-self."

"Yeah, well, I'm in a bit of a funk, so I'm allowed to mope."

"Speaking of funks, what's eating your sister?"

"What do you mean?"

"Doesn't she seem out of sorts?"

Gavin did think she seemed angry, an obvious result of her drug use, but he couldn't tell his mother this. He wasn't sure what to make of this quieter, darker version of his little sister. She had changed so much since he'd last seen her. Now she was so tense, so unsmiling, so uninterested in people, even her family. Yesterday, drinking and wan-dering around the city, something they had always enjoyed so much, seemed to her like an inconvenience, as if there were so many other places she'd rather be.

"She seems lonely," Gavin finally said. "It probably isn't easy living overseas."

"Which is why you'd think she'd be happy to be home. Instead she just seems annoyed. She snaps at me every time I try to talk to her. And I'm still upset she didn't come to Mass last night."

"Have you talked to her about it?"

"No."

"Well," Gavin said. "That might be a good place to start. You both tend to be a little passive-aggressive."

She shook her head. "I just want us all to have a nice time together."

"I know, Mom," he said, placing his hand on her shoulder. "Me too."

JONAH

H E   S A T   O N   T H E   F L O O R   of the walk-in closet, thumbing through banded stacks of cash, wondering if there was any way to counteract the terrible act of betrayal they represented. It seemed unlikely. He considered giving the money to a local charity, but while that might assuage his own guilt, it would do little to remedy the situation in which he was now complicit. In fact, it would probably only make things worse. He was on the hook to deliver fifty thousand dollars, and there was no way around that unfortunate truth. He decided he needed to talk to Marcus, not to confess but to get his thoughts on whether there was a future for him back in Gabon.

"Did I wake you?" Jonah asked.

"Merry Christmas," Marcus said, sounding surprised to hear from him. "I take it you're back in Chicago."

"I am."

"How is it?"

"Cold. And crowded. How are you? Feeling better?" He hadn't spoken to Marcus in months, and he sounded markedly older, his voice tinny and frail.

"I've recovered for the most part, though I still have headaches from time to time. My doctor isn't convinced they have anything to do with the malaria, though."

"What's the news back in Nashville?"

"I'm a bit out of the loop, seeing as how I spend most of my time begging for money."

"Any success on that front?" Jonah asked, staring at the cash.

"We received a small grant from the National Science Foundation. It's enough to float us for the next six months."

"Does that mean I can go back?" Jonah asked. He already knew he was going back, if only to deliver Slinky's money, though he also hoped Marcus would agree to let him continue his research.

"I don't know," Marcus said. "Is that a good idea?"

Marcus had a knack for posing questions that weren't really questions at all, but rather thinly veiled critiques. Clearly, the answer he was fishing for went something like: *No, Marcus, I think I've shown myself to be profoundly irresponsible and staggeringly lazy, and it would probably be best for all of us if I spend the spring semester performing grunt work in the lab while I lament the incredible opportunity I somehow squandered.* But Jonah wasn't about to give him that. "Why wouldn't it be?" he finally said.

"I received an email from Laurent. He said you ran into some trouble."

"It was nothing."

"That's not what Laurent said."

"Laurent tends to exaggerate. It was a very minor thing." Jonah had hoped Laurent would be discreet about the arrangement with Slinky. Jonah wasn't sure how much Marcus knew, but he wasn't about to offer up any additional information.

"I'm wondering if we should let things cool down a bit before sending you back," Marcus said.

"I think someone needs to be on the ground over there. Our presence is one of the few things keeping it from being open season on the elephants."

"And you'd like to be that person?"

"Of course. You and I are the only ones who really know the area."

"There's Laurent."

"Laurent has a family. He doesn't have time."

"If I do send you back, I need to see a little more productivity. It was radio silence for a while there toward the end. We're operating with limited finances, and I need to know you're actually working."

"I'll upload the new recordings in the next few days," Jonah said. "I think you'll find some interesting stuff in there. There's been a lot of activity in the last couple weeks. Lots of new faces. The head count had been dropping for a while, but it started picking back up right before I left. I also noticed a few tuskless elephants, which I'd never seen before. New faces. What do you know about that?"

"You're kidding," Marcus said, his voice coming alive with excitement. "You're certain?"

"Absolutely," Jonah said, feeling a little swell of pride.

"Females, I presume?"

"That's right."

"Did you get photographs?" Marcus asked excitedly.

Jonah hesitated. "No, unfortunately not. I was having issues with the camera."

"Oh," Marcus said, clearly disappointed. "Well, that's interesting, I suppose, though scientifically useless."

"Sorry," Jonah said, taken aback by the sharp reaction.

"How's the thesis coming along?" Marcus asked.

"I'm planning to spend some time in the library while I'm back here. I've been taking lots of notes."

"Notes aren't going to impress your thesis committee, Jonah. If you want to graduate in the next decade you need to put pen to paper. The research is only valuable insofar as you're able to analyze it and formulate some sort of defensible conclusion. And at the moment, I'm beginning to have some concerns."

For someone with no children, Marcus had the unique ability to badger Jonah in a way that even his own parents couldn't. "I get it," he finally said. "So where does this leave me?"

"Let me talk it over with the rest of the committee and I'll get back to you. In the meantime, please spend some time in the library. Give me a good reason to send you back."

"Okay, sure," Jonah said, and hung up. He wondered if he should have just told Marcus everything that had happened, his arrangement with Slinky, the meeting with Andre, the myriad ways he'd sullied their research and betrayed their subjects. And Marcus probably would have believed him, maybe even assured him that his actions, in light of such duress, were excusable. But that wasn't enough. He wasn't returning because he needed to be absolved by Slinky or Marcus or the judicial system, but rather by the elephants themselves.

He stepped out of the closet and heard voices in the kitchen, his mother and brother, he guessed. Needing to pee, he tried the bathroom door but it was locked.

"What?" Sam's voice called.

"You almost done in there?" he asked.

"No."

"What are you doing?"

"I'm getting out of the shower."

Under normal circumstances, Jonah would have taken her word for it even though he hadn't heard the shower running, but Gavin had planted this idea of drugs and now he couldn't help but wonder what was really happening on the other side of that door. Recognizing that there was nothing he could do about it and, more important, that it was really none of his business, he walked to the living room, where Gavin and his dad were watching a parade on the television.

"Merry Christmas," he announced.

"Merry Christmas, kiddo," his mom said. "Who were you talking to in there?"

"Someone from school," Jonah said, pouring himself a cup of coffee.

"The guy from yesterday?" Gavin asked pointedly.

Jonah sat in the recliner across the room. "Different guy, actually."

"And it went well?" his father asked. "They're happy with your work over there?"

"I think so," Jonah said. His phone vibrated in his pocket and he removed it to find a text from Gavin. We need to talk to her. When?

He shot his brother a look from across the room, then typed a response. You do it.

Gavin shook his head in disbelief, then began punching at his phone. You're an ass.

You're only gonna make things worse.

How could they be any worse?

Their dad, who sat between them in the living room, looked up from the television every time one of their phones vibrated. "What are you two conspiring about?" he finally asked. Their father had a sixth sense for when something was amiss in the family, and Jonah suspected he was on to them.

"Just some highly classified Christmas business," Jonah said with a friendly smile.

"Right," his dad replied, rolling his eyes.

His mom entered from the kitchen and sat on the arm of the recliner. "So how much longer will you be there?" she asked. "In Gabon?"

"Hard to say," Jonah said, slipping his phone back in his pocket.

"Do you have any interest in getting a regular job—back here in the States?"

"Maybe real estate?" Gavin added. "Mom has a lead on some real estate work."

"Oh, lighten up, Gavin," she said. "I was half kidding."

"Yes," Gavin said. "But only half."

Jonah considered it. The idea of a nine-to-five might have seemed appealing a few days ago, when he was being chased out of Africa with a suitcase full of ivory, but a couple days in Chicago reaffirmed his distrust of cities. It was nice being around his family, sure, but the noise and the people and the general griminess of urban areas upset his inner rhythm. And despite the bout of laziness that had plagued his last few weeks in Gabon, he really did, more than anything else, miss the elephants. "I don't think so," he finally said.

SAMANTHA

S HE'D SPENT THE PAST HOUR in the bathroom, under the pretense of a long shower, though at some point she would be called
forth to participate in the Christmas holiday, a harrowing prospect.
She was hoping for a call from Max, just a quick hello, anything that
might motivate her to stay clean, but in lieu of that she was content to
sit on the tile floor, using the hairdryer to blow warm air across her
face while debating whether to flush the remaining drugs down the
toilet. With or without, clean or sober, there was no future she de-
sired. She had nothing to look forward to. This drug had ruined everything. It had killed Atticus and destroyed her career and now it
threatened to estrange her from her family. She had no sense of what
came next, of where she would go from here. After the holiday, her
brothers would leave and her parents would return to work, at which
point she would be left scrambling for an excuse as to why she wasn't
headed back to Moscow. She'd tried calling Max earlier that morning,
but he hadn't answered. She assumed this was a conscious act of avoid-
ance, which, on a professional level, she accepted, but which, on a
more human level, broke her heart.

She looked at her phone: 8:40 A.M. She knew that something
needed to change, and until she expelled the drugs from her life, noth-

ing would. So now was the time. *Goodbye to all of this,* she thought, retrieving the small bag of drugs hidden in her makeup bag and flushing it down the toilet in a well-intentioned act of restraint she would soon regret. She popped a Klonopin to take the edge off, then changed into her workout clothes, slipped quietly out the front door, and went to find the gym, where she would attempt to exercise the demons from her body.

SHE ALMOST STOPPED AFTER the third mile, but three miles wasn't enough, so she pushed on to four, then five, until her heart was ricocheting in her chest and her legs gave out and the treadmill deposited her, like a piece of airport luggage, on the gym floor. She looked up and saw a woman standing in front of a weather map on a small television mounted to the wall.

"You okay?" came a voice.

Sam saw a man standing over her. He had a pair of earbuds hanging around his neck, his face slick with sweat.

"I'm fine," she said. "I just tripped."

"Careful now," he said, helping her to her feet.

"Yeah, thanks." She grabbed a paper-thin hand towel from a wicker shelf and wiped her face, then sat on an orange balance ball and drank water from a paper cone. The man who'd helped her— the only other person in the gym on Christmas morning—returned to the elliptical machine. Gyms were sad places, and gyms such as this one—windowless, in the basement of an apartment complex, with too few machines to be taken seriously—were particularly sad. Today was day one. Tomorrow would be day two, and so on and so forth until at some point she could stop counting. But she also knew it might be a while until she could stop counting. Maybe never. That's how it was for some people—every day a struggle. Or, if not a struggle, a series of very important choices that, if not carefully considered, could negate all the choices that had preceded it.

———

BACK AT HER PARENTS' APARTMENT, she felt better. Or marginally better. She didn't want to tear off her skin, so that was something. The exercise had helped, and the smell of her mother's cooking revived her appetite. Gavin was setting the table, while Jonah and their father watched a football game in the living room. Overnight, a handful of gifts had materialized beneath the tree.

"Merry Christmas," her mother announced.

"Merry Christmas," Sam said, hugging her mom from behind. "I'm sorry."

"What are you sorry for?"

"Everything." Sam wasn't sure why she was apologizing, but it seemed necessary.

"Well, there's no need to be sorry," her mother said. "All is forgiven on Christmas morning."

It was a nice thing to say, but Sam didn't believe it. Forgiveness seemed like a distant concept she wasn't entitled to, at least not yet.

"You're all sweaty," her mom said.

"I went to the gym."

"Well, go clean up. Breakfast is almost ready."

She showered and changed back into her pajamas, because that's how she'd always done it on Christmas morning for as long as she could remember, and perhaps what her life needed was a return to tradition. She brushed her hair just enough to be presentable, then went to the kitchen and joined her family at the table, which was spread with croissants and fruit, as well as the egg casserole her mother made every year.

"You went to the gym on Christmas morning," Jonah said. "I applaud your ambition."

"I'm turning over a new leaf," Sam said, draping her napkin across her lap. "This looks delicious."

"Fill up," her mom said, "because we aren't eating again until dinner."

Gavin looked to Sam. "Why?"

"What?" she asked.

"Why are you turning over a new leaf?"

She shrugged. "I don't know. I just feel like I've let myself go." There was a pointedness to his question that made her uncomfortable.

"Yeah," Gavin said. "I know the feeling."

"I think you both look a little thin," her mom said. "You need to eat."

"What's the food like over there?" her dad asked. "In Russia."

"Lots of meat," Sam said. "So I eat lots of salads."

"I don't know that I've ever had Russian food," her mom said. "Is it good?"

"Very," Jonah said, somewhat unexpectedly. The collective gaze turned toward him. "Russian food that is."

"When have you had Russian food?" Gavin asked.

"Few times," Jonah said nonchalantly.

"Name a Russian dish."

"Goulash."

"That's Hungarian."

"White Russian."

"That's a cocktail."

"Cocktails are food."

"No," Gavin said, "they aren't."

"Pass the fruit, please," their mother said.

And so it went. After breakfast, they migrated to the living room, where their mom distributed the gifts, a role the kids had always coveted but which now held little interest for any of them. When they were younger, Gavin and Jonah used to wake Sam up in the middle of the night, and the three of them would sneak downstairs to see what Santa had left under the tree. They would use steak knives to make little slits in the gifts, just enough to see what was inside before carefully re-taping them shut. They were so close then, yet so distant now. Sam felt as though she hardly knew her brothers anymore, and she suspected they felt the same way. She still hadn't seen Gavin's show, and she couldn't say with any certainty what Jonah did over in Africa. They rarely spoke anymore—not because they didn't want to but because their lives had sent them in such divergent directions— and if it weren't for the homeward pull of the holidays, she wondered when she would ever see them.

The day passed in a quiet leisure, everyone entertaining themselves with football games and phone calls to friends. That afternoon, they went to a movie together—a disastrous science fiction spectacle—and though the movie was unwatchable, Sam was grateful for the two hours she spent immersed in someone else's problems. Afterward, they returned home and ate turkey and stuffing and scalloped potatoes—Sam eating only a few bites of the potatoes—then pumpkin pie, and drank the port their father brought home from a trip to Lisbon. As the day darkened and the holiday came to its conclusion, the sense of optimism she'd felt that morning began to wane. Max wasn't going to call, and the drugs weren't going to release her, and all the fear and dread she'd experienced upon arriving in Chicago came rushing back.

That night, she couldn't sleep, though she rarely slept once the drugs had faded and she was left to confront the yawning pit of sobriety. It was shortly before midnight according to the clock on the nightstand, and she got out of bed and walked to the living room, where Jonah was asleep on the couch, the canned laughter of a studio audience floating from the television. She moved to the kitchen and opened the refrigerator without desiring anything it contained. She opened and closed the cupboard doors, poked her head inside the pantry, looking for the thing she knew she wouldn't find. She felt mildly possessed, as if there were something directing her body, guiding her from one corner of the apartment to the next. She went back to her bedroom, dressed, slipped into her coat, then the hallway, then the elevator. Once outdoors, she walked south to Jackson Street and took the stairs underground. She boarded an empty Red Line train to 95th/ Dan Ryan. She had no destination in mind, only the need to keep moving to a place other than where she had been.

The train pulled to a stop at Forty-Seventh Street, and a homeless woman boarded with an IKEA bag overflowing with assorted treasures. She was dressed in a down jacket and sweatpants and rubber boots. She had somehow fit three different stocking caps onto her head and was staring intently out the window, muttering a silent prayer. "I hope you die for Christmas," the woman said.

Sam wasn't sure if the directive was intended for her or some imagined nemesis, but she kept her head down, staring at a circle of gum stamped to the floor. The woman began again, louder now, turning to Sam and pointing a dirty, calloused finger in her direction. "You hear me?" she yelled. "I got so much love in my heart, I swear to God. I got so much love in my heart, but ain't none for your ass." She stopped, wiped away a tear, and began again. "I hope you die for Christmas!"

The woman paced up and down the car, howling obscenities. When she reached one end of the train, she turned and shuffled back toward Sam. She stood above her and looked down at the top of Sam's head. "You hear me, bitch? I hope you die for Christmas!"

"Please stop," Sam said, head bowed, careful not to make eye contact.

"You listening to me?"

"Leave me alone. Please."

"Die for Christmas!"

"Go away!" Sam screamed. Her eyes filled and she felt an intense fear, not only of this woman, but of her future, the impossible task awaiting her. She didn't want to be in Chicago, but she didn't want to be in Russia either. She wanted to be back on the plane, forever circling the globe, high above the cesspool of her circumstances. Instead, she was alone on a dark train, suffering through the menacing homily of a madwoman.

The train slowed to a stop and Sam stood to leave, but the woman grabbed her arm. "Listen to me," the woman said, and for a moment, they stared at each other, two broken women on a train in the fading hours of Christmas. "I got so much love in my heart. I really do." The woman went in for a hug, but Sam pulled free and slid through the closing train doors. From the platform, she watched the woman's face disappear as the train carried her away.

She found the stairs and walked to the street above. She passed a laundromat that was closed, then a diner, also closed. She was looking for a face that could help her, but this was an unfamiliar part of the city and you had to know where to look for such faces, so she finally returned underground, to the dark warmth of the subway station. She stepped onto the platform and watched trains arrive and depart, the doors whooshing open for no one, then clapping shut and departing as quickly as they had arrived. If only she could control her longing, a longing that went so much deeper than the immediate desire for drugs, a longing for a release from her self-imposed prison, the fiction of her life. As she sat on a bench watching a rat pick at a discarded muffin, she tried to identify when the unraveling had begun. She could say it was the night when Atticus first offered her a taste, but even then something had been set in motion, a need still too small to identify but whose roots had already taken hold in her body, its tendrils strangling her volition, choking out the light.

She looked up and saw him standing above her, the face she'd been looking for, the stranger who could set her right. "You look like you need a friend," he said.

SHE OPENED HER EYES and saw a dog, a large one, some kind of retriever, lying next to her on the bed, its furry, copper head resting on her thigh. She looked around the room, which she quickly realized was a hospital room, and located her brothers sleeping in plastic chairs, backlit by a large picture window overlooking the roof of an adjacent apartment building. She sat up and the dog lifted its head, looked at her with a face that offered little explanation. *How did I end up here?* she wondered. And then, aloud, to the dog: "Who are you?"

"That's Cooper," said a nurse dressed in Christmas-themed scrubs. She approached and chucked the dog behind the ear. "He took a real liking to you."

The dog looked up at her briefly, then returned his head to her lap. "What's it doing here?"

"We bring him around to cheer up the kids," the nurse explained. "For some reason, he really wanted to see what was happening in your room, so I brought him in and he hopped right up in bed with you. You were sound asleep, of course, but Cooper didn't care." The nurse looked at the dog. "Did you, Cooper?" She moved and spoke in a way that suggested this was all very common, a young woman and a therapy dog sharing a hospital bed on the morning after Christmas.

"Is everything okay?" Sam asked.

"You tell me," the nurse said, punching some buttons on the monitor above Sam's head. She remembered very little from the night before. She remembered riding the train and the homeless woman yelling at her and then the man with the drugs, but nothing after that. "How did I get here?"

"A subway worker found you unconscious on the train platform. You were barely breathing. The EMT administered Narcan, which saved your life. Do you remember what you took?"

Sam shook her head.

"It doesn't matter. That's for someone else to sort out. The important thing is that you feel better."

"Do you?" Jonah said, straightening in his chair, blinking awake.

"What?" Sam asked.

"Feel better."

She wasn't sure. *Compared to what?* she wondered. She had no reference point. She was warmer certainly, more comfortable lying in this bed than she probably was on the concrete floor of the subway station, but it would be disingenuous to say she felt *better*. Mostly what she felt was a mixture of confusion as to what exactly had transpired and gratitude that she was still alive to wonder at such things.

"I'll let you guys have some privacy," the nurse said. "A doctor will be in shortly to check on you." She placed a clear plastic bottle on the tray next to Sam's bed. "We'll also need a urine sample for the toxicology screen whenever you feel up for it. Come on, Cooper," she said, and the dog hopped off the bed and followed her into the hallway.

"What time is it?" Sam asked.

"Almost noon," Jonah said, standing and stretching.

"How long have you been here?"

"I don't know. Since early morning?"

"Somebody called you?"

"They called him," Jonah said, nodding toward Gavin, who was now awake, running his hands through his hair. "Apparently, you had him listed as your ICE contact in your phone."

It was possibly the only responsible thing she'd done in the last year. In a way she'd always feared this scenario might come to pass, and she figured that if something terrible did happen, Gavin would be better equipped to handle the news than her parents. "Do Mom and Dad know?"

"No," Gavin said. "And we went to considerable lengths to make sure they didn't find out."

"Thank you," she said. There was a moment of silence as she considered the situation, what might happen next.

Jonah approached and took her hand, rested his forehead against hers. "What's going on?" he whispered, and with this simple gesture, she broke open.

"I don't know," she said, feeling the pinch in her throat, the tears coming down her cheeks.

Gavin walked to the other side of the bed and took her other hand. "We love you," he said. "We love you and we want to help you. But you have to *want* our help."

"I know," she said. "I do."

"Okay," Gavin said, standing and walking to the window. "Then we need to figure out a plan."

"What do you mean?" Sam asked.

"I think you know."

"I'm not going to rehab if that's what you're suggesting," Sam said, the mood in the room shifting abruptly.

"I think you should consider it," Gavin said, walking back to her.

"I have. It's not for me."

"Then who's it for?"

"Drug addicts."

"Which doesn't describe you?"

She hesitated. "No."

Gavin scoffed. "Yet here you are in a hospital. How do you explain that?"

"I fucked up. Someone gave me something bad." That part must have been true. There was no other explanation for how she'd ended up here. She looked around the room, wishing that dog would come back to distract her from her brother's incessant questioning.

"Look, Sam," Gavin said. "I love you, but it's pretty obvious that your way of navigating this thing isn't working."

"Can we discuss this when we get home?" Jonah said, pacing the room. "Let her rest."

"No," Gavin said. "We can't. We need to figure this out now." Gavin turned back to Sam. "I found a clinic in Lincoln Park. I spoke with one of the women on the phone and she suggested you come by for a visit. I can go with you if you want."

"That's not gonna happen," Sam said. She was already feeling better, and she didn't see why she couldn't do it on her own terms. This was just a slipup, albeit a pretty severe one, but she would turn it around.

"Why?" Gavin asked.

"Because I told you I'm not going to rehab. I can do it on my own."

"It might not be a bad idea," Jonah said. "Maybe just see what they're all about."

"I know what they're all about," Sam said. "They're about sitting in a circle and holding hands and talking about their fucked-up lives. I'll get on the next flight back to Moscow before I'll do that."

"That's mature," Gavin said, rubbing his forehead.

"Fuck you both. I don't enjoy being attacked like this."

"Maybe you should have thought about that before you pumped yourself full of drugs and nodded off on the Red Line."

"Don't be so dramatic."

"I'm being realistic. According to the police, that's a fairly straight-forward accounting of what happened."

"You're being the self-righteous older brother. And it's obnoxious. Besides, you can't *make* me go to rehab."

"You're right," Gavin said. "But a judge can. It's called court-appointed rehab."

"So you're gonna have me arrested?" Sam asked.

"If that's what it takes."

"That's blackmail," Jonah said.

"Exactly," Sam added, relieved to have an ally.

Gavin looked to his brother. "Well, fuck, Jonah, I'm kind of at a loss here, so maybe you could suggest something."

Jonah stood and walked to the window, put his hands behind his head. "There is one other idea." He paused, staring out the window.

"Okay . . . ," Gavin said, "what is it?"

Jonah turned back to his siblings. "Have either of you heard of iboga?"

Sam and Gavin shook their heads.

"It's sort of like a psychedelic, but not exactly," Jonah said. "It comes from the iboga tree, which is native to Gabon. This guy I work with—Laurent—he's from the Babongo tribe, and he actually told me about it a few months back. It's used during a spiritual ceremony called Bwiti. Laurent did it when he was younger. It's a rite of passage.

"Anyway, it was discovered to lessen the withdrawal symptoms of opioid addiction. Don't ask me how it works, but it does. At least for some people. I did some research yesterday, and there's all kinds of high-end ibogaine clinics popping up in Costa Rica and Mexico. Fancy beachfront resorts, celebrity rehab–type shit. But it's different in Gabon. It's more spiritual than medicinal there. But the drug works just the same."

"What are you suggesting?" Gavin asked.

"I'm saying Laurent offered to arrange it," he said, looking to Sam.

"Sounds a little bit like cultural appropriation," Sam said, trying to imagine the optics of inserting herself into a West African spiritual ceremony she knew nothing about it.

"Maybe it is," Jonah said. "But seeing as how you don't seem particularly interested in your own culture's approach to dealing with this, you might want to try someone else's. And besides, Laurent offered and when someone offers help, you should take it. So, what do you think? You interested?"

At the moment, she was interested only in getting out of this hospital, but she also knew that wasn't going to happen without concessions on her part. And based on Gavin's suggestion of rehab, she figured she might as well hear Jonah out. "What's it like?"

"To be perfectly honest," Jonah said, "it sounds pretty miserable."

"It's a hallucinogen?" Sam asked.

"Yeah."

"Like LSD?"

"Much stronger than that," Jonah said. "One of the articles I read described it as something more like an exorcism."

"So it's witchcraft," Gavin said dismissively.

"No," Jonah said. "But it *is* rough. Apparently, it's a forty-eight-hour nightmare that results in a complete reformatting of the brain. Also, you should probably know that it's administered with no professional medical oversight. So, you know, not exactly FDA approved."

"Sounds like a terrible idea," Gavin said.

"It's not really your decision to make," Jonah shot back. He turned to Sam. "Look, I don't claim to be an expert on this, but people swear by it. And if Laurent says he can arrange for you to do it safely, then I think it's worth considering." He paused. "What do you think?"

She wasn't sure what to think. She knew Gavin was right. Her way of dealing with this wasn't working, but she also wasn't about to set foot in a traditional rehab facility. She had nowhere else to go. She couldn't imagine hanging around Chicago, and she wasn't welcome back in Russia. "How long would we be gone?"

"I don't know," Jonah said. "It's kind of an ordeal getting over there. A week, maybe longer?"

"And how exactly *are* we supposed to get over there?" Gavin asked.

"I'd suggest an airplane," Jonah said.

"No shit. But I'm currently unemployed, so an international flight to Africa isn't exactly in the budget."

"We'll figure it out," Jonah said.

"Maybe you could pay for it with your stolen money," Gavin said.

"It's not stolen," Jonah said. "Just dirty."

"What money?" Sam asked.

Jonah shook his head. "Look, I don't want to get hung up on the details. We'll figure it out. I just want to know if you're interested or not."

"It sounds extraordinarily dangerous," Gavin said.

"Well," Jonah said, "Sam doesn't seem particularly interested in *your* idea."

"*His* idea," Sam said, "isn't an option."

"And this is?" Gavin asked, incredulous.

"Maybe."

"Look," Jonah said. "I know it's a little unorthodox, but what do you have to lose? If it doesn't work, then you come back here and at least you got to see West Africa. I'm going back regardless, so it might be nice to have some company. Do it for me. Please?"

Sam stared out the hospital window. "Iboga?"

"Research it if you want," Jonah said.

But she didn't need to research it. She already knew she would go because the truth was that she was afraid of what she'd become, of what she was capable of doing to herself. She'd drifted so far, and she wanted nothing more than to break this opium spell, which would require something drastic, a violent shock to her system. For the past year, she had repressed the truth, hidden the reality of her addiction in the tiny compartments of her soul, but now it was time to unlock those doors and take a long, hard look inside. It was time to regain dominion over her body.

GAVIN

THE TRIP LACKED ANYTHING RESEMBLING a proper itiner- ary, which Gavin noted a half dozen times in the intervening days. A quick Google search of the country alerted him to the poten- tial health risks—yellow fever, malaria, typhoid—which he and Sam attempted to address with a quick trip to a travel clinic, where they received a half dozen vaccinations and a prescription for Lariam, the anti-malarial drug whose side effects, the doctor warned them, in- cluded hallucinations and unusual thoughts or behavior. Whatever that meant. Their parents were under the impression that each of their children was returning to their respective lives, and great effort had been taken to maintain this illusion. So three days after Christmas and less than forty-eight hours after retrieving Sam from the hospital, Gavin, Jonah, and Sam stood in the foyer of their parents' apartment, luggage already in the hallway, saying their goodbyes.

"I wish you could stay a little longer," their mom said, clearly upset that two of the three of them were leaving earlier than planned. Gavin had originally told her he was leaving New Year's Eve, and Jonah had claimed to be staying till after the new year. Only Sam had been up-front about needing to leave so soon after Christmas, and Gavin was feeling some intense guilt about the complexity of the lies required to pull this off.

"Me too," Sam said, "but they need me back there earlier than I thought."

"I still don't understand why you're all leaving at the same time," their dad said in a tone that suggested he could smell their lies.

"We don't *have* to," Gavin said. "But I'm going that direction anyway, so it just makes sense. Besides, you don't want to get out in this weather."

His dad shrugged, though if in response to the weather or their simultaneous departure, Gavin couldn't say.

"Will you please let us know when the ballet opens?" their mom asked Sam. "We really want to come out there, but we need to buy our tickets soon."

"I know, I'm sorry," Sam said. "I should know once I get back."

"And please be careful out there," she said to Jonah.

"I'll do my best," Jonah said.

Once the *goodbye*s and *love you*s and *until next time*s were delivered, they stepped into the hallway and took the elevator to Gavin's car in the parking garage. Outside, it was snowing and windy and Gavin had the feeling that something wild and unpredictable awaited them on the other side of the world. Whether this trip was blatantly reckless or absolutely necessary was a question he still couldn't answer. He had joined the expedition because he had nothing else to do, or at least that's what he'd told his siblings, but the truth was that he couldn't shake the feeling that he was somehow to blame for Sam's addiction, and he'd decided, while watching his sister sleep in a hospital bed, that until something changed, he wasn't letting her out of his sight.

As they drove in silence to the airport, he was reminded of the summer before tenth grade, when his buddy Donnie appeared at the Brennan house with news of some big shit going down at the arcade. The arcade's owners were trying out a happy hour of sorts, whereby they were exchanging nickels for quarters, a regular video-game fire sale. Gavin's parents had left for the afternoon and Jonah was at a friend's house, which meant Gavin had been tasked with babysitting Sam, who was seven at the time. Gavin explained his situation, but Donnie insisted that he just bring his kid sister with him. "We'll bike it," Donnie said. "She's got a bike, right?" Sam had a pink Spice Girls bicycle with purple tassels dangling from the handlebars. She'd never ventured much farther than their driveway and Gavin wasn't sure how roadworthy it was, but Sam said she was up for an adventure, so the three of them pedaled down the quiet residential streets of their suburban subdivision and into the fast-moving traffic of Highway 12. They kept to the edge of the shoulder, but every few minutes a tractor trailer would scream past, the draft pushing them toward the tall grass in the ditch. Gavin knew he was being irresponsible, but the physical proximity of his sister instilled in him the belief that he had a certain amount of control over the situation, and he wanted to believe the same was true now.

Gavin eased the car into the long-term parking garage. He turned off the ignition, and the three of them sat in silence, listening to the tick of the radiator, the rattle of cars passing over metal plates in the garage floor. Gavin looked in the rearview mirror, first at his sister's face, the mystery of it, then to a family passing behind the car, the mother and father each pulling rolling suitcases, a young boy dragging a small one shaped like a race car.

"I don't know if I can do it," Sam finally said.

"What do you mean?" Jonah asked, turning to her.

But Gavin knew what she meant. He looked to Jonah, who then understood.

"Do you still have some left?" Gavin asked.

Sam nodded.

"Jesus, Sam," he said. He wanted to ask how she'd managed to find more despite everything they'd just gone through, but it was a useless line of inquiry. "Once more and then that's it," he said. "Then we get on the plane and no more, right?"

"Yeah."

"Promise?"

"I promise."

"Okay," Gavin said. He turned to Jonah. "Okay?"

"Okay," Jonah said, hesitantly, as if unsure what he was agreeing to.

Sam removed a makeup bag from her suitcase and arranged the instruments on her lap. Gavin watched through the rearview mirror, the sliver of needle, the spoon, the complicated reality of what until now he'd only imagined. It looked so complex, like a surgeon's prep, and his heart sank when he imagined his sister doing this alone, in Russia, day after day after day.

Sam looked up and caught his eye in the mirror. "Please don't watch," she said.

Gavin looked down at the steering column. He heard the click of a lighter, then the squeak of leather as she moved about in the back seat. A moment passed, and then he reached his hand back toward her, and she took hold of it. "Now?" he asked.

Sam nodded. "Yeah."

PART THREE

JONAH

HE SAT IN THE DINING car with his sister, a game of dominoes spread between them, the black shadows of the forest flickering past in the window. They were on an overnight train to Franceville, scheduled to arrive at dawn. Jonah stared at the threads of dominoes splayed across the table, strategizing his next move. It was shortly after midnight and most of the other passengers, Gavin included, were asleep in their seats.

They had arrived in Libreville late that afternoon and taken a taxi to the train station in Owendo. The driver warned them about the recent terrorist attacks, something to do with the newly elected president. Jonah hadn't really been following the election, though he'd heard from Laurent that it had been strongly contested, violent protests sprouting around the city. The cabbie suggested they keep away from large crowds, avoid public venues. Gabon had a reputation as a politically stable country, a relatively safe place for Westerners, so Jonah figured this was just a case of a paranoid cabbie and an overly protective police force. He'd looked at Sam and Gavin, dismissing the warning, but he could tell they weren't convinced.

After arriving at the airport, they'd eaten at a restaurant next to the train station, some variety of beef Jonah couldn't place, then boarded an ancient yellow train that hurled them deep into the heart of the country. He had hoped to catch the express, but their timing was off, so they were stuck on a slow-moving thing that stopped frequently at places that were not train stations. He'd been overcome with a terrible anxiety the first time he'd taken this train, so many months ago, unsure what he was getting into, and he felt something similar now, a special kind of culpability for dragging his siblings into his perverted orbit.

Jonah had arranged for Laurent to meet them at the train station. The plan was to decompress at his place for a day, which would give Jonah enough time to deliver Slinky's cash before they set off for the Bwiti ceremony. Slinky had wanted to meet at the restaurant, but Jonah was hoping to shield Laurent from his dealings, so he suggested the handoff take place at his camp in the forest, to which Slinky had agreed.

The train lurched to a stop at the station in Ndjolé. Through the window, Jonah noticed a man stepping aboard. He was white, in his mid-forties, with no luggage, an odd thing at such a late hour, in such a remote part of the country. A moment later, the train jolted back to life and the guy entered the dining car. He took a seat at a table next to Jonah and Sam.

"Possible to get a drink at this hour?" he asked. His accent was British, but he had a cocksure air about him that suggested he was more than just a tourist.

Jonah pointed to the bar at the end of the car.

The man smiled and made his way down the aisle, swaying with the motion of the train. Jonah got a whiff of his sour stench as he passed. He wore khaki cargo pants and a T-shirt advertising a Gabonese bank, and his hair, which curled out beneath a baseball cap, appeared stringy and unwashed. He possessed the crazed, slightly malarial look of someone who'd spent an extended amount of time in the forest, and Jonah recognized something of his former self in the man.

"No bartender tonight?" he called back.

The bartender, who Jonah had struck up a conversation with earlier in the evening, had checked out an hour ago, but left the refrigerator unlocked and told Jonah to leave money for whatever they drank. "He closed up for the night," Jonah said. "Honor system."

The man smiled, pulled a few francs from his wallet, and placed them on the table. "Can I get you something?"

"No thanks," Jonah said. "We're about to call it a night."

"Something for the lady?"

Sam shook her head.

"Suit yourself." The man walked back to his table and lowered himself into his seat with the exaggerated motion of the elderly. He popped the cap on his beer and released a dramatic sigh, watching Jonah and Sam continue their game.

"Your move," Jonah said.

Sam wore a chunky wool cardigan despite the heat, and she kept putting her hand to her mouth to mask long, exaggerated yawns. She claimed to have come down with a cold, but Jonah knew she was most likely suffering from withdrawal. He wasn't sure what to do aside from keeping her company. He'd never considered himself a caretaker—he could barely take care of himself—but he was hopeful that she might feel better once the ceremony was underway.

"Dominoes," the man said, taking note of their game. "Too much math for me. More of a chess guy, myself." He took a long pull on his beer. "American?"

"What?" Jonah said.

"You're from the States?"

"Yeah."

"I can usually tell." He extended his hand to Jonah. "Edwin."

Jonah shook the man's hand. "Jonah."

Sam made her move, then looked to her brother. "Your turn."

"I live in London most of the year," Edwin continued, "though lately I've been spending a lot of time here. I've got some business with the Gabonese government that keeps me on the move."

"Oh yeah," Jonah said, more out of courtesy than any real interest in what he was saying. He considered the board, but there was nothing for him, so he drew from the boneyard.

"Where are you from in the States?" Edwin continued.

"Chicago," Jonah said, not looking up from the game. The guy obviously wasn't getting the hint.

"Windy City," Edwin said, as if summoning a memory. "I visited once in the late nineties. Cold city full of warm people. That's how I remember it. May I ask how you ended up on this train tonight?"

"Tourists," Jonah said curtly.

"Is that right? Gabon isn't known for its tourism, but I admire your sense of adventure. Kenya is the obvious place for tourists. Kenya or South Africa. People want to see the animals, the big five. They want luxury camps and sundowners in the bush. Don't get me wrong, a safari is a wonderful thing, but I applaud you for taking the road less traveled. Tourism is a real boon for countries like Gabon. Of course, it doesn't help when we have this kind of political unrest. It's important for people like you to spread the word, let the West know that Gabon is a friendly place full of kind people." He looked to the bar. "The kind of place that still uses the honor system."

Jonah was tired of listening to this man speak as if he were the tourism ambassador. "We should get some sleep," Jonah said to his sister.

"Let's finish the game," she said.

"What do you think of this train?" Edwin continued. "I don't care for it so much. Too slow. Quite dangerous as well. Last time we hit an elephant." He illustrated this by punching his open palm with his fist. "Damn thing exploded all over the train. Took almost three hours before we were moving again. The conductor had to wipe the windshield down with his T-shirt. That's an image I won't soon forget." He paused to drink from his beer. "You probably don't know this, but we have a serious poaching problem here in Gabon. It's taken quite a toll on the elephants."

Jonah had tuned the guy out, but this last statement commanded his attention. Edwin drained his beer and went to retrieve another. "Yes, poaching is a real concern here," he said, swaying with the motion of the train. "The ivory smuggling is out of control, keeps getting worse. Chinese are part of the problem, but it goes much further. Vietnam, Philippines, even the U.S., where you'd think people would know better."

Jonah didn't like where the conversation was headed. He swept the dominoes into the small metal box and stood to leave. "I think we're done for the night. You have a good one, okay?" He motioned for Sam to follow.

"It was a pleasure meeting you," Edwin called after them. "Enjoy the rest of your trip."

They made their way back to their seats, where Gavin was snoring, his head resting against the window. The train didn't have proper sleeping compartments, but it was half empty, so they had most of the car to themselves. Jonah took a seat in the row behind his brother, and Sam settled into the two seats across the aisle. Beneath his feet was his backpack containing a week's worth of clothes and fifty thousand dollars of someone else's money.

"Night," Sam said, pillowing a sweater between her head and the window.

"Good night," Jonah said. His sister looked broken, defeated, a shell of her former self, and Jonah immediately regretted bringing her here. He was only beginning to realize the magnitude of her sickness, and he wondered if an obscure drug was really the best medicine, or whether Sam might be better served by a Western-style detox program like Gavin had suggested. As the train hurtled them into the forest, Jonah looked to his sister staring blankly out the window and felt a crushing guilt for leading her into something he knew so little about.

"Jonah," Sam finally said, very softly, without looking at him.

"Yeah?"

"How worried should we be about what the cab driver said—the violence and all that?"

This was not the question he was expecting, but it was one for which he at least had an answer. He wanted to confess, to tell his sister everything. He wanted to tell her about the money in his backpack, about Slinky and Andre, and how he was beginning to think this Edwin fellow was somehow involved in all of it. He wanted to tell her about the terrible situation in which he'd implicated himself, if only to illustrate the insignificance of her concerns compared to everything else that could possibly go wrong. Instead, he smiled and said, "Not very."

SAMANTHA

IT WAS RAINING WHEN THEY arrived in Franceville, a violent purging of the sky that fell faster than the ground could take it. Small ponds were forming in the fields outside Sam's window, and she watched an elderly man trudge through rust-colored mud, leading a cow toward a copse of trees. When the train settled at the station, Jonah and Gavin grabbed their bags and made their way onto the platform. Sam followed them into the station, which was surprisingly simple compared to the bustling ones in Europe. There were no travelers wheeling suitcases, no electronic billboards displaying schedules, no intercom announcing arrivals and departures. It wasn't much more than a concrete box, and she was taken aback by the paucity of the place, the cavernous silence. It was unoccupied aside from a woman painting her nails behind the ticket counter and two young boys kicking a soccer ball against a wall.

She followed her brothers to a bench, where Jonah dropped his backpack. "We'll wait here for Laurent. I spoke to him yesterday and he said he'd meet us here."

"Do we have a reservation?" Gavin asked.

"For what?" Jonah said.

"The hotel."

"I told you. We're staying at Laurent's restaurant."

"A restaurant?"

"Yeah." The kids' soccer ball rolled over to Jonah, and he kicked it back to them.

"Does he have beds at this restaurant?" Gavin asked, rifling through his duffel bag, searching for something.

"He has a couch. And I have my sleeping bag."

Gavin looked up. "You can't be serious."

"But I am."

"This is bullshit," Gavin said, removing the phone charger he'd been after.

"You'll survive." Jonah pulled his phone from his pocket and checked for messages. "I'll go look for him. You guys wait here."

"I need to eat something," Gavin said to Sam. "You want anything?"

"I'm good," she said.

Gavin disappeared and Sam sat with her head in her hands. She hadn't brought anything besides a few Percocets, which she'd polished off on the two flights over here. Her muscles ached and she felt terribly cold despite the equatorial heat. She had downplayed the extent of her addiction to her brothers, though she knew Jonah was on to her. She'd barely slept, spending most of last night pacing the train car and making frequent visits to the bathroom. She had hoped that maybe it was just motion sickness, but now, back on solid ground, the waves of nausea continued, crashing and receding, until she finally stood and ran to a nearby trashcan to vomit. The woman at the ticket counter called over to her, but Sam couldn't understand her over the sound of her own retching. When she was done, she wiped her mouth with the back of her hand and looked up to the see the woman standing next to her.

"*Êtes-vous malade?*" the woman asked.

"Bathroom?" Sam said.

The woman pointed to a door marked TOILETTE, and Sam shuffled toward it. She cupped her hands under the tap and rinsed her mouth,

then splashed water on her face and looked in the small mirror above
the sink. She did not look good. She was pale and her eyes were bloodshot and faint bruise-like splotches were blooming on her cheeks.
This was already turning out to be significantly more difficult than
she'd imagined, though she now realized she hadn't really considered
the physical repercussions of going cold turkey. She needed to either
go home and find more drugs, or get started with whatever sorcery
Jonah had in mind, because what she was currently experiencing was
unsustainable.

She heard a knock at the door, followed by Gavin's voice calling
her name. "Sam?" he said again. "You okay?"

"I'm fine," she called back.

"What's going on?"

"I'll be right out." She fixed her hair and tried to compose herself.

"You need anything?"

She opened the door to find her brother holding a bag of chips and
a bottle of water. "What happened?" he asked.

"I got a little nauseous," she said, stepping past him.

Gavin nodded toward the woman sitting at the ticket counter.
"She said you were puking."

"Yeah."

"You're really sick, huh?"

She went to retrieve her bag. "I don't feel spectacular."

"Is it because of the drugs?"

It was actually the lack of drugs, but she wasn't about to admit
that. "It's just motion sickness. I should be fine now."

Gavin handed her the water and she drank. "Where's Jonah?" she
asked.

"I don't know. He isn't back yet."

"I think I need some fresh air," she said.

They grabbed their luggage and found an empty bench outside.
The rain had ceased and the sun was now breaking through the clouds,
pressing down on them with renewed purpose. Across the road was a

gas station, where two men worked under the hood of a busted pickup while a teenage boy leaned against one of the pumps, smoking a cigarette and watching indifferently.

"Is this what you expected?" Gavin asked.

"I don't know what I expected," Sam said.

A skinny dog approached from the gas station and began drinking from a puddle in the road.

"I expected more elephants and fewer stray dogs," Gavin said.

The dog wandered over and sniffed Sam's leg. She gave it a chuck behind the ear.

"I wouldn't pet that thing," Gavin said.

"Why?"

"It probably has rabies."

"I doubt it has rabies."

"I hope those vaccinations work," Gavin said. "Knowing my luck, I'll get fucking typhoid."

Sam didn't know what typhoid felt like, but she imagined it was preferable to whatever she was currently experiencing. She had a sudden longing for her old life back in Russia, the routine, however toxic, that she'd designed for herself. She realized now that she didn't care for new experiences and unfamiliar places. She liked knowing the shape of her days, the tasks that were expected of her. Before leaving Chicago, she'd sent a curt email to Nikolai telling him to go to hell, and another, kinder email to Max, apologizing for all the damage she'd caused. He'd written back to tell her that the production was moving forward, though it wasn't the same without her, a nicety she didn't totally believe. Nikolai had been right. She *was* replaceable, and so she'd been replaced, most likely with Marguerite, his Parisian pawn. It had been hardly more than a week, but those people seemed so far removed from her life.

Gavin paced the road in front of the station. "Where the hell did Jonah go? This is ridiculous. I don't even know where we are."

"We're in Franceville," Sam said, pointing to a sign affixed to what appeared to be a post office.

"Doesn't seem particularly French."

Suddenly, as if summoned, a white truck appeared from around the corner. It pulled to a stop in front of the station and Jonah emerged, along with the driver, who, Sam realized, was the Englishman from the train. Standing behind them were two men in camouflage military fatigues.

"Where the hell have you been?" Gavin said. "We've been sitting here with our fingers up our asses."

"There's been a change of plans," Jonah said. He had a troubled look about him, and Sam got the impression that he'd been reprimanded by the Englishman who now stood next to him, holding his backpack.

"Is this your friend?" Gavin asked.

"Different friend," Edwin said.

He spoke with an authority and formality absent from the night before. Gone was the disheveled wanderer who'd peppered them with questions about their travels. This was a man in charge of something, though what exactly that was Sam couldn't say. "What's going on?" she asked.

"Get in the car," Edwin said. "Jonah can explain on the way to the hotel."

"So we *are* staying at a hotel?" Gavin asked, sounding more relieved than he should have been.

"You two are," Edwin said. "Jonah has some business to tend to."

GAVIN

THE HOTEL WAS NICER THAN he'd expected, a once glamorous building that refused to go quietly. Jonah led them to the lobby, where he spoke surprisingly decent French to the woman at the front desk. Edwin stood a few feet back, like a skeptical parole officer, while the two rangers waited at the hotel entrance. Whatever business Jonah was involved in was turning out to be considerably more nefarious than Gavin could have imagined. "I'd like to know what's going on," he whispered to his brother.

"Not right now," Jonah said. The receptionist handed him a key and directed him to the elevator at the other end of the lobby. He turned to Edwin. "Can I show them to their room?"

"Five minutes," Edwin said, stepping aside.

The elevator ride was their first chance for Jonah to speak freely, and Gavin wasted no time. "Can you please tell me what the fuck is going on?"

"It's a long story," Jonah said, "and I only have five minutes."

"Who is that guy?"

"I'm not sure."

"But you're going with him?"

"I don't have a choice."

"What did you *do,* Jonah? Is this about that money?"

"What is this money you keep talking about?" Sam asked.

"It's nothing," Jonah said. "I just need you guys to hang tight until I get this squared away. I'm sure it's just a simple misunderstanding."

The elevator stopped at the fifth floor, and they made their way to their room at the end of the hall. It contained two double beds, a small desk, and an old television. A wall AC unit dripped water into a plastic bucket on the linoleum floor. Gavin pulled back the curtains and looked out onto a field of palm trees and half-constructed concrete buildings. He'd been here less than a day, but his impression was that Gabon was a country with a serious lack of follow-through. It was shortly after noon, and a tide of clouds had blotted out the sun. "How does this factor into our original itinerary?" he asked.

"It doesn't," Jonah said.

"But I assume you have a plan."

"Not at the moment, but I will soon."

"When will you be back?" Sam asked, flipping through a worn magazine she'd picked up off the desk. Some color had returned to her face, and she looked slightly better than she had at the train station.

"Soon," Jonah said.

"So we're supposed to just sit here and wait for you?" Gavin asked. "What happened to the guy who was supposed to pick us up? Your friend we were gonna stay with?"

"I can't get a hold of him, but I left a message telling him to meet you here. I gave him your name and room number. I also told the woman at the front desk. He probably just got held up. If worse comes to worst, you can sleep here tonight and I'll meet you at his place in the morning."

"And what are we supposed to do until then?" Gavin asked.

"Hang out by the pool. The restaurant's supposed to be nice."

"This is unreal," Gavin said, appalled by his brother's insouciance. "If you insist on involving us in your sketchy bullshit, you could at least have the decency to tell us what's going on."

"If I knew I would tell you," Jonah said. "But I honestly don't. I'm sorry."

"You've got until noon tomorrow," Gavin said. "If you aren't back by then, Sam and I are returning to Chicago and proceeding with my original plan."

"No, we're not," Sam said, hanging a shirt in the small wooden armoire.

"Yes, we are."

"I'll be back," Jonah said. "I promise." He tossed a wad of francs on the desk and made for the door. "Dinner's on me."

"That's so generous of you," Gavin said as the door slammed shut.

BECAUSE THE AIR CONDITIONER was broken and because there was no working fan and because they could think of nothing else to do, they took Jonah's advice and spent the afternoon by the pool. It was small, yet surprisingly clean, ringed by a chain-link fence and a few plastic loungers. They were the only ones there.

"So what happened with Renee?" Sam asked, sitting along the edge of the pool, kicking her legs back and forth. She looked shockingly thin in the orange one-piece bathing suit she'd bought from the gift shop, and for the first time, Gavin noticed the bruises stamped on her forearm.

"She's camping in Joshua Tree," he said, hiking his jeans up to his knees and sitting next to Sam at the pool's edge.

"I thought she was coming to Chicago with you."

"She was supposed to. But then we got into a fight and she decided to spend Christmas with friends."

"That seems drastic."

"That's Renee."

"So you broke up then?"

Gavin ran his hand along the water. "I don't know. I haven't spoken to her in a while."

"I think that means you broke up."

"Probably."

Sam lowered herself into the pool. "I never really liked her if that's any consolation."

"It's not, but I appreciate your honesty."

She swam to the other end, then circled back to her brother, her hands gripping the pool's edge. "So Mom told me not to ask about your show, but I'm going to anyway."

"That's very obedient of you," Gavin said.

"Why did they cancel it?"

"Because it wasn't very good."

"Yeah, Mom sent me a DVD with some of the episodes. It's pretty bad, no offense."

"Yes," Gavin said. "That seems to be the consensus."

"So what are you gonna do now?"

"That, Sam, is an excellent question." And one for which he had no answer. The plain truth was that the auditions were coming less frequently these days, and there was no denying the trend would continue. He often wondered if he should cut his losses and find a more stable line of work like his mother suggested, but he had no experience aside from a few stints in the hospitality industry. Sam's talent was undeniable, and though she'd dug herself a mighty hole, Gavin believed she would eventually climb out. And Jonah, if he wasn't arrested, would continue his elephant thing, which, though Gavin didn't understand it, appeared to have some merit. Jonah had degrees and Sam had talent, whereas Gavin had nothing but failed relationships and the wreckage of an unremarkable acting career.

"I'm sorry," Sam said, scooping a beetle from the water's surface and gently placing it along the pool's edge.

"For what?" Gavin asked.

"For all of this."

"You don't have to apologize."

"I know I don't, but I want to. Or maybe I just want to explain myself. Either way, just hear me out." She took a deep breath, as if she were about to say something she'd been rehearsing. "Do you remember when I was little—maybe five or six—and I used to hide in that closet we had in the basement?"

Gavin laughed, because he remembered it very clearly. "You were a strange kid."

"And remember the time I locked myself in there?"

Gavin nodded. "I still don't know why there was a lock on a coat closet."

"Exactly. But the point is, there *was* a lock. And I *knew* there was a lock. And I'd been told not to play in there because we all knew how easy it was to get locked in there. But for whatever reason, I did it anyway. I guess I wasn't thinking, or I didn't believe it would happen, whatever. It doesn't matter. Somehow, I locked myself in there, and I remember it being so dark, darker than anything I'd ever experienced. And I was pounding on the door for an hour, but nobody could hear me because you guys were all upstairs. I remember crying so hard that I worried I would use up all the oxygen and suffocate and die in that closet." Gavin could see her bottom lip start to tremble. "So that's what happened," she continued. "I locked myself in that fucking closet again. And now I can't get out, and I hate myself for being in this position." She wiped her eyes with the back of her hand. "I don't know why I'm telling you this. I guess I just don't want you to think that I'm a bad person. This isn't who I am. This isn't me."

Gavin shook his head. "I don't think you're a bad person, Sam."

"But *I* do."

"Then you need to forgive yourself."

She turned her head and looked off into the distance. "I don't know how."

Gavin reached his hand out, and she took it, resting her forehead against the pool's edge. He couldn't tell if she was still crying. He wasn't sure what to say and so he said nothing, instead turning his attention to a turtle struggling to make its way over a crack in the concrete.

After a moment, Sam dipped her head beneath the water in a kind of emotional reset. When she surfaced, she pulled her hair behind her ears and exhaled. "Sorry, I just needed to say that."

"Feel better now?" Gavin asked.

She nodded.

"You hungry?"

"I could probably eat something. What did you have in mind?"

Gavin was about to suggest they try the hotel restaurant when an orange flash stretched across the sky and a charge of hot wind shoved him into the pool. When he finally surfaced, he looked back at the hotel and saw a smoking black hole where the restaurant used to be.

SAMANTHA

THERE WAS GLASS IN HER MOUTH. That's the first thing she noticed. She spit out water and a shard of window came with it. She waded toward the edge of the pool, her vision frayed, her mouth tasting of blood and chlorine. She looked to Gavin, who was climbing the stairs of the pool. Smoke billowed from what was left of the hotel.

"What happened?" she yelled, though she knew the answer.

"Are you hurt?" Gavin called back.

"I'm okay."

"Stay there. Don't move."

Sam lifted herself from the pool and tried to make sense of the scene. Everywhere she looked were blackened pieces of things she could have identified thirty seconds ago, but which now struck her as complete nonsense. *Disjointed* was the only word she could think of. She watched a man emerge zombielike from inside the smoking mess, holding his hands in front of his body, his face glazed with blood. Feathers floated on the water. A charred spoon smoldered in the grass. She began walking, despite Gavin's orders, toward the blast zone, the ground littered with small pieces of concrete that burned her feet like tiny coals.

Another man ran from the smoldering hotel, yelling "*Allez-vous en! Allez-vous en!*" Sam didn't know what he was saying but the fear on his face convinced her to turn around. The man grabbed her by the arm and pulled her away, and it was fortunate timing because a few seconds later another smaller blast went off, and it appeared that any unlucky soul left inside the restaurant was no more.

In the ensuing chaos people with varying degrees of injury fled from the ruins of the hotel. A woman Sam recognized as the receptionist escorted an elderly man by the arm, while two members of the kitchen staff—young men in chef's whites—wrapped a woman's leg with a tablecloth. A little girl, maybe eight or nine, sat in the grass with her head in her knees, seemingly unharmed but crying uncontrollably. Sam looked over and saw Gavin trying to restrain a man with skin dripping from his forearms from sinking his burning limbs into the pool water. She paced in circles in the grass, unsure what to do.

An ambulance arrived on the scene, and a woman with what looked like a toolbox ran to the man with melting skin. She sat him on the ground and began dressing his wounds. Two paramedics entered the hotel with a dispiriting lack of urgency, as if they'd resigned themselves to a purely janitorial role.

Sam looked up and saw her brother walking toward her wearing a pained expression. "What is it?" she asked.

"My back," he said.

She spun him around, inspecting for injuries, and that's when she discovered the splash of crimson, bubbling skin printed across his back.

"Jesus," she said.

"Is it bad?"

She had to will herself not to gag. "I think it probably looks worse than it is."

"It burns like hell."

"You need to go to the hospital."

Gavin craned his neck to get a look at the mottled skin. "Find something to bandage it with."

"I don't know how."

"Then find someone who does," he snapped.

Sam ran to the ambulance, which had now been joined by two others. A procession of police trucks and military vehicles was arriving from down the road. Sam motioned to one of the female medics, who rushed with her over to Gavin. The medic went to work on his back while Sam leaned close to her brother, holding his hand because she could think of nothing else to do.

"Are there still people inside?" Gavin asked.

"I don't know," Sam said. "More ambulances are showing up. It looks bad."

"We never should have come here," he said. "This was a terrible idea."

SAM SAT IN THE HOSPITAL waiting room, surrounded by a handful of locals, most of whom, like herself, were either guests or employees of the hotel. Sitting across from her was a young woman on a cellphone, speaking hurried French. When the woman hung up, Sam asked if she had any details on what had happened, but the woman greeted her with a blank, uncomprehending stare. Hoping to get some clarity, Sam walked over and questioned the receptionist, whose limited English did little to clear up her confusion.

She began walking the halls. Her body still vibrated and she couldn't shake the images now lodged in her mind, all that blood and destruction. She was looking for the restroom when she noticed a nurse exiting a storage closet, so she poked her head in for a closer look. What she discovered was an unlocked cabinet containing an assortment of pharmaceuticals. She scanned the shelves of pills, trying to decipher the French labels, all those vowels, each bottle only marginally different from the one preceding it. She wasn't picky, any opioid would suffice: Percocet, Oxy, she didn't care. And it wasn't entirely uncalled for either, because she had survived an *explosion,* after all, so yes, she was entitled to something for the pain. She found a bottle labeled OXYNORMORO, which sounded pretty similar to Oxycontin, then swallowed one and emptied the rest into her pocket. *That'll do,* she thought.

Stepping into the hallway, she nearly ran into a lean, youngish man being pushed in a wheelchair. "Sorry," she said, moving around him.

The man's right leg was set in a cast, but despite the obvious pain he must have been in, he wore the large, cheerful smile of someone grateful to be alive. When he saw Sam his eyes lit up. "You must be her," he said, clapping his hands together in the manner of someone receiving terrific news. "You must be Jonah's sister. Oh yes, thanks to God!"

Sam wasn't sure what to make of this jolly, injured man who seemed to think he knew her, but seeing as how he was confined to a wheelchair she assumed he was harmless. The female nurse who was pushing him smiled at her.

"I know your brother," the man continued, reaching up to shake her hand with both of his. "I'm Jonah's friend. My name is Laurent. I'm here for you. I'm very happy you're alive."

"You're the guy who was supposed to pick us up?" Sam asked.

"I came to look for you at the hotel," Laurent said. "I was in the lobby, but then—*BOOM*—there was the explosion." He illustrated this by making a blooming motion with his hands. "Next thing, I'm on the floor, trapped under concrete. And now my leg," he said, shaking his head. "It's no good."

"Jesus," Sam said, shocked that he'd been inside the hotel at the time of the explosion. "I'm so sorry."

"But *you're* okay?" Laurent asked.

"Yeah," Sam said. "I'm fine, but my brother Gavin has some pretty serious burns. The doctors are looking at him now. Thankfully, we were outside when it happened."

"Oh, good," Laurent said, relieved. "And where is Jonah?"

"I was hoping you'd know that. He dropped us off at the hotel and left with some British guy. You know him?"

Laurent shrugged.

"He wouldn't tell us much," Sam said. "Just that you'd be by to pick us up and take us back to your restaurant. We weren't sure if you were coming."

"Yes, but I was late because my car was having trouble. I'm very sorry this happened to you. I don't know what's going on. As you can see, everything is very strange now."

Strange was the operative word. Between the military-style police force in Libreville, Jonah's apprehension at the train station, and the massive explosion at the hotel, there hadn't been a moment of normalcy since arriving in this dizzyingly foreign country. And now here was the man they'd been looking for, this incredibly kind man whose generosity and unfortunate timing had placed him at the center of the blast zone. Sam was shocked that he still wanted anything to do with them.

"Sam!" a voice called. She looked behind her and noticed Gavin approaching from down the hall. He walked delicately, as if balancing something on his head, and he wore old sneakers and a T-shirt with the words GABON TELECOM printed in an orange sans serif font, a donation from the hospital, she guessed.

"What did the doctor say?" Sam asked.

"She applied some kind of gel. I'm supposed to come back in a few days to change the bandages." He looked down at the man in the wheelchair. "Who's this?"

"I'm Laurent," he said, extending his hand. "Jonah's friend."

"What happened to your leg?" Gavin asked.

"He was at the hotel," Sam said. "During the explosion."

"Fuck," Gavin said. "But you're okay?" He looked down at the cast. "I mean aside from your leg?"

"Yes," Laurent said. "I will be fine. Your brother though . . ." He shook his head, dismayed. "He seems to be in some kind of trouble."

"I know," Gavin said. "Do you know what's going on?"

"I think he got caught up with some bad people," Laurent said.

"That's an understatement," Gavin said.

Two hospital workers pushed a gurney down the hall, and the nurse maneuvered Laurent out of the way.

"What do we do now?" Sam asked.

"Well," Laurent said. "I have to see the doctor, but afterward we can go to my restaurant and wait for your brother."

"I'm actually thinking just the opposite," Gavin said. "I think we should get back on that train and go home. I have no desire to vacation in a war zone."

"Gavin," Sam said. "You're being ridiculous. We can't leave without Jonah."

"Actually, we can. He got himself into this. He can get himself out."

"Don't be an ass."

"*I'm* being an ass? We almost died earlier. We never would have been at that place if it weren't for him. This was his stupid idea, and it's not going very well."

"Go," Sam said to Laurent. "Get your leg looked at. We'll wait for you in the lobby."

JONAH

THEY BOUNCED ALONG A MUDDY logging road, splashing through rivulets of rainwater, the forest alive with birdsong. Jonah and Edwin were in the back seat, while the two rangers sat up front, chatting in French. Edwin pulled a loaf of bread and a jar of peanut butter from a military issued backpack. "You grow sick of the food out here," he said, using a Swiss Army knife to lather a slice of bread. "But you probably know that."

"I was on a strictly noodle-based diet," Jonah said.

Edwin offered Jonah the jar of peanut butter. "Sandwich?"

"I'd prefer an explanation."

"You're a smart guy, Jonah. Academic like yourself, I figured you would have put the pieces together by now."

"I have theories, but I'd like facts."

"Sure," Edwin said, biting into his sandwich. "Let's get you caught up."

Edwin explained that he was a former soldier in the British Army who had become dispirited by the poaching crisis. Five years ago, he quit his job with a private contractor and established an NGO called the Elephant Conservation Task Force. With support from INTER-POL and the International Fund for Animal Welfare, Edwin and his team of rangers spent their days tracking key players in the ivory trade.

Their work spanned twelve nations and involved hundreds of officers from a spectrum of NGOs, customs agencies, airport security, and various ministries of tourism. As a result of this unprecedented inter-agency cooperation, they'd been able to monitor trafficking routes as well as survey ports and markets, all of which had culminated in the seizure of nearly two tons of ivory in the past six years. But despite their success, large populations of elephants were still being slaugh-tered every month, most of them in West African nations like Gabon.

Edwin had been tracking Slinky's network for three months but had uncovered nothing aside from a handful of ghost stories. It wasn't until customs agents in Chicago detected ivory in Jonah's luggage that they had their first solid lead. U.S officials contacted INTERPOL, who in turn contacted Edwin. Rather than arresting Jonah at the air-port, they elected to play the long game. They tapped his phone, which led them to Andre, who, Edwin explained, had been arrested while Jonah and his siblings were sailing over the Atlantic. Edwin said that while he took a certain amount of pride in the confiscation of eighty pounds of ivory, his real interest was in choking out the source, which was why they had decided to sit back and wait for Jonah to re-turn with Slinky's money.

Jonah looked at the vegetation blurring past the window. He felt like a fool for believing things could have gone so smoothly. It had all seemed too easy, too good to be true, and it turned out it was. Every-thing that had happened in Chicago had been a farce, orchestrated by unseen hands, a carefully designed operation resulting in this, the thing he'd feared all along. "So you knew about this the whole time I was in Chicago?"

"Of course," Edwin said with a smile. "Did you seriously think you could smuggle eighty pounds of ivory in a suitcase without any-one noticing?" It was a rhetorical question, so he didn't wait for a re-sponse. "What can you tell me that I haven't already covered?"

Jonah scrambled to think of something non-incriminating to say. "Just that I was unwillingly caught up in this, which I assume you al-ready know. My interest is in studying elephants, not killing them."

"Which is why I find this so ironic," Edwin said.

"It wasn't a choice."

"You could have said no."

Jonah shook his head. "If you know anything about the man you're looking for, you would understand why that wasn't an option."

"When did you last speak to him?" Edwin asked, his tone shifting from condescending to interrogative.

"I thought you were listening to my phone calls. You should know the answer."

Edwin smiled and tossed the remainder of his sandwich out the window. "Tell me about Osman."

"I was hoping you could do that," Jonah said.

"I understand you met with him."

"I watched him cut a man's neck, but I never had the pleasure of shaking his hand."

"This was in Libreville?"

"Yeah."

Edwin began writing in a small notebook he pulled from his backpack. "Where?"

"An abandoned factory of some kind. Garment factory or something like that." Aware that he was being cross-examined, Jonah imagined everything he said being repeated back to him in a courtroom. "Am I under arrest or what?"

"Not yet," Edwin said, continuing to write. "So was it your first time meeting him—this Osman fellow?"

"First and only."

"He's involved with Boko Haram," Edwin said, looking up from his notebook. "They use the ivory to finance their operations."

"I know. Slinky told me."

"What else did he tell you?"

"Just that Osman is a savage, which is quite a statement coming from a man who used a dull machete to hack the face off an elephant."

"But he knows him?"

"He knows *of* him," Jonah said. They passed a small village, where a group of men eyed them suspiciously.

"So they don't work together?" Edwin asked.

"I thought you said you were listening to my phone calls? These were all things he told me—and apparently you—when I spoke to him in Chicago. I know nothing more than what he told me over the phone. Slinky worked with Mateo, the guy who drove me to Libreville, the one Osman killed. Mateo was an employee of my buddy Laurent."

"Who's Laurent?"

"That came out wrong," Jonah said, trying to walk it back. "Laurent isn't involved in any of this. I want to make that clear. What I meant was that Mateo worked at the bar Laurent owned. It turned out he also moonlighted for Slinky. He's the one who drove me to Libreville. And he's the one who met with Osman, though from what Slinky tells me it wasn't a meeting he'd personally authorized. It sounds like Mateo went behind Slinky's back and tried to sell the ivory to Osman, but Osman didn't want to pay for it so he cut his neck."

"Do you know what he looks like?" Edwin asked.

"Who? Osman?"

"Yeah."

"He's an older guy, in his sixties, I'd guess. Walks with a hunch and travels with a big posse. Wish I could tell you more, but like I said, our time together was brief."

"It's no mystery that Boko Haram is behind the political unrest," Edwin said. "They tried to work their way into the government through the election, but their puppet candidate didn't fare so well. Luckily, the Gabonese people were sharp enough to see through the charade. But I guess when your guy loses by forty points, you lick your wounds by reverting back to what you do best."

"I'm getting the impression this is about more than a few dead elephants."

"It *is* about the elephants, for me at least. But there are many other people involved now, people whose interest in Slinky and Osman goes far beyond elephants." Edwin slapped Jonah on the shoulder. "You poor sap. You have no idea what you've gotten yourself into, do you?"

THEY EVENTUALLY ARRIVED AT a small concrete building hidden in the forest. It looked like a one-room schoolhouse, with an enormous satellite dish perched atop the roof. A uniformed soldier greeted the truck.

"*Bonsoir,*" Edwin said, shaking the soldier's hand.

"*Il y a eu un incident,*" the soldier said. "*Venez voir.*"

"What kind of accident?" Jonah asked.

Edwin followed the man into the building, while the two rangers sitting up front stepped out for a smoke. Jonah sat in the back seat, watching a deranged rooster hammer at the dirt. He thought about calling Gavin or Sam to see if Laurent had finally shown up, but Edwin had confiscated his phone back at the train station. A few minutes later, Jonah heard the thump of helicopter blades approaching, and he stepped outside and discovered a military chopper hovering above the compound, kicking up a cloud of dust. The pilot touched down in a grassy clearing ringed by a half dozen dirt-colored military jeeps. Edwin appeared from the building and went to join his rangers, who were no longer smoking but standing at attention. As the blades continued spinning, bending the branches of the surrounding trees, a man in a decorated military uniform descended the steps, escorted by three armed soldiers. He was a tall, muscular man with wire-rimmed eyeglasses and a green military beret. Edwin shook the officer's hand and followed him inside.

"Hey!" Jonah yelled after them, but the men had already disappeared. He looked to the rangers, who had wandered over to chat with the soldiers from the helicopter. "What am I supposed to be doing here?" he yelled in French, but his words were swallowed by the thwack of helicopter blades. The men didn't seem particularly

concerned with his detainment, so he walked to the building where
Edwin had gone and pushed open the door. The room was unfur-
nished save for a small folding table and a weathered Gabonese flag
pinned to the wall. Edwin and the officer and a couple soldiers stood
around the table, listening to a garbled French voice emanating from
a handheld radio. *"We've got seven confirmed dead, but that number could
rise. Casualties are in the dozens. Most are being taken to the local hospital."*

"Are we collecting evidence?" the officer asked.

*"We're doing forensics, but it's pretty obvious that Edwin's team was the
target."*

"When did it happen?" Edwin asked in French.

"Shortly after one P.M."

"How does this affect my mission?"

"It doesn't."

Edwin looked up and saw Jonah standing in the doorway. "Get
out!"

"What's going on?" Jonah asked.

"I said *leave*."

"Tell me what happened!"

Jonah felt an arm around his waist, and then he was being dragged
out of the room. "Take him back to the truck," Edwin yelled.

EDWIN RETURNED THIRTY MINUTES later and joined Jonah in the
back seat while the rangers loaded the truck with an alarming cache of
weapons. It seemed whatever was about to happen would be violent,
though Jonah hoped his involvement would be purely administrative,
like a witness fingering a bank robber from behind the safety of one-
way glass. A few minutes later, the rangers hopped in the front seat
and steered the truck into the forest. It was growing dark now, the
headlights splashing across tree trunks. "Tell me what you were talking about in there!" Jonah yelled.

"There was another bombing," Edwin said, as if it were becoming
a regular occurrence.

"Where?"

"Libreville."

"And you think Osman had something to do with it?"

"It seems pretty likely. But that's someone else's concern."

"What's *your* concern?"

Edwin pulled a map from his backpack and spread it across his lap. "Finding Slinky."

"And you want me to take you to him?"

"Exactly."

"So I'm the bait?" Jonah asked, disturbed by what he was hearing.

"Don't think of it like that," Edwin said, studying the map in the dull glow of the truck's interior light.

"If you think he's just gonna roll over, you're mistaken."

"I don't expect him to roll over." Edwin nodded to the rangers sitting up front. "That's why I have these guys."

"So you plan to kill him?"

"Of course not. I never set out to kill anyone, but I'm willing to if that's what it takes." Edwin turned to Jonah as if he were about to deliver some significant news. "Here's the thing you should understand about me, Jonah. I've spent the last five years of my life chasing people like Slinky for very little reward other than the fleeting sense that my work is making some kind of positive impact. I've had two of my guys killed and I've personally taken bullets to the leg, shoulder, and stomach, the last of which nearly killed me. Yet every time I apprehend one of these bastards, they pay off some government official and return to the forest a month later. The problem is there's a low-risk, high-reward structure in place. What do you think Slinky would be doing if he weren't hunting elephants? He'd be slumming it in the oil fields twelve hours a day like anyone else with a grade school education. He's no fool. He knows there's a tremendous amount of money to be made so long as he greases the proper palms. So why not, right? What's he got to lose? My goal is to correct that type of thinking, make sure people like Slinky understand that there are consequences to their actions. I'm a pretty reasonable guy, Jonah, but there's nothing that enrages me more than the slaughter of helpless animals. I think you'd probably agree with me on that."

"Of course," Jonah said, strangely moved by Edwin's speech.

"I know quite a bit about you, probably more than you realize. And despite what you've done, I do believe your story. But there's some pretty damning evidence connecting you to Slinky, so unless you want to test your luck in the courts, you're going to play for our team. Understood?"

Once again Jonah found himself hostage to someone else's agenda. "Sure," he said. "Whatever you want."

"First thing I'd like you to do is call Slinky and set a time for us to meet tomorrow, preferably somewhere remote." Edwin handed Jonah's phone to him.

"Now?"

"Please."

Jonah dialed, hoping for voicemail, but Slinky picked up after a few rings. "Elephant Man," he shouted into the phone. "You are back. How was everything? You have a nice time in Chicago?"

"I have your money," Jonah said. "Let's meet at my camp tomorrow morning like we discussed."

"Of course."

"I'll be there at nine."

"Very good. I appreciate what you did, Elephant Man. I think maybe you and me, we can do more business together. I'll make it worth your time, huh?"

"I don't think so."

"Okay, sure. We'll discuss tomorrow."

Jonah tapped his phone off and looked to Edwin. "Can I make another call? I need to check in with my brother and sister."

Edwin nodded, and Jonah dialed. After a few rings he was greeted by Gavin's curt voicemail message, instructing him to leave a brief message. "Call me back," Jonah said. "Let me know if Laurent showed up. I'll be there tomorrow if everything goes as planned. I'm sorry about all this. I'll make it up to you." He handed the phone back to Edwin.

"I'm curious," Edwin said. "Why did you drag your brother and sister into this?"

He wanted to explain that he'd intended to get his sister clean, return the money to Slinky, and resume his peaceful existence studying elephants in the wild, but he realized how naïve that sounded. It wasn't as if he had some grand plan that Edwin had derailed. It was more like a half-baked itinerary sketched on a cocktail napkin in a taxi on the way to the airport. "I don't know," he said, shaking his head. "It wasn't supposed to turn out like this."

THEY ARRIVED AT LAURENT'S an hour later. Jonah went to retrieve his camping gear, but the door was locked and the place was dark. He hoped maybe they were asleep, exhausted after the long train ride, but Laurent rarely locked the place, and it became clear that his siblings had not arrived. He walked to the house behind the restaurant, where Helen was sitting on the front porch, chatting with a friend. "Helen," he called, hurrying toward her. "It's me, Jonah."

"Jonah," she said, squinting into the darkness. "What are you doing here?"

"I'm looking for Laurent. Have you seen him?"

"He's not with you?"

"No," Jonah said, looking around, hoping he might materialize from the dark.

"He called from the hospital. He was very worried about you."

"The hospital?" Jonah said. "Why was he at the hospital?"

"Because of the explosion."

"What are you talking about?"

She stood and walked over to him. "You don't know?"

"Helen, what explosion are you talking about?"

She shook her head at the tragedy of it all. "There was an explosion at the hotel. The one you told him to go to—where your brother and sister were waiting. Laurent was looking for them when it happened. I thought you were there, no? They took him to the hospital. His leg is broken."

"So where are Sam and Gavin?" Jonah asked, flushed with panic.

"I don't know. He couldn't find them."

"When did you talk to him?"

Helen shook her head, trying to remember. "Maybe three, four hours ago."

Jonah felt a rage blooming in his chest. He charged back to the truck and discovered Edwin's sleeping body pressed against the passenger-side door, which he wrenched open. Edwin rolled out and fell to the dirt. "You fucking liar," Jonah yelled. "Tell me what the hell is going on!"

The rangers jumped out of the truck and drew their guns, shouting French profanities. Edwin crawled to his feet and ordered the men to lower their weapons. "I nodded off there for a minute," he said with a sleepy smile.

"You said the explosion was in Libreville. You lied to me."

"I didn't want to worry you," Edwin said, dusting himself off.

"Where are my brother and sister?" Jonah shouted.

"I don't know. We're trying to figure that out."

"What do you mean you don't know?" Jonah was pacing, burning with the idea that his siblings might be dead. "How do you not know? How the fuck is this possible, Edwin?"

"There was an explosion at the hotel."

"I know that! What kind of explosion?"

"A large one," Edwin admitted. "But there's nothing that leads us to believe your siblings were injured."

"But there's also no proof they weren't. Or worse."

"Correct."

"Have you tried calling the hospital?" Jonah asked. "Have you tried to do *anything*?"

"I have," he said with a quiet resignation. "The lines are jammed."

"Surely, there's something you can do besides tell me everything is fine! I need more than that."

"I'm sorry," Edwin said, and his voice at least suggested he meant it. "I wish I could."

"Then take me there," Jonah said, determined to do something.

"The hospital?"

"Yes!"

"You won't get in. It's on lockdown for fear of another attack. We'll get word soon. Until then, all we can do is wait."

"Fuck!" he yelled, feeling thoroughly useless. He went and sat on the porch of Laurent's restaurant, the place he'd spent so many afternoons nursing beers, waiting for batteries to charge. Everything that had gone wrong thus far could be classified as a string of inconvenient setbacks, but the news that his brother and sister may have died in the hotel where he'd instructed them to wait was enough to level him. He'd spent the past ten years on college campuses and had learned nothing about what it meant to be a responsible adult. His carelessness had endangered everyone he loved. He put his face in his hands.

"Look," Edwin said, shining a flashlight at his feet. "I understand you're worried. I don't blame you. But I really believe they're fine. I was told the explosion took place in the restaurant and most of the fatalities were confined to the kitchen staff. Information is trickling in, and I've requested to be notified as soon as we have confirmation that they're okay. Because I'm certain they *are* okay. But in the meantime, we still have a job to do, and I need you to focus on the task at hand. We need to get moving."

"That's easy for you to say," Jonah said.

"Come on, Jonah. It's getting late."

Jonah gathered his camping gear from the restaurant and went back to Edwin and the two rangers, who now had large backpacks hoisted over their shoulders, automatic weapons strapped to the sides. By the light of their headlamps, they set off into the forest, Jonah leading the way. It was never a good idea to hike at night due to the chance of spooking an elephant, and so they filled the silence with their voices. Jonah asked Edwin about the genesis of his organization, which he seemed happy to discuss.

Edwin explained that he had spent two years trying to figure out where ECTF fit in the constellation of wildlife NGOs. He interviewed high-ranking officials at some of the more well-known outfits, and from what he could tell most were a well-intentioned but toothless collection of bureaucrats with an impressive fleet of SUVs. Their offices, which resembled five-star hotels, were fortified complexes situated next to embassies, as far removed from the front lines of the ivory trade as he was from his home back in London. When he inquired about what they were doing to enforce the existing laws against ivory poaching, he was told about the workshops they conducted with government officials, the educational groundwork that had been laid, their strategic ten-year plan.

"Workshops," Edwin said, shaking his head at the insanity of it. "Poachers are mowing down elephants with machine guns and these idiots are conducting workshops. Can you believe that? If the projections are accurate, there won't be any elephants left to protect in ten years, yet there's no sense of urgency from these guys." Edwin used a machete to hack his way through a tangle of understory creeping across the trail. " 'The government is impossible to work with,' " he mimicked, in a whiny, nasally voice. " 'We can't tell the government what to do.' " He scoffed. "So that's when I took matters into my own hands."

Edwin went on to explain how he'd channeled his frustration into what became his first undercover operation. He arranged a meeting with a local poacher looking to unload six elephant tusks. Edwin fixed a hidden camera to his backpack and met the poacher at a hotel in Libreville, where he was presented with the product. He told the poacher he would meet him there the next day with the money, then went back to the police chief and showed him the video, demanding that he do something about it. The chief finally relented and assigned two of his officers to go with Edwin to arrest the man. The guy ended up only serving six months in prison, but the operation proved a moral success, giving Edwin the confidence to press forward.

"Then what?" Jonah asked.

"We secured seed money from donors back in London," Edwin continued. "And I recruited a recent Cambridge graduate to act as a legal advisor. People started taking notice. Turns out there are a lot of young people disillusioned with the 'air-conditioned apathy' of traditional NGOs. We have an aggressive approach here at ECTF, one that doesn't always sit well with other conservancy organizations, but I think our results speak for themselves. We currently have investigations underway in four West African nations, but this is the largest and most pressing. I can't get into the details, but we have reason to believe that if we're able to nab Slinky, then Osman and other key members of the trafficking ring will soon follow."

THEY ARRIVED AT JONAH'S camp shortly after midnight. He pitched his tent, while Edwin and his team set up a separate camp a quarter mile down the trail. Sleep was useless, and Jonah spent most of the night contemplating the consequences of his errors. His mother used to talk about the dark hours she spent lying awake, fretting over her children, and Jonah finally understood what she was talking about. It was a terrible thing not knowing. It was a terrible thing to let a mind wander unleashed through the catacombs of possibility, because it somehow, invariably, always found its way to the thing it feared most.

When he was a kid, his mom used to read to him from a book of children's Bible stories. His favorite was an elementary retelling of the Book of Jonah. He liked to imagine himself as Jonah, the rebel who instead of going to Nineveh to tell everyone to stop being bad, defies God and gets on a boat with a bunch of sailors and ends up being swallowed by a whale and spending days thrashing around inside its belly. And that's how he felt now, trapped inside a prison of his own making. But in the Bible, the whale spits Jonah out after three days, and he more or less gets on with life. He remembered his mom explaining the moral of the story, which had something to do with obedience and how good people sometimes do bad things, but that God forgives all.

It seemed reasonable as a five-year-old, but now, almost twenty-six years later, he wasn't so sure. Despite his Catholic upbringing, he'd fallen away from the church in recent years, but with nothing left to comfort him, he folded his hands, looked to the canvas ceiling of his tent, and prayed for a peaceful resolution, for the safe return of his brother and sister, for a salvation he probably didn't deserve.

GAVIN

HE AWOKE WITH A CAT next to his head, a feral-looking calico that glared at him as if demanding an explanation for his presence. He swatted it away and watched it leap onto a table, where it folded itself into a ball. He stood and stretched, his neck stiff from sleeping facedown in a nest of blankets on the floor. He went to the bathroom and removed his shirt and tried to inspect the large bandage covering the burns. He washed his face in the sink, then walked to Laurent's office, where Sam was still sleeping. He had offered her the couch, a flourish of generosity he now regretted. It had been impossibly dark when they'd arrived, but now, as he made his way outside, the village revealed itself.

The sun was making a slow climb over the surrounding forest, stippling the land with fragmented light. A teenager piloting a bicycle draped with bananas passed by, and he watched a woman grilling something over an oil drum. He wanted to call his brother, but his cellphone had disappeared in the explosion. The early morning stillness offered a moment of clarity, a chance to reflect upon his situation, which, he concluded very quickly, was fucked. He felt panicked not knowing where he was, the way he used to feel waking up in the bed of a strange woman after a night of heavy drinking. Standing on Laurent's porch, in his boxer shorts, somewhere in West Africa, his thoughts narrowed to how he might escape. He went back inside and shook Sam awake.

"What?" she said, surfacing from sleep.

"Get up," Gavin said. "We need to get moving."

"Is Jonah here?"

"That's what we need to figure out."

Gavin walked back outside, where he saw Laurent hobbling down the road on a pair of crutches, smiling despite his new handicap.

"Good morning, friend," Laurent called. "You sleep well?" Standing next to Laurent was a slightly younger man balancing a tray of fruit. "We brought some breakfast. You like mangoes?"

"Thanks," Gavin said, reaching for a slice.

"Your sister—she's still sleeping?"

Sam stepped outside, running her fingers through her hair. "Good morning, Laurent," she said. "How's your leg?"

"There's some pain," Laurent said. "But not too bad."

"Have you seen Jonah?" Gavin asked.

"My wife said he showed up last night—before we arrived—but then he went to his camp in the forest. She said he was with the Englishman."

"Do you have a phone I can use?" Gavin asked.

"Sure," Laurent said, handing him an ancient flip phone.

Gavin realized he didn't know his brother's number. "Do you happen to have Jonah's number?" he asked.

"We always spoke in person," Laurent said with a shrug.

Gavin turned to his sister, who shook her head. "I can barely remember my own."

Gavin handed the phone back to Laurent. It burned him that Jonah hadn't upheld his promise to meet them there, but what bothered him even more was that he was now in a situation where he couldn't uphold *his* threat of getting on the next plane back to the States.

"I'm sure he will be back soon," Laurent said.

"I doubt it," Gavin said.

"This is my cousin Remy," Laurent said, introducing his companion. "He is the one who will take you for the Bwiti."

"*Bonsoir*," Remy said. He looked to be in his late thirties, with a sharp receding hairline and a patchy beard. He wore sandals and a loose-fitting dashiki. A leather apron was tied around his waist and his arms were sleeved with colorful bracelets. He offered a smile that suggested his day was off to a significantly better start than Gavin's.

"Before we go, we should discuss the fee," Laurent said.

"What fee?" Gavin asked.

"I told your brother he would have to pay for this. We don't have to settle it now, but Remy and the tribe will need to be compensated."

"I'll let Jonah settle up on that," Gavin said.

Laurent nodded, seemingly satisfied. "Should we go now?" he said, motioning to his car.

"What about Jonah?" Sam asked. "I don't think we should leave without him."

"He can meet us there," Laurent said. "He knows the way to the village."

"Before we follow you into the jungle," Gavin said, "can we discuss what this involves?"

"Of course," Laurent said. "I thought your brother told you, no?"

"He gave us *his* version," Gavin said. "I'd like to hear yours."

Bwiti, Laurent explained, was the name of the spiritual ceremony based around the ingestion of iboga, a powerful hallucinogen that allowed one to revisit the consequences of past actions in order to gain a better understanding of one's true self. His version sounded even more ridiculous than Jonah's, like some new-age hippie speak, but they'd traveled halfway across the world for this, so it seemed pointless to back out now. And besides, Sam appeared willing to give it a try, which was more than could be said for his suggestion.

"You," Laurent said, looking at Sam, "are the *banzie*. You will follow the *n'ganga,* your Bwiti mother, who will guide you to the places you need to go."

"And who is this person?" Sam asked.

"For you, this will be Remy's wife. Her name is Grace."

Remy nodded and smiled.

"How long does it last?" Sam asked. "The ceremony?"

"Two days."

"Oh, wow. Anything else I need to know?"

Laurent went on to explain that though it was very safe, Sam would need to sign a release form absolving Remy's tribe of responsibility should something go wrong.

"Like what?" Gavin asked.

"Just to be careful," Laurent said, dismissing Gavin's concern. "There shouldn't be any problems."

"Yes," Gavin said, "I really hope there aren't any problems seeing as how we're in the middle of nowhere. But just to be clear, what do you mean when you say 'should something go wrong'?"

"It's nothing really," Laurent assured him.

"Well, it's obviously something if you want her to sign a release." Gavin looked to Remy, then back to Laurent. "What are you guys not telling us?"

Laurent looked at the ground, then back to Gavin. "There have been instances of death, but this is very rare."

"Jesus," Gavin said, shaking his head. Jonah's version hadn't mentioned death and it further enforced his belief that this ceremony, like everything else that had occurred thus far, would turn out badly.

"Very small," Remy added with a smile and a little pinching motion of his fingers.

"I should hope so," Gavin said, annoyed that he was just now learning about this.

"And besides," Laurent added. "Sam is young and in good health."

Gavin looked to his sister to gauge her reaction to the news. "You sure you want to do this?"

"Is there an antidote in case things go wrong?" she asked.

Remy flashed Laurent a confused look.

"An antidote," Gavin said. "She wants to know if there's a way to make it stop—if there's a problem."

"No, no," Laurent said, shaking his head. "Nothing like that."

JONAH

"KNOCK, KNOCK." JONAH OPENED HIS eyes to shadows in the tent canvas. He hadn't slept more than a few hours last night, and now that morning had arrived, he wanted only to recover the sleep that had eluded him. Instead, he pulled on a shirt and unzipped the tent to find Edwin standing outside, backlit by the sun.

"Morning," Edwin said, holding a half-eaten banana.

Jonah stepped out of the tent and began lacing up his boots. "Have you heard anything?"

"They're fine."

"How do you know that?"

"Because the deceased have been identified and they weren't on the list." Edwin shoved the rest of the banana into his mouth and tossed the peel on the ground.

"Can I see the list?"

"I don't exactly have it handy, Jonah, but I'd be more than happy to show you once we get back to town. Of course, by that time your brother and sister will most likely be waiting for you."

Jonah wanted to believe him, but he couldn't shake the suspicion that Edwin was lying to ensure Jonah's cooperation with the mission. Regardless, there wasn't much he could do about it now. The two rangers approached from down the trail, rifles slung over their shoulders.

"What's with the guns?" Jonah asked.

"If everything goes smoothly, there won't be any shots fired."

The idea of being shot wasn't something Jonah had considered until now. While Slinky wasn't a paradigm of good faith, Jonah felt relatively confident that so long as he handed over the money, he'd let him go. But Edwin's presence, along with heavily armed men hiding in the trees, complicated the calculus in a way that unsettled him. "Nothing has gone smoothly thus far."

"That's not a winning attitude, Jonah," Edwin said, digging through his backpack. "Take your shirt off."

"Why?"

"So I can mic you," he said, removing a wireless microphone.

"No way," Jonah said. "I'm not wearing a mic."

"Yes," Edwin said. "You are."

"What if he sees it?"

"He won't."

"How can you be sure?"

"Because I've done this before," Edwin said. "Now take off your shirt."

Jonah removed his shirt and Edwin taped the microphone to his chest. "It's not a gun, but it's potentially a lot more damaging. Make sure you speak clearly so we can pick up the conversation. Keep him close if possible. He seems like a chatty fellow, so let him talk as much as he wants. Encourage it. Explain what happened to Mateo. Ask about Osman—see what he knows. The more he talks, the stronger our case."

"And where will you be while this is happening?"

"I'll be in that tree over there," Edwin said, pointing. He turned to the rangers. "These two will be in the bushes behind your tent. We'll have eyes on him the whole time. Once you hand over the money, we'll make the arrest."

"And then what?"

"Then you're done."

"It's that easy?" Jonah assumed there had to be a catch. He wasn't

entirely sure Edwin didn't plan to have him arrested once he'd apprehended Slinky.

Edwin shrugged. "Why not?" He looked at his watch. "We've got
about twenty minutes. Good luck."

The men disappeared into the forest and Jonah sat on a tree stump.
He watched an orange-breasted waxbill dart between trees and heard
a talapoin monkey barking at him from somewhere overhead. With
everything that had happened, he hadn't given much thought to the
elephants, though he resolved to make a trip to the bai once he'd ex-
tricated himself from this mess.

The distant groan of a motorbike ushered him to his feet. Edwin,
who was crouched in dense vegetation fifty meters away, flashed him
a thumbs-up, an insultingly flippant gesture in light of what was about
to transpire. Jonah crawled inside the tent and grabbed the backpack.
When he stepped back outside, he saw a man who was clearly not
Slinky approaching on the motorbike. He was younger, mid-twenties,
a tall, statuesque guy with sharp cheekbones and exceptionally white
teeth. He pulled up next to Jonah and silenced the bike. "You him?"
he asked, dismounting.

"Who are you?" Jonah asked.

"Sterling."

"Where's Slinky?"

"He sent me instead."

"That wasn't what we discussed."

Sterling shrugged.

Jonah looked past the man, hoping to get eyes on the rangers in
order to deliver a signal that this wasn't shaping up the way he'd expected, but he couldn't locate them. "I talked to him yesterday," he
said to Sterling. "He told me he'd be here."

Sterling reached for the backpack, but Jonah pulled it away.

Sterling laughed. "Let's not have a problem."

"I'll give the money to Slinky. No one else."

Sterling pulled a pistol from his waistband and pointed it at Jonah.

"Okay, okay," Jonah said, raising his hands. He had incorrectly assumed this guy was some harmless errand boy. "Put the gun away."

Jonah shimmied the pack off his back, and Sterling holstered the gun in his waistband. As Jonah was handing over the bag, he heard Edwin and his men charging toward them, shouting *"Baisse-toi!"*

Sterling reached for his gun and that's when Jonah saw a muzzle flash out of the corner of his eye. Sterling's body jolted in the manner of someone releasing a violent sneeze, then collapsed to the ground. As Edwin and the soldiers rushed in, Jonah stood above the man, watching blood leak from his head and pool in the dirt. "What the hell was that?" he shouted at Edwin. "I thought you said there wouldn't be any shots fired."

"I just saved your life, pal," Edwin said, leaning down to check for a pulse. "You could be a little more gracious."

"That wasn't even him!"

"What do you mean?"

"That wasn't Slinky," Jonah said, incredulous that Edwin wasn't able to recognize the man he'd been tracking.

"Then who was it?"

"I don't know. One of his guys."

"I thought you said he was meeting you here."

"That's what I thought too. Maybe he got spooked—I don't know." Jonah took off his shirt and peeled away the microphone.

"Well, this is a fucking mess," Edwin said, grabbing the bloody backpack from off the ground and slinging it over his shoulder.

"Yeah," Jonah said, tossing the microphone at Edwin. "*Your* mess."

JONAH LED EDWIN AND his rangers back to town. He'd witnessed his second execution in two weeks and though he felt no sadness at the man's death, he was disturbed by the recklessness of Edwin's method, his cowboy approach to wildlife law enforcement. As the centerpiece in Edwin's strategy—if one could call it that—Jonah worried he may become a necessary casualty in whatever happened next. And there would be something next; Edwin had assured him of that.

Back in town, they settled at Laurent's restaurant, where Jonah found Helen tending to a stew in the kitchen. She told him that Laurent and Jonah's brother and sister had shown up late last night, shortly after he had set off into the woods. "They left this morning to go to the Bwiti," she said. "So do not worry. Everything is good."

"I told you," Edwin said, standing in the door of the kitchen.

Jonah wrapped his arms around her and kissed her on the forehead. It was the confirmation he'd been waiting for. "Did Laurent go with them?" he asked.

"And Remy too," Helen said. "They waited for you this morning, but when you didn't come they left."

"Thank you, Helen." Jonah walked to the dining room and helped himself to a beer. Edwin placed a call to an INTERPOL agent back in Libreville, trying to explain the botched operation. Jonah took a special satisfaction in knowing that for once he was not the cause of the shit storm swirling around him. Because there was nothing for him to do at the moment, he stepped onto the porch and drank two more beers in quick succession. Edwin, who normally possessed the steely composure of a military general, was scrambling around like an understaffed restaurant manager. As the day wore on, Jonah's exhaustion from the night before caught up with him, and he lifted his feet onto an overturned plastic bucket, tossed an arm over his eyes, and drifted into a delicious sleep.

"JONAH," A VOICE WHISPERED.

He blinked awake and saw Helen standing above him. "Hey," he said, sitting up.

"I'm sorry to interrupt your nap, but I need to talk to you about your friend. The Englishman." She scanned the surroundings to make sure Edwin couldn't hear what she was about to say.

"What's up?" he asked.

"Slinky was here this morning," she whispered. "He asked if I had seen you, but I told him no. He asked me if I'd seen another white man, but again I said no. But he did not believe me and became very angry. He said I was lying. I'm very sorry, Jonah, but I think he knows about this Englishman. I think he knows what is happening with you."

"It's okay, Helen," he said, trying to reassure her. "You didn't do anything wrong." Someone must have tipped Slinky off after seeing Edwin's truck drive through town late last night, which would explain why he'd sent a decoy in his place. Jonah had considered this possibility and even thought about relaying his concerns to Edwin, but he figured it wasn't his place to manage the logistics. Gossip traveled quickly around here, so he was a little surprised that Edwin, with his years of experience, hadn't been a little more inconspicuous when rolling through town late at night in an unfamiliar truck.

Jonah walked back inside. Edwin was sitting at a plastic table drinking a beer, a map spread before him. "Someone tipped him off," Jonah said.

"I figured as much," Edwin said.

"So now what? My cover's blown."

"If he wants his money, he'll be in touch."

"And what do we do until then?"

Edwin turned to Jonah and smiled. "We wait."

SAMANTHA

R EMY DROVE THEM THROUGH A labyrinth of untamed for- est, a winding dirt road devoid of markers and signposts. Sam had felt safe in town, but as they ventured deeper into the forest, she was overcome with a pinching anxiety. The road tossed her stomach around, and her head throbbed. She'd resisted the urge to pop another Oxy, and she hadn't eaten anything all day, part of the purging process Remy said was necessary in order to purify her body for the journey ahead. And what was this journey? She didn't know exactly. She'd avoided researching anything about the ceremony for fear that she might back out, instead trusting that Jonah would guide her through it. And now Jonah was nowhere to be found. This was a problem, not just immediately, but in general, this reliance on other people to make decisions for her. Growing up, most everything had been managed by other people—parents, ballet instructors, tutors— so that she could focus on dance, but now that dance was gone, she found herself unequipped for the messy responsibilities of adulthood. In the past few years, everything in her life—including this impromptu trip to the other side of the world—had been hastily arranged, and she had no one to blame but herself.

They arrived at the village three hours later. A few dozen people stood around a handful of mud huts with thatch roofs, awaiting their arrival. Remy and Laurent went about shaking the hands of the villagers, presenting the men with gifts of tobacco, the children with balloons. Sam and Gavin watched from a distance until Laurent motioned for them to come forward.

"This is Grace," Laurent said to Sam. "She will be your Bwiti mother."

Grace was a short, thin woman dressed in a purple sarong and a floral headscarf. She had a warm, maternal smile. "Very nice to meet you," Sam said, shaking the woman's hand.

"You are ready?" Grace asked in heavily accented English.

She wasn't ready, but she also wasn't sure if she ever would be, so she said, "I think so."

Grace smiled and took her hand. "Come."

IT BEGAN WITH A BATH. Sam removed her clothes and followed Grace and six other tribeswomen to the river, where she was lowered into water so cold it made her heart flinch. Grace described it as a spiritual cleansing, but it struck Sam as something like a backwoods baptism. Afterward, she was loosely wrapped, from shoulders to knees, in white cloth and escorted back to the village, where men in raffia skirts pounded frenetically on small drums, a schizophrenic rhythm that did little to calm her nerves. There were people touching her, guiding her, speaking in a language she didn't understand. She hadn't even ingested the drug and she already felt disoriented.

She looked to Gavin, standing some distance away. She could see the concern on his face, and though she tried to hide it, she was having second thoughts as well. It was a three-hour drive back to Laurent's place, followed by a dozen more to the airport in Libreville. She knew something unpleasant awaited her, and despite Remy's assurance that everything would be fine, it was difficult to quiet the possibility that it might not be. She knew it would take only one small look to Gavin, a nod that she wanted out, and her brother would whisk her away.

But then what? Where would she go from there? Back to her old ways, of course. She couldn't go back there.

An antelope horn was blown, setting the ceremony in motion. A woman approached and painted Sam's face with white kaolin, a cold paste that cemented on her skin like a face mask. She was led to a hut and seated in the center of a circle formed by six village elders. Grace arrived with a plate containing a dozen small brown mounds that resembled meatballs. Sam opened her mouth and when the first one touched her tongue, the reflex was immediate. It tasted like dirt, or spent coffee grounds, or what she imagined battery acid might taste like. She had ingested psilocybin mushrooms a few times, but this was something else entirely. When her stomach tried to expel this thing it did not want, Grace covered Sam's mouth with her hand. A moment later, she ate another one, then two more, and when she gagged again, Grace yanked her head back to keep the drug from escaping. "This is the first part," Grace said. "We call this the dying stage."

Some time passed—it was hard to say how long—and the drug settled in. Grace placed a small mirror on the ground, and when Sam looked at it she did not recognize what she saw. *Hello? Who is this?* She felt feverish, nauseous, not that different from the dope sickness that plagued her withdrawals. But then something else happened. She felt her veins contracting, the blood choking in her body. There was a burning sensation in her chest, as if her organs were being electrocuted. Her heartbeat slowed and her vision echoed and then suddenly, violently, she jerked forward and expelled the contents of her stomach.

Now the world was breaking apart. Pink currents of electricity, something like a Tesla coil, fractured her vision. The walls of the hut separated like a continental drift, leaving deep crevasses of black, through which a cold wind blew. She willed her mind to stitch the scene back together, and slowly, almost imperceptibly, it repaired itself. Her body vibrated. She could not move. Her surroundings were reduced to sounds and textures. She watched the dull, amorphous outline of a man playing a mouth harp. A few minutes later, Grace administered the flood dose and Sam was no longer swimming but instead being catapulted through a kind of pneumatic tube of past experiences, a patchwork of memories, the most vibrant of which coalesced into still life tableaus that branded themselves onto her psyche.

The day we buried Grandpa and got drunk on bourbon, and shot potato guns from the deck, and you guys told me we were celebrating a life well lived, but I couldn't see it that way through the tears. How do you celebrate an absence? *I'd asked, and you both looked at each other because you didn't know, but you were my brothers and so you tried.*

Early November, late nineties. The abandoned house with a trampoline and a half pipe dusted with leaves. No one skates it anymore, *you said, standing at the top, board perched on the coping, Jonah egging you to drop in, but you never dropped in. I danced* The Nutcracker *on the trampoline while the season's first snow began to fall.*

The time I was chased through a field by an angry bull, and I climbed up a tree and stayed there until it was dark, and you both came hollering with flashlights, and Jonah carried me down and Gavin wrapped me in his sweatshirt, the one that said MIDWEST IS THE BEST, *and I still believe that.*

I am ten, I am six, I am nineteen, I am twenty-six. I am thriving, I am learning, I am cocksure, I am lost. I am the girl inside the closet.

A HAND ON HER SHOULDER, Grace standing above her. "Walk."

Grace led her to a clearing in the forest. Her legs were stiff and she had to command them to do their job. Birds flew overhead like fighter jets. Trees pulsed with energy. The sun radiated against her flesh. She was shaking, her internal temperature rising and falling. She felt exhausted, ravished, as if her body had been scrubbed on a cellular level. This wasn't a detoxification; it was an acid wash. Her soul became a physical thing, swelling and contracting, pressing against her skin. Her mind no longer comprehended linear time, and she wondered if she would ever escape the drug's grip. Grace christened her with the flower of a parasol tree, then opened her hand, revealing more iboga. "Open," she said.

Sam shook her head. "No more."

"You are stuck," Grace said. She placed her hand on the back of Sam's neck and brought their foreheads together. "Push through," she whispered.

"I can't," Sam said, shaking her head, convinced she was dying.

"You must," Grace said, holding her chin in her hands.

Sam reluctantly opened her mouth.

"Now the hard part," Grace said, pressing the iboga against her tongue. "Stage two. The lifting of the curse."

"Please," Sam whispered, tears streaming down her cheeks. "I don't want to do this anymore."

"Down," Grace said, helping Sam onto the ground. Kneeling, Sam looked up at Grace, whose eyes were closed to the sky. "*Apongina,*" Grace said to no one, to the heavens. She took Sam's hands and ran them along the sides of her own chest, slid them beneath her arms, then cupped them in front of her face and blew. Grace then pressed her own hands together, said a few words under her breath, and threw them wide in thanksgiving. She began reciting an incantation in her native tongue, though whether it was a condemnation or a prayer, Sam couldn't say.

When her speech was finished, Sam opened her eyes.

"Go visit the dead," Grace said. "Tell them what you know. Ask for forgiveness."

"I don't know how."

"Follow this," Grace said, tapping a spot in the center of Sam's forehead. "I am with you."

Sam closed her eyes. She felt herself falling through her past, her time in Russia, New York, finally landing in the living room of the loft that night when she and Atticus had stumbled home in the pre-dawn light, silently raging at each other over some injustice neither could properly articulate. The fight had arisen in the back of the cab, something about leaving a party too soon, or maybe staying too late, even at the time it was unclear. What *was* clear was that they were both unhappy, casting blame at each other, Sam accusing Atticus of dragging her into his poisoned atmosphere, Atticus accusing Sam of enabling his addiction, which had swelled and arranged itself into a kind of scaffolding that now encased his life. "You don't care what happens to me," he'd said, fixing a dose on the living room couch. "You're not trying hard enough," Sam had shot back, though she knew the advice was equally applicable to her. Compared to her boyfriend, she'd been in a better place back then, though of course there was no good place on the opium spectrum. She slammed the bedroom door and fell, fully clothed, onto the bed, where she slept until she was awoken the next morning by the groan of a garbage truck on the street below. She walked to the living room and discovered him slumped on the couch, his chin resting against his chest, the needle in his arm. She ran to him and shook his shoulders, bellowing, pleading, then finally apologizing.

But now, back in Gabon, her eyes flicked open and she put a hand to her forehead, sweating, breathless. Grace helped her to her feet. "Where am I?" she asked.

"You are still here," Grace said. "You are still in this world."

GAVIN

HE SAT AGAINST A TREE, watching a woman bathe a small child in a pail of water. The baby smiled at him, and Gavin smiled back. He wondered what the woman thought of this foreign white man loafing around her village, without any real task or place to be. Everyone in the village was doing something—chopping wood or harvesting cassavas or bathing children—but Gavin had been sitting on his ass for the last two hours. The problem was that he wasn't needed. He wasn't needed in Los Angeles and he wasn't needed in New Mexico and he certainly wasn't needed in Gabon. He'd come here to help his sister, yet there was nothing he could do for her. Sam had been inside the hut for hours, but his requests to see her had thus far been denied. *Everything is fine,* they told him. *She is strong.* He knew she was strong—he didn't need to be told that—but it was the uncertainty that bothered him, not being able to observe the process. This whole procedure struck him as flagrantly regressive, this misguided belief that drug addiction could be cured through the administration of other, more exotic drugs. It wasn't that he was against alternative medicine, but this was something far more primitive, and that's what bothered him most.

According to Laurent, Sam would likely be out for the rest of the day, probably longer, so he took a walk around the village. He imagined how sweet it would be to stumble across a cold beer and an air-conditioned room, or, on a more practical level, a glass of water and some bread to fill his stomach. Some company might also be nice, someone to chat with, but he imagined Laurent was the only person who spoke any English, and he was busy having his leg inspected by the village doctor. Gavin passed a schoolhouse with a half dozen kids sitting on little stools and then, farther along, two men repairing a thatch roof.

He followed a dirt road out of town, finally stopping to rest at a wooden bridge straddling a narrow creek. He took stock of his surroundings, the forest thrumming with birds, stretching outward in every direction. He was a long way from the table reads and oyster dinners of Los Angeles, and maybe that was a good thing. City life dulled the senses, masked the specific hardship that results from extended time out of doors. Part of his reason for coming here—aside from his sister's recovery—was for the plain adventure of it all. Jonah was by far the more daring of the two of them, and he secretly admired the bit of wild man in his brother. They were so similar in some ways, yet so different in others. "Spend too much time in a city," Jonah had warned him on the train ride into the forest, "and one day you'll wake up dickless with a sixty-dollar haircut." Gavin had gone quiet at the warning, because his haircut—which included a glass of Islay scotch—cost ninety dollars after tip.

A vehicle approached from down the road. Gavin stepped aside and watched a battered truck cross the bridge, then pull to a stop in the middle of the road. A man stepped out and began walking toward him. Unlike the villagers, he was dressed in Western attire, camouflage cargo pants and a faded T-shirt. He was muscular, his face splotched with old acne scars, his nose spongy and red like a barroom drunk. "Hello," he said, lifting a hand in greeting.

"You speak English?" Gavin said.

"Of course," the man said, drawing nearer. "You must be Jonah's brother, yes?"

Gavin wasn't totally surprised that this man assumed he was related to the only other white man in the village, but it seemed odd that he knew Jonah's name. "You know my brother?"

"Yes. Jonah is a friend of mine. I saw him this morning."

"Where?"

"Back in town," he said, jabbing a thumb in the direction from which he'd come. "He arrived after you left. You just missed him."

"Is he coming here?"

"I don't know. He would like you to call him."

"Do you have a phone I can use?"

"In my truck," the man said, motioning. "Come."

As he followed the man back to the truck, Gavin rehearsed the righteous medley of profanities he would unleash upon his brother, tuning the cadence, finessing the verbiage. He thrilled at the sweetness of his anger. "So how do you know Jonah?"

"We work together," the man said, leaning into the cab. He tossed an empty beer bottle onto the ground, then an empty pack of cigarettes, before finally emerging with a phone.

"You work with elephants as well?"

"Sort of," he said, handing Gavin the phone.

"So you know Laurent then?"

The man smiled. "We're old friends."

"Any idea who this English guy is? He seems like trouble. I'm not really sure what's going on, but I think my brother got mixed up in something bad."

"Yes. It appears this way."

"Do you have his number in here?" Gavin asked, scrolling through the phone. When there was no response, he looked up and noticed two men exit from the passenger side of the truck. "Oh, hey," he said, surprised.

"These are my friends," the man said.

The men approached. Gavin extended his hand to shake, but was greeted instead with a fist to the face. His knees buckled and he fell to the ground. Someone lodged a knee into his shoulder, then his arms were drawn behind him and tied with a length of rope. His mouth tasted like dirt and blood, and he felt a hole where a tooth should be. He tried to ask what he'd done to deserve this, but his mouth wouldn't make the words, and the men were speaking quickly to one another in a language he didn't understand. He lifted his head to get a look at his assailants, but someone didn't like that idea and slammed it back to the ground, grinding his face into the dirt. Next thing he knew, a blindfold was wrapped around his eyes and he felt himself being lifted off the ground and rolled into the bed of a pickup truck, where he lay coughing and smarting as the gate slammed shut. Seconds later, the truck jolted to life and began rattling down the road.

SOME TIME LATER, he was pulled from the back of the truck and taken to a windowless room furnished with lion pelts and ivory tusks and a dozen hollow-eyed gorilla skulls. His face and body ached from the beating he'd received from men who, it turned out, were not Jonah's colleagues after all. The blindfold had been removed and his hands were now free. He stood slowly, touching the lump on his head, which he imagined was purple and bulbous. He pounded on the door a few times before sitting back on the floor. The only light came from a hole in the thatch roof, a rectangle of blue just large enough for his body to squeeze through if only he could figure out a way to get up there. Aside from the inventory of animal parts, there was nothing of substance to stand on, no furniture he could arrange into makeshift scaffolding, and he felt the full weight of his impotence settle upon him.

He'd nearly drifted back to sleep, when a wash of light flooded the room and he looked up to see a young man standing in the doorway. He was a thin, light-skinned teenager with a placid, almost sympathetic face. He placed a cup on the ground, then turned and hurried from the room, locking the door behind him.

Gavin lifted the cup and drank without considering its contents. It wasn't cold, but it was water and he was grateful for that. Beneath the cup was a small piece of paper folded in half. He opened it and read the words: *Do what they say.*

Do what who says? No one had told him anything thus far, so what, he wondered, was with the coy advice? He'd gladly do whatever anyone asked of him so long as he could gather his sister and hightail it out of this place. It didn't take a detective to determine that some fuckup of his brother's had landed him here, so as far as Gavin was concerned, Jonah could devise his own extraction plan.

An hour later, his captors stepped into the room. Each guy held a machete in one hand, a two-way radio in the other. They led him outside. He had assumed he'd been taken to some kind of village, but aside from the small shack, he could make out no other structures, and it appeared he was being housed in something like a remote hunting cabin. They didn't say anything as they led him through a half mile of wet and tangling rainforest, before finally descending an embankment to a small fishing boat floating along the edge of a wide, slow-moving river. Sitting in the boat was the boy who'd brought him the water as well as the man who'd accosted him at the village, the man he'd mistakenly trusted. "Welcome," the man said.

"Who are you?" Gavin asked in the most subservient voice he could muster. The two men with machetes shoved him into the boat, which was cluttered with empty water bottles and a tangled nest of fishing line.

"My name is Slinky," he said, unleashing the boat from a nearby tree. "I'm Jonah's friend. I've brought you here to help me."

"I apologize for whatever my brother has done to you," Gavin said, "but I don't think I can be much help. I know almost nothing about his life here. And even less about whatever he's gotten himself involved with."

"Your presence is all I need," Slinky said with a tight smile.

"So this is a kidnapping?" Gavin asked. Being kidnapped implied that Slinky would need to keep him alive rather than dump him in the river once he realized he was useless. So really, a kidnapping was good. He could take direction. As an actor, that's all he'd ever done. This was just a new role, that of the shiftless yet obedient hostage.

"Sure," Slinky said, yanking the pull cord of the outboard motor.

"Let's call it that." The other men stepped aboard, and Gavin took a seat on a cooler that smelled strongly of fish, while Slinky, sitting tall in the lone captain's chair, maneuvered the boat down the river.

"So what did he do?" Gavin asked Slinky. "My brother."

"He has some money that belongs to me," Slinky explained, peering downriver. "I sent someone to get it, but there was a problem."

"So you're the guy he met in Chicago?" Gavin asked, piecing the story together.

"That was my cousin, actually."

"Okay," he said, still confused. The river narrowed and Gavin had to duck to avoid the tendrils of mangroves bending toward the boat. "Where are we going anyway?"

"To work," Slinky said, nodding to a clearing up ahead.

"I assume you're the one who blew up the hotel?" Gavin asked.

"No, no," Slinky said, smiling. "Those were terrorists."

"You're not a terrorist?"

Slinky shook his head.

"Then what are you?"

Slinky paused to consider his answer. "A merchant."

THERE MUST HAVE BEEN a half dozen of the enormous beasts lying dead in a forest clearing. They reminded Gavin of smoldering tanks abandoned after an unsuccessful battle. They rested on their sides, squat legs pointing stiffly outward, like overturned plastic figurines. He tried to avert his eyes from the massacre, but the carnage surrounded him. Four or five guys stood atop the elephants, hacking at the flesh, blood-soaked bandannas tied around their faces. They sang along to an Afro-funk tune blasting from a small radio, breaking occasionally to wipe blood from their foreheads and drink from a canteen passed around the ranks. Gavin watched from the sidelines, horrified at what he was witnessing. After the elephant's faces had been removed, the tusks were separated from the jaw, rinsed in the river, and stacked like cords of firewood in the bow of the boat. It was a ruthlessly efficient operation, bordering on industrial, and Gavin quickly realized that he was witnessing a routine day in the life of professional ivory poachers.

He heard a sharp whistle and saw Slinky waving at him, a bottle of beer in one hand and a satellite phone in the other. Gavin walked over to him.

"You should help," Slinky said.

"I don't know how," Gavin said, recognizing the absurdity of his excuse.

"It's very easy." He motioned to the men hacking at dead elephants. "They can show you."

"I'm sorry, but I can't take part in this. I'll do whatever else you want but not this."

"That's what your brother said before I convinced him otherwise."

Gavin heard a mewling sound and peered into the forest, where he discovered an elephant calf shackled to a tree. Metal cuffs connected by chains were fitted around its legs, keeping the animal from moving more than a few feet in any direction. Two small nubs of dentin protruded from its wrinkled face. Its eyes said, *Kill me now please.*

"He's very small," Slinky said, "but my buyers—they sometimes like the small pieces. We found this elephant standing next to his dead mother, crying like a little baby." He laughed and threw his empty beer bottle at the elephant's head, where it landed with a thud and fell to the ground. "We're not sure what to do about this one. Maybe we will let it grow big, or maybe we will kill it now." He pulled a handgun from the waistband of his pants.

"Okay, okay," Gavin said. "Tell me what to do."

"Go help him," Slinky said, nodding toward the boy.

Gavin walked over to the kid, who stood ankle deep in elephant parts, working the tusk back and forth like a loose tooth. "What's your name?"

"Oliver," the boy said.

"I'm Gavin," he said, lifting the sole of his shoe, which was stuck with something damp and fleshy. He raked it on a large rock. "I was told to help. What should I do?"

"We have to break it loose," Oliver explained, as if it were plainly obvious.

Gavin looked down at the mangled elephant. The surrounding dirt was stained a deep crimson, and flies swarmed around the opening where its face had once been. Gavin stepped alongside the boy and grabbed the tusk and together they began pushing and pulling until it broke free of the skull with a loud crack.

"Very good!" Slinky yelled, hoisting an enthusiastic thumb in the air.

Gavin looked at the elephant's eye, which was open wide, a single streak of blood running forth like a tear.

"Go on," Slinky yelled. "Take it to the boat."

Gavin tossed the tusk over his shoulder and carried it to the river. When he reached the boat, he stacked the tusk alongside the others, then lowered his arms into the water and washed the blood from his hands.

J O N A H

H E CONVINCED EDWIN TO TAKE him to the village under the pretense that Laurent might have some information on Slinky's whereabouts. It was late afternoon, and Laurent and Remy were chatting outside a hut. Jonah stepped out of the truck and walked over to them. "What happened to your leg?" he asked, motioning to the cast.

"At the hotel," Laurent said.

"Jesus, Laurent. I'm sorry. I had no idea."

A man Jonah didn't recognize stepped forth to introduce himself. "Remy."

"Nice to finally meet you," Jonah said.

"These are your friends?" Laurent asked. Edwin and his men stood a few feet back, surveying the villagers, who seemed unsure what to make of their presence.

"Not really," Jonah said. "But I'm sort of stuck with them for the moment." He looked around the village. "Where's Sam?"

"Inside," Laurent said, motioning to the hut.

"How is she?"

"She's fine. But she is not done yet. She has more work to do."

"And Gavin?"

Laurent looked to the ground, shamefaced. "This is what we're still figuring out."

"I thought he was with you?"

"He was," Laurent said. "But not anymore."

"What do you mean?" Jonah asked, incredulous. "Where could he have gone?"

Laurent looked at the expanse of forest surrounding the village. "Many places."

Jonah wanted to ask how he'd managed to lose one of the two people he'd been entrusted to watch, but there was no use in pointing fingers, especially since his own negligence was the catalyst for their maligned journey. "Can I speak with Sam?" he asked.

"You can try," Laurent said.

Jonah ducked inside the hut and found his sister lying on the ground, a metal pail filled with what smelled like stomach fluids resting next to her head. Her hair was wild and her face, which had been painted white, was now stained with a mixture of dirt and tear tracks. She looked like a bereaved clown after a night of heavy drinking. He placed his hand on her shoulder and roused her awake.

"Jonah?" she said, opening her eyes. She tried to sit up, but her stomach wasn't up to the task and she made another contribution to the pail.

Jonah held her hair back while she finished, then wiped her mouth with his shirtsleeve. He looked up and saw Grace standing in the doorway holding a bowl of water. She walked over to Sam, knelt next to her, and placed a hand on her forehead. Grace began whispering in Sam's ear, while another woman used a palm frond to fan incense in her face. "What are you doing?" he asked.

"She must rest," Grace said.

"When will this be over?" Jonah asked.

"Soon." Grace motioned toward the door. "Please. Let us do our work."

Jonah placed his hand on Sam's shoulder and kissed the top of her head. "I'll be back," he said. "I love you."

Back outside, Edwin was talking on the phone, while the rangers were inspecting something beneath the hood of the jeep.

"Who's he talking to?" Jonah asked, but the men ignored him.

Laurent appeared, holding his cellphone out to Jonah. "It's your brother."

"Gavin?" Jonah said, taking the phone.

Edwin ended his call and turned his attention to Jonah.

"Where the fuck are you?" Gavin yelled through the phone.

"Where are *you*?" Jonah asked.

"I'm floating down a river in a boat filled with elephant tusks."

"What happened?"

"I was kidnapped," he said curtly. "By that Slinky guy. He said you have his money. He wants it back."

"Put him on," Jonah said. There were a few seconds of rustling before Slinky's voice greeted him on the other end.

"Bad Elephant Man," Slinky said. "You were doing so good, but then you try to make trouble. Why you making trouble for me?"

"I still have your money," Jonah said. "You can come get it whenever you want. But if you hurt my brother, I swear to God I'll dump it in the river."

"I heard about your new friend," Slinky said.

There was no use in lying. His cover was blown. "They know about it, Slinky. They knew all along. They knew as soon as I landed in Chicago." He looked back to Edwin, who was shaking his head, silently imploring him to shut his mouth. "They've been tracking you for months," Jonah said, turning his body to block Edwin, who was reaching for the phone. "They've already arrested Andre, and they're coming for you next."

"You idiot," Edwin muttered.

"Good," Slinky said. "Tell them to bring my money."

"How about *I* bring your money?" Jonah said. "And you release my brother in exchange. Isn't that how this is supposed to work?"

"I don't know. You've turned into a real killer, Elephant Man. I'm not sure I can trust you after what you did to Sterling."

"That wasn't my idea."

"No matter. I still can't take the risk."

"Then how do we resolve this?"

"There's a place in Franceville called The Dream Factory. It's a nightclub in the city center. In the bathroom is a storage closet that will be unlocked. Leave the money there. I'll be by to collect it, and if you haven't kept any for yourself, I will release your brother."

"When?" Jonah asked.

"Tonight. But if you mention any of this to your new friend, we will have a very big problem. And by we, I mean your brother."

The call went silent. Jonah handed the phone back to Laurent.

"What's going on?" Laurent asked.

Jonah realized that Laurent, like his siblings, had been doing what was asked of him without much explanation, and Jonah knew that if he didn't level with him soon he might lose one of his only comrades. He told Laurent about his arrangement with Slinky and his time together with Mateo, mercifully omitting what had become of his employee, and then skipping ahead to his return and subsequent involvement with Edwin. As Jonah unfolded his story, Laurent shook his head in the manner of a disappointed father. "Why didn't you tell me any of this?"

"Because there's nothing you could have done. I was blackmailed. And if you had known, it would have made things worse. I was trying to protect you from this. You *and* your family."

"Does Marcus know?"

"Nobody knew anything until now. I was trying to keep it that way." Jonah looked to Edwin, who was calmly rolling a cigarette on the hood of the truck. "I blame *you* for this."

Edwin shrugged. "Blame whoever you want."

Jonah tossed the backpack over his shoulder and began walking toward Laurent's car.

"Where are you going?" Edwin said, looking up.

"To get my brother."

"I don't think that's a good idea," Edwin called after him.

"Why's that?" Jonah asked, walking faster.

"Because it could interfere with our plan."

"I don't believe you *have* a plan," Jonah yelled back.

Edwin caught up with him, grabbed him by the shoulder. "I think you should reconsider what you're about to do. We're putting a plan together that will allow us to get your brother back safely. I'm asking you to please let us do our work."

"Get off me," Jonah said, shaking free. He opened the door of Laurent's car and stepped inside.

"Jonah!" Edwin yelled after him. "I strongly urge you not to do this!"

GAVIN

THEY FLOATED DOWN THE OGOOUÉ River, the sun slipping behind hills of lemongrass. Oliver piloted the boat, while Slinky and the rest of his shipmates were gradually falling under the spell of palm wine. The dressing on his wounds had begun to peel away, his T-shirt now chafing against the burned skin, and a dull throbbing pain issued from somewhere toward the back of his neck. He was supposed to have returned to the hospital to change out the dressing, and he couldn't help but imagine the wounds becoming infected. He hadn't eaten anything other than the mangoes earlier that morning, and aside from the small act of mercy shown by Oliver, he hadn't had anything to drink. "Do you have any water?" he asked Slinky.

"Lots of water in this river," Slinky said with a hearty laugh.

"Do you have any water that won't rot my gut?"

Slinky pulled a canteen from a duffel bag and tossed it to Gavin. "Next you'll want something to eat."

"Are you offering?" Gavin asked, suddenly hopeful.

"No."

Gavin finished drinking and set the bottle down at his feet. It was warm, with a slightly metallic taste, but he was grateful for it nonetheless. "Where are we going?"

"To deliver this product."

"And then I can leave?"

"Only if your brother obeys the rules."

"There are rules to this?"

"There are always rules," Slinky said. "And so far, your brother hasn't done a very good job following them."

GAVIN SAT BACK IN the boat and stared at the stack of tusks hidden beneath a blue tarp. There was no denying his complicity in the act. He'd done what he'd done, and he would have to live with that. He wanted to blame his brother for putting him in this situation, but the truth was that he'd traveled here under his own volition, without any clear role, the only one in the family unable to justify his passage. He'd proved himself to be perfectly useless, a burden more than anything. He'd come to help his sister, but he hadn't considered the possibility that she didn't need his help. Only Sam knew what Sam needed, and it was foolish to think he had any control over that. It was foolish to think he could convince anyone to do anything. He couldn't convince Renee to want children, and he couldn't convince Mariana to want *him*. He'd spent most of his life trying to micromanage the emotional lives of other people, a tactic the futility of which he was only now realizing. "What you don't understand," Renee had once said to him during one of their more heated arguments, "is that you're most effective when you disappear."

Oliver steered them into a cove hidden under cover of dense vegetation. He then waded to shore and pulled the boat aground, allowing Slinky to step onto dry land. Gavin waited in the boat, unsure what was expected of him. Two jeeps approached from the forest and pulled to a stop along the riverbank. A tall, wiry man in a pinstripe suit stepped out of the first jeep. His skin was smooth and unblemished, his thick hair carefully coiffed in a back comb, and he possessed a hushed and delicate air that reminded Gavin of the musician Prince. Hands were pumped, then Slinky pulled the tarp from the ivory and streaked his flashlight across the tusks. "One hundred twenty kilo-grams," he announced.

Prince pulled his phone from his pocket and snapped a picture of the tusks. "Twelve total?" he asked.

"Yeah," Slinky said.

Prince jabbed at his phone. "Sending this to my client for ap-proval." A moment later, he turned to Gavin. "Who's that?" he asked, seemingly annoyed to find an unexpected white man sitting among his product.

"Don't worry about him," Slinky said.

"I'm worried," Prince said.

"He's nothing. A nuisance."

Prince looked down at an incoming message on his phone, then nodded his approval. "Okay. Load it up."

Slinky's men began loading the tusks into the jeeps.

Prince looked to Gavin. "He should come with us."

"Not a chance," Slinky said.

"What do you intend to do with him?"

"Ollie," Slinky said, handing his pistol to the boy, "you stay with the American. If he tries to run, shoot him. I'll be back in a couple hours."

"Okay," Oliver said, sitting up a little straighter in the boat, hold-ing the gun awkwardly, as if it were a small, unpredictable animal.

A moment later, the men piled into the jeeps and drove away, leav-ing Gavin and Oliver alone. With everyone gone, the sounds of the forest asserted themselves, the barking of distant monkeys, the trill of an unseen bird.

"Low man on the totem pole, huh?" Gavin said.

"What do you mean?" Oliver asked in heavily accented English.

Gavin finished what was left in the canteen. "It means he doesn't tell you anything."

"He tells me things," Oliver said, registering the slight. "He's my dad."

"That's your dad?" Gavin said.

"Yeah," Oliver said. "And I hate him as much as you do. Probably more."

Gavin tried to arrange this new information into something he could understand. "Then why are you here?"

"I don't have a choice," Oliver said. He went on to explain that he lived in Libreville with his mother, who had moved there after leaving Slinky for what Oliver explained were obvious reasons. But a few times a year Oliver was forced—due to some legal maneuvering by his dad—to spend a few weeks back in his hometown. Oliver hated everything about the place—the boredom, the food, the absence of friends—but it was the awful business of elephant poaching that he most despised. He suffered it only because he feared his father's legendary temper, which he'd been subjected to on more than a few occasions.

Gavin had suspected that Oliver, unlike his father, was not an executioner. While the rest of Slinky's men had taken a perverse pleasure in disassembling elephants, Oliver had moved with a ruefulness that suggested he was ill-suited for such heinous labor. And the fact that he'd brought him water for no apparent reason other than a vague sense of sympathy hinted at a generosity Gavin imagined being able to exploit.

"So the elephant guy is your brother?" Oliver asked.

"Who? Jonah?"

Oliver nodded. "I see him around town sometimes. At Laurent's place. My dad stole his camera and gave it to me for my birthday."

"Oh," Gavin said, unsure if the kid was looking for an apology or just an acknowledgment.

"Tell your brother I'm sorry about that." Oliver laughed. "I should have known my dad would never actually *buy* me a real gift."

"That was shitty of him," Gavin said. "Your dad, I mean."

Oliver shrugged, as if he were used to it. "Like I said, he's an asshole."

———

AN HOUR PASSED, THEN another and Slinky still hadn't returned. Gavin leaned against a fig tree, flicking ants off the toe of his shoe, while Oliver paced back and forth in the darkness.

"You really think he's coming back?" Gavin asked.

"Why?" Oliver said. "You don't?"

"I don't know." Gavin wasn't sure what the play was, but he assumed Oliver knew the geography better than he did, and if there was any chance of making it out of here he'd have to rely on the kid. "How far is it to town?"

"Ten kilometers?" Oliver said. "Maybe less."

"You think we could make it?"

"Tonight?"

"Do you really want to sleep out here?" Gavin asked. He could see the kid turning it over in his mind. "Here's what I'm thinking. You and I start walking. I know it's dark, but the moon's bright enough and I think we can make good time. If we see your dad's truck, I'll run into the forest and you just tell him that I beat you up and took the gun."

"He's never gonna believe that."

Gavin stood and approached Oliver and struck him hard across the face. He swung again, this time connecting with his bottom lip, which burst open and began trickling blood down his chin.

"*Putain!*" Oliver said, holding his face in his hands.

"I'm so sorry," Gavin said. He'd never punched anyone before, and he felt terrible for what he'd done. "I had to do that so your dad would believe your story."

Oliver turned his back to Gavin, quietly whimpering.

"Are you okay?" Gavin asked, leaning closer to get a look at the kid. "Let me look at it."

Oliver turned and swung at Gavin, landing a fist just above his right ear, a tough piece of skull he imagined must have stung the kid's hand more than it hurt his head.

"Feel better?" Gavin asked.

"Yeah," he said. He stood and began walking toward the road. "Let's go."

They followed the jeep trail that Slinky and the rest of the men had taken: a narrow, winding road pocked with patches of rainwater. They hiked in silence, Oliver hesitantly leading the way, stopping every so often to rest, occasionally doubling back when the road split and they lost their way. Oliver showed himself to be very much a city kid, flinching and jumping at the slightest rustle and movement, waving his gun at the surrounding forest like a skittish bank robber trying to manage a room full of hostages. After a few kilometers, Gavin began to question the logic of leaving. He remembered being lost once while exploring the Grand Canyon with his college girlfriend. The trail they'd been following had disappeared into a dry riverbed, and they spent hours bushwhacking through desert scrub brush before finally realizing they should just return to where they'd lost the trail and wait for help to arrive, which it eventually did. The only problem with applying that logic to his current situation was that help wasn't coming.

"So what are you doing here anyway?" Oliver asked, attempting to fill the silence. "In Gabon?"

"I came to help my sister," Gavin said, "but I haven't been very helpful."

"Is she sick?"

"Sort of. But she's getting better. She's a very strong woman."

"I don't have any brothers or sisters," Oliver said. "What's it like?"

What was it like? Gavin had never considered the question. He thought of his siblings like appendages, things that had always been there and he imagined always would be. "It's like . . . ," he said before stopping.

Oliver turned back to him, awaiting his reply.

"It's like a part of yourself you can never really know."

AS THEY HIKED, GAVIN'S mind drifted back to his childhood. When he was sixteen, his parents went to a conference in Orlando and left him in charge of Sam, who was eight at the time. Jonah had gone to a friend's cabin in Wisconsin, so it was just the two of them together for the weekend. On Saturday night, Gavin rented *Spice World* from Blockbuster and set her up with a tub of popcorn in front of the TV in the living room. A couple of Gavin's friends—Richie and Nick—showed up with boxes of beer, waving to Sam as they descended to the basement. Gavin warned his sister that she wasn't allowed to come downstairs, said to call him on the intercom if she needed anything, and that if she ever mentioned any of this to Mom and Dad she would be one very Sorry Spice.

More kids arrived later in the night, most of whom Gavin didn't recognize and definitely hadn't invited. They entered without knocking, dumping beer in the refrigerator, oblivious to the little girl dancing along to the television. Gavin moved around the house, frantically trying to manage the situation, which was quickly spiraling out of control. He looked out the window and saw a line of cars stretching down the street, a mass of teenagers walking toward his home. The music grew louder as more kids arrived, a thumping he could now feel through the carpet. The kids wore shoes in the house, which was a blatant violation of their mother's policy, and they smoked cigarettes in the kitchen, which was so completely against the rules they didn't even have a policy for that. When the party outgrew the basement and began overtaking the rest of the house, Sam retreated to her bedroom. Pretending to be a neighbor, she called the police to file a complaint. When the cops arrived, the party drained through the back door, a wash of drunk teenagers fleeing into the cornfields bordering their property. Gavin had been drinking gin and orange juice all night, so that by the time the party had died, he was sitting on the floor of the powder room, a thread of saliva hanging from his mouth, something awful brewing in the toilet. Sam knocked gently before poking her head in. "Are you okay?" she asked.

He said he was not okay, he was fucked, completely fucked, because not only was the carpet ruined but someone had stolen a twenty-year-old bottle of scotch from their dad's liquor cabinet, plus a

Nintendo controller, maybe both. Sam didn't say anything, at least not that Gavin remembered. Instead, she helped him up to his room, where she tucked him into bed, then stayed up late cleaning the house. When he awoke the next morning, she was making pancakes in the kitchen. Sitting on the kitchen table were two Advil, a glass of orange juice, and a note that read *You owe me big time*. And he did. He'd spent his life trying to repay that debt, trying to rise to his sister's level of grace, but he never could, and it destroyed him to think that even now, so many years later, when she needed him most, he had tried once again, and once again he had failed.

SAMANTHA

NOW SHE WAS DEEP UNDERWATER, swimming through the amniotic fluid of her soul. What she found was Samantha, but a better, more honest version of Samantha, the person she aspired to be. She was separated from her ego, desiring nothing. The sharp edges from earlier had given way to a slow-moving carousel of pastel hues. Time had ceased to exist. Had it been five minutes or five days? No idea. All she knew was that it had been awful for a while, but now it was less awful. She felt a hand on her shoulder and surfaced to find Grace sitting next to her with a bowl of water. She took a drink and felt the liquid cascade down the walls of her stomach. A crown of leaves was placed upon her head and then Grace and the other woman lifted her to her feet and out into the night.

Outside, more women joined them, everyone singing a happy tune as they descended toward the river. Leaving the hut had sobered her up a little and, though her limbs were still numb, she felt strangely lucid, as if observing herself from a comfortable remove. When they reached the river, she was stripped naked and passed through a structure made of sticks. "This is the third stage," Grace said. "Rebirth."

Let it begin, Sam thought. *Show me a new life.*

———

AFTERWARD, THE WOMEN ESCORTED her back to the village. Grace fed her another small dose of iboga, and Sam swallowed it without difficulty. A young girl placed flowers at her feet. An elderly woman blew pipe smoke in her face and caressed her cheek with a dry, calloused hand. The world had snapped into sharp focus and she experienced a divine clarity. She had spent the day examining her life as if it were an object she could hold, critiquing it in a manner that felt beautiful and without judgment. Something profound was happening, and though she didn't understand the mechanics of this drug, she felt as if she were finally stepping into the light.

Men dressed in the hides of wildcats played the *mougongo,* while others kept rhythm with small drums. A woman lifted Sam to her feet and led her to the center of a circle formed by villagers holding torches made from tree bark. A chant went up and they began dancing around her, orange cinders trailing them like comet dust. There was something celebratory about the spectacle, an air of victory, and though she didn't know what had been won or by whom, she wanted to believe she had broken free of her shackles, those beastly urges that had ruled her for so long. She fell in line with the mass of swirling bodies and began clapping her hands, pulsing, exultant.

The ceremony faded as the night wore on. Grace approached with a blanket under her arm. She took Sam by the hand and together they walked down to the river and sat on a large rock under the light of the moon. "You will sleep here tonight," Grace said. "This is the final stage of your journey. In the morning, you will return to the village. There will be nothing to speak of then. The ceremony will be complete."

"Will I feel normal again?"

"If the ceremony has worked you will never feel normal again. Normal was your old self. That person is dead. This is a new life."

Grace handed Sam a blanket. "*Bonne nuit,*" she said, disappearing into the forest.

Sam spread the blanket on a patch of grass next to the river. It had been years since she'd slept outside under the stars, but despite all the creatures circling around her, she wasn't afraid. She had walked to the edge of this world, then returned unharmed. She rested her head on a mound of leaves, pulled the blanket around her, and fell quickly asleep.

JONAH

Driving through Franceville, he passed the burned shell of the hotel, now guarded by a half dozen tanks and military trucks. It was hard to imagine anyone making it out of there alive, and the scale of the destruction made him flinch at the gravity of what Sam and Gavin had endured. It was almost ten o'clock, eerily dark save for the splash of an occasional streetlight, and he registered a notable tension as he drove these streets that had once been alive with commerce.

He passed Laurent's place, then continued into the city center, where he finally located the nightclub. He parked the car, shouldered the bag of money, and headed inside. The club was nearly empty, save for a clutch of prostitutes in citrus-colored miniskirts lounging on a velvet sofa, sipping Orange Fanta from highball glasses. The dance floor was shrouded in the colored exhaust of a smoke machine, and as he made his way toward the bar he could feel the women's eyes stalking him like wolves in a predawn fog. He took a seat on a stool and ordered a beer. Two men dressed like construction laborers sat at the other end of the bar skipping dice. They didn't look at him, though he knew they registered his presence, the way everyone registers the presence of a foreigner in a place foreigners don't belong.

Jonah drained his beer and headed to the men's room. He was

parked at a urinal when he suddenly felt hands on his shoulders. His heart clinched. He turned around expecting to find a gun but instead was greeted by the smiling face of a woman massaging his back. "Feel good, yes?" she said.

"No, thank you," he said, zipping his pants.

"More?"

"Not interested."

"Come." She took his hand and led him toward a stall.

"Please don't." He tried to make for the door but the woman blocked his way. Her lips were stained an iridescent orange, either from the soda she'd been drinking or some tropical shade of lipstick. She placed one hand on the doorframe, the other on his crotch. "Let's have a nice time, yes?"

"I can't, but thank you," he said, pushing past her. He sidled back up at the bar. *Fuck,* he thought. He'd have to try that again.

He scanned the bar and noticed an elderly man who looked an awful lot like Osman sitting at a table in the corner. Jonah looked away, then turned back to confirm his suspicion. It was most certainly Osman, elbows on the table, head bent over the dull glow of a cellphone, the bulbous hunch of his back pressing against his shirt. A moment later, Osman's two henchmen, the ones who had killed Mateo, pushed through the door and pulled up chairs at his table. Jonah wasn't sure if Slinky knew what he was walking into, but either way, the situation was about to devolve into something he would rather not stick around for. He needed to ditch the money and get out of this place, but the route to the restroom would funnel him past Osman's table and there was almost no chance he would forget the face of the American who'd stolen his ivory. Jonah took a pull of his beer and looked the other direction. The prostitute who had propositioned him was chatting with her friends, probably regaling them with stories of the nervous white man.

A moment later, a guy bearing a striking resemblance to Prince entered the bar. Slinky and his crew filtered in behind him, and the group settled in around Osman's table. Prince made the introductions.

Jonah tried to glean bits of conversation, but their voices were smothered by the bassline of a hip-hop song. Jonah turned his attention to a talent show playing on the television behind the bar, a Gabonese version of *American Idol*. And that's when he heard the shriek. He turned and saw the look on the prostitute's face, a look that said: *What the fuck is this?*

He spun back and saw the bartender aiming a gun at Osman's table. The front door split open and a dozen men with guns charged into the club. Jonah heard three loud pops followed by three more. The prostitutes scattered like birds on a wire, but it wasn't until bottles of booze began exploding above the bar that Jonah finally dove to the floor. Slinky took cover behind a pool table and got off a few rounds, but he was now on his own, his men spread out, some lying on the ground, one holding his stomach in a futile attempt to keep the blood from spilling forth. Jonah crawled behind a bank of speakers, where he watched men in thick-soled boots sprint across the Technicolor dance floor. In a curious shift of loyalty, Prince and another soldier had Slinky pinned to the ground, hands cuffed behind his back. One of Osman's men charged forth and punctured Prince's thigh with a buck knife. Edwin, who had now joined the melee, grabbed the man by his shirt collar and peeled him away. Prince removed the knife from his leg and grabbed a pool cue, delivering three sharp blows to the man's head, the last of which snapped the cue in half and stilled the guy's body. Jonah grabbed the backpack and crawled to a storage room, where he found one of the prostitutes cowering behind a keg of beer.

"How do we get out of here?" he asked.

She shook her head, not understanding.

"*Sortie?*"

She pointed to a metal door. Jonah pushed through it and stepped into an alley clogged with police cars and military vehicles and a dozen commandos with guns pointed at him. He put his hands in the air and waited for what came next.

———

JONAH SAT AT A metal table, surrounded by Edwin and three government officials, in a windowless room deep within the police station. He'd been told it was just a formality, that he'd be released after answering a few questions, though the only question *he* wanted answered was where he could find his brother. Edwin said they were in the process of retrieving Gavin, but first they needed Jonah to recount his time in Gabon. He began with the origin of his research, his relationship with Laurent, how he became involved with Slinky, all the sordid details of his messy life. He recounted the story of the past couple weeks, omitting a few details, exaggerating others. It was the first time he'd really assessed his situation with any kind of distance or objectivity, and he was appalled by how easily one thing had led to another, the accumulation of bad decisions. The men seemed generally satisfied with his story, and, after signing some documents he didn't totally understand, told him he could leave.

"Before I go," Jonah said, sliding the documents across the table, "maybe you could explain what just happened."

"Sure," Edwin said, tucking the papers into his back pocket. "What do you want to know?"

"Everything."

"Right," Edwin said, settling in for the telling.

Prince's real name was Vincent, and he was one of Edwin's undercover agents. He'd spent the past year posing as a Cameroonian ivory broker, forging connections between poachers on the ground and shadowy groups with connections to the expanding Asian market. A week ago, he followed a lead to Libreville, where he met some Nigerians who claimed to work for a man named Osman. The Nigerians took Vincent to a strip club outside of town, where he found his target sipping Cristal with a flock of attractive young women. Osman told Vincent about his contacts in Asia and how he was looking to get his hands on more ivory, and Vincent told Osman about a Gabonese poacher named Slinky who would probably be willing to part with his product for significantly less than market value.

As for the Slinky half of the equation, that required some bluffing on Vincent's part. He'd never actually met Slinky, though he did drink a beer with one of his lieutenants at a bar in Libreville. Vincent was told that Slinky's Chinese connection was currently indisposed and that he now found himself with a surplus of product and a shortage of buyers. Vincent said he knew a rich Nigerian who might be interested, and for a few days it seemed as if two of the key players in the West African ivory trade would converge in a delightfully convenient manner. But when Vincent tried to arrange the meeting with Slinky, his calls went unanswered and it appeared the transaction wasn't going to happen after all.

"So what changed?" Jonah asked.

"Nothing for a while," Edwin said, "which is why we proceeded with our original plan to use you to get to Slinky."

"And we know how that turned out."

Edwin shrugged, as if he didn't have an opinion on that.

"But then Vincent received a phone call," Edwin continued. "This was when we were in the village. Slinky had changed his mind, said he wanted to meet after all, and suddenly the operation was back on. Vincent got in touch with Osman's team and the meeting was set."

"So there was really no reason for me to be at the club. All the crap with me delivering his money, that was all pointless. You were planning to arrest him anyway."

"Exactly."

"Why didn't you tell me that? Why'd you let me walk into a firefight?"

"If you remember, I did try to prevent you from going. I told you I was working on something. I asked you to give me some time."

"If I'd known your plan involved shooting up the place, I might have reconsidered."

"It was out of my hands. Like I said when we first met, there are a lot more people involved now. I wasn't at liberty to divulge details of the operation."

"What happened to Osman?" Jonah asked.

"Dead."

"And Slinky?"

"He was escorted away by some nice men from INTERPOL."

"So you're done with me then?"

"You've completed your duty," Edwin said.

"Good. Then take me to my brother."

Edwin hesitated. "We're still working on that."

"I thought you said you were in the process of retrieving him."

"Yes," Edwin said. "But it's a process."

GAVIN

WHILE OLIVER SEEMED CONFIDENT THEY were moving toward civilization, Gavin couldn't shake the feeling that they were just wandering. He kept hoping that the next bend in the road would offer a view of distant lights or at least a paved stretch of highway, but each step only heightened the pain in his feet, which were blistered from the shoes he'd been given at the hospital. He wasn't sure what time it was, though he knew it was getting late. Oliver had estimated ten kilometers, which Gavin—due to his limited knowledge of the metric system—assumed was somewhere in the vicinity of five miles, though he guessed they'd already gone that far, and they were no closer to town. He was thirsty and hungry and growing certain they were irretrievably lost. His vision was doing this strange thumping thing, like the cone of a bass speaker, and he wondered if he was beginning to hallucinate, which would certainly explain the elephant standing in the road.

Gavin stopped and peered into the darkness. *Was it an elephant?* There was something there, quieter than an automobile, larger than a human, but it wasn't until it shook its head, its tusks catching the moonlight, that his suspicion was confirmed. "Oliver," he hissed, and the boy turned back to him. Gavin pointed ahead.

"*Merde*," Oliver said, registering the animal's presence. He drew his gun.

The elephant moved a few steps toward them and lifted its trunk, though whether in greeting or warning, Gavin couldn't say. A second later, it pinned its ears back, curled its trunk inward, and the message was made clear. On a certain level, this made perfect sense. The elephant had come to exact revenge, to trample them both to death, thereby restoring a kind of moral order to the universe.

Oliver moved slowly backward until he was standing shoulder to shoulder with Gavin, the gun still trained on the animal. "Should I shoot it?"

"No," Gavin said, strangely calm despite the situation.

A moment passed, though it seemed much longer, and the two parties stood in the road, trying to divine the other's intention. Gavin was alternately terrified and awestruck by this creature that until now he'd seen only in pieces. He raised his hands in the air in a show of both surrender and strength. The elephant, unimpressed, took another step forward. Gavin and Oliver took another step back.

"What do we do?" Oliver asked.

"Stay still," Gavin said. "It could try a bluff charge." Gavin didn't know what he was talking about. He'd heard this was common with bears and hoped that elephants were inclined to similar acts of mercy.

"If it takes another step, I'm shooting it," Oliver said.

"That pistol won't do shit except make it angrier."

The elephant scratched its foot in the dirt, exhaled something like a snort or a cough. Oliver grabbed hold of Gavin's arm with his left hand, the gun shaking in his right. The elephant raised its trunk once more and growled a guttural kind of war cry, at which point a flash of light framed the elephant in backlight. The animal turned toward the source of the light, which Gavin quickly realized was a jeep bouncing toward them from down the road. It began honking and flashing its headlights, a cacophonous mix of light and sound that sent the elephant lumbering into the forest.

The truck braked to a stop, and Gavin raised his hand to shield his eyes from the headlights. His first thought was that Slinky had returned to cut his throat, but the men who emerged from the jeep wore berets and military fatigues, and Gavin realized they were park rangers. They approached slowly, guns drawn, instructing Gavin and Oliver to stay put. Oliver threw his gun to the ground and positioned himself behind Gavin, as if he planned to use him as a shield should the men start shooting. One of the rangers scooped Oliver's gun from the ground, while the other inspected them both for additional weapons. A few seconds later, a white man emerged from the back of the jeep, followed by another white man who looked an awful lot like his brother.

"Jonah?" Gavin said, unsure if it was really him.

"You okay?" Jonah asked, scanning him with his flashlight.

"I'm fine," Gavin said. "What's going on?"

"We came to get you." Jonah turned to Oliver, a vague look of recognition spreading across his face. "Don't I know you from somewhere?"

"The camera," Oliver said.

"Right," Jonah said. He looked closely at Oliver's lip, which was swollen and crusted with dried blood. "What happened?"

Oliver nodded to Gavin. "Him."

Edwin approached with the two rangers. "Told you we'd find him," he said to Jonah.

"Can someone tell me what just happened?" Gavin asked, alternately baffled and relieved.

"Come on," Jonah said, walking back to the jeep. "I'll explain on the way."

EDWIN DROPPED THEM OFF at Laurent's restaurant, where they planned to sleep for the night before heading to the village to retrieve Sam the next morning. Jonah explained that Sam was still deep in the throes of the iboga, but that she was in good hands. He then plucked a couple beers from the refrigerator and handed one to Gavin. "*Bonne année!*" he said, tapping his beer to Gavin's.

"What?" Gavin asked.

"Happy New Year."

"Tonight?" Gavin looked at the clock on the wall. It was a few minutes past midnight. The days had all run together since arriving here, the last few in particular, and he now realized he'd spent New Year's Eve wandering through the forest. Fitting in one sense, profoundly depressing in another.

"Sorry about all of this," Jonah said. "Things spiraled outta control."

"It's fine."

Jonah seemed surprised by his answer. "You're not mad? I figured you'd be complaining about this for months."

Gavin shrugged. "We're alive, right?" He moved to the kitchen and began rummaging through the refrigerator, where he found a bowl of stew, which he ate while standing at the bar.

Jonah, meanwhile, was in Laurent's office, removing pillows from a cabinet and placing them, along with an assortment of blankets, on the couch. Gavin watched him unroll his sleeping bag on the floor, then emerge a moment later to bid him good night.

"You can have the couch," Jonah said.

"Thank you," Gavin mumbled, still shoveling food in his mouth.

"Good night," Jonah said and closed the door behind him.

WHEN GAVIN FINISHED EATING, he took his beer and stepped onto the porch. He wasn't tired, though it was well after midnight and he knew he should be. His body still thrummed from the chaos of the last couple days, and he suspected it might be a while before his mind would spin down enough for sleep. He'd come here reluctantly, but now that their trip was drawing to a close he didn't want to leave. He felt strangely content despite everything that had happened. He hadn't thought much about Renee or his life back in L.A., and he figured that probably revealed something about his attachment to them. He hadn't thought much about Mariana either, or really anyone aside from his siblings, and he suspected that was a good thing.

He walked down the road, passing dark, quiet houses, then turned onto a street lined with restaurants and storefronts. The distant thump of music emanated from somewhere down the way, so he continued past an electronics store and a bakery, eventually arriving at the source of the music. He stopped and looked through the windows of what appeared to be a banquet hall. A deejay was spinning music beneath a large disco ball, while a crowd of people moved around the dance floor. He heard laughing from somewhere nearby and turned to discover four women in purple dresses and floral head wraps snapping selfies with a cellphone. Gavin immediately realized they were bridesmaids and this was a wedding. A wedding on New Year's Eve. He was reminded of that other wedding today, or maybe it was tomorrow—hard to say with the time difference—the one in New Mexico.

Gavin watched the celebration from a distance. One of the women noticed him staring and saluted him with her wineglass. He smiled and saluted back with his beer. Then he turned and started back toward Laurent's.

SAMANTHA

Sₕₑ AWOKE IN THE TALL GRASS along the riverbank. The sun had crested the trees and she felt surprisingly refreshed. A few feet away from her, a young boy waded in the water. She waved to him, but he disappeared beneath the surface and didn't emerge until he'd reached the opposite shore and disappeared into the trees. She removed the robe she'd been wearing and walked carefully into the water, her feet melting into the river mud. Monkeys barked overhead and she felt the scaly brush of a fish against her leg. She washed the white kaolin clay from her face and scrubbed her arms and legs with a banana leaf she found sailing across the water's surface. She floated on her back, eyes closed to the sun, her body drinking up its warmth. She felt a complete lack of desire, not just for drugs but for anything besides her immediate surroundings: the river, the sun, the trees. The last two years had been shrouded in black gauze, but now, suddenly, the shade had been drawn and the world presented itself with a clarity she hadn't believed possible. Had she been cured? Hard to say. She suspected the reckoning wasn't complete, but this wasn't the time to concern herself with future tasks. There was no telling what would come next and she didn't care. Right now, for the first time in as long as she could remember, she was content.

She swam back to shore and dressed. Her shoes, the only remnant of her old life, were wet and muddy, but she put them on anyway and began hiking back to the village, past the pineapple grove and the stand of padauk trees. She saw kids shouldering pails of water and a couple of men roasting meat over a small fire, and some women hanging laundry out to dry. The celebration from the night before had been replaced with the workaday tasks of village life.

She found her brothers sitting with Laurent in the shade of the schoolhouse. "Good morning," she said, approaching.

"There you are," Jonah said. He stood and threw his arms around her.

"When did you get back?" she asked.

"Early this morning. Had to go get this guy." He nodded to Gavin.

Sam turned to Gavin. "What happened?"

"I disappeared for a while," Gavin said.

Sam wasn't sure what he meant by that, but she smiled anyway. "Well, I'm glad you're back."

"So how was it?" Gavin asked.

"It was *awful*," she said. "Awful but necessary."

Grace approached with a bowl of jackfruit. "Better?" she asked.

"Much," Sam said, taking a piece. "Thank you for everything. You were a very good Bwiti mother."

"So that's it?" Gavin said to Laurent. "It's done?"

"The withdrawal symptoms will subside," Laurent said, "but her work is not complete. The Bwiti is just the beginning. Sam must continue the journey. She must continue the hard work."

"I understand," Sam said, and she did. Work was nothing new to her. Hard work was what had granted her access to the cutthroat world of professional dance. It's what had landed her at the Joffrey at sixteen and the New York City Ballet two years after that. Hard work was what had defined her life until recently, and though she knew the path forward would be long and lined with temptation, she finally possessed the will to try.

"So what was it like?" Jonah asked. "The iboga?"

She couldn't say what it was like, because it was unlike anything she'd ever experienced. It wasn't a dream, because the sensations were too real, too strong, and it wasn't real life either, because the things she saw were not of this world. It was a walk through the darkest part of her soul, but also a reminder of the happiness she'd once known, such shining joy that it nearly brought tears to her eyes just thinking about it. It was impossible to explain, so she decided not to try. "I don't know if I'm ready to talk about it just yet," she finally said.

"Understood," Jonah said.

"It's not easy to explain," Laurent added.

"When did *you* do it?" Sam asked.

"When I was a young man." He shook his head. "But never again."

"Yeah," Sam said with a smile. "That's kinda how I feel too."

"So now what?" Gavin asked.

"I think we should go see about the elephants," Jonah said.

THEY ARRIVED AT THE BAI early that evening and sat on the observation deck, eating what was left of the smoked fish and plantains Laurent had packed for them. Rain had fallen earlier, but now the clouds were beginning to part, the sun painting the sky a silky orange. The plan was to spend the night there, enjoy a bit of peace before returning home. In the morning, they would return to Franceville, where Sam and Gavin would catch the train to Libreville, then a couple flights to Chicago. Gavin said he planned to drive back to Los Angeles, would try to wrangle a few auditions, maybe adopt a dog. Jonah's plan was to stick around for a while to monitor the situation with the elephants, then, assuming everything remained calm, head back to the States to work on his thesis. Sam wasn't sure what came next for her. Some kind of restart was all she knew, and she savored the idea of a blank, uncluttered future.

"How do you know if they'll show up?" she asked, staring out at the empty bai. The three of them sat next to one another, their feet dangling off the edge of the platform.

"I don't," Jonah said. "I sometimes spend whole days waiting up here."

"Do you ever get lonely?" she asked. "I think I'd lose my mind if I lived out here by myself."

"Most of my time was spent questioning my sanity."

"It must be scary when the sun goes down."

"You'll soon find out."

"It's funny to think about you living out here," she said.

"What do you mean?" Jonah asked.

"I just never really had a clear picture of your life—what you do on a day-to-day basis. I knew you were doing research, but I always imagined you in some kind of lab."

"This is it," Jonah said. "This is the lab."

"Look!" She pointed to two elephants emerging from the forest. Trailing behind them were three young calves.

"You're in luck," Jonah said. "Here they come."

"They're stunning," Sam said, floored by the majesty of these creatures she'd seen only in zoos.

"The big ones are the matriarchs," Jonah explained.

"And the little guys?" Sam asked.

"Siblings most likely."

Two more adult elephants arrived, but unlike the rest, they were tuskless.

"Those guys don't have tusks," Sam noted with a little frown.

Jonah couldn't be sure if they were the same two he'd observed the last time he was here, or if these were new additions, but he removed his camera and snapped a few pictures to show Marcus. "This is something I just started noticing," he said. "Nobody really knows for sure how it happens, but the thinking is that because of all the poaching, the gene pool's being altered to such a degree that some of the females are born without tusks."

"That's awful," Sam said.

"Yes and no. I mean it's terrible that it's happening, but if that's what it takes for the species to survive, then maybe it's okay."

"But don't they need them—their tusks?"

"Not necessarily. *We* notice the change, but if they're born that way then it's all they know. It's evolution, albeit human-motivated evolution, but still. They adapt. They learn to live without."

"Yeah," Sam said. "I guess so."

The two matriarchs began drinking the mineral water percolating from the ground, while the calves splashed in the mud, spraying water from their trunks like rowdy schoolchildren.

"What happened to the males?" Gavin asked.

"They usually leave and form bachelor herds when they reach adolescence," Jonah said.

"Smart animals."

"Will the calves leave when they get older?" Sam asked.

"Some will," Jonah said. "Some won't."

"That's a little sad."

Jonah shrugged. "Such is the life of a forest elephant."

As the last bit of color drained from the sky, a silence fell upon them. It had been a long time since they'd spent this much time together, and though nobody wanted to ruin the moment with an acknowledgment, Sam knew that something unspoken had passed among them. As kids, they used to spend whole afternoons watching planes take off from the commuter airport down the road from their house, oblivious to the way moments become memories and memories become things no one talks about anymore. How had the distance opened up? Where had it come from? Sam couldn't say, and it was unlikely her brothers could either. But now, in Gabon, on the first day of a new year, that distance was momentarily collapsed as they watched elephant calves jostling in the mud, limbs crashing, tiny trunks knocking, struggling to make sense of all that common blood between them.

ACKNOWLEDGMENTS

I'd like to thank my parents: my mom for encouraging me to read; my dad for instilling in me the work ethic required to finish a novel. Thanks to my brothers, my first friends, the loyal and constant presence in what was an occasionally itinerant childhood.

It's likely you wouldn't be holding this book if my agent, Emma Sweeney, hadn't plucked it out of the slush pile, shepherded it through many rounds of revisions, and then, through a stroke of what seemed like magic, made a dream come true. Thanks to everyone at ESA, including Margaret Sutherland Brown and Hannah Brattesani.

Many thanks to my editor, Susanna Porter, whose sharp eye and keen instincts elevated the novel in ways I could not have done on my own. This book is immeasurably better because of her. A special thanks to everyone at Ballantine and Random House, especially Emily Hartley.

Jonah's work with forest elephants was loosely based on *The Elephant Listening Project,* and I'm grateful to Peter Wrege, the director of the program, for consulting on matters relating to Gabon and forest elephants.

Steve Almond has taught me more about the craft of writing than almost anyone else, and his notes on a very early draft pushed the book in the direction it needed to go.

Many thanks to the following people who read various iterations of the novel: Andrew Hume, Dustin Hammes, David Heinz, Cheryl Spraetz, Lauren Westerfield, Zack Quaintance, Josh Denslow, and Mark Douglas.

A very special thanks to my love, Sondra Hammes, for encouraging me to keep going when there were plenty of reasons to stop. And lastly, to my sweet boy, Quinn, for putting it all in perspective, for making it all worthwhile.

ABOUT THE AUTHOR

BRADY HAMMES is a writer and documentary film editor. His short stories have appeared in *Michigan Quarterly Review, Guernica, The Rattling Wall,* and *Landlocked.* He lives in Los Angeles by way of Colorado and Iowa.

bradyhammes.com